Give My Love to Charlie

The Life of an Anthropoid Ape

ABOUT THE AUTHOR

William, the younger son of a Bournemouth solicitor, was educated at Canford School, sojourned six months in West Africa under the aegis of a Winston Churchill Travelling Fellowship in the category of 'Exploration and adventure', and later read law at the Inns of Court School of Law in London, qualifying as a barrister. He was called to the Bar by the Middle Temple in 1980.

William has been involved in publishing for many years, and has written several books. He wrote the first distance learning course on proofreading and copy-editing, and now runs an online training course (www.LearnFreelancing.com). He has also worked as editor-in-chief for a large group of Internet publishing companies.

From the depths of Africa…
'aliquid semper novi'

Give My Love to Charlie

The Life of an Anthropoid Ape

WILLIAM CRITCHLEY

FIRST ENGLISH BOOKS

First Published in Great Britain in 2013 by:
First English Books
11 Newton Road
Poole BH13 7EX

ISBN-13: 978-0-9551437-6-2

Copyright © 2013 William Critchley

The right of William Critchley to be identified as the author of this work has been asserted by him in accordance with the Copyright, Designs and Patents Act 1988.

No part of this publication may be reproduced, stored in a retrieval system, or transmitted in any form or by any means, electronic, mechanical, photocopying, recording, or otherwise without the prior permission of the publisher.
All rights reserved.

Cover design: Tom Parrett at MarqueePrint.com
Cover image © Can Stock Photo Inc./muha04
Reverse: Esengi children © the author
Typesetting: Ian Taylor, taylorthorneprint.co.uk
Copy-editing and proofreading: Michèle Clarke, Liz Shaw
Printed and bound in Great Britain by CPI Antony Rowe, Eastbourne, East Sussex, main text in 12 pt Times New Roman

A CIP catalogue record for this book is available from the British Library.

All characters appearing in this work are fictitious.
Any resemblance to real persons, living or dead,
is purely coincidental.

Dedication

For Robert Mason (mining engineer, game warden, fur trapper in the Yukon for the Hudson Bay Co., 'Mountie', Royal Canadian Mounted Police) who first introduced me to the magic of West Cameroon, and the forest reserve of Takamanda; and to Jacqueline Lois Sunderland-Groves, M.Phil., who also studied the Cross River gorilla (*Gorilla gorilla diehli*) and the Nigeria-Cameroon chimpanzee (*Pan troglodytes ellioti*) in that country; Professor Tetsuro Matsuzawa; to Jane Goodall for being a real-life inspiration; the people of Cameroon; and for '*Domus*', the Honourable Society of the Middle Temple

*The Takamanda National Park is a protected area in Cameroon, set up in 2008 in order to protect the endangered Cross River gorilla. An older protected area, known as the Takamanda Forest Reserve was established in 1934 and covered an area of 676 sq. km.

'The charm of West Africa is a painful one. It gives you pleasure to fall under it when you are out there, but when you are back here, it gives you pain, by calling you. It sends up before your eyes a vision of a wall of dancing white, rainbow-gemmed surf playing on a shore of yellow sand before an audience of stately cocoa-palms, or of a great mangrove-walled bronze river, or of a vast forest cathedral, and you hear, nearer to you than the voices of the people round you, nearer than the roar of city traffic, the sound of that surf beating on the shore down there, and the sound of the wind talking in the hard palm-leaves, and the thump of the natives' tom-toms, or the cry of the parrots passing over the mangrove-swamps in the evening time – and everything that is round you grows poor and thin in the face of that vision, and you want to go back to the coast that is calling you, saying as the African says to the departing soul of his dying friends, "Come back, this is your home".'

From a lecture given by Mary Kingsley to Cheltenham Ladies College

'One of the gladdest moments in human life is the departing upon a distant journey into unknown lands. Shaking off with one effort the fetters of habit, the leaden weight of routine, the slavery of civilisation, man feels once more happy. The blood flows with the fast circulation of youth, excitement gives a new vigour to the muscles and a sense of sudden freedom adds an inch to the stature.'

The Life of Sir Richard Burton by Thomas Wright (1906)

'We carry within us the wonders, we seek without us. There is all Africa, and her prodigies in us.'

Religio Medici by Sir Thomas Browne, MD (1642)

'With such assurances, it is much to be lamented that those philosophers who are yet believers virtually deny to man the prerogative of his high descent, and of his *natural affinities*. They class him simply as an animal, forming part of the brute creation, as a genus allied to the monkey, as an order of quadrupeds, or an essential part of a zoological circle, surrounded by apes and baboons.'
On the Natural History and Classification of Quadrupeds by William Swainson (1835)

'The history of the chimpanzee, or African oran, is still more imperfectly known. It inhabits similar wild and inaccessible regions, under the same latitudes, in tropical Africa; but chiefly in the forests bordering the great river Gaboon.'
William Swainson, ibid.

'There is grandeur in this view of life, with its several powers, having been originally breathed into a few forms or into one; and that, whilst this planet has gone cycling on according to the fixed law of gravity, from so simple a beginning endless forms most beautiful and most wonderful have been, and are being, evolved.'
On the Origin of Species by Charles Darwin (1859)

'As humans we can identify galaxies light years away, we can study particles smaller than an atom, but we still haven't unlocked the mystery of the three pounds of matter sitting between our ears.'
President Barack Obama announcing proposals for a $100 million brain-mapping project, BRAIN (Brain Research through Advancing Innovative Neurotechnologies) Initiative, 2 April 1913

Acknowledgements

First and foremost, I would like to thank my father Robert Lewis Critchley (1911–1985) for buying the plane ticket that took me to West Cameroon, almost half a century ago, to spend three months as an assistant game warden, and generally learn about life at the same time.

Thanks are also due (all mentioned, with one or two exceptions, no longer hold these posts) to: Chris Foncham, one-time Forestry Officer at Mamfe, Mr S.C. Tamajong, Chief Conservator of Forests, Lt-Col L.T. Valentine, Ministry of Agriculture, Dick Boteler, Chief Leprosy Officer, Mamfe; to Jacob Mbianda, Smoky Joe, John Ebai, Gabriel Amele, Florence Moliki; Robert Mason, mining engineer and game warden, who needed two planes to fly out of Cameroon when he left, one for himself and one for his luggage; to Alastair Robertson, financial controller of the Cameroon Development Corporation, Wally Cranfield, ranch manager on the Obudu Plateau in Nigeria, Major-General H. A. Lascelles, former Director General of the Winston Churchill Memorial Trust; my good friend Ken Rowles; Jonathan Leather; the ship's doctor on board SS Tarkwa whose name I forget; Dr George Schaller, zoologist and primatologist, Dr Jane Goodall, Jane Goodall Institute (JGI) UK, and Monkey World in Wareham, Dorset, for the space to wander and reflect on the life of chimpanzees.

To my skilful editors Michèle Clarke and Liz Shaw go my sincere thanks. Last but not least to my three children for believing in the story – before they had even read it!

PART I
BRINGING UP CHARLIE

ONE

Dr Waldren had been a general practitioner for almost twenty-five years. His small-town practice had yet to be replaced by a polyclinic, a fact which provided a morsel of satisfaction. His working week was now part-time, with retirement only a few years away. He wanted more time for his 'hobbies' and projects, more time to spend in his own unique purpose-built laboratory. Most of all he wanted to continue with his plans for some bizarre experiments.

The last call he had to make that morning in June was to a Mrs Emily Settle, an elderly lady who lived quite alone in an apartment block on the outskirts of a minster town in the county of Dorset. The block was not grand. It had the look of a building that wouldn't last much longer, one that would soon fall into the clutches of developers, especially as the most of the residents were as old as his patient. One by one they would gradually pass away.

When the last resident died, the building would be boarded up, he thought, weeds would colonise the concrete driveway, and a prominent sign read: SOLD or ACQUIRED FOR CLIENTS. It would be emblazoned confidently in the lettering of one of many development companies, successful in the area before the credit crunch – like one the doctor had read about in the local newspaper which had employed over seven hundred men before its boss went bankrupt.

What was to be torn down would be replaced by modern flats, albeit with bedrooms and bathrooms not much bigger than the cages built for monkeys and chimpanzees in the local zoo, though that was later closed down on health and hygiene grounds.

The zoo was small and badly run. Dead animals in whiffy cages put a lot of people off their walks in the park. Children balked at the smell of urine and decomposing bodies, even if the animals were dressed in furry coats.

Dr Waldren paused a moment on the steps to Mrs Settle's flat, thinking of that sign he'd seen on a property website: '*Traditional construction with concrete floors throughout*'. It described a new build by the sea, just ten miles away. Three million pounds for concrete floors! Not expensive wood flooring (although probably overlain with marble) but concrete. It made him so angry.

With three million pounds he could carry out hundreds of experiments – enough for several lifetimes. Despite this nagging ambition, there was really only *one* major experiment Dr Waldren still wanted to do. The problem was if he only attempted it, he'd risk disgrace, quickly followed by expulsion, from the General Medical Council.

Dr Waldren was not a criminal. He prided himself on never having the mindset to become one. Usually smartly dressed in dog-tooth, country-style jacket, brown trousers, brown shoes and striped college tie, he valued old-fashioned precepts like honesty and virtue, though he averred that what most believed as everyday 'truth' was intangible, and unknowable.

He felt certain he had, more often than not, sided with truth rather than untruth, and that he had tried all his adult life to do what was right. In the case of one of his experiments, however, he correctly foresaw he was, to put it mildly, getting close to the bone.

Relentlessly the good doctor worked towards this ineluctable goal, as a person afflicted with obsessive compulsive disorder is unavoidably trapped in a habit or series of habits, in the grip of a disease. In Dr Waldren's case the task was much more complex.

As he rang the doorbell, a faint and frail voice called out, 'Come in!' Dr Waldren pushed open the door. He was immediately met by the smell of old age – faint odours persisting in the air, in the fabric of the curtains, even in the wallpaper, on chairs. A harsher odour would indicate cleaners, trying to hide the smell with cheap perfume or furniture polish. The smell just hung there, silently, relatively innocuously, but as real as a person's reputation in the world. Once born and made, brought into existence, it was hard to hide.

Emily Settle was an elderly patient of 93 who Dr Waldren had cared for over three decades. He knew what to expect. She'd be lying flat out in her bed, complaining of feeling faint and feeble, although if asked to stand up, she could do; and then point out that as a young girl she'd climbed most of the peaks in the Lake District – 'in hobnail boots', she said.

'And how are we today, Emily?' asked the doctor pleasantly. 'Having any problems, are we?'

'No, not really,' Emily answered, looking straight at Dr Waldren from her bed, her white hair in need of a wash and comb. 'I've got this pain, just here.' She pointed to her stomach, and her mouth opened, as if mimicking the sudden onset of pain.

Dr Waldren asked her to lie still so he could examine her. He pressed lightly on her stomach, asking if that hurt. 'We'll have to lift your dress a little; I know you'll understand, so we can see what's going on.'

Emily lifted her colourful dress to show off her gaunt legs, and then pulled it higher. She wore no underpants. The doctor scarcely noticed what someone described as her 'cleft', topped off by sparse white pubic hair. The doctor prodded Emily again but this time she made no sound. Briefly his hand touched the wrinkled skin of her belly. There came into his mind then a ridiculous, fleeting thought, that many years ago when the world was young, and he'd been too, how a man such as her husband would have caressed that same body, found comfort between her then beautiful thighs, now so aged and grim. There was no succour now. It was so silly that he dismissed the idea immediately.

'Looks like you'll be all right. Just a little sore skin, nothing to worry about. Try to spend a little less time in bed. It's not good for your circulation, you know, to be inactive for long periods of time.'

Dr Waldren told her she could pull her dress back down and, as he wrote out a prescription for the soreness, Emily told him how years before she had walked most of the Wainwright walks in her hobnail boots, and how she'd gone swimming in Lake Coniston on the day she married.

'Have you got someone to collect your prescription?' asked the doctor, in a hurry to leave. It was his last call out for the day, and he wanted to return to work, his real work. At least it was very real to him, much more real than checking the bodies, hearts and pulses of his elderly patients.

Emily said her carer would collect the items on the prescription.

Dr Waldren said his goodbyes and let himself out. Eagerly he turned the key in his Rover 825 Sterling. He'd be home soon. After a twenty-minute drive, he swung the car into the driveway of his house, a relatively (for the area) modest but still desirable three-bedroomed detached property. It had a large, rose-edged garden at the front and a larger garden behind where tall oaks shaded a single fruiting apple tree.

He heard a familiar sound as he parked the car by the garage. It was his favourite black and white spaniel frantically yelping with pleasure at the sight of her master, scratching a window pane with her paws.

Dr Waldren found the front-door key. 'Get down, there's a good girl,' he said letting himself in. The dog acquiesced with a sullen look in its dark brown eyes.

He placed his doctor's bag on the side table with a drawn-out sigh, his eyes immediately looking through the back window in the kitchen, towards the garage. Inside was his 'experiment'. He'd had the garage soundproofed, which was just as well as the neighbours would have heard some dreadful howling and screaming noises on occasion, and the sound of limbs thumping against a metal cage.

Dr Waldren had constructed a kind of reinforced polytunnel, which reached from one side of the garage across a corner of the back lawn straight to the French windows at the rear of the house. He could slide open a small window of thickened glass, and hear down the polytunnel, instantly being able to know how the inmate inside the cage in the garage was doing.

The dog was sniffing furiously at the small glass window. 'Get back, Helga! Get back,' Dr Waldren cried. Helga reluctantly moved away. The doctor knelt down, pulled back the glass window a few centimetres, then a little more, and called out. '*Charlie?*'

The dog sprang back into life, barking as if possessed by a demonic spirit.

There came a scream from inside the polytunnel, from deep within the garage. Then another high-pitched scream echoed towards them – the deeply fearful and wild holler of an anthropoid ape.

*

Dr Waldren felt relieved and slammed shut the small glass window. Charlie was clearly very much alive. He sat in an armchair by the fireplace, while Helga snuggled her nose between his right thigh and the armchair. He stroked her head, saying, 'All right girl, all right', pondering how to begin his great experiment.

Charlie had been 'donated' by a colleague, spirited out of the local zoo before it was closed by the council. It was actually less of a donation and more of the doctor's persuasive but forceful charm that led to his being Charlie's guardian. When the doctor heard a chimp was left behind, he'd stepped in fast, offering to care for the animal until a permanent home could be found, perhaps at an animal sanctuary. (There was an ape rehab centre just twenty miles away, in a wooded part of heathland skirting the harbour shores.) He'd had to offer a bribe of £2,000 to ensure complete confidence.

African apes had long fascinated him, ever since he'd watched a television programme made by the famous Dr Louis Leakey, in Africa. Dr Leakey had held in his hands the skull bone of a hominid ancestor, an ancestor more than one million years old. It was an intact cranium of *Homo erectus*. From that moment he'd been hooked.

Homo erectus (Latin for 'upright man'), an extinct species of the genus *Homo*, is believed to have been the first '*hominin*' to leave Africa. Typically, a male would have weighed around 60 kg, stood 1.8 m high, and flourished in Africa and Eurasia from 2 to 0.3 mya (million years ago). *Homo erectus* was 'one of the most successful and long-lived species of the *Homo* genus', a fact that had once made Dr Waldren cry. Where had their success got them, Dr Waldren asked himself? Looking at the weathered cranium held up by Dr Leakey on that television programme, so many years before, he'd wondered what else was left, since the species was utterly extinct.

Then it had dawned on him, or rather comprehension came, much as those early fossil discoveries in the Olduvai Gorge in Africa's Great Rift Valley had light and new understanding suddenly cast upon them by a newer and more intelligent branch of the same family – their discoverers – that all had not been lost because faint traces, even if in altered forms, must have been passed on in the genome shared by all modern humans.

*

Homo erectus probably knew how to control fire, used relatively sophisticated tools, and had a fairly large cranial capacity of 850 to 1,100 cubic centimetres (cc), the latter figure overlapping with modern human brain size. Males were significantly larger than females (known as sexual dimorphism), and in more 'recent' times, it is also possible that the species might have interbred with modern humans.

Fascinating as this all was, the doctor was still more intrigued by man's closest living relative, the chimpanzee, there being just two extant species of apes in the genus *Pan*: the (more) common or robust chimpanzee *Pan troglodytes*, found in West and Central Africa and its smaller cousin the bonobo (*Pan paniscus*), found only in the Congo, well known for its precocious sexual behaviours, nearly every opportunity for gratuitous sex being taken.

There are four (possibly five) subspecies of *Pan troglodytes*. The eastern or long-haired chimpanzee (*Pan troglodytes schweinfurthii*), found in Burundi, the Central African Republic, Rwanda, Sudan, Tanzania, Uganda and Zaire, inhabiting dry savannah to rainforests up to 6,000 feet in altitude.

The central or black-faced chimpanzee (*Pan troglodytes troglodytes*) is found in the Central African Republic, Rwanda, and Zaire but also in Congo, Gabon, Nigeria and Cameroon. Its habitat range includes rainforests and open woodland forests.

The western or masked chimpanzee (*Pan troglodytes verus*) inhabits Ghana, Guinea, the Ivory Coast, Liberia, Senegal, Sierra Leone and Togo and its habitat range includes riverine forests, semi-deciduous woodland and rainforests up to around 6,000 feet.

The Nigeria or Nigeria-Cameroon chimpanzee (*Pan troglodytes vellerosus*, from 2009 known as *Pan troglodytes ellioti*) is the rarest (and most threatened subspecies) and found only in eastern Nigeria and western Cameroon.

Dr Waldren was intrigued to learn that each night, like the gorilla, chimpanzees build a nest made with branches and leaves up in a tree. It was strange to think that 'home' for an ape in the wild is where you construct your nest each night. Does it mean a life of wandering from place to place, from tree to tree? Apes have no fixed abode, only a territorial area in which to roam. Day nests for napping, sometimes on the ground, are also made.

In the extant hominoids surviving today are humans (the genus *Homo*), chimpanzees (genus *Pan*), gorillas (genus *Gorilla*), orang-utans (genus *Pongo*), and gibbons (four genera of the family *Hylobatidae*). The separate 'tribe' known as *Hominini* has just two members – humans and chimpanzees.

Dr Waldren knew that humans and chimpanzees had a very similar genetic inheritance; humans and chimpanzees share about 98% (not allowing for gene repeats and mutations) of the same genes (and 100 per cent of the same blood groups). That does not mean that we are 98 per cent chimp, and chimps are 98 per cent us, or does it?

About 7 to 10 million years ago chimps and humans (and gorillas) also had a common ancestor. Chimpanzees may well have interbred with humans resulting in hybridisation, before the final divergence into two distinct, separate species some 6.3 to 5 million years ago. The latest estimate from analyses of genetic drift and recombination, using the mathematically esoteric Markov model, suggests that humans and chimpanzees fully diverged or speciated into two separate species around 4.1 million years ago, although this figure has again been revised to 7.5 mya, using a new method measuring mutations per genome per generation. Most of this knowledge is relatively new, as chimpanzees have only been studied in the wild for the past 60 years.

The common chimpanzee and the bonobo cannot swim, although bonobos seem more adapted to foraging in river water. Some scientists have proposed that the formation of the Congo River around 1.7 mya led to the speciation of the two species. The bonobo ancestors south of the river were separated from the ancestors of the common chimpanzee to the north. A neat theory Dr Waldren opined: how, in that epic heart of darkness, the immense snaking river uncoiled, water could separate out two species. *Marlow on the one side of the bank, and Kurtz on the other.*

The Sanaga River in central Cameroon also seems to serve as a phylogeographic division between two subspecies of chimpanzee (this being the study of the processes controlling geographic distributions of lineages by constructing the genealogies of populations and genes). Genetic analyses indicate these two subspecies last shared a common ancestor about 600,000 years ago. (It is well known that chimpanzees are chary of crossing large rivers or open water though they will happily play in shallow, surface water, and smaller streams.)

So what happened, Dr Waldren concluded finally, on the dry and dusty plains of Africa millions of years ago, was still showing up aeons later, locked into the genome of both species. It was a sobering thought. If that were true, chimpanzees must have shared virtually the same genes as Jesus. If that were true, how did God 'assemble' Jesus the man? From which gene pool did He conjure up the genes? Not being at all religious, Dr Waldren was not bothered with such questions. He asked them only out of simple scientific curiosity.

Whatever the genetic similarities, chimps had not been blessed with the same brain size as humans. *Homo erectus*, the last archaic human, saw a large leap in cranial capacity, much bigger than chimps, but the brains of modern humans are larger still. A typical reading or value for a modern human would be in the range 1350 or 1400 cc. *Homo erectus* had a brain volume of around 1000 cc. This organ needs much to sustain it. The human brain is only 2 per cent of body weight but it takes up to 20 per cent of available energy, a big demand.

The brain of a chimpanzee is small in comparison – between 300 and 500 cc. Gorillas average 500 cc, and more, up to 700 cc. However, brain size loosely correlates more to body size than intelligence.

So the chimpanzee that Dr Waldren was caring for was not that bright, if compared, for example, with *Homo erectus*. Chimpanzees have been used in all kinds of scientific experiments, some involving concepts of language and communication, and they have been rocketed into space.

Chimps in the wild have been observed fashioning basic tools to dig ants out of termite mounds, crack open nuts with wood or stone hammers, and make 'spears' to kill bushbabies. They are not meat eaters in the main but occasionally chimpanzees hunt other animals or chimps from groups outside their own, and if they catch one, will tear the animal apart with their sharp teeth, devouring the meat voraciously. Chunks of meat may be torn off with their teeth or hands. If the prey is small, the skull may be bitten open, blood sucked out, and the brain consumed. With larger prey, bigger bones may be cracked open to extract the marrow, and sometimes the brain scraped out of the skull using a wodge of leaves.

*

As if subconsciously to prove the point, Dr Waldren pushed Helga away, got up from his chair and inspected the contents of his fridge. It was stocked with fruit and several legs of lamb. The doctor pulled out one leg, pale blood dripping onto the carpet, which Helga licked, and then walked towards the entrance to the reinforced polytunnel. Once again he drew back the glass window. He bent over slightly, confident that he would soon be relieved of the leg of spring lamb. *'Charlie!'*

Helga was watching too, through the back window of the dining room. The polytunnel, all of its components and measurements, from tube diameter, wall thickness, steel tensile strength, width and hoop spacing, specifically chosen by the doctor, rocked and swayed from side to side as Charlie negotiated the journey between his cage in the garage and the small opening at the end of the polytunnel.

In moments Charlie's muzzle appeared, two wild dark eyes staring back towards the doctor. Helga barked again, as if rabidly possessed. 'Shut up girl,' the doctor said with concealed menace, the low tone of his voice immediately noticed by Helga. The dog whined as if in sudden pain, and backed away.

Dr Waldren positioned the leg by the window opening. Charlie grimaced, and then let out a piercing shriek. He was clearly hungry. Dr Waldren opened the glass window, enough to begin to push through the meat; you could see Charlie hanging back, almost licking his lips, because he'd gone through the 'charade' before. He knew he'd have to wait until Dr Waldren had pushed enough of the leg through the opening for him to be able to sink his teeth into the meat, and then drag away meat and bone.

Charlie's jaws clamped around the lamb's leg, and with a grunt he turned, and was gone. Helga whimpered quietly to herself. Dr Waldren straightened up, then washed his hands in the kitchen sink. It was a habit he could never surrender; it had been ingrained by his early years of medical school training, and ward rounds in numerous hospitals. He searched for a clean cloth to wipe his hands. He found one in a cupboard, and then sat down in the same chair, calling Helga over.

'Come, dear girl,' he called to the dog, who was clearly pleased to see the back of Charlie, and to be with her master again. Reaching towards a small table to his left, on which sat a pristine bottle of malt whisky and a glass, he unscrewed the top, and poured himself a drink. It was time to relax, time to start making plans for the next great project.

Dr Waldren was about to accomplish a monstrous surgical procedure, and Charlie would discover the destiny thrust upon him.

TWO

Charlie tucked into the leg of lamb inside his cage, having carried it back through the polytunnel. He sank his sharp molars into the fleshy leg, nipping the meat first in order to tear off neat strips, and making feeding grunts. The meat on the leg reduced by about half before Charlie began to lose interest. He tossed the bone aside, as one might discard an object found on the foreshore of a beach that turned out to be nothing special.

Charlie yawned. He scratched idly at his flanks with both hands, pausing to look round his cage. There wasn't much room. Dr Waldren had made the cage himself, and it took up much of the garage space. Two horizontal wooden poles had been placed inside the cage. Charlie used these as improvised swinging posts. When angry he swung from one pole to the other, and then completed the movement by thrusting his legs upwards, against one side of the metal cage, which shook, making rattling noises, and Charlie felt better.

Charlie's keeper could only approach the cage from the front and one side, as it had been placed flush against the garage walls to the right and back. The right side of the garage's sloping roof also had a window cut into it, about five feet by three, in order to give Charlie the benefit of sunlight. A shutter could be drawn across this from a pulley at the side of the garage door – an invention by the doctor to shut out daylight as necessary, such as trying to calm Charlie down if he displayed his fierce temper.

Charlie's attention turned again to the gnawed leg of lamb. The doctor would be coming to remove it before too long, and clean the floor of his cage, and Charlie sensed that. Charlie picked up the bone, sniffed it briefly, and then shuffled towards the front of his cage, which was also the best place to attract his keeper's attention.

Holding the leg bone in his right palm, with his opposable

thumb wrapped around it, Charlie brought it behind his head, then forwards with a great thrust, smashing the bone against the metal cage. The cage rattled and shook on its foundations, flimsy even by the standards of third-world country zoos. Again Charlie smashed the leg bone against the metal wiring, and at the same time began to hoot repeatedly, following this with a long-drawn out shriek.

Inside the house Helga jumped up from her basket, whining. Dr Waldren stirred in his chair, knowing that Charlie was calling him, but waiting for one last crash of noise to justify rising from his comfortable chair after a day's work at the surgery. 'Goddamn,' he said to himself, getting to his feet. Dr Waldren went into the kitchen and out of the back door. He looked down the drive, as if to check for the presence of strangers, and being satisfied no one was there, he walked quickly to the garage.

He unlocked two mortise locks on the garage doors, paused to catch his breath, and opened the right-hand door. Charlie saw him, and screamed as if a momentous event in his life had just happened, which in a way it had. Dr Waldren swiftly went in, closing the door behind him. He tugged at a switch. A beam shone over the cage, illuminating Charlie in a pool of soft yellow light. His pelage or fur shone an inky brown-black with the sheen of health, having none of the grey flecking associated with older chimps. He was still young, in the prime of life.

Dr Waldren's face lit up with enjoyment and excitement every time he came face to face with Charlie. This time was no exception. Charlie was his own special project. He had waited years for this. He was impatient to get started. Charlie softened his stare when he saw the doctor standing by his cage, the chimp's gestures indicating appeasement and pleasure.

Dr Waldren looked at Charlie but then averted his gaze, knowing that direct stares between primates, as they were doing, constituted a threat. Charlie looked back too, a little wistfully. The chimp could have no inkling, surely, that his life was soon going to be changed forever.

THREE

Back in the house, Dr Waldren opened up his purpose-built laboratory with a special key. The lounge had the curtains permanently drawn, on purpose. Who would want to see a table, with a 'patient' upon it, and in this case, as Dr Waldren told himself, the creature etherised? Whether the evening was spread out against the sky was not important; what was spread out on *his* table, awaiting new medical procedures – that would count.

He switched on the lights. A quiet humming came from the machines, and a clean smell, as if everything in the room had been washed. In the middle of the room was a basic operating table that he'd bought from a mail order medical supplies company. It might only have been a basic operating table but it could also be seen as an alternative kind of altar upon which the doctor offered up his latest procedures, so he might win the praise of his professional equals. Behind the table's head hung an expensive monitor for measuring vital signs such as heart rate and blood pressure, an electrocardiogram (ECG) device, and a finger slip for measuring the patient's pulse rate and oxygen saturation level, a pulse oximeter. Behind the monitor in a corner stood a portable oxygen tank, ready to use, with leads. Supplemental oxygen was available via a nasal cannula.

Dr Waldren's mind was racing, thanks in part to the whisky he had just consumed. He was thinking about the evolution of early mammals, all of 200 million years before, when there was a leap in brain size.

*

Small creatures, nocturnal mammals, appeared and were many times cleverer than reptiles, four or five times as much, and this increase in intelligence is largely, although not exclusively, due to a new development in the brain – the cerebral cortex – a thin layer of cells enveloping or covering the forebrain, and responsible for that most remarkable of phenomena: conscious thought. As if to underline the importance of the this organ, Dr Waldren had read that between a third and a half of all our genes deal with the brain.

Even if you were a patient, thought the doctor, before you were etherised upon a table, your conscious thoughts were incredibly special, unique to you, and they helped make a map of the external world, which was also internalised in your brain or mind. The cortex, the doctor knew, is unique to mammals. Birds, for example, which were believed to have evolved just after mammals, and which had developed brains of equivalent size, do not possess a cortex. The cortex is necessary for creating the reality that an individual organism experiences; it is a machine for constructing reality, and this is the only reality available to every mammal possessing a cortex. The brain uses it to make representations of the world visually accessible to its owner. Streams of sensory information input need processing – arranging, analysing, decoding – to then be turned into a way of looking at the world. All our senses are involved. These demands led to the evolution of the cerebral cortex, which in modern mammals can reach 40 per cent of brain volume. In humans, the cortex accounts for an incredible 70 to 80 per cent of brain volume.

The senses provide the data, the raw information, which the brain then turns into a kind of mental map of the world. The point of these evolving functions has been to create an ever more complete picture of reality. Language also developed in humans, perhaps through the need for communication, and this may in turn have led to introspective consciousness, something unique to humans. 'Yes,' Dr Waldren thought to himself, 'the ability to ask something as simple as "To be or not to be?" has also helped, through the use of language, to extend our perceptions of reality.'

There was much more. The burial of the dead. The positioning of the dead body, the gifts for the afterlife. The evisceration of internal organs and their mummification, along with the bodies from which they came. Their bodies were hairless in the sense of not being covered with mammalian fur. They walked fully erect. Their ears had large external lobules. They had chins. Their hands were small but their arms had exquisite musculature. Whatever term or word they used, the idea of 'posterity' must have been understood. They made music…they talked using complex language structures. They wept at things that could not be seen. They appreciated beauty, and searched for something called truth.

*

Dr Waldren looked down at the operating table. It was draped with a cotton and lint covering and it was so clean that no dust had fallen on it – at least to the naked eye. It would not be long now, the doctor mused. Not long before he attempted to create another kind of reality. *Charlie was going to be the guineapig.*

How strange! What was it about guineapigs? Easy to operate on, quick to breed he supposed.

Dr Waldren drew in his breath sharply, as he considered the medical experiment contemplated for so many years. 'Oh brave new world! Oh brave new world!' he suddenly exclaimed. 'That hath such, such…' He broke off the sentence, unable to say the word 'people'. Then he said, 'How many goodly creatures, like this poor ape, my own dear Charlie!'

FOUR

Josephine Waldren, like her husband, practised as a GP but had moved away from the marital home for the past two years. Her friends called her Jo for short. Her husband, so she told her friends, put his work first, and his marriage a reluctant second. She had decamped to a house twenty miles away, far enough to ensure she did not meet him on 'home territory' but near enough to find him in less than forty minutes if need be.

She had decided to confront George, at least to try to ascertain if he still cared for her because, in truth, she liked his company. He might be a little severe, occasionally withdrawn, but on the whole he was a focused individual, energised, driven. She liked driven men. It was so simple. She sat back. They did the driving.

She could perhaps give him another chance, if, and it was a big if, he'd come round to see things a little more her way.

'Hey, George,' she'd called out when she parked her car. At a side window Helga frantically scratched the glass, barking her head off. George was nowhere to be seen. She opened the back door with a spare key, a precaution she had insisted upon when they split up. 'If I have a key,' she thought, 'I can walk back into George's life at my own choosing. I won't have to ring the bell like a stranger.' Inside the kitchen, there was no sign of George. Helga bounded towards her, crashing into her legs, yapping and nipping at her shoes. 'George!' Jo shouted. 'Where are you?'

George emerged from his laboratory with a sheepish grin on his face.

'George, what is it now? What *exactly* is going on? Are you with someone?'

'Hi, Jo! Are you joking? If you don't believe me, come inside and look.'

'I believe you,' Jo said, immediately making for the lab door as if she knew she'd find someone on the other side. When she entered the room, there was nobody there unless, she imagined blithely, a poltergeist were hiding in one of the lab cupboards. There was just peace, incredible quiet, apart from the background hum of machines. In the evening the lights were set on a dimmer. It was still fairly easy, even then, to see no one else was there.

Jo walked towards the centre of the room, towards the operating table. She looked at it, and then she turned to George. 'You're planning something George, aren't you? Come on now, what is it? Private hospitals are pretty rare, you know, unless run by big companies or health groups. What do you want to do here? This is not exactly a BUPA annexe where you can go to town on whatever medical procedures you like!'

George's face had reddened but bravely he put on a front. 'I just made this so I could...well, I don't know.'

'What do you mean, you don't know?' insisted Jo.

'It's not something I want to talk about.' The doctor's voice had an edge to it, toned down, entirely unwilling to divulge anything of value. It was slightly menacing, as if he wouldn't tell Jo no matter how many times she asked. In fact, he had advised her, without saying anything directly, she should press him no further.

Jo stared angrily at George but George held his ground, venturing nothing. She was still pretty in her mid forties – even after all the long hours she'd spent on ward rounds before becoming a GP. When she smiled, her face had an elfin quality that George had gone for in a big way. She smiled a lot because she'd fallen in love with George; in fact she smiled so much George proposed to her inside two weeks.

Jo smiled through her teeth. 'Are you sure there's nothing you can tell me?'

George relented slightly. 'You must swear to tell no one. Not a soul.'

Jo knew she'd win some ground at least. She grinned, her front teeth like an ad for tooth whitener. 'I love you George, you know that.'

George considered this unimportant. He was figuring out how much to tell her. She could know *about* Charlie, but not what he planned *to do* with Charlie. 'I'd like you to meet someone,' he said, with an air of someone who owns a big secret, and is proud of the fact. 'Come through. His name is Charlie.'

Jo's face took on a confused, blank look. Heavens, was Charlie a secret lover, she mused? She knew that couldn't be true. George was resolutely heterosexual. Thinking that the house seemed empty, she wondered where George could be hiding Charlie. What was Charlie made of? Was he a child's toy?

'Step this way, Jo.' She followed George into the small dining room at the back of the house. George opened the French windows and walked onto the patio.

Jo almost tripped when she saw the transparent polytunnel. 'George, oh my God, George, what's *that?*'

George put a finger to his lips, indicating she stay silent. He took a cane stick resting against the side of the garage, and used it to beat on the polytunnel – a series of rhythmic taps – then stood by her side, looking straight at the polytunnel.

From inside the garage there came a muted squeal, or was it a shriek, Jo wasn't sure. Whatever it was, it was odd, very frightening, not exactly sinister, but strange. George tapped again, just once, and immediately another muted, muffled shriek reached their ears. 'Look there,' George said, pointing the length of cane about a foot away from the garage wall, down the polytunnel. A black shape emerged and metamorphosed into a black head. The head was small, covered in brown-black hair. It turned into a face like a grinning gargoyle. It had two sharp eyes, a flat nose, then a mouth opened, showing long, yellow, canine teeth. Jo screamed.

Charlie looked at the figures beyond the tunnel and hesitated. Normally he might scamper down the tunnel and wait by the window, knowing he would probably get something to eat. There was just enough room to turn round in the polytunnel, so if no food was forthcoming, as occasionally the doctor became temporarily absorbed with another task, Charlie would return to his cage.

George did not often 'call' Charlie in the way he had. Inside the garage, he occasionally let the ape out of his cage because Charlie was still a young chimp, and George felt he could trust him. He also fed him by hand inside the cage, often with fruit, and also with organic nut and date bars from the supermarket, which Charlie loved. He tried a variety of food and found that seeds, nuts, celery, fruit, eggs, and even handfuls of leaves and wild flowers, were always popular. The ape also liked a spoonful of acacia honey at night. Figs were a special treat, as was pawpaw.

In view of the experiment he had so carefully planned for Charlie, although he had not exactly fleshed out all the details, because of the immense complexity of the idea, it would be necessary to get Charlie used to the house, so he could be taken into the room with the operating table without trouble. He needed Charlie to get acclimatised to the room, though it had occurred to him it might be easier to drug the animal inside the garage, and then carry him into the operating theatre. He'd have to think about that.

Charlie was not used to seeing anyone other than the doctor, so he hung back in the polytunnel entrance, hesitant, unsure, not feeling safe.

Jo's mouth dropped open. She had stopped screaming but the blood seemed to rush to her head with the shock of seeing a creature, almost half-human, half-ape meeting together in such a grisly apparition. It was not as if Jo was unused to shock, blood, pain, even death – those things only doctors get to see – but she had become conditioned to such things, not to this *strangeness*. Jo felt her legs give way, and she fell in a huddle on top of the polytunnel, bouncing off a little, as if it were an unusual kind of bouncy castle. Now it was Charlie's turn to scream.

FIVE

Jo felt her face smash against the smooth reinforced plastic of the polytunnel. Her face was just above the plastic, and then her nose was buried in it. She'd turned her face to see Charlie, black, squat and huddled there, as if he'd been held in place by invisible superglue. Charlie was as still as the night in the Cameroons, which had once been his home. West Cameroon, to be exact, some miles from a town called Mamfe, where the urban sprawl ended and the wild bush began.

*

Charlie had been playing in a clearing with his mother. In the trees above, colobus monkeys had sounded the alarm, a scout monkey having been the first to see two hunters picking their way towards them along a forest trail. Charlie's mother had grabbed him, and she'd started to swing away and upwards, trying to gain height, looking for sanctuary in the tree canopy. But the tree cover was sparse, and one of the men had aimed his gun, an ancient Dane gun, at Charlie's mother. She took the full blast in her right shoulder, and crashed down through thin branches to the forest floor, not dead but in great pain, whimpering between screams of anguish and terror.

The hunters were pleased. They would have bushmeat to sell. The young chimp, captured alive, would make them more money. While one reached out over Charlie's head, Charlie still clutching the air trying to feel for his mother, before the net closed above and around him, the other hunter looked at Charlie's mother, at the red blood spilling from her shoulder into the red earth of the forest floor; he saw the hole in her flesh that would never heal, and her eyes – that was always the worst, because the forest people, the Igbo, believed in spirits of the dead in the forest; in the mother chimp's eyes was the same fear and distant longing and great sadness that the hunter had seen in his grandmother's eyes, when she lay dying in a hut, not more than a few villages' distance from Mamfe.

The hunter swung the stock of his Dane gun, smashing it against the mother chimp's skull. All that protection, so carefully managed by the chimp's body to protect the vital organ within, came to nothing. The bone splintered with the impact of the blow; Charlie's mother was dead.

While Charlie cried in his heart because he was too frightened to utter any sound, his mother was skilfully impaled on a sharp stick so she could be carried back to the village, on the shoulder of a hunter. Her head hung down, pointing towards the ground. When the hunters moved off, drops of blood from Charlie's mother fell to the dry earth. Charlie looked on hopelessly and helplessly, from the other hunter's back, where he lay imprisoned in a net. At least he was alive, his mother nothing more than a carcass to be smoked over fire.

Back in the village Charlie's mother was adroitly skinned, her body suspended for several days, so the meat would be well hung before being butchered and smoked.

Into the black night the villagers fired their Dane guns, dancing round a fire, drinking palm wine; shouting, singing, carousing, the party lasting until dawn. One hunter wore a heavy ship's bell round his middle, which he'd tied with rope, the same rope he used to trap duikers, the little forest antelopes. The bell had rung out mournfully the whole night, always the same note, insistent, pounding in his head, like a church bell tolling, on and on until dawn came and the whole village collapsed into sleep.

Charlie saw her no more. He was carried back to Mamfe, the hunters always seeking to hide the young chimp from the officers of the combined Forestry and Wildlife Departments, built on a knoll on the outskirts of the town, where the river was crossed by a rickety wooden bridge.

He was driven to Kumba, hidden in the back of a dilapidated Land Rover. The Land Rover diverted to a bungalow not far from a volcanic crater lake called Barombi Mbo. Charlie was still imprisoned by the net. A man reached in, pulled Charlie from the back of the Land Rover, and threw him and the net into a garage. It was dark inside, darker than the forest north of Mamfe. Charlie's eyes were bloodshot and they bulged with fear.

*

Charlie screamed when Jo's face turned towards him. Yet his scream contained more anger than fear. He had grown up since being caught in the bush near Mamfe. He'd been housed and looked after fairly well, smuggled into England almost a year later. By chance he'd ended up in the zoo near the doctor's home, a relatively free creature, safe from medical labs, vivisection, drug-testing, and all the other woes of animals imprisoned by humans. His territory may have been tiny but he was an animal growing in confidence, especially since he had begun to trust Dr Waldren.

He was angry with Jo for invading his territory, which consisted of a cage in the garage and the polytunnel, for her invading it so clumsily, so abruptly. Charlie hunched up his shoulders, thrusting his head up against the plastic of the polytunnel, his mouth open wide, baring his strong teeth. When he saw the creature sprawled over the plastic tunnel didn't stare back at him, or use any sudden or aggressive gestures but merely lay there with downcast eyes, Charlie relaxed. Dr Waldren picked Jo up, and put her down bottom first on the grassy lawn. Her eyes opened when Dr Waldren pinched the lobes of her ears. Only Man has these large lobules on the external ears. All extant apes and monkeys don't develop them, and the only use Dr Waldren knew for them in humans was that pinching one slowly between your fingers was a good way to wake someone from sleep. It has been suggested that large lobes meant a long, or at least longer, life but there was no scientific proof, as far as he knew.

Jo's eyes opened. For a moment she saw nothing other than the blur of blue sky overhead, and heard the rustling leaves of a silver birch at the back of the garage. Her eyes found George, gratefully.

Then she sat up. 'For God's sake, George, you could have told me Charlie was an ape, a chimpanzee. He scared the hell out of me!'

SIX

Calm was soon restored to the Waldren household (something of a euphemism, since the household only consisted of Dr Waldren and Charlie. Jo had left him, and their two children were both at university, living more or less independent lives.)

Charlie sloped back down the polytunnel and disappeared into his cage in the garage. George helped Jo into the kitchen. He made two mugs of tea, without milk. Jo sipped hers gladly, and colour came back to her face.

George looked at her solicitously. 'That gave you a fright, didn't it?'

Jo burst out laughing. 'You could have told me, George, you were looking after a chimpanzee, an ape for Christ's sake. You've had some odd patients in your time, but Charlie just about takes the proverbial biscuit! Please don't tell me you're trying to extract hormones from that poor animal to make some old man happy.' Jo was referring to multispecies tissue transplants carried out by a French surgeon, of Russian extraction, a Dr Serge Voronoff. He was famous in the 1920s and 1930s for a new technique – grafting monkey testicle tissue to the testicles of men seeking 'rejuvenation' – in other words, transferring monkey parts to humans. Before this he had worked in Egypt, studying the effects of castration on eunuchs.

'No, Jo, I'm not talking about Voronoff, the surgeon of "monkey gland" fame, or should I say infamy, the doctor, who in the pursuit of scientific knowledge to overcome the effects of aging with hormonal substances, injected himself with extracts from ground-up dog and guineapig testicles, under his skin. Nice thought, isn't it? No, he was pretty incredible Jo, as you know.'

'I feel sick but go on,' Jo said, pulling a face as if she were swallowing ground-up dog and guineapig testicles herself.

'Voronoff was no slouch. He transplanted thyroid glands from healthy chimps into humans who were thyroid deficient; he got hold of the balls of executed criminals, and transplanted these into millionaires who thought they'd end up younger. Viagra was a long way off.'

'Ugh,' Jo said. 'You mean he cut the balls off dead men – a criminal like the Kray twins? Who would want to use their balls anyway? It's true then, what I said, using monkey glands to make some sick old millionaire happy, with a hard-on!'

'That's more or less it. He carried out over five hundred transplants, on monkeys, chimps, guineapigs, sheep, goats, a bull too. The idea was to graft the balls of younger animals into older animals, so he'd slice off a few millimetres of testicle, mainly from chimps and baboons, and implant the thin tissue into the scrotal sac of his old patients, who were either dictators or millionaires. They gave him so much money he took over the entire floor of a large hotel in Paris, and staffed it with all kinds of flunkeys – secretaries, chauffeurs, valets, and even two mistresses.'

'You mean they paid out all that money just to get a hard-on?' she asked, incredulously.

'Not really. The scourge was senility, and how to overcome it. The grail was rejuvenation. It had no aphrodisiac effects, but it was claimed it improved their sex drive, perhaps made men live longer, have more energy. It was before the discovery of testosterone. The research was not that far-fetched.'

'Wow,' Jo was really amazed. 'They didn't teach me any of this at medical school, although I've heard of Voronoff.'

'That's not all,' George said, a little wearily. 'It never is. The same guy set up a monkey farm on the Italian Riviera. He employed a former circus animal trainer, a keeper, to run the place.'

'A monkey farm?' Jo asked, her eyes wide open with disbelief.

'That's right,' George said. 'Monkey glands were the in-thing in the 1920s. They were fashionable, just as lobotomies and male circumcision were at one time. This guy Voronoff also tried transplanting monkey ovaries into women; once he transplanted a human ovary into a female monkey, then attempted artificial insemination with human sperm – his own or a criminal's – who knows? The experiments didn't work. There were no half-human, half-ape hybrids born.

'There was another mad professor in the 1920s who caused an international scandal, a zoology professor by the name of Ilia Ivanov. He wanted the Soviet government to fund a project to hybridise humans and apes using artificial insemination. He'd already carried out all kinds of hybridisation experiments on the usual suspects – guineapigs, rats, mice, rabbits. Ever heard of a zeedonk, a liger or a humanzee?'

'George, I'm just a GP you know, not a zoology professor.'

'Okay. Point taken. A zeedonk is a zebra-donkey hybrid, and Ivanov created one. He got interested in creating ape-human hybrids, like a humanzee. He actually asked the Bolshevik government for money, including funds for him to organise an expedition to Africa to collect apes, so he could bring them back, and get them to mate with humans, well not exactly mate with humans, as some Neanderthals did, but use artificial insemination to create a kind of monster hybrid.

'Ivanov travelled to Guinea in French West Africa in 1926 but when he reached a primate centre there, he found none of the chimps had reached breeding age, so he returned to Paris, spending some of the summer with our old friend Voronoff. Together, that summer, they took a woman's ovary and transplanted it into a chimp. The chimp had a name. Nora. Poor Nora had some human sperm put inside her. I've no idea who the donor was. Nothing happened. Then Ivanov returned to Africa, captured some chimps, and inseminated at least three of them, again without any result. Then he hit on another twist. He wanted to inseminate women with chimp sperm but how could he get them to agree?'

'Pretend it was some sort of medical experiment I suppose,' said Jo, still captivated by George's story.

'That's just what he did but the French governor refused to

allow it. With about twenty chimps he'd captured in the jungle, Voronoff hit on the idea of getting Russian women to help him, so he set off, of all places, for Abkhazia, the unfortunate neighbour of Georgia. He landed with just four chimps and immediately began searching for local women who would volunteer to carry half-ape babies…'

'…sorry to interrupt you George,' Jo said, 'but all of a sudden and half in jest, I don't know what's worse. Carrying a half-ape baby or being shagged by some of those hairy brutes at medical school!'

'Come off it, Jo!' George was smiling now. 'I'll just finish this story – I don't know what it's got to do with Charlie. Anyway, five or six women came forward but by the time that happened, the apes in his ape nursery had had a hard time of it, so when Ivanov was ready to inseminate the women, there was only one ape left – an orang-utan. All the others had died. Do you want to know what the orang was called?'

'Tarzan,' piped Jo, thinking that George would find it funny.

'That's right!' George answered her. 'That's right!'

Jo looked like she was stuck with a plum in her mouth, because she wanted to burst out laughing. 'Tarzan?'

'Yes,' George replied, a little glumly. 'Tarzan of the Apes, aka Lord Greystoke. What a corny story but it's absolutely true!'

'Go on,' Jo urged.

'Tarzan the orang had a brain haemorrhage at the wrong moment, maybe it got too much for him, so all the women ended up being spared the ape sperm. The ape died. Ivanov got hold of some more chimps in 1930 to try the experiment again but by then Ivanov had fallen out with the authorities. There was a purge on scientists. He was exiled to Kazakhstan after that, but his career was at an end and he died soon after.'

'Fuck me, George. That's one hell of a story. Sorry to swear but it's just so crazy, isn't it?'

'Yes, you're right,' George acknowledged. 'And I'll tell you another thing. I've seen pictures of Voronoff. He looks pretty spritely, big flowing moustache, got all his hair, though he was in his fifties. His face looked young, very young. It's possible he may have stitched some chimp balls into his own scrotum, if you ask me. He probably fried some for breakfast too.'

'George, stop it please. I'm beginning to feel sick.'

There was suddenly silence. Jo looked at George, and George just stared into the garden, as if he were meditating. Jo realised that George still hadn't told her *why* he'd got Charlie imprisoned in his garage or *what* he was going to do with him. Jo saw the small glass window that opened through the wall of the back room. 'What's that for, for heaven's sake?' she asked. When no answer was forthcoming, she saw that the window would slide open, so she pulled the plastic button stuck on near the rim of the glass, and a hole appeared as she moved the glass back.

George took a step back, and said, 'Christ.' The polytunnel was moving from side to side as if it had been galvanised by a tornado. It was Charlie, throwing his weight around in the tunnel. Then he rushed up to the small window, where he would sometimes collect food. He could just get his mouth through the opening. Charlie's mouth opened, and there came into that room a hideous scream.

George didn't bat an eyelid. He'd gotten used to it but Jo was so scared her heart fluttered in her chest, as if in a bout of atrial fibrillation. Involuntarily, she passed several drops of urine, feeling the slight wetness on her body, and she felt ashamed, not for 'wetting' herself but because she was angry for being so frightened. All that rational training I've had, she thought, just went out of the window, and down my pants.

George sensed she was upset. He took a banana from the kitchen, peeled it, and shoved it towards Charlie's mouth. Charlie took it with surprising delicacy, puckering his lips over the ripe fruit, as if he were afraid he might harm it. He turned, and shuffled back through the polytunnel.

SEVEN

Helga escaped into the back garden. Dr Waldren opened the patio doors, and she sneaked out when he wasn't looking. Helga had seen Jo collapse onto the polytunnel, and growled when she saw Charlie. She'd been terrified of Charlie's scream but now there was no sign of him. The dog started sniffing round the garage wall, where the polytunnel had been cut through to make an entrance and exit for Charlie.

She scratched the wall of the garage with her front paws, squealing like a frenzied pup, punctuating this every few seconds with half-suppressed barks and yelps. Dr Waldren decided to investigate, the noise was disturbing, and if Helga tore a hole in the garage, so Charlie escaped, how could he explain it the neighbours, who in any event were already curious about Dr Waldren. They could see little of his back lawn because of tree cover, but he did seem to wander in and out of his garage rather a lot, sometimes with a bunch of bananas, and this was odd, unless he was storing fruit. If he kept rabbits or guineapigs in the garage, would they eat bananas?

'Get back, Helga!' Dr Waldren shouted angrily. The black and white spaniel desisted but there were deep ruts in the wood where the dog's claws had scraped the side of the garage.

Jo had come out to see what the commotion was about. 'Why is Helga so keen to get inside, George? That's where you keep Charlie, isn't it? Are you going to show me inside now?'

George took her arm, leading her through the side gate to the front of the garage. Again he turned to look down the drive, towards the road, as if scouting the territory for intruders. Then he rushed towards the garage doors, undid the heavy locks, opened one door, and ushered Jo inside. Helga nipped in as well, hiding inside a cardboard box George had left out for her when she'd been a puppy.

Dr Waldren had no need to switch on any lights because sunlight still streamed through the roof opening. They could easily see Charlie. He had retreated to the far corner of his cage at the back of the garage.

Jo stood entranced. She scrutinised the great ape. The animal was clearly not fully grown, his arms long, his legs short, his fingers and hands looking also elongated, covered with dark, rubbery skin. Body hair stopped on the hands only just above the knuckles.

Charlie's face was mottled with brown, his ears stood out, and the raised ridge above his eyes, called the supraorbital crest, made his brown eyes, which were quite close together, appear more deeply set. There were a few white hairs around his mouth; the nose was tiny, virtually flat, and his mouth had an odd pinched look, like an old man's, the upper part rounded and prominent, as if Charlie had taken half an orange and stuck it between the skin of his mouth and gums.

Jo thought of the times she'd pretended to be a chimp at primary school; the trick was to stick your tongue down over your bottom front teeth, curl it into a ball, so the lower part of your mouth bulged out, and scratch under both arms, while making pretend 'pant-hoots' or grunts – imitating a chimpanzee.

*

In chimpanzees, the pant-hoot is a common form of vocal communication, a series of loud calls, which rise and fall in pitch, and often end in a scream. Both males and females use this call. The pant-grunt is a series of soft, low grunts – often given or made by a subordinate chimpanzee to a dominant one, perhaps in response to a charging display – where the chimp behaves like a lunatic, running, pulling or grabbing at branches, throwing branches or stones in the air, as well as drumming, slapping, stamping, kicking, and screaming. This behaviour is normally associated with chance or random meetings with old ape 'friends' not seen for some time, or to keep a group subordinate, especially where the male is the dominant alpha male.

Charging displays have also been witnessed in heavy rainstorms when the rain sheets down, through the forest canopy, and tiny rivers of rain quickly gather underfoot. It might be the rain that makes the chimps display, but it is more likely to be the thunderous noise of tropical storms, the bright bolts of lightning hurtling to the forest floor, like a primeval form of chaos that temporarily disrupts their lives.

*

All this time, Dr Waldren had been standing beside Jo, calling to Charlie softly, in an attempt to reassure him. 'Charlie boy, you're a good chimp today, Charlie boy, Charlie boy...'

The ape, however, suddenly came to life, perhaps wanting to show off, perhaps because Dr Waldren had another human beside him. Charlie took a running jump at the front of his cage, swung over one of the two horizontal bars, and ended up crashing against it. He kicked out wildly, making the flimsy cage rock and shake, his mouth wide open, screaming. Helga emerged from her cardboard box and joined in. The noise was terrible. Then, as suddenly as the noise started, it stopped. Charlie was gazing intently at Jo. His hair seemed to have fluffed out around his head and shoulders making him seem larger.

Charlie gently shook one of the bars, stretching out his arms, rocking from side to side. Then he sat down, his legs flexed and slightly splayed. He was still gazing directly at Jo, sitting more hunched than before, and swaying his shoulders. You could hardly miss Charlie's testicles because they were so huge, relative to his body size, about four to five times the size of a man's. Just as Jo was about to titter at the sight of them, a bright pink, thin, stick-like object with a tapered end – a very erect penis – stood out alarmingly, showing up against Charlie's black hair and the pale skin on his thighs.

'I think he fancies you,' George said.

'You are joking!' Jo looked horrified.

'He's displaying signs of courtship initiation,' George told her.

Charlie was up to something because just then he 'flicked' his penis, contracting a muscle to make it tap up and down rapidly. It seemed to dance in the air like a magician's wand.

'That's part of male chimpanzee behaviour when trying to initiate copulation,' Dr Waldren said. 'But, in Charlie's case, I don't think he actually means it. It's probably just displacement activity. If it were for real, he'd be hoping you'd present your rump to him, as in the lordosis reflex.'

'My hindquarters and gluteal folds are my business, George,' Jo joked saucily, but in the back of her mind she was starting to feel uneasy. All the talk about Voronoff and Ivanov, capturing wild chimps to boost the sex life of ageing millionaires, implanting chimp ovaries into random women, inseminating women with chimp sperm, George's strange companion in his garage, and the fact that he'd set up an operating table in his own house, it was all starting to look a little weird; Charlie's bobbing little stick of a penis only served to make it worse, as if instead of sticking up two fingers, Charlie was cocking a snook at the world via 8.5 cm of revoltingly pink flesh.

EIGHT

'Come Jo, let's give Charlie a rest. Good boy Charlie. Stop playing with yourself too. Maybe he gets lonely. No female chimps. I've got to clean his cage out, hell, I'll do it tomorrow.'

'What's that bone, George?'

'A lamb's bone – it was – a leg of lamb. Charlie eats meat from time to time. Chimpanzees are omnivores, just like us really. Actually,' George added as an afterthought, 'frugivore, fruit-eater, is probably more accurate for its cousin, the bonobo.'

As George locked up the garage, Charlie let out a howl of discontent, at least it sounded as if he weren't too happy.

George was reluctant to go back in the house, perhaps trying to intimate to Jo that it was time for her to leave. But Jo didn't want to leave. She wanted to get to the bottom of George's little experiment, so she asked George to make her some coffee before leaving. George agreed.

'Jo, I know you want me to tell you what I plan to do with Charlie, but I just can't,' George told her, his arms folded across his chest, hoping the gesture of stubbornness would make its point. 'You know we don't have that many secrets between us, but Charlie is, how shall I put it – at the moment – his future is hypothetical. There's no way of telling if what I plan will work. It's never been done before. If you just happen to mention it to someone, or any other doctors, that would probably be the end of my career.'

George looked downcast, almost hunted, Jo reflected. He hadn't shaved for at least four or five days, yet there was something about him, an air of excitement, the way his eyes shone when he talked about chimpanzees, and other primates, their history, human history, *our* history, Jo thought to herself, there was something about him beyond the ordinary; he was clearly an inspired man.

'Okay, George, I won't press you just now. Not yet. Tell me instead something else, why do chimps have such big balls? Such a thin penis?'

George smiled. 'You're right to be curious. Chimps have evolved them to cope with "sperm competition". Copulations with males are frequent – they're known as multimale copulations – so in order for sperm to compete, there has to be plenty of sperm capacity. Put another way, the sperm competition that results from multimale copulations must have favoured the evolution of large testes, relative to body size. The thin penis is peculiar. It's called "filiform", which means "threadlike". It's very long. Precopulatory displays involve the male displaying his penis in front of females, flashing if you like. Females also use the external genitalia for display, that's visual communication. At just the right time in the female's menstrual cycle, there is this pink sexual skin swelling. Females also have orgasms.'

'I hope this isn't your main area of interest, George?' Jo said. 'Or maybe it is.'

'No need to tease, Jo, not at all, but scientific curiosity extends into all corners of life. By the way, the average male chimp makes one intromission, and in five to ten seconds, it's all over – 8.5 to 9 pelvic thrusts until lift off.'

'Lift off?'

'Ejaculation. In Uganda, chimps have been observed wiping their penises or penes with leaves, after sex. In the Budongo Forest, to be exact. It's called postcoital penis cleaning.' George smiled wryly. 'Quite a lot of human females do the same, I believe. Male chimpanzees can also hang in the tree canopy and masturbate using a foot. Their own naturally, not one picked up from the forest floor! The opposable toe wraps round the thin but very long penis, a remarkable sight.'

Jo tried to imagine a hairy foot wrapped round a chimp's penis but found it forgettable. She felt overwhelmed by the facts, and her imagination stirred. Chimpanzees and humans shared a lot of DNA, over 98 per cent. If chimpanzees evolved further and at an improbable point in the future developed their own Internet, she couldn't imagine anything more horrible than 'chimp porn'. And yet, instead of interminable hours of porn showing humans having sex, at least with chimps every clip would all be over in five to ten seconds. Great! Jo suddenly felt she liked chimpanzees a little bit more.

'Forget the coffee, George. Next time will do.' Jo got into her car, a black VW polo. She reversed out of the drive, opened a window, and called out, 'Give my love to Charlie!'

NINE

George was left alone in the drive, pondering. He had cleaned out Charlie's cage earlier, feeding him with more nut and date bars from the supermarket. He had a little time but not much. The idea he had in mind for Charlie's future was becoming less appealing by the hour. He liked Charlie. A bond was unquestionably developing between man and ape. There was no Hippocratic Oath to be sworn for animals, although he had recently read about proposals by the Spanish parliament to pass a new law granting apes 'human rights'. It urged that 'non-human hominids', such as chimpanzees, gorillas, orang-utans and bonobos should enjoy the right to life, freedom, and not be tortured. This was largely the outcome of the foundation in 1993 of the Great Ape Project

George also controlled Charlie, marginally. A small daily dose of tranquiliser was necessary, he had decided. A chimpanzee is so strong, so unpredictable. What constraints had developed, George opined to himself, to rein in or keep a check on behaviour? Surely nothing like humans experience. Chimpanzees react to life with undefined rawness. Social controls or constraints existed to an extent in chimpanzee groups but there were no laws, as humans know them, other than 'the law of the jungle', which was a literary tale for the most part, and which also had gone, since the natural cycles of animals in the wild had been so disrupted by man.

If their reactions were so fast, like lightning because their inherent emotions are quite so ungoverned, would that explain the precocious Ayumu (son of Ai), the infant savant, the chimpanzee who has demonstrated extraordinary 'higher levels of cognition', by showing how to press a touch-sensitive screen in the right order, after memorising in milliseconds random sequences of numbers shown? No human taught him; he just watched his mother.

*

Chimpanzees and bonobos are our joint closest living relatives. George knew they are so close that humans can accept a blood transfusion or a kidney. He reminded himself to bring a mirror into the garage so Charlie could look at himself. Chimpanzees quickly pass the 'mirror self-recognition test', using mirrors to check their teeth (usually 32 in total, as with human dentition) or examine parts of their body they couldn't see without a mirror. (Other animals to have passed the test, which measures self-awareness by determining whether an animal recognises its own reflection, as an image of itself, include all the great apes, some species of dolphins, and elephants. An extension of this is the 'mark test', using a colour marker spot, often on the face.) George thought it might help Charlie's self-awareness. However, when he contemplated the ape's future, he wasn't so sure it was such a good idea.

Britain was the first country to afford legal protection from animal experimentation. Experiments, Dr Waldren knew only too well, on chimpanzees, orang-utans and gorillas were forbidden. There were mandarins in the Home Office who would have him arrested, if they found out what he planned for Charlie. He'd be in a cage himself. His career would be in ruins. Was it worth it?

*

Dr Waldren shivered. It was time to contact a colleague who was also a friend, of sorts, a friend with whom he shared rooms when reading medicine at university. Both had belonged to an amateur dramatics society, known as 'The Little Theatre'. Whereas George had earned success and the professional respect of his fellow medics, Christopher Grailing MD had broken the rules, and been suspended from practice by the GMC.

*

Doctors occupy a position of privilege and trust in society, and are rightly expected to uphold proper standards of conduct at all times. Christopher had his case heard before a 'Fitness to Practise' panel. First it was being uproariously drunk, knocking together the heads of two surgeons he'd met in a bar – alcohol-fuelled violence that was wholly unacceptable despite his remorseful apologies. His behaviour had 'fallen significantly below those standards of conduct expected of a member of the medical profession'.

Then it was displaying 'sexualized behaviour' towards a patient, this defined as 'acts, words or behaviour designed or intended to arouse or gratify sexual impulses and desires'. Chris had grabbed a patient (he had been seeing her socially for drinks) in his surgery, fondling her breasts, very nearly exposing himself, and wishing he had (although the Panel did not know that). This amounted to a breach of the previous warning placed upon him by the GMC.

The third error made by Chris was stealing ketamine from a treatment room, while under the influence of alcohol, to the extent of being totally wasted. The Panel determined that Chris's fitness to practise was impaired pursuant to Section 35C(2)(a) and (c) of the Medical Act 1983 (as amended), 'by reason of misconduct and caution'.

The Panel found it necessary in the public interest, and in order to maintain public confidence in the profession, to suspend his registration with immediate effect. Chris had been unable to earn a living. Suspension from the register of doctors has a punitive upshot. A doctor may not practise during the period of suspension (18 months for Chris), and so cannot earn a living as a doctor.

Chris had drifted from London to Oxford, a city where he felt strangely at home, though he had not studied there, and was not 'an Oxford man'. Within a few weeks, he had blagged part-time work as a city guide, showing tourists round the colleges. Then he'd taken a job at the imposing John Radcliffe Hospital, a modern white-tiled edifice on Headington Hill, overlooking the city. No one checked his references, and if they had, they certainly hadn't checked very carefully; Chris emerged as hospital porter and possible trainee mortuary assistant. He'd said he was really keen to learn; the job as trainee mortuary assistant had been suggested as an option. He'd given a different home address, and altered his middle name. It seemed to do the trick.

Working as a hospital porter meant the suspended doctor had

virtually to become another person. The doctor's persona, the social graces of his profession, had to be hidden; no more friendly smiles, compassion and understanding. His social skills needed lobotomising. Porters at the hospital tended to be monosyllabic, gruff, taciturn, thick-skinned, slightly menacing in their black trousers and heavy black, lace-up boots. For a porter to get on quietly with the job, and not be noticed, it was arguably better to wear the hang-dog's permanent expression of resignation, bitterness, even indifference, a sullenness only broken by the occasional cackle of a laugh or a '*Whoops, sorry mate*', when accidentally knocking a trolley carrying a patient up against a ward wall.

*

George found him in a pub off the High Street, the gently curving street known in Oxford as 'The High'. Walking down a narrow alleyway, George tumbled into a pub, searching in the gloom – and there he was – Christopher Grailing, dragging deeply on a cigarette, surreptitiously pouring neat whisky from a hip flask straight into a pint of beer.

'Hiya!' said Chris cheerfully, reminding George of middle aged checkout ladies in Tesco he could just as cheerfully murder.

'So there you are, you old bugger!' George slapped him heartily on the back. Chris set off into a spasm of bronchial coughing that sounded utterly dreadful. 'This was my favourite pub too, some years back. It seemed a good place to start looking. How the hell are you?'

Chris stared at George as if George were jointly responsible with the 'powers that be' for all the ills in the world – including his hacking cough, his sore, red-rimmed, rheumy eyes, and the fact that his beer glass was all but empty. There was a kind of malign accusation in his eyes, as if Chris were seeking someone to blame. 'As far as I know I'm still very much alive,' Chris answered. 'And what are you looking for?'

George said, 'You'll never guess,' quickly deciding to add

nothing more. 'Let me get you a drink,' not such a brilliant idea he thought, as if encouraging Chris to damage his liver even further. George went to the bar, and came back with two streaming pints. On the way to the bar he'd glanced up a flight of stairs, catching a glimpse of an oil painting in a gilt frame with a strangely haunting face. He stared until recognition came. It was Percy Bysshe Shelley when a young man, almost a boy, the picture a famous portrait by Curran, dated 1819. Oh, '*Cor Cordium*', he found himself saying aloud, '*Heart of Hearts*', the words part of an inscription on Shelley's gravestone in Rome. Shelley had been sent down from Oxford he remembered, for publishing an obscure tract on atheism, and famously only ever attended one lecture. To balance this lamentable fact, he did spend sixteen hours a day reading in his room. Did he not once say or write, George thought to himself, that poets were the unacknowledged legislators of the world? Then it was as well that Shelley would never know what he'd planned for Charlie.

Chris's face showed a glimmer of a smile as he supped his pint. George, however, was in tentative mood. He wanted to trust Chris, to have someone to unburden his plans to, but would Chris trust him? When Chris heard what he planned to do for Charlie, when he was told exactly what was needed for his experiment…

'I know about the suspension, Chris,' George began. 'Worse things happen at sea, or in the operating theatre, or the surgery. I know it must be tough for you now.' (That was a dig, and George knew, because it was in his surgery where Chris had almost displayed his manhood to the female patient.)

'So, what is it George? It must be important if you've come all the way to Oxford.'

'Where do you work?'

'At the Radcliffe, as it happens. Nothing grand. Pushing bodies on trolleys.'

'Do you have access…?' George stopped mid sentence. He was actually quietly horrified by what he was about to ask.

Chris was leering at him, the beer still wet on his lips, his nicotine-stained fingers sloppily cradling his glass. '*Bodies?*' Chris asked, almost reticently, in an offhand way, as if discussing cuts of meat at the butcher's.

George looked at Chris's eyes, first one then the other, unsure which one to home in on, or both, as a display of intended sincerity. He realised it made no difference. Chris Grailing's eyes were equally glazed over. He was best described as a sozzled alcoholic, albeit with something approaching a 'heart', inside him. 'Not bodies, Chris. Parts of bodies. *Heads*, to be exact!'

'I'd say you're taking the frickin' Mickey, George, if I didn't know you better. What *kind* of head parts do you have in mind? Ear, nose, throat? Eyes?' Chris spoke in a manner a jury might construe as apologetic. It was because he didn't want to know the answer.

'You have a head on you, Chris, don't you?' George asked with a certain amount of authority.

'I should fucking well hope so,' Chris replied with comparable intensity.

'I'm looking for a brain,' said George. 'A sober one, mind. Male, youngish, and of course, still alive.'

'Seriously, George?' Chris strangled the words as if gulping for air. His hands were shaking uncontrollably. Then he added, 'Did you get that story from someone…who had no business in the telling of it?'

It could be delirium tremens, George thought, except there was no sweating, acute anxiety, confusion or hallucination. He cleared his throat. 'Fucking serious, Chris.' It was his turn to look crazy. 'I want a brain, a human brain! You got any ideas?'

Chris swallowed involuntarily. There was nothing in his mouth to swallow. He turned his head round, to the left, then to the right, as if looking for an anchor for his own brain to latch on to, to feel something remotely approaching normality, to feel sane.

TEN

After leaving the pub, the two men found somewhere good to eat in St Aldate's, a Thai restaurant selling a remarkable green paste chicken curry, not far from Tom Tower; this is the famous landmark entrance, gatehouse to Christ Church College (to many known as 'The House', from the Latin temple or house of Christ); it is deserving of its old name 'The Faire Gate', as it conceals so much pomp and finery, and further south there is the pleasure of green meadows. Feeling bloated from the food and drink, George and Chris walked back towards The High, turning right at Carfax Tower, then past St Mary the Virgin's Church, ambling along St Mary's Walk, with All Souls on their right, Brasenose and the old Bodleian Library to the left.

Chris had recovered from his drinking session. He was keen to find out more from George. As they passed the entrance to Brasenose College in Radcliffe Square, Chris stopped to look through the gateway, noticing the porter in his lodge, and the green quad beckoning behind, sunlight flooding the ancient stones. 'Money in it, is there George?' Chris asked quietly, his eyes taken by a girl with an older man, perhaps her father. Chris gave her the usual male look-over – legs, bottom, curves, breasts – and then finally her face. However, when he looked into her eyes, and realised what lay behind those eyes, encased in a skull, and that George Waldren, his GP friend, was looking for body parts, for a human brain no less, he suddenly felt sick to his stomach.

'Enough money to pay the rent for a couple of years,' George replied. 'There's more if you'll help me with the operation.'

Chris was unable to respond. He was thinking that there was more money, much more money to be made by creating something like Damien Hirst's diamond-encrusted skull, titled 'For the Love of God'. Buy any old skull in a taxidermy shop, send it to a workshop, encrust with 8,601 flawless diamonds worth £12 million, polish the original teeth, no ugly amalgam fillings, and then give it a new price tag, £50 million. Not a brain in sight. Nothing inside the skull but vacuous, empty space.

A living brain was a different proposition altogether. Veins, arteries, canals, glands, fat, blood vessels – the human brain was a very fragile organ, the cornerstone of the nervous system. Think upon it as the command and control centre, a processing centre for nerve information, home to more than 100 billion neurons, or nerve cells. Given the money, Chris thought, it would be easier to construct another 'For the Love of God' than to deliver George a living human brain.

'The architecture, as you know George,' Chris began, 'has none of this certainty. The only certainty – no there isn't one – but I suggest viewing the miniscule skull in the ante-chapel here, near the Deer Park, where you won't find any deer. It's so neat it's almost pretty. I found it on my last visit. It says all there is to say about life and death. Ask one of the porters to show you if you like, they always remember a face. You could come back in twenty years and someone would know you. Especially the butler, always attired correctly, always ready to enquire your business.'

It was then that both men paused to look through the gateway of Brasenose College, both distracted, if not mesmerised, by the patterns of sunlight continually falling into the quad. Chris continued. 'To get back to the problem, you can't have a brain without a head, and to be alive it needs a body. You're asking me to deliver a body, someone alive – not a kind of Unipart brain box, all wrapped up in ice and ready to go. I don't do bodies, George. Not for hell's fire.'

'Why not? Just think. You'll be helping me to create something remarkable, something the world has never seen before, something actually new under the sun, that all those scientific professors and students, those whose dead souls line these hallowed Oxford streets, or at least their memory, with their crazy experiments, their air pumps and electrical machines, galvanic troughs – do you know they were called "stinks men" – could never have dreamed of. Admittedly they were more chemists than surgeons but Christ almighty George, what I will do is going to make one hell of a stink! You'll see. You can be part of it. Chris, help me, please!'

Chris just stayed silent, pursing his lips as if in pain, and they left Brasenose, to walk into the street, not far from Wren's sundial on the library wall of All Souls, All Souls of the Faithful Departed, of Oxford. Then he spoke, to the polite embarrassment of those in the street, a mixture of students and tourists. 'For all the brazen gods, what is this you ask me? Is it not written,' his voice growing louder and more clamorous as they walked past All Souls, as he pointed an accusatory finger in the direction of Wren's creation on the north wall of north quad, 'is it not written, "The hours perish, and are reckoned to our account?" *Pereunt et imputantur.* How will you, how will *you* account for what you intend to do with a man's mind, his poor precious brain, inside his bloody head?'

'Come now, Chris, there's no need for that language. Save it for later, when I tell you what I'm going to do.'

'You'd better tell me soon, Georgie boy. The brain is the most complex organ in the human body, responsible for all our thoughts, every single one of them, our memories, feelings, actions, experience of the world, George. That's big stuff, that not-so-hollow crown. One point four kilograms of jelly-like mass, a tissue mass. I know George. No two brains are alike. Our brains form a million new connections every second, every second of our lives. And you want one. You want me to deliver one to you, on a plate too, and alive!'

This time it was George's turn to keep silent, and he held his peace.

ELEVEN

Charlie was lying back on the floor of his cage inside the garage. A little light shone through from the opening in the roof, and Charlie was quite content to lie there, his arms stretched out in a position of relaxation, his large testicles bunched up either side of his pink penis; this is what was showing, and it wasn't much. He had no wish to move but a momentary annoyance was a black fly that seemed trapped inside the cage. Every so often it flew round his head. Charlie snatched and missed every time but the effort seemed to deter the fly from buzzing around until a good fifteen seconds had passed, and then it appeared again.

Charlie seemed oblivious, perhaps because he was enjoying the warm sunlight more. He closed his large eyes, scratching only occasionally underneath one arm. In the daze that followed, Charlie might have dreamed of his mother in Cameroon hung upside down on a hunter's pole, her blood dotting the forest floor in big, bruised lumps, or so it seemed to Charlie when a hunter had gathered him in a net, and taken him. He might have dreamed of his mother cradling him in her arms, playfully biting his toes, rolling upside down on the forest floor, while Charlie clung to her fur, his mouth wide open, big ears splayed; perhaps Charlie, mischievously, might have attempted to escape from his mother but she would reach out a black, furry arm, her hand with its very long, mottled brown fingers clasping young Charlie's foot, dragging him back to earth. A mother's love extends to apes too.

Who knows if chimps can dream? If they could tell us, what would they say?

While Charlie lay there, silent, still, only moving occasionally to brush aside the fly that still bothered him, and felt in the dream his mother's puckered lips on his mouth, there was a noise from outside the garage, a car driving in, and Charlie instantly tensed, his body arching. He rose up, his head towards the door of the garage, the upper body tight, taut, ready for challenge. Although he was young, and living in virtual isolation, he displayed all the characteristics of a young alpha male; he was growing in strength, becoming his own chimp, even in the bleak confines of Dr Waldren's garage.

Charlie started to pant-hoot, that strange noise made by chimps when something in the group isn't right, when there is danger, when the unexpected looms close, when other groups are heard vocalising in the distance, even when finding lush fruit trees in the rainforest. Then, they become excited and wish to express... what? Feelings of fear, hope, anger, lust or love? The emotions of a chimpanzee are unlike humans. They do not cry, they have no tears or tear ducts, and as far as we know they do not ache from the heart. Charlie had as much as cried once, when his mother was killed in front of him, when life had been shot from her by a hunter's gun; and though he knew nothing of his heart, in what strange valleys the rivers of his blood were pumped, something deep inside him felt pain when he lost his mother.

*

Scientific evidence now supports the existence of many traits that are undeniably human in non-human primates, such as the discovery that chimpanzees can exercise empathy and altruism by providing comfort to other chimps they know are stressed. Chimpanzees bond with members of their group with grooming activities, caressing, stroking, play behaviour, and sex. Empathy and sympathy, described as 'pillars of human morality', may also belong to the domain of the great apes. Animals, some scientists believe, are conscious, and suffer as we do.

*

Charlie's pant-hoots reached an ear-splitting climax just as the garage door was shaken. Jo saw the locks and remembered she could get the keys from the kitchen. Returning to the garage with the keys, she unlocked the garage doors, and slipped inside. Charlie was standing on two legs as she walked in. He thumped his cage with both feet, and then dropped down on all fours, shoulders hunched, swaying rhythmically from side to side.

'Hello Charlie, it's me. How are you?' Jo called out. She had lost her fear of this great ape. Her face broke into a smile as she approached his cage. Charlie relaxed as soon as he saw her. His upper lip oddly curved up for a moment over his mouth; perhaps it was Jo's perfume. The ape looked at Jo with great concentration, sitting back on his haunches, pressing his face against the steel wire bars. He pushed a finger through the gap between the thin bars, and Jo instinctively touched it, rubbing her own fingers back and forth over the mottled brown skin. Charlie loved it. His face rested against the cage, enjoying the tactile massage of Jo's fingers. It seemed to her that Charlie's eyes nearly closed over, she imagined with something approaching happiness, contentment.

After a few moments Charlie rolled onto his back, still leaving a finger loosely in Jo's hand. With his other hand, he scratched near his scrotal area, as if indicating a request for grooming. Jo, perhaps unwisely, reached one finger through the bars and scratched Charlie's thigh. Charlie uttered soft grunts, clearly delighted with the attention. His eyes opened again, and he looked at Jo with very large brown eyes, flecks of gold in liquid pools, the tiny points of light coming in from the skylight above them.

'Aren't you beautiful, Charlie? So beautiful.' Jo was quite taken with Charlie's charms. 'Heaven knows what George Waldren wants with you, I hope you'll survive it, whatever it is. God, you poor creature. I'm worried for you!' Jo noticed a bunch of bananas hanging on a rack. She broke one off, giving it to Charlie, who pant-hooted again at the sight of the fruit. Jo considered whether it was safe to let Charlie out. She thought how nice it would be to cuddle him. He could hang on to her waist or neck, grip round her body with his legs, but then she remembered he was no longer a young chimp. He could be dangerous.

There wasn't time to think about it as Helga, who had escaped from the house, started scratching at the garage door, barking like a demented demon. Charlie flung the banana aside, stomping hard on the floor of his cage, screaming with what appeared to be rage. Helga managed to nose her way into the garage, Jo not having properly locked the garage doors. She stood trembling in front of Charlie's cage, legs quivering, a low mournful growling beginning. Not to be outdone, Charlie took one great leap against the side of his cage opposite the dog, and crashed against it with his head. Recovering from this, Charlie swung both poles in his cage as hard as he could, and rushed to the front to confront Helga. His upper lip drew back in a frenzied snarl, displaying his strong, robust canines, which projected far above (and below) their tooth row. Helga whimpered, her tail well and truly between her legs, or at least it would have been, had it not been docked.

Jo knelt down to push Helga away but the dog turned round, so that her hind quarters were nearer to the cage. Charlie saw the opportunity – to grab Helga's tail stump. He would not let go. Poor Helga! She howled, doing her own version of a dog pant-hoot that was both miserable and pathetic. From the noise you'd think a canine torturer was pulling her claws out one by one.

The whimpering, yelping, almost crying sounds from Helga only served to make Charlie angrier. Helga dug her claws in but failed to get a grip on the concrete floor. She was pulled back against the cage.

'Charlie,' Jo shouted. 'Stop it!'

Charlie looked at Jo and then at Helga. Suddenly he let go and Helga shot forward, as if fired from the barrel of a cannon. She started to run but only got as far as the garage door, which she neatly crashed into, head first. Still whimpering, she scrambled past one of the garage doors, and fled.

Jo was utterly unsure about what to do next. Unsure about why George kept a live male chimpanzee in his garage, why he'd set up a makeshift operating theatre in his house, why he talked so much about his 'experiment', without explaining a single thing.

George would have to answer soon, very soon. She could wait no longer.

TWELVE

George had invited Chris down to Dorset. It seemed the best way – show him the goods, as it were – and take it from there. There would also be time for Chris (he took a week off) to dry out a little, if that were possible. The money was attractive. Ten thousand pounds, and more, if the 'experiment' worked. There would be more money, George explained, because in the event of success, the media would be beating a path, more likely a motorway, to their door. They would be famous.

George drove back first, and Chris followed, after four days, on the train. George was angry because at the station, he found Chris tottering and teetering on the platform, and smelling like a distillery in the Western Isles. He had been told to get off at Poole but Chris had only got as far as Bournemouth.

'Get in the car, you old soak,' George admonished, when he eventually found him. 'When are you going to leave that stuff alone? You don't need me to tell you that your liver is already a burnt-out case, well, strictly that's your lungs, but your liver, it's got to be a swollen sclerosed wreck by now.'

'I'll take your fucking advice when asked for, thank you,' Chris announced with a slur. That was the problem with alcoholics. They put so much feeling that often came out as resentment into things – imagine a boozed-up Peter O'Toole on crack – but you can often push them over with not much more than a bent straw. 'I need a drink, anyway, because I'm freaked out by what you want from me. You said a male. Do you mean a schoolboy, on life support? Body dead but brain alive, instead of the other way round? And what's wrong with a schoolgirl? Slightly more interesting from a dissection point of view.'

'Shut up, Chris. How can you talk like that? You lost the best job in the world, for what?'

Chris's chin slumped down on his chest. 'You're right. Too right. Dr Chris Grailing MD, currently suspended, for taking horse shit and displaying in front of a patient who was fucking fit. Oh bollocks! Dr Chris Grailing MD, imbiber extraordinaire, sozzler and sot, suspended by the GM-fucking-C.' Chris began to snigger, and the snigger turned to a belly laugh. 'Dr Chris Grailing MD suspended, but a frigging hung drawn and quartered Dr Grailing when they find out your little secret. George's experiment. Dealer in brains, body parts. Body snatcher. No, brain snatcher!'

George was silent. When something got Chris worked up, you couldn't stop him talking. This was more like chess, the moves had to be worked out well in advance, and the greatest game of all was the experiment. A bit like playing God really, George pondered inwardly. *Playing Darwin and Dawkins*. A sub-chapter for *The Ancestor's Tale*. 'Dr George Waldren's experiment with human and animal consciousness breaks entirely new ground. History must be rewritten.' Those hours that Chris had referred to on Wren's sundial at All Souls, would he, George Waldren, not account for them in his own unique way? Even if the hours perished, something would remain. George preferred silence. There was nothing to explain just yet.

'I'll be your accomplice, my old mate,' Chris announced suddenly, in a maudlin fit of camaraderie. 'Count on me, George, as long as you're Burke and I'm Hare.'

'Oh,' said George casually. 'Why?'

'Burke was hanged, you burke. Sixteen, or was it seventeen murders in all? Hare escaped with his life, testified against Burke. Skin from Burke's body was used to make a leather binding for a small book. God knows what's in that book, *Burke's Skin Memoirs*. The book is in a room at the Royal College of Surgeons, Edinburgh. Incredible really, the surgeon who bought the bodies, he got off scot-free, because there was no evidence against him – that he knew where the cadavers were coming from.'

'Trying to tell me something, Chris? The medical school at Edinburgh University has Burke's skeleton. It's in the anatomy library. I know. Get this Chris, rather you than me. And if there's a book in this, I hope it's your skin and not mine they use to bind the book!'

Chris snorted but said nothing more about the famous body-snatchers.

As they turned into the driveway, George couldn't help wondering about his guilty secret, just *what* was in the garage, that creature he'd locked up in a cage, with whom his mind was beginning to wrestle. How would he explain everything to Chris, indeed where to begin?

Helga welcomed them but George was uneasy. Helga might give the game away before he had a chance to explain anything. Chris wanted to kick the dog off his trouser leg when it jumped up but he was too unsteady on his feet.

'That's Helga,' George explained. 'Resident barker. My dear friend, too. She's all I've got with Jo away and the children at college.'

George took Chris upstairs with Helga snapping at his heels. He let Chris into the spare bedroom, except it was more akin to offloading a limp body. Chris slumped onto the bed like a corpse, as one of Burke and Hare's victims might have crumpled up before rigor mortis set in.

'Come on, Helga, let's leave him to recover. Come downstairs, now!' Helga's little tail stump wagged gladly, apparently none the worse for Charlie's wrenching in the garage.

George sighed. What to do now? He told himself he wasn't really much better than Chris, just more in control, as he took down a bottle of malt, and poured a double, sinking gladly into his favourite chair.

He decided to have an early night too. He couldn't be bothered to feed Charlie now. That would have to wait until morning.

THIRTEEN

That morning came. Out in the harbour seabirds danced over the waves, and yacht pennants caught in sea breezes tinkled against their masts. At six o'clock a fox slunk through the garden, his nose picking up Charlie's scent. The effect on the fox was to send it running for the nearest hedge, and a gap in it, to escape.

In the kitchen Chris Grailing made some filter coffee. He'd unexpectedly woken very early, his head clearer, and he was hungry. He was startled to see several bloody legs of lamb in the fridge, and more in the freezer. He took some milk from the fridge, found the sugar bowl, and went into the dining room. In one corner on a sideboard was a huge pile of bananas.

Cradling his coffee as if to warm his hands that October morning, Chris looked out of the French windows. Surprisingly, a few shrivelled apples on the solitary apple tree still clung on though the branches were dancing too, like the waves, in the October wind.

He wasn't prepared when it happened. He'd noticed the long polytunnel contraption, for that's what it was, how it snaked from a wall in the garage to a wall of the room he was standing in. He'd seen it begin to shake, a dark shape inside relentlessly moving through the tunnel. He'd put down his coffee, as if to concentrate more. The dark shape stopped. A bristling, receding chin rested against the end of the tunnel, at least it looked like a chin, with hairs, both white and black, and lips, the kind you'd kiss only in an extreme nightmare.

Chris gingerly touched the plastic, then having seized on the button, drew the opening back. Charlie had come for breakfast.

'My God! I'm going mad!' Chris's eyes were white with fear. He fainted, slipping onto the floor in a desultory heap. Charlie reached through the opening, pulling at one of Chris's hands, drawing it towards his mouth. His teeth closed over the fingers on Chris's right hand with a playful bite. Chris came round. He screamed. Charlie copied him, sounding off a series of mighty pant-hoots.

Dr Waldren heard the commotion. He jumped out of bed, and ran downstairs, immediately sizing up what had happened. 'Charlie boy! That's enough.' He reached for a hand of bananas, and thrust a couple of ripe ones towards Charlie's open mouth. The ape's lips closed on the unpeeled bananas, just as he nearly always did, with surprising delicacy. His dark brown eyes took in first George, then Chris, and with a single grunt, he turned and was gone.

George pulled Chris over to an armchair, and lifted him in. 'You've got it. That's my secret. I can't hide it from you any longer. That hulking brute is *Pan troglodytes*, a chimp, cave dweller. Charlie boy. Isn't he the greatest?'

Chris's face was blank. 'Gave me one hell of a shock,' he said.

'So he should. You, me, and him, we all share a common ancestor, from about six or seven million years ago.'

'Well, he and you might, not sure about me,' ribbed Chris with uncharacteristic good humour. But then his mood changed, a characteristic of alcoholics. 'Who cares about the past? We're living in the goddamn present, the here and now. Why, George? Why the hell keep a chimpanzee in your back garden?'

'George is my – my student. I'm studying him. Problem is, to carry out the experiment I want to attempt...I need to remove something from Charlie, and replace it with...' he paused, quite unsure of what to say '...something else.'

'Uh-uh!' Chris stared at George, his rheumy eyes watering fast. 'Is this where I come in? I provide you with what? A human body and you swop them? You want to find the best way to dispose of one body, say the chimp's, and replace it with another?'

George just stared at him silently.

'No, that can't be right, old chap. You want the person to be alive, don't you?'

George took Chris's coffee away, and came back with a fresh cup. 'Here, try that,' he said. 'And listen.'

Chris rubbed his eyes as if to see straight. He took a gulp of coffee, and said, 'Fire away. I'm all ears for this crazy plan of yours.'

Just then, Helga, who had been pretending to snooze on the dining room carpet, jumped up barking. They heard a car door slam, then the front door banged shut and in stormed Jo, looking pretty, her cheeks pink, almost obscenely healthy, thought Chris.

'Hello boys,' Jo smiled warmly, obviously pleased she had found both men in. 'Are we discussing something important? Have you seen it yet, Chris? The beast in the garage with the big balls. Actually, he's not a beast. He's really very sweet when you get to know him.'

'Tell you later, Chris,' George muttered under his breath but Jo heard him.

'Come on now, George. We want to know all about it. The bloody experiment! Don't keep us waiting any longer. We want to know, don't we, Chris? George, speak up. We're waiting!' Jo was now really worked up, her feet planted firmly on the ground, her earnestness and female determination obvious. Chris noticed how the points of her breasts stirred and gently shook when she spoke, and he liked that.

'He's just about to tell me, Jo. He can tell you too, can't he?' Chris was getting into the swing of things. 'George, Jo and I are *not* leaving this room until you tell us just what the devil's going on in your garage. For Christ's sake, George, a grown chimpanzee at the end of a plastic tunnel, trying to bite my fingers off! Those legs in the fridge, lambs' legs, and this pile of bananas, they're for him, aren't they? I suppose you want to feed him a human brain. Turn him into a sort of cannibal. You can see it now, can't you,' he said sarcastically. "Ape devours human body parts, brain first. Scientist doctor explains all." We're listening George, aren't we Jo, and we're sitting comfortably, so begin.'

George sat down on the nearest chair, as if glad to be about to get the whole thing off his chest. So George began to tell them, and as he talked, a kind of shocked silence fell in that room and even the excitable Helga seemed to hold her breath.

FOURTEEN

'There was a room at school – in the biology lab – that's where it all started. In fact, the cabinet was in a corridor at the back. Inside the cabinet were the usual fossils and trophies, the skeleton of a frog, so delicate, almost a work of art, two heads of New World monkeys, one smaller than the other, they looked almost cheerful. But it was next to the monkey skulls where I saw, gazing out at me, this grotesque, monstrous skull, although it was only grotesque when, as an impressionable schoolboy, I considered my own mortality. I would go, eventually I thought, from one miracle, the miracle of this present life to another forlorn place, the place of death. Perhaps I'd end up in the same cabinet, if I chose to donate it – my skull displayed there too, next to the other one – and people might say – masters, boys, girls, old boys, old girls on Open Days – "Look, there's George! The one that did the experiment with the chimp!" But who would know about the other skull, how it got there, where it came from? Would anybody care?'

Chris looked almost cross. 'Look mate, we're not expecting a philosophical monologue about your school days. Maudlin memories of your alma mater. You're supposed to be explaining what's going to happen to poor old Charlie, right?'

'Okay,' George agreed, 'but I'll just tell you about the skull. It was found in a hat box in an old Victorian mansion. The skull was weathered, as if it had been left out by the seaside or something like that, it had a heavy ridge at the back, very distinct grooved sinuses, and worn, almost flat teeth. The biology master told me first they thought it might be an Inuit skull, an Eskimo, but a department in the British Museum told them it was from Polynesia. It's an odd feeling to hold a skull, not just when you're a medical student. Just by the door of the biology lab is a skeleton, donated by a Chinese man. It was when I went outside, and walked over the lawns back to School House, that was my boarding house, after the name changed, I thought I'd like to study medicine.

'The way we fired the .303s on Field Days, someone would have need of a doctor. Incidentally, the RSM's booming voice came through gaps in his front teeth. When a boy questioned the extent of the empire, he whistled back, "British Empire? You can throw a rifle from 'ere to China – got a man there to catch it!"

'It was so good to be alive, to be young. I felt who could not treasure every moment of life, of living, especially when you're young? Though the food made us gaunt in those dear stones. Remember the feeling, Chris? It was as good as being a god, wasn't it?

'Later that night I thought more about what it means to be alive. I suddenly thought what would a man do to save himself, or put another way, if a doctor could save a terminally ill person, and give him or her life, even if in another form, could I ever do it? Would it be worth it?

'How many times have you heard someone say, "One thing led to another"? It's what happened to me. I'd wanted to do general surgery. I was also interested in palaeontology, especially in our nearest relatives, probably because as you know, primates are facing an extinction crisis. If it's not habitat loss, then they're being eaten to extinction – anthropogenic disturbance and predation. Charlie in there,' George continued in earnest, pointing to the garage, 'in Africa he'd just be bushmeat, or made into juju charms for good luck. Bushmeat can provide up to 80 per cent of protein in people's diets. I have no time for that tired old expression, "There but for the grace of God go I", you know, but no African thinks like that. It's food. At present rates of bushmeat consumption, the great apes will be extinct in twenty years. Of course people need to feed their families. There's over a million tons of bushmeat taken out of Congo basin forests every year.

'When you eat a chimpanzee you're eating 98 per cent or so human genes, or at least genes we share with them. Can you eat a gene? Look, it's just meat on the bone to the average African. I know it's not as simple as that. We share half the same DNA as a banana – and I've lots of those – in the garage.'

'It's depressing,' Jo said, trying hard to conceal a glorious smirk, 'but so what? You've got a live chimpanzee living in your garage. You don't have permission to keep it there, to keep it anywhere. Experiments on chimps are banned in this country.' Jo looked angry.

'Shut up, Jo,' Chris called out from a slumped position on the sofa. 'Give the poor man a chance to speak.'

'Thank you, Chris,' George said quickly. He stroked his chin thoughtfully, wondering how to start telling them what was going to happen to Charlie. 'My experiment is essentially a cross-species transplant.' George paused, waiting for an outcry but there was none. Chris looked very serious, and Jo seemed worried. 'I take a brain, half a brain to be precise. That is, I perform a hemispherectomy on a young male, who is essentially terminally ill, very terminally ill, not expected to last for more than a few days, or hours, at most. Ideally, and more realistically, comatose, with no hope of survival, and on life support.

'Concurrently, I perform a hemispherectomy on the donee, being careful to match up the same side of the brain, in other words there will be one left hemisphere and one right hemisphere in the final outcome. This is an incredibly complicated procedure, and may easily lead to a fatal conclusion. In fact that's what will probably happen. Stem cells will be harvested, from both sources, and used in the hope they might help to stabilise and even improve the outcome for the patient. How they will interact is not known. There will need to be some cranial enlargement, again an entirely new procedure, because the donor hemisphere will be too large to fit comfortably within the donee. I am not entirely sure how this can be accomplished yet. In essence, what you will have is human brain tissue transplanted into the brain of a chimpanzee, the space for this being made by the hemispherectomy.

'As to what will happen if the creature survives and how it will behave cognitively, that is a complete unknown, but I have no doubt it will be of immense interest to science, especially to students of primate behaviour, and even human behaviour. Textbooks will need to be rewritten, studies in neuroethics will flourish. This is a totally unique, human–primate experiment. If this is not the bravest of brave new worlds, tell me. Apart from that I know in my heart it's absolutely wrong to use chimpanzees in invasive medical research. There's no justification for it any more. That leaves *me* in a very awkward place.

By the way, and I'm sure you have guessed by now, the subject, the principal subject for this experiment is in my garage now.'

'Charlie!' Jo and Chris screamed in horrified unison. 'Charlie!'

There was complete silence. Helga's eyes darted about the room, ears flattened, her little body trembling.

'You're going to butcher that poor chimp!' Jo cried. 'That poor chimp in there, living on bananas and lambs' legs. What about the other poor bastard? You won't be allowed to practise as a doctor ever again if you cut someone's brain out – while they're still alive! That's murder, isn't it, even if they are terminally ill?'

Then Helga did a strange thing. She crawled over the carpet to the sanctuary of George's shoes, inching along on her belly, front paws stretched out, hind legs scrunched underneath. In the relative safety of the space next to George's brown shoes, Helga let out the most mournful howl. It was a horrible wail of a howl, and it made the skin on Jo's arms and neck prickle.

George buried his head in his arms. Chris actually sat up on the sofa. Jo was wide-eyed. But as soon as Helga stopped her yowling, there came an altogether more alien sound. Instead of just sounding fearful, the scream was of the primordial deep-jungle, the Lost World of the primeval, an ape separated from the human race by six million years of evolution yet sharing now, in the eternal present, virtually the same genetic make-up.

Charlie's nose was snuffling by the polytunnel opening. He was butting it with his head. If he could break through, he'd get food. His teeth soon found it very easy to tear open the end of the polytunnel, even if only in neat strips, the way he stripped meat from a bone. Before long, there was enough room to poke his head through the opening. As soon as he got his head through, he pant-hooted with all the excitement. Helga dashed for the nearest corner, trying to hide in a space that couldn't be hidden in, so she only scraped her head against the wall. Charlie made such a noise that Jo held her hands tightly over her ears, while Chris cuddled up against the sofa, evidently afraid.

Only George stood there tall, even proud, as he surveyed the scene. Charlie, his growing physique filling out handsomely, could have been the dominant alpha male in the troupe in Dr Waldren's dining room, because everyone waited on Charlie, anxious for his next move.

FIFTEEN

First came the head. The shoulders of the chimp battered the glass hatch at the end of the polytunnel. It gave way. After the head, a black hairy arm dropped through, then another, pushing past shards of glass, seemingly with no ill effect. Charlie slipped through the opening as the astonished onlookers held their breath. He came through like a contortionist. He was long and so big, Jo thought, but she dared not take another look.

Charlie moved determinedly towards the centre of the room. His gait was quadrupedal, moving on all fours, 'knuckle-walking' with his front hands, his shoulders hunched. In fact, he was remarkably self-composed for a chimpanzee that had just walked into a room with three human beings in it.

Charlie's eyes were wide open, and he'd pushed his lips into the shape of an 'O', like a pout. He was looking straight at Dr Waldren. His mouth opened, the corners drawn back, showing his teeth, almost as if mock grinning. When Dr Waldren did nothing but simply stare back, Charlie dropped his lips so they covered his teeth and glared fixedly at Dr Waldren.

'Do something, George, will you?' Chris pleaded.

'What the hell am I supposed to do?' Dr Waldren answered with a hint of terror in his voice. 'Feed him a goddamn banana?'

The doctor looked anxiously around the room, saw a banana on the dining room table, took it slowly in his right hand, and held it out to Charlie. The ape uttered a series of soft, low grunts known as pant-grunts. He swayed from side to side, stood up on two legs, his shoulders still hunched, his hair fairly bristling. Then Charlie lifted both arms. Dr Waldren was hoping Charlie would take the banana but so far he had just ignored it. 'That's called a bipedal swagger,' George ventured, his voice tone displaying anxiety. 'These guys are really strong, about three or four times stronger than a human, probably more.'

With a sudden lunge, Charlie grabbed the banana from Dr Waldren's hand, screamed, and hurled the banana over a shoulder. It smacked against the wall behind him, and then fell limply onto the floor. Charlie had seen Dr Waldren's coffee mug. He dropped down on all fours, knuckle-walked towards the sideboard and with his right arm reached up for the mug. His fingers delicately closed round it. He pulled it down to look inside. His lips pouted again, this time to grip the rim of the coffee mug.

'Atta boy, Charlie,' Dr Waldren said softly. 'Help yourself.' George's voice seemed to unfreeze everyone temporarily, even Chris, supinely aghast on the sofa. He helped himself to some of George's whisky – straight from the bottle, doubtless having decided it was not safe to start walking round looking for a glass.

Charlie appeared to like the taste of the coffee. It made his lips curl and move up and down over his teeth. Conceivably it was the sugar. When he'd drunk a little more, once again the arm holding the mug shot in the air, and the mug crashed past George and into the dining room door. It smashed into dozens of pieces.

'Charlie's just had his homecoming,' Jo said. 'One hell of a party.' She began laughing uncontrollably, perhaps from fear. Suddenly, Charlie bounded across the room in a strange kind of loping gait. Jo froze. Charlie sat on his haunches at her feet, wrapped an arm carelessly around her and then under his other arm for a good scratch, his long black, mottled fingers almost reaching his back. He looked up at Jo. His eyes and mouth were wide open but this time no teeth were showing.

'I told you he likes you,' George barked. 'I think he wants to play.'

So as not to seem intimidating, Jo gingerly sat down in a chair next to Charlie. Charlie shifted on his haunches. He put a hand on Jo's bare knees, and stroked them. He lifted her skirt slightly away from her body. Then he ran his fingers over her legs, stopping now and then to look closely at a mole or the faint hairs on her legs.

'He's grooming you,' said Dr Waldren. 'He's looking for insects to remove from your skin.'

'Thanks a lot, George but I don't have any ticks on me right now.'

'Never mind about that. Just stay calm. Maybe you should examine Charlie for ticks, see if you can find any.'

Jo stretched out an arm self-consciously and touched Charlie's pelage. She pretended to prise the fur apart very gently with her fingertips, as if looking for juicy insects to eat. Charlie pulled something from Jo's skin and put it in his mouth.

'You see! George cried. 'He *has* found something.'

'Be serious,' Chris interrupted. 'If I had a brute like that searching through my private parts, or near them, I wouldn't be inclined to move very far. Have you looked at his teeth? Very long and very sharp.'

'Jo has nothing to worry about,' George began. 'Charlie is an affable animal. He hasn't, as far as I know, been mistreated when young. This is all about social grooming, which is where one individual removes parasites or dead skin from another. It maintains social bonds. It's also proof of friendship. A chimp, by the way, has the same number of hairs as a human but the chimp's are just thicker, wirier.'

Jo glanced up, her face a picture of submissive pleading but Dr Waldren was having none of it. 'Get grooming Charlie while we decide what to do next!'

Jo dutifully bowed her head and began searching Charlie's forearms. She was forced to pretend she found something like a tick every now and again, for she put a finger to her mouth as if to lick something off, and Charlie was watching her.

SIXTEEN

Jo sat very still in the chair. Charlie had stopped grooming her legs, and suddenly embraced her, putting both arms around her back, but without any pressure or squeezing. He turned to look at Jo, his mouth pouting.

'Looks like you've met your match at last Jo,' Chris called out sarcastically from the sofa. Jo seemed reluctant to answer him, perhaps because Charlie was a little too close for her liking.

George was speaking excitedly. 'Just look at that! He's really so gentle. Do you know the difference between chimps and bonobos, their cousins? Of course there are many but one of the main ones is that bonobos live in female-dominated or female-centred societies. They use sex instead of aggression to settle their differences and enforce social order. The females also practise lots of genito-genital rubbing. So there's this partially apocryphal story that bonobos go in for altruism and free love.

'Actually it's not absolutely true. In the DRC, bonobos have been seen hunting duiker, the small forest antelope, eating them alive. They didn't bother to kill them, just pulled out the stomach and intestines to eat there and then.'

'George, for Christ's sake stop it, please! How can you go on about bonebos or booboos – whatever you call them – when you can see I'm in such a really awkward situation?'

'Bonobos, if you don't mind. I was only saying that, well, if Charlie falls out with you in a hurry, it might be better if he were a bonobo and it would help if you were one too, of course. I know that's crazy Jo, and don't blame me too much. It's the whisky and my interest in the subject. You'd merely have to go into the presentation posture, show your hindquarters, to solicit mating, and that might be the end of it, or there could be what's called reassurance mounting...'

'…look out George,' Chris interrupted. 'Charlie's after you.'

Charlie had indeed abandoned Jo, and knuckled-walked determinedly over to George, his pelage bristling with colour and sharp points of light. It was because he was healthy and in his prime. George sat down quietly on a piano stool so as not to alarm Charlie.

Chris stood up. 'George, I can tell you are uncertain of your next move. Can I give you some advice? The position you are in could either be described as a black swan or a Markov chain – at least, those are two interpretations of it.'

Sweat was beading George Waldren's forehead. He so wanted to swear at Chris, give him a mouthful but he dare not excite Charlie or take any risks. Instead he just gazed blankly at Chris, and in a soft voice said, 'What the hell are you talking about?'

Chris evidently enjoyed the chance to show off, especially when George was under pressure. 'A black swan,' he began somewhat smarmily, 'is an event that you cannot predict on the basis of past experience. You can't make absolute predictions. Having the Markov property means that, given the present state, future states are independent of past states. The description of a present state fully captures the information that…'

'…what kind of balls is that?' Jo interrupted tetchily. She seemed, at least temporarily, to have recovered from the attentions of Charlie. (Charlie had other ideas. He went back to Jo.)

'What I mean is that no one in this room appears to be able to control or predict what happens next,' Chris blurted out. 'That is, *who* is going to get hold of Charlie and lock him up?'

When George heard this, his demeanour abruptly changed. 'I will take Charlie,' he announced in solemn tones, 'because Charlie and I have a date with fortune – I dislike the word "destiny" – but that's what it is. Charlie's destiny awaits him now, or at least very soon. Charlie, my boy,' he called. 'Come here!'

Chris was about to giggle and smirk, thinking how the chimp wouldn't take the slightest notice but, he'd be damned, Charlie did. He loped over to George, and crouched readily by his feet.

George held out his hand, and Charlie took it. 'Let's get you *home*,' George said, unable to conceal the irony in his voice. 'I'm sorry it's not a nest in a tree in the deep, dark forest but it's all we have right now. Come Charlie, let me take you back to the garage. It's time you had some food and rest.'

The ape grunted, and if this was by accident or, uncannily, actually in agreement, no one could tell. Charlie then performed some strange bobbing movements, push-ups with arms bowed, accompanied by more pant-grunts.

George left the dining room leading Charlie by the hand. Charlie put an arm round George, who felt a sudden pain in his chest. It was the emotion. He had come to love Charlie. But, in his heart (and he knew in what strange valleys pumped *his* blood), he was unsure if the medical 'procedure' he had planned for Charlie was in reality very cruel, unworthy of such a magnificent anthropoid ape.

He considered how much his love for Jo had grown over time, even though they had separated. Yet the love of surgery beyond what had previously been attempted lured him on with a terrible fascination he felt powerless to resist.

Perhaps the pain also came from his own agony, the moral dilemma of any scientific journey into the unknown, the Faustian tilt, the more so because he held the power of life and death, rather life *or* death over the ape. He loved Charlie too much to harm, to hurt him…yet supposing his experiment led to new knowledge, a paradigm shift in learning, was he prepared to sacrifice Charlie's life for it?

SEVENTEEN

Dr Waldren came back from the garage, having 'bedded' the chimp down for the night. Chris had attacked another whisky bottle, and went back to reclining full length on the sofa. Only Jo seemed animated. She told George she wanted to learn more. The chimp had fascinated her.

George was pleased to have a potential convert to his cause. 'Jo, this animal is, well, he's my brother. Heavy, he ain't! As they say. Do you want to know how it goes?'

Jo looked puzzled. 'Go on, yes, tell me.'

'Kingdom, Animalia. Phylum, Chordata. Subphylum, Vertebrata. Class, Mammalia. Order, Primates. Suborder, Haplorrhini. Family, Hominidae. Genus, *Pan*. Species, *Pan troglodytes*.' George was overcome. He could barely speak. "Family, Hominidae", that just about says it all, doesn't it?'

'You're crying, George! I've hardly ever seen you like this before.' Jo took George in her arms, holding him tightly. They might live apart but she still appreciated him, if only for the man he was.

'I know about taxonomic levels, George. The most incredible filing system ever devised, thanks to Linnaeus. Do you know how to remember the eight major taxonomic ranks? I'll tell you. "Dignified Kings Play Chess On Fine Green Silk." Remember that, George?'

George spoke, oblivious of the tears streaming down his face. 'I prefer, "Dumb King Philip Crawled Over Five Girl Scouts, instead of Domain, Kingdom, Phylum, Order, Class, Family...' George stopped. He was crying because of the experiment he had planned. As a doctor it went against his natural instincts and all his training.

*

Charlie was in a thoughtful mood in the garage. 'Thoughtful' is not the right word to use, of course, because ascribing human feelings to animals, or anthropomorphism, is unacceptable from a scientific perspective and anyway, as far as is known, chimpanzees do not consciously 'think', although mind reading, the beginnings of morality, the ability to make tools, the possession of a kind of culture, and of emotions and personality, even empathy, have all been linked to primate studies.

Take morality, for example. A classic study conducted as long ago as 1964 found that hungry rhesus monkeys refused food they had been offered, if taking that food meant another monkey received an electric shock.

Charlie was keeping very still. His eyes opened and closed rhythmically, as if in a trance. Perhaps he was remembering his time in Cameroon, in the mist-clad rainforests, in the forests of Takamanda, a few days' hike from Mamfe. *A land of ferns and mosses, orchids and bromeliads, of epiphytes in the forest canopy drunk on the wetness of the equatorial rains and the warmth of the tropical sun. A land of eternal summer, of everlasting flowering.* The time when his mother cared for him, although how a chimpanzee would describe, even if able to, the animal that was his mother or his father...

There is a story of a disabled boy from Kano, Nigeria who is believed to have been adopted and raised by a troupe of chimpanzees when aged just two. It's likely the child would have been breastfed by a nursing chimp mother. Hunters found him with a family of chimps and brought him to a children's home in Kano. He is thought to have spent almost two years with the chimpanzees. Months later he was reported as still leaping like a chimpanzee, clapping his hands over his head, cupping his hands as chimps do, and not speaking any language but making pant-grunts and other chimpanzee-like noises.

Charlie's eyes stayed open. He was watching a spiral of dancing sunlight coming in from the roof window. How close he had been to the sun, to its warmth, in the way it showed him his home in the forest, which at night turned to a nest in a tree where everything would be forgotten in the dark, or a glimmer of a moon, until the sun came again in the morning.

In the same sunlight moved the other creatures of the forest: antelope, monitor lizard, civet, pangolin or scaly anteater, genet, water chevrotain, python; chameleons, dragonflies, and geckos; many kinds of monkeys including red colobus, olive baboon, red patas, mona, mangabey, and drill; birds including the African grey parrot, francolin, hornbills, bulbuls, kingfishers and a myriad more; crocodiles lurked in some of the rivers, there were shy and wary forest elephants, often heard but not seen, and even more rarely, western or lowland gorillas whose habitat reached right up into Nigeria and the Obudu Plateau. The gorillas in this area, in the border region of Nigeria and Cameroon, a small and isolated population of Cross River gorillas, had only recently been recognised as a subspecies (*Gorilla gorilla diehli*).

Charlie's life in the forests had been brief but long enough to see most of the things there that could be seen, long enough to have time to feast on fruiting trees, to learn hunting skills, and even to pant-hoot with extreme excitement when finding, and reacting to, his first waterfall. The forest was criss-crossed with streams, and further to the north where montane forest predominated, there was always water to drink from running brooks that cascaded down the steep, tree-covered hills.

If you had been able to look at Charlie then, without being observed, you would have seen how relaxed he was, how 'thoughtful' were those liquid brown eyes, or at least they were full of repose, in a way that only animals are able to be, as the poet Walt Whitman wrote, 'so placid and self-contained'. Charlie didn't sweat or whine about his condition, he was not demented with the mania of owning things – there were many lines from the poem that would fit Charlie, except part of one line: 'Not one kneels to another…' Dominant alpha males did make sure that lower-ranking animals effectively did kneel to them by eliciting submissive gestures.

Charlie was complaining of nothing. His eyes still had that

peaceful look, the tranquillity when all is well in the immediate present, and no predators are lurking. He had lost his mother to hunters with Dane guns but the memory of her was receding. He had lost his natural life in the forest. If he missed anything, it was the daily foraging for food, for titbits in the grass, or fishing for termites with twigs, or cracking open nuts with stones, even using sharp stones as cleavers to open fibrous fruit plants or heavy ones as anvils – all the exploring, the day-to-day life with his troupe, and the companionship of other chimpanzees. Now all that was lost but he had food and shelter, and a certain kinship with Dr Waldren. He was still lonely. Food and shelter were not everything.

Into Charlie's mind came a memory from the past when he had trekked with his troupe beyond their usual range. He had heard a strange noise at dusk, above the noise of bizarre-looking hornbills whooshing away on their great wings, and in a forest clearing the troupe had gathered, about eleven individuals, huddled together anxiously because the dominant male had gone on ahead; not far away, this male had screamed a series of pant-hoots, and then come charging back to the group, pulling up ferns, cracking branches, uprooting anything he could find to pull from the ground. Then he gestured ahead, and the troupe sidled off and that's where Charlie first saw the sheet of white water tumbling over a high rock.

It moved like an animal or a living being, powering over the rock face, crashing down into a dark pool, thundering as it went, white spray spreading into the air. Charlie felt damp mist on his face, tiny droplets of water spray. Transfixed for a while, he and the other chimps stood still to gaze at the moving wall of water. In response Charlie jumped onto a hanging vine, climbed it and pushed himself out into the spray. The noise of the water was increased by the wind rushing through rock fissures. After swinging backwards and forwards on the vine, and getting his pelage wet, he jumped down, walking upright into the water, his coat bristling in threat display. He hurled small rocks into the waterfall, and then retreated to a larger rock downstream. There, hunched on the rock, the ape gazed back, staring at the water plunging over the sheer rock face, and he stayed like that for many minutes.

*

Jo had held George in her arms, and then she'd had to go. Only Chris stayed on. He had little time left, and would soon have to return to Oxford.

'George, can you give me a lift to the station later?'

'Yes, of course.'

'When do you want me to start…on this project of yours?'

George almost jumped out of his chair. 'You mean you'll come with me, on the experiment?'

'I'm in. But it might take time. You're looking at months. I'm still not sure how this will work, or even if it's possible.'

'Make it possible,' George said in earnest. 'For Charlie. Actually, that's not right. I mean for the purposes of scientific knowledge. You know where Charlie comes from? He's actually a subspecies of *Pan troglodytes*. There are not too many of them left, just a few thousand. Habitat fragmentation, the Ebola virus, deforestation, the commercial bushmeat trade will kill them all off in time. Most Africans ask only one question, "Does it taste good?"'

'What kind of subspecies is he George?'

'*Pan troglodytes vellerosus*. You want the taxonomic history and morphology too?'

Chris nodded, suddenly quite keen.

'Charlie comes from a special geographical area, loosely the area between two rivers, the Niger and the Sanaga, that's between Nigeria and western Cameroon. The earliest description of these chimps dates to 1862. A chimpanzee skin had been collected by a certain Captain Richard Burton, the British consul to Fernando Pó. Burton got the skin from Mount Cameroon, which on its lower slopes is abundantly forested. It was once prime chimp habitat. He was struck by the fur or pelage of this creature, he thought it more abundant than usual, softer, the back was more brown than black.

Burton sold the skin to the Natural History Museum in London. A researcher named J.E. Gray named it after its fur, *vellerosus*, furry. Charlie belongs to this subspecies. He was found in the Cross River area of Cameroon.'

'George, does any of this matter?' Chris asked.

George looked angry. 'For Chrissakes Chris, it matters. If Charlie is going to have the kind of medical procedure I've planned for him, the least we can do is to respect where he comes from, where his home was, what kind of animal we are dealing with.'

Chris agreed. Alcohol, he thought, was almost unattractive by comparison. George was going for it – an experiment that involved a live human brain, a young male. If George wasn't mad, he might just accomplish the unthinkable. He would go with George, his friend, all the way.

EIGHTEEN

Chris caught the train back to Oxford the same night. He'd decided that somehow or other he must control his drinking habit. Nevertheless, as the train pulled in to Oxford, Chris was already imagining a fresh pint overflowing on the bar in a favourite haunt – the old, 'historic pub' on The High reached via an alleyway.

Chris had only minimal interest in literature or poetry, except where something really obsessed him. Unlike George, he probably wouldn't have cared much for Shelley's portrait, or his memorial hidden away nearby. He was more concerned about his present ridiculous job, and how he might lose it – if he followed through with Dr Waldren's absurd plan. He wanted to return to medicine one day, that was sure, but right then, the only job security of note came through the job at the hospital. The money wasn't good but at least it kept a roof over his head.

He caught a bus from the station to The High. On a whim he decided to visit another old pub, reached via New College Lane, under the 'Bridge of Sighs', and then left down a small alley. The tavern, a tiny low, beamed ceiling affair sat snugly alongside the old city wall. Chris ordered a pint, and took it out to the beer garden. He lit a cigarette, thinking the spiral of warmth in his hand was the single source of heat until rusty braziers began to burn furiously, staffed by a student working part time to earn money for uni. He watched a young girl with blonde hair and an impish face toast pink marshmallows. In the night air, Chris saw the faces of others, their laughing faces, their teeth. It was really odd, he thought. He wondered why he noticed their teeth. Was it to do with body parts? Like those traditional healers in South Africa called *Sangomas*, some of whom in their blind ignorance thought that lips and genitals, testicles, intestines, all would heal and bring money.

The victims of these 'Muti Murders' should preferably be young; they should feel pain when they are killed; better to be tortured before being killed because then the medicine of the private parts would be so much stronger, more powerful. Torturing when the victim is still alive makes those parts more effective, so they believe. The ritual murders promise health and good fortune. How dare they call themselves *healers*? It was an insult to his profession, to every qualified doctor anywhere in the world.

Chris smoked his cigarette but felt nothing. Although he was not able to practise as a doctor, he *was* still a doctor. Surprisingly, he felt for Charlie as much as he felt for the poor human who would have half his brain removed, though in the circumstances whether half or a whole brain were taken away made no difference, the patient was going to die anyway. George had told him not to worry. Death would be unavoidable due to terminal illness or trauma. Whether it happened ten or five or fifteen hours earlier or later made no difference, or if it did, it was hardly quantifiable in terms of the person's lifespan.

Chris knew even so the argument did not hold water, medically, philosophically or morally. He decided in an extraordinary moment of altruism that he would not be able to deny anybody fifteen hours of life. He was not a body snatcher and never wanted to be.

*

In Great Britain over 15 million people have already signed up to the NHS Organ Donor Register. They can leave someone a future in the form of a heart, lungs, kidneys, pancreas, liver and small bowel but not a single person has so far agreed to donate a brain. It takes courage for the imaginative to sign a piece of paper declaring, 'I want to donate my heart.' There were as yet no forms you could sign, stating, 'I want to donate my brain.' Not yet. It was too personal. The operation was probably just about technically possible but it would be so complicated that it would make open heart surgery seem routinely mundane.

*

Chris sipped slowly on his pint, unwilling to hurry anything. He was thinking how curious it was that Oxford always talked about its much loved sons but never, or only rarely, of its daughters. The sons were always famous (sometimes infamous) but the daughters merely distinguished. It was as if the sons were the inheritors of the great academic tradition – and then Chris remembered Oxford was also the home, as Matthew Arnold had said, of lost causes and impossible loyalties. He was thinking that George could have a lost cause even before he started. His loyalty to him might very easily become impossible if it meant the taking of human life. Then there was Charlie. How was this strange saga to end? Probably with a dead human and a dead chimpanzee.

The logistics were frightening. The 'window of opportunity' to conduct the operation George had planned was far less than that for a heart transplant, which was about four hours, six hours at the most. With no oxygen the brain dies in minutes. One solution might be some form of super cooling of the brain tissue, and then there was the difficulty of conducting such an operation simultaneously. He was hardly going to be able to smuggle a drugged chimpanzee into the John Radcliffe Hospital or drive a comatose human being down to Dorset, so the two could be on separate operating tables, side by side, to make the operation easier and more feasible.

There were also the difficulties likely to be encountered without expensive state-of-the-art equipment. Chris had read about a horse in Australia with a compound leg fracture. Surgeons in Oxford could see the 'patient' by webcam, look at the digital images, and communicate information immediately around the world. Digital imaging and MRI scanning were increasingly essential tools. George and Chris were going to rely on only basic medical skills and basic equipment.

It was just like attempting the impossible, Chris considered quietly, looking at some marshmallows sizzling on a skewer inside one of the braziers in the garden. The heat made them congeal together so individual shapes metamorphosed into one amorphous lump. Deconstructing *that* operation would be impossible too. Chris's mind was suddenly flooded with doubts, and a nagging anxiety brewed inside him, so that he overrode his earlier intention to drink less, and ordered another pint.

Chris smiled at the barmaid, a young girl of about eighteen with short black hair and a cream, sequined bandanna. She was pretty but Chris hardly noticed her, his attention focused on the enormity of what George had in mind. A partial brain transplant, from human to non-human primate, would work best. The barriers to accomplishing this feat would be much less than for a full brain transplant. Chris felt his head swim. How could he ever get his head round it?

He glanced again at the girl. He was looking at her head, imagining the neural structures deep within. Her brain was able to marshal millions upon millions of individual nerve cells to produce behaviour, and even the cells themselves could be modified by their environment. It was curious to think that one of medicine's greatest remaining challenges was to understand the biological basis for consciousness, and the mental processes by which we are able to perceive, to act, to learn, to remember, to feel emotions.

George had mentioned that it would be better to remove the right hemisphere, most of it, because there was evidence that the remaining hemisphere would compensate for the loss. Removal of the left hemisphere might have different results. In humans the left hemisphere is dominant, and George thought it might be the same for chimpanzees, although that was guessing. The major focus of interest was going to be the addition (the replacement of what was taken out) of part of a human right hemisphere implanted into the non-human primate recipient. George was probably going for a partial cortical removal so as to achieve better anatomic preservation of the remaining hemisphere, and reduce long-term complications overall.

Nevertheless, the chances of success were incredibly slim. Preventing overwhelming blood loss was just one area of concern. The microsurgery involved demanded the highest skills. Avoiding neurological catastrophe when removing part of the right brain hemisphere was just one potential disaster on a list longer than the surgeon's arm. Chris reckoned George was simply biting off not so much more than he could chew – but enough to choke him.

Chris had a good idea what George wanted to achieve. Was it possible to move a human 'identity' to another body – a non-human body – by transferring part of a live human brain? The outcome might either be a damp squib or very stormy. It was unlikely to be somewhere in between. It might be closer to Frankenstein's monster than he cared believe. But then he thought of Charlie, and he felt his confidence coming back. It was wrong to think about Frankenstein. The profound question of consciousness was a better subject. Mind was matter. They just needed to join the parts to make it work. There was even a chance the ape might become more than an ape – after the operation.

NINETEEN

Jo awoke from a horrible dream. She'd been into the garage to feed Charlie but he was waiting for her by the door. His coat was bristling, his stance confidently bipedal, and there was this strange pink spiky thing sticking out, flicking up and down. She thought she was quite happy to be separated from George at that moment, when she awoke. If she'd been with him, George would probably have his own spiky thing to confront her with, first thing in the morning, or last thing at night. The trouble with penises, and the male sex, she thought, is that they needed too much servicing. She didn't really object. What she didn't like was all the rubbing and scratching, all the man-hours devoted to stimulation, so that the organ could achieve its ultimate function.

She had to admit that chimpanzees, especially bonobos, fascinated her, even if in a gruesomely sexual way. The way those bonobos took every opportunity to rub genitals together, to mount furiously, and to suck off any male or female who was around, left her cold. Imagine a blow job with a bonobo!

The last patient she had to see had cancelled. She could go home. On the way home, Jo decided instead to see George. It took her about forty minutes to make the journey. When she got to the house, she saw the garage door open, correctly guessing that George had taken Charlie outside. He was in the back garden, walking quietly with Charlie holding on to his left arm. Charlie walked a mixture of gaits, sometimes quadrupedal, sometimes bipedal, it seemed as if he kept reaching up to George, trying to be like him. They stopped under the apple tree. George saw that there were a few late October apples, red and shiny, so he let Charlie climb up for one. They seemed happy together. Jo held back, not wanting to intrude. When she saw them reach the bole of an oak and sit down together, their backs against the tree, she gasped.

They acted so close, she thought, like father and son, like two friends.

Charlie saw her first. He hooted, and then made a greeting call. George pulled on Charlie's leash. He didn't want Charlie to make a noise.

'Am I interrupting something?' Jo called out.

It was strange because both George and Charlie replied at the same time; Charlie with a single scream, and George just said, 'Hi Jo, come on over, won't you?'

'Chimps' tea party?' Jo said laughingly.

'Come and join us.' George beckoned to a garden chair. 'Sit yourself down, Jo. You know, Charlie is enjoying some special time with me. I don't know how much longer he's got.'

Jo sat on the wooden chair just a few feet away from George and Charlie. She was surprised to see how earnest George looked, and how Charlie's coat was gleaming. The light from the sun was waning, it would soon be dark. 'How long is it, George?'

George sighed. 'It's down to Chris now. It depends how long it takes him to find a...' he hesitated '...a donor.'

Charlie had slowly gathered up his leash while George and Jo were talking. Quickly, he seized it from George's grasp, and holding the leash in one hand, bowled over with surprising agility and speed to another oak tree. Transferring the end of the leash to his mouth, he began to climb the trunk like a practised climber.

In moments he was in the tree canopy, which consisted of five oaks, a copper beech and a sycamore, brachiating like an arboreal acrobat. Charlie moved fairly effortlessly, and George wondered how he was so fit when most of the time he just sat inside his cage. He stopped where there was a break in the branches, where the leaf cover was sparse. He could see over the roofs of houses, and behind them the dark blue of the sea.

Charlie noticed only the colour of the sea, not that it was water. His eyes focused back on the red and green leaves around him. Autumn had tinged them with russet and gold streaks but, unlike the small red leaves in the Cameroon forest that were often younger and more nutritious than green leaves, these were hard to the touch, and not worth the eating. Charlie spat out a handful.

Breaking over a small island out in the lagoon, a turgid moon sent long white-gold rays glittering over the harbour, floating like a shattered upturned mirror. Charlie looked at the moon and the intense colours of the evening, then spontaneously pant-hooted. The pant-hoots had a singing, melodious quality about them, more like a softly individual uttering into the dark and coming peace of nightfall than any wish to share information with other chimps.

George looked up into the oak trees, with Jo at his side, trying to call Charlie down. Charlie was intent on the moonscape, the light playing on the water, as if he were pondering, considering the natural events in front of him, a kind of reverence for life, for the natural world.

'Come down, Charlie, come on!' shouted Dr Waldren. He was worried about the neighbours. Not too much by the one further up the road, next door on the right; he was a DIY fan and could usually be relied on to have his nose deep in a DIY problem. The other side was more dangerous. The old lady liked to hobble in her garden, as best she could, even when it was cold. The sight of a dark shape like a hunched up gargoyle, a chimpanzee in an oak tree at the end of her garden, might induce a heart attack. If still alive and talking by the time the paramedics arrived, the game might be up.

'Charlie boy, it's dinner time,' Jo called out.

Up in the tree canopy, Charlie saw the night darken. In the wild he would have made a nest. He looked down, urinated, the urine pattering over the dry leaves, some splashing Jo below.

'Charlie, you bastard! I mean, can't you be more careful where you put it?'

Charlie shinned down the tree, and then danced. He was proud of himself. You could see it in his bipedal swagger, the way he lashed out at a tree stump with both feet. The ape calmed down. He walked quietly towards George, holding out an arm, and as George was about to take hold of it, Charlie reached out to pat George on his arm. Just as quickly, he scampered back to the oak tree he had moments before descended. It was like a game of tag and chase.

Exasperated, George strode over to the oak tree. Charlie dodged behind it neatly, clearly enjoying a game of chimp hide-and-seek, vocalising with shrieks of delight. George decided it was time to play games too, so in the gathering darkness he lay down on the wet grass, still as a statue. Charlie's face peered back from behind the oak tree, and then he knuckled-walked over to George.

George had closed his eyes. Soon he felt warm breath on his face as well as something moving down his cheek. Charlie had to be crouching over him protectively, fingering his face with one of his long, brown, mottled fingers. '*Hoo, hoo*,' Charlie cried and George opened his eyes. Immediately Charlie held out his arms to embrace George on the ground.

'He loves you!' Jo said. 'Thank God.'

George stood up, still holding one of Charlie's hands. He was careful to pick up the leash. Then George walked Charlie back from the garden towards the house, and from there, after a nice ripe banana, it was easy to get the ape back in the garage. He went into his cage without a murmur. George handed him another banana. Charlie retreated to a corner of the cage, huddled up against the wires, and ate the banana.

George said, 'Well done, Charlie boy. Well done.' Then he shut up the garage, and he and Jo went inside the house.

Charlie drank some water from a trough in his cage. He picked up the banana skin and casually threw it over a shoulder. It didn't go far. The ape lay down on his woollen blanket, ready to sleep.

George had forgotten to close the roof covering. In the darkened garage, Charlie looked up at the light from the roof window. There was starlight, tiny lights, much the same as the light-points in the night sky above the Cameroonian forest, but not as bright as he had known, not as strong as Van Gogh had painted the starry night.

In Africa it had been like Gauguin with his splashed primary colours, swirling stars above a Rousseau jungle – had he been able to describe the tropical night in human words. Later, when Charlie fell asleep, a big golden moon moved across the opening in the roof, and if you could have seen it, you would have seen Charlie's face and pelage painted with gold flecks, as if he were swathed in moon dust like a golden fleece.

TWENTY

While Chris went to work, pushing trolleys in the John Radcliffe Hospital, and trying to get on the mortuary assistant's extra training course, Jo and George Waldren had spent the night together. Jo had met George on the landing outside the spare bedroom, which she had opted for, having scant interest in the ex-marital bed. She'd seen George standing there, his penis startlingly erect. 'Oh God,' she said to herself, 'it's that pink thing again.'

George pretended to know nothing about the large filament of flesh pointing in her direction, and Jo had done likewise, so nothing had happened, although in the morning much the same thing occurred again on the landing. This time, Jo seemed overcome by something, as she knelt down and very swiftly engulfed George's manhood in her mouth. After a while George uttered a long low moan, and two hundred million motile spermatozoa jettisoned onto the carpet. 'Look what you've done now, George,' Jo said cockily, as if it had nothing to do with her. 'That's just for old time's sake, you know. Nothing else. Now maybe you can keep your mind on your work?'

'Jo, how could you, for heaven's sake? It's perfectly natural to get erections from time to time. Did you have to?' George dressed, still talking with Jo.

'Did you have to show me quite so pointedly?' Jo chuckled. 'I think there was an element of sexual display in that.'

'From whose side?' George quipped. 'Well, I've no complaints, Jo. However, it's not so much fun for some of the male chimps that have trouble making the females conceive. RPE is often used to collect sperm samples for analysis. Sometimes they're trained to use an AV, and then they don't need RPE.'

'Describe the acronyms please George, RPE and AV?'

'Rectal probe electrostimulation. It works pretty well. Durrell tried it on gorillas successfully in his Jersey zoo. Naturally the animals were anaesthetised first. It wouldn't be much fun trying to give a gorilla RPE if it were bouncing around in front of you. AV is simpler. It's an artificial vagina. The point of the experiment was to demonstrate that oocyte sperm penetration; well, put it this way, the sperm swim differently in ejaculates collected by RPE than ejaculates collected by AV. They swim in a more convoluted manner. Seems they don't like being brought out, roughed up, by a rectal probe – electrically charged. Can't say I blame them.'

'For goodness sake, George, I think I'll skip breakfast. Let's feed Charlie instead, shall we?' Jo was trying to put a brave face on it. She couldn't imagine what came over her. The move on George was precipitate, to say the least.

George saw that Jo had become quite fond of Charlie. She could help with the operation. It was a chance, George considered, to get her onside. He'd need someone competent to nurse Charlie over the first few days, if not weeks of recovery.

'Will you help me with Charlie?'

It was a direct question. She was good at them. She didn't waste any time. 'I don't think you've really convinced me of any compelling *raison d'être*, have you? You know experiments on the great apes are banned. You must realise your chances of success, even if you could get hold of a donor, are virtually nil. You don't have the equipment, the facilities, even if you knew what you were doing.'

'I'm working on the donor problem,' George answered in a taciturn manner. 'It's also occurred to me that I might need to look elsewhere, not rely on Chris in Oxford. I had an idea last night, an idea for an alternative donor source, if Chris can't make it.'

Jo looked at George enquiringly, hanging on the explanation she knew George would give.

'Those Dignitas people, you know the ones that ship themselves over to Zurich for an assisted suicide? They take people suffering from depression as well as the terminally ill. So they may be depressed but their brains are still working. You can't get any sort of donor unless they're brain dead, which isn't any use. Brain stem death. Isn't that the case? I believe it is.'

'Yes, that's right as the law stands. Don't tell me. You want to persuade a person who thinks life's not worth living to donate his or her brain instead, before they're quite dead. They would have to be pretty depressed to agree to that, wouldn't they? In fact, they'd be so depressed, I don't think you could trust them.'

'You know we're ahead of our time. Twenty years from now, maybe less, it'll be easy. You'll plug into Microsoft or Google in the clouds. They'd find you a virtual donor, no problem. Surgeons will do the job remotely, non-invasively, it'll be so simple!'

'Stop dreaming, George. How many years did you train as a surgeon? I doubt it would ever be enough. The only luck you'll get is the "stick a patch on here" kind, sorry to be so rude, or a miracle. Yes, that's it. You are absolutely going to need a miracle to make this work!'

George Waldren was a very determined man. Nothing quite stopped him until *he* decided it couldn't be done. 'Jo, my father, I never believed him, he told me that whatever I did in life, I should do it, it sounds corny now, to the best of my ability. I wrote to him when I was away at school. He hardly ever wrote back. That made me listen to him even more, as you know. I'm working as a GP now but when I was in surgery, I felt as if I were cutting for him. He died early, didn't he? So I was cutting away all the stuff that might kill other people, the same stuff that probably killed him, I was cutting it away *for* him. Because I loved him. Hell, I missed the old man for a time.' Tears came into George's eyes.

'I still love you too, you know, you crazy bastard!' She held George close for a moment, but he pushed her aside.

'When I was at home I used to read through my father's books. All kinds of books he left. "I loved you so I drew these tides of men..." You know. T.E. Lawrence. "I drew these tides of men into my hands and wrote my will across the sky in stars, to earn you freedom, the seven-pillared worthy house, so that your eyes might be shining for me when we came." Hell, I can still remember it. I didn't know then Lawrence wrote it for an Arab boy he'd fallen in love with. But it was poetic. Only a poet could write stuff like that. So, when I was working as a surgeon years later, I was the one drawing the tides of men into my hands, their bodies, and I was cutting them free from one disease or another, and I was doing it because I loved my father.'

'The hell you did, George. Don't think you ever loved me that much though. You've never told me that before. That's serious shit, isn't it?'

'I couldn't even admit it to myself, Jo.'

'I do remember. Does that surprise you? He also had something worthwhile to say about men who dream. "All men dream, but not equally." The ones that cause all the trouble are the men who dream by day, because that makes them dangerous. They dream with their eyes open. The dreamers of the day, "for they may act their dreams", that's how I think it goes, "with open eyes, to make it possible".'

'That's right, and you're a dangerous woman. Were you dreaming a few moments ago, with your eyes open too?'

Jo blushed, tossing her hair to one side, as if to make the thought go away. 'Let's go and see Charlie, shall we? George, it's not too late to give him away, so he can have a decent life. The ape rescue centre is near here, isn't it? Charlie would do well there. He'd have a life. If you want my honest opinion, he's either going to end up very dead, or paralysed.'

'I know you're probably right,' George sighed, 'but I just don't like to turn back, give up. Charlie is just one life. You know the Salk vaccine developed in the 1950s? Have you any idea how many monkeys were used to perfect the vaccine for humans, to eradicate polio? One hundred thousand Rhesus monkeys!' George thumped a table, as if to ram home his point.

'The argument is unsound, George. How do they say it? "It should be allowed by courtesy, but not pressed in argument." Let's see what Charlie thinks about all this.' She lifted the garage keys from their hook, and walked fast, out of the kitchen door, with

George following. George used a foot to keep Helga inside. She had gone into a corner to sulk, ever since George and Jo had sex on the landing, but had tried to escape into the garden.

Jo opened the garage doors. A very strange sight met their eyes. Charlie had also retreated into a corner of his cage with his back to the garage doors, like a sad old hunchback, and he'd pulled the woollen sleeping blanket over his head, as if to blot out the world.

TWENTY-ONE

George and Jo stared at the huddled bundle. Only because they knew it was Charlie were they able to visualise inside the blanket, and form a picture of the ape within. If you didn't know Charlie was there, that shape could have been anything. It was getting near to Halloween: was it a ghoul, a zombie, a hobo, an escaped dwarf? It could have been anything, and it wasn't moving.

George was the first to speak. 'Charlie boy, what's happened? What's the matter?' George shook the wire bars of Charlie's cage but there was still no response, which was unusual for a chimp, as some sort of threat display, at least a behavioural reaction, would be expected. There was no sound, apart from George's steady breathing, and Jo's sharp, indrawn breaths.

Jo tried next. 'Charlie, you haven't anything to fear. Why don't you turn round, take that silly blanket off your head. Charlie, don't...'

'...Jo, for chrissakes!' George broke in. 'Charlie doesn't speak English. He doesn't even speak Pidgin English. He's from West Cameroon. He can't understand you.'

Jo looked crestfallen. 'I was just trying to help,' she said.

George's face softened into the beginnings of a smile. 'It's no use talking to him as you might talk to someone in your surgery. This is a wild creature, semi-tame, but still wild.' George rattled the cage again, shouting at him through the wire bars. 'Come on, Charlie, we can't wait all day! Charlie, stop pissing about. Come here, please!' George was looking angry now, but there was no response from Charlie.

'Chrissakes yourself, George Waldren. You tell me not to talk to that animal, that chimp, because I'm human and *it* won't understand me, and then you do just the same thing! Is that blatantly crazy, and sexist, or what?'

'Oh, I don't know,' George said, exasperated by Charlie's antisocial behaviour. 'Maybe he's forgotten who he is. What he is. I'll go inside, get a mirror, fetch me a glass. Show him. Remind him who he is. Jo, stay here, will you? Stay here a moment. I'll be back.'

George left the garage. Jo looked back and saw George going inside the house. She was more relaxed now. She took off a shoe. She scratched the side of Charlie's cage with it. Charlie responded. He let out a strange cry that Jo had never heard before. It sounded like, '*Wrra, wrra!*'

This sound, if Jo had known, is made by chimpanzees when there is deep fear or alarm. Then Charlie half looked over his shoulder. Jo could just see his eyes under a beetling brow, the rest of his brooding face hidden behind the blanket. Charlie glanced at her. She heard him softly utter, '*Hoo, hoo.*' Then he turned his back again. It was like a lamentation. There was great silence.

George Waldren soon came running from the house with a mirror tucked under his arm. It was quite big, shaped like a ship's porthole. 'Christ, Jo, any change?'

'None whatsoever,' Jo sighed. 'He's come over all peculiar.'

'Son of a bitch! Poor goddamn ape. What's got into him?'

'He looked round once, let out this fearful cry. I've never heard him like that before. It sounded dreadful, like really sad.'

'Charlie!' You could hear the frustration in George Waldren's voice. '*Charlie!*'

Charlie moved his head very slightly, as if he were straining his ears to hear from underneath the blanket.

'Look, he moved!' George was suddenly animated. 'Charlie, come and look at this, will you?' George almost ran the length of Charlie's cage, trying to reach him but there were boxes filled with books in the way. He moved them with the alacrity of bailiffs repossessing goods. 'Get me some light. Hurry, Jo!'

She searched for a wall light, and found one. She turned it on, making the grey-brown figure of Charlie seem oddly large, and more threatening. 'Careful. George. Don't try to stroke him through the bars. He's not in the mood.'

'I won't, don't you worry. I just want to show him this, so he can see his face. He might come to his senses. He'll recognise himself. You know, it's called the mirror self-recognition test.' George got round to the side of the cage. If he held the mirror at the back, in a gap between the garage wall and the ape's cage, Charlie should be able to see himself in the mirror, if he bothered to look, if he bothered to open his eyes. 'You okay there, Jo?'

'Don't worry about me. Let's see what Charlie does.'

'Okay,' George muttered.

It might have seemed that George was in the middle of some great experiment. The concentration on his face was pronounced. First of all, he tapped the side end of the cage with the wooden-backed mirror, as if to gain Charlie's attention. Inside the blanket there was a sudden stiffening of the posture of the ape. George leaned over the end of the cage, at head or skull height for the chimpanzee. He held up the mirror, so that it faced Charlie head-on. 'Look at this, my boy,' he called out. 'Who's that?'

Charlie's head, or at least what was presumed to be his head under the blanket, jerked forward. The blanket still covered him, so George didn't know if he could see the mirror. But the part of the woollen blanket nearest to the mirror came forward a few inches until stopping just in front of the wire bars.

George held his breath. He moved the mirror slightly, from side to side, to make the image in the glass clearer, adjusting the view Charlie might get. George saw Charlie tweak the blanket, move it a little. Then Charlie pulled the blanket away from his head, so it hung round his neck and body.

George waited.

Charlie was looking directly at the mirror. He grabbed the wire bars right in front of the mirror, as if trying to bring the mirror closer. He turned his head from side to side. He was still looking.

'Looks okay,' George said. 'It seems like he knows himself. It's working.' George smiled but the smile on his face was instantly wiped off.

Charlie's face seemed to boil. *'Wrra! Wraa!'* Charlie cried.

'Wraa!' It was a desperate clamour, a mixture of pain and distress, the sound of terrible fear, loss, and abandonment.

George looked ill. 'Christ almighty, Jo. He's spooked himself!'

Charlie screamed as he gathered up the blanket and put his head back inside it, then he leapt to the other corner of the cage, and fell down, his arms flailing the floor of the cage, still screaming as if demented, his chest convulsing as if racked by giant sobs.

'Do you think chimpanzees can know the future?' Jo asked. 'I mean could they feel it?'

'I doubt they could,' George answered in a voice that seemed lost. 'We use words. They don't have a language. We know it as premonition. For them, it may be more like unquantified dread. Do animals know they are going to die, when a man comes up to them with a knife, to slit their throats? Or a pig is met with a man with a stun gun? I don't know what they're called, but you know what I mean. A steel bolt goes into the brain. Abattoir workers used to stick a straw in the hole in an animal's head, and twirl it round. If there was no movement, the animal was dead.'

'I don't want to hear any more, George,' Jo interrupted. 'I am tempted to say, if you prick him, will he not bleed? If you tickle him, will he not laugh...?'

'...and if you poison him, will he not die?' George put in quickly. 'I know Jo, and if wronged, he can make no revenge.'

'What about reading faces, can apes do that? Like anthropoid seers? Surely there isn't such a thing.'

'Dogs and humans look left, at the right-hand side of a face, to judge emotion – it's called left-gaze bias. It's supposed to be easier to read a person's face that way. I couldn't read Charlie's face but he did. He saw himself. He saw what might happen to him. That's what I think. Christ, Jo, maybe it's wrong, of course it is, wrong to cut out the chimp's brain, part of it. God, this is getting heavy.'

'I think I know what you want to say,' she answered. 'You're a doctor, and not a vet, but paramount to you, as a doctor, must be the welfare of the creature in your charge, your ambit, your control, your aegis – call it what you will. You have a duty of care to that creature, as much as if Charlie were human. I don't think you know what you've got yourself into. You're going to find it very difficult to override being a doctor, aren't you?'

'We'll see about that,' George said. He got hold of a stick and prodded the now seemingly lifeless shape of Charlie. 'Come on, you freckled whelp of a chimpanzee! We'll see about that.'

TWENTY-TWO

Chris had gone for a walk. For two days he'd pushed trolleys with and without bodies in the John Radcliffe Hospital. He'd made two visits to the morgue. He knew that brain surgery in the hospital was not common, although it was a large hospital with over 700 inpatient beds. It also housed many departments of Oxford University Medical School.

In the new West Wing, the neurosciences unit specialised in neurology, neurosurgery, and specialist surgery such as craniofacial surgery, with state-of-the-art operating theatres. A dedicated children's hospital was another addition. The Oxford functional neurosurgery unit looked after the alleviation of movement disorders, such as Parkinson's disease, as well as phantom limb pain and anaesthesia dolorosa.

The neurosurgery department also treated brain lesions, skull base tumours, and spinal cord diseases. The surgery team had an international reputation. Chris began to doubt he'd ever find a way of getting hold of a human brain, *part* of a human brain, he kept telling himself, as if that weren't quite so bad. Even if he were able, what use would it be? They say at medical school that of all the soft tissues in the body, after death the brain's the first to vanish, the uterus the last. It would be a race against time to get the brain into a lab, and with bureaucratic red tape and paperwork in abundance, it wouldn't be easy. In fact, it would be as good as impossible.

Chris decided to clear his head. He crossed Magdalen Bridge and escaped into the Botanic Gardens. October had only a few days left. There was not much to see: the punts in the Cherwell roped together, some half-filled with water, all the summer's flowering dried up. There was apparently more biological diversity in the Botanic Garden than in rainforests or other biodiversity hot spots but you'd hardly know it. A fountain played into a circular pond inside the walled garden, attended by four wooden seats inviting company. Chris stood still, closed his eyes and listened. There was something innately peaceful about the sound of falling water in a garden. It was noon. He had heard the ten bells in the bell-chamber of Magdalen's great tower sonorously ring their hourly chime in E major, the complete run of chimes, followed by the single strike bell sounding the hour. Then there was just the pleasant noise of water again, trickling from the fountain.

Chris soon returned to The High, wishing for once he had a bicycle. He crossed over the road, and walked along Long Wall into Holywell Street, glimpsing an entrance to New College through which a few students rode on bicycles. He didn't want anything to drink, just to clear his head and work out his next move. He passed up the chance to turn into the tiny passage to the pub where he'd seen the doughy marshmallows coalesce into an amorphous lump, and instead turned up Parks Road, on his left the proud vistas of gardens that led to Trinity College and St John's.

When he got to the Museum of Natural History, a crowd of young German students was listening to a guide. Chris made his way through the small crowd, and went in. A few girls were entranced by a stuffed cheetah. Lightly they stroked its skin, hoping it wouldn't come alive. The forty-foot monster that was *Tyrannosaurus rex* was a big hit, as were other dinosaurs. So was the dodo (known as 'Alice's Dodo'). There were lots of skeletons of animals grouped together – elephants, camels, horses, rhinos, deer, a bluefin tuna and a giraffe. Chris tried to imagine what they would look like, clothed in their living skins, alive, breathing, all running. You'd be back in Jurassic Park.

He visualised the skeletons, the specimens, coming randomly alive – apart from the fish – as they would merely thrash around in the absence of water. (Perhaps a bladderfish alive would be even more horrible than a dead one.) But, if everything else came to life, the chimpanzees, gorillas, orang-utans, gibbons, marmosets and macaques smashing their way out of their glass boxes, the cheetah snarling and leaping onto the back of a crocodile that opened a cavernous mouth and thrashed its tail, the camels running flat-footed between the aisles, the deer and moose trying to dodge between the columns, and elephants and the mighty dinosaurs beginning a feverish charge round the galleries, and if the birds got out of their cages – parrots, parakeets, ostriches, eagles, hawks – what might happen? The dodo!

Terror, pandemonium, the screams of children, museum staff, it would be worse than biblical bedlam. The high glass roof would amplify the screams. Life would be incredibly vocal. Who or what would die first? What or who would be eaten first? There would be a fearful noise and an utter wailing confusion – instead of the pleasant hum of a busy place innocently visited.

None of that mattered when Chris had his brainwave. It was when he saw a man being pushed in a wheelchair, an elderly man whose forelimbs were shaking. Chris had no doubt of the cause or his diagnosis. The man had Parkinson's disease.

*

The soft, whispery voice he heard was hypophonia; the drooling, tremor, and movement disorders were caused by degeneration of nuclei in the dopamine-producing nerve cells in the brain stem. When brains are dissected, the most important section is the substantia nigra, literally 'black substance', and in this small area the size of a thumbnail at the base of the brain, scientists concentrate their research. The loss of dopamine-secreting cells here leads to hypokinetic movement disorder, and the terrible disease known as Parkinson's or the shaking palsy.

Chris had read about a new donor programme, set up to receive donated brains. Only about six hundred people had agreed so far to donate their brains for research but making off with a donated brain immediately after death was a lot better than killing someone, or cutting them open when still alive. The chances were that the operation wouldn't work anyway; Chris would still get his money. If the chimp lived, who would really know if the operation had been successful? It was unlikely the chimp would undergo such a behavioural change as to appear human, or be more human than ape, less ape than human. Who would know if the partial brain transplant had 'taken'? It was such a long shot Chris decided it wasn't worth worrying about.

The Oxford Natural History Museum had done the trick, imagining those convulsing creatures coming alive, seeing the man with the shaking palsy. Chris felt his mood improving fast. He caught a bus back to his flat in Headington and switched on his laptop. He typed *donate brain* into Google. There were 46,100,000 results. Chris then tried, *tissue bank*, and at number three in Google was what he was looking for. A quick search through the site index confirmed the existence of a tissue bank at Imperial College, and they were looking for entire brains.

As well as studying and dissecting brains, the tissue bank needed 'control' brains. They collected only about four or five brains a month but in extremes of weather, when it was either very cold or very hot, the number of brains available increased.

To get at the brains without disfiguring the donors, a small flap has to be cut at the back of the head, the skin peeled over the top, a hole cut in the top of the skull. Then the brain is lifted out and the skin peeled back, so no one can see the brain has been removed.

Brains harvested in this way have to get to a lab within 24 hours. The whole process is regulated by the Human Tissue Authority and death has to be properly certified and registered. Section 32 of the Human Tissue Act 2004 makes it an offence to have commercial dealings 'in bodily material, such as organs or tissue, for the purposes of transplantation'. If you get caught the penalty is a fine or up to a year in prison. Not much of a penalty. Chris continued with his research. It seemed the tissue bank had to be informed of the death of the registered donor, and then the body would be transported to the hospital nearest the place of death.

A pathologist and lab technician would 'retrieve the tissue'. Then a member of the on-call team collects the brain tissue from the hospital, and takes the tissue back to a London hospital for 'processing and storage'.

*

It was time to ring George. 'George. Hi. I think I can really help you this time.'

George sounded pleased. 'I've placed my faith in you, Chris. So what's the deal?'

'Can't tell you everything now. I'll confirm later. Basically, we're looking for someone who wants to donate some tissue – whether they like it or not.'

'Fair enough,' George said.

'Sooner or later, I'll get the tissue organised. We might need to produce some documents and make them work for us, if you know what I mean.'

'You mean forgery?' George asked.

'That's right. I'm going to be part of a team, the on-call team responsible for transporting the stuff. I will be self-employed, George.'

'Meaning?'

'Meaning I'll be the team myself. Arrive early, very early before the other team gets there. I have to be someone else.'

'Impersonation?' George thought quickly. He could see it working already. 'It doesn't have to be someone young,' he said. 'More or less anyone will do, but bear in mind the younger the better. Once you get the brain, you'll have to give it blood, and take care of oxygenation. It'll be a perfusion job. Maybe we won't be able to do that after all. We might just have to rely on the ice. Later we'll have to freeze it at -85°C. That's unless we use it right away. Come to think of it, we might have to do just that. Operate the moment we get home. Christ almighty, Chris, it's a fucking lot of trouble for a chimpanzee, for chrissakes!'

Chris hadn't had a drink all day but he began to laugh. George joined in. 'Who says being a doctor's boring?' George must have hit the whisky because soon after hearing from Chris, he was flying high, as high as a kite.

TWENTY-THREE

The towers and dreaming spires of Oxford have seen, and still see, countless experiments, some bizarre, others at the forefront of science. Boundaries are continually being pushed back. After the success of one Japanese team effort to clone mice from cells that had been frozen for 16 years, there had been speculation that this meant extinct species like the woolly mammoth could be brought back from the dead.

Chris made up his mind to rid himself of his drink problem, at least by slow 'reverse incremental steps', he told himself. One reason was that he needed to be much more observant. He began to study the clothes and habits of everyone around him, from distinguished surgeons to tea girls pushing trolleys and mopping floors. He watched drivers come and go with blood samples, urine and specimen samples for the pathology labs, hospital notes or X-rays. Apart from a small badge, a tie, black trousers and white or blue shirts, no one ever seemed to check drivers delivering or collecting material. They usually asked for a piece of paper to be signed, and then they were gone. The blood samples were neatly packaged in small boxes. Chris saw the drivers bang on a window, and be handed a chit and the blood in a red canvas box.

He'd ask George to find out more from the tissue bank. Get the forms for prospective donors. Ask questions. Uncover the small facts they needed to know for success. It would be Chris's job to slip in unrecognised, almost unnoticed, to sign for the brain tissue.

*

George meanwhile was getting nervous. He had been so confident after Chris rang but was it only the confidence of malt whisky skewing his judgement? How far were they going to get with a missing brain? He thought about substituting the brain of one of his own patients, someone who might die at home. He could get the brain out with some forged forms but that wasn't really likely. His own health wasn't so good. He was taking statins to bust the cholesterol clogging his arteries.

Charlie was getting on his nerves. The poor creature had become morose in his cage. Charlie seemed to have given up meat. George had thrown out most of the lambs' legs. The friendly chimp who happily plucked an apple, walked with George beneath the oak trees, climbed aloft amazed by the sunset now seemed to care for little except the occasional banana and the comfort of his woollen sleeping blanket.

*

Charlie missed other chimpanzees. He was unable to function as he should, solely on his own. Chimpanzees live in multimale-multifemale groups, often defined as fission–fusion organisation. Fission occurs, for example, when a group splits up to forage in the daytime; fusion results when the returning members come together again at night as a group to sleep.

Group sizes are typically between 40 and 60 members, the numbers in constant flux. Membership of a dynamic chimp group confers many benefits but none accrued to Charlie. For several moments, when he climbed an oak tree in the back garden, he must have felt something like the once-known joy of being in the forest, being a living part of it. The forest was a place where Charlie belonged, among the creepers, the vines, the teeming ferns, the giant trees with their buttressed roots on which he could kick and drum with something akin to happiness, the ripe fruits he could gorge on, the leaves and flowers he could eat, the water to drink from streams, roots to dig up. There was the early morning mist, the start of every new morning. He could chase butterflies, scream at snakes, play. The forest was like something alive, with the insistent, incessant background noises of insects, birds and other animals. The forest spoke to Charlie, or used to, and when it spoke to him, he uttered cries back, and hooted with something like joy. At night he would sleep in trees, relaxing in a nest of his own making. He would sleep soundly; sometimes through the canopy he could see the star-points of light in the Cameroonian night sky, and always around dusk the forest would be enveloped in a haze of purple mist, a kind of luminous inky violet, which was the tropical night, bearing in upon those still left in the forest, one vast mass of mingling shade, and dark shadows.

When the rains came in the wet season, Charlie would pass hours, huddled with his troupe, the rain beating down over their backs, and there would be silence apart from the heavy pattering of rain drops sheeting through to the forest floor. The red earth smelled a wholesome, rich smell so that you could just lie down on it, be content, and the ants, well they were food. No matter how heavy the rain, the sun would eventually break through, and more mist would rise from the pelages of the chimp troupe as they dried out in the sun's heat.

Now, he could hardly sleep at night except fitfully. His limbs were heavy, although he had not used them to climb or carry anything. His mouth was continually dry. In the forest he was able to interpret day or night in his own way, according to his own 'laws' of the forest. He could 'read' it as a human might read a book. In the cage in the garage there was nothing to do. There was only emptiness, an ache inside him like a valley the rain could not reach.

*

In the meantime Chris slowly stopped drinking quite so much. He made enquiries. When a donated brain is collected, the matter is placed in moist tissue, and then put in a container with ice blocks to keep it cool. Later it is cut up and frozen in supercooled liquid. The main preservation task takes place back at the laboratory. Large freezers store the brain tissue in special inventory systems and trays.

A member of the lab staff from the Tissue Bank calls for the brain tissue. No uniform is worn but the person collecting the brain will have Tissue Bank identification and paperwork.

The brain is cut up into small pieces before freezing – whole brains are not frozen in one piece. Without a blood supply, irreversible brain death sets in within six to ten minutes. Supercooling the brain is the only way to preserve the tissue, and then only in the short term.

*

It was in the evening of November 5th, when half the sky around Oxford seemed lit up with fireworks that Chris got the call from George. 'Hi Chris! We're close. Do you want to know how close?'

'I'm just about ready.'

'There's a guy coming in pretty soon.'

'Christ, George. How do you know?'

'I've got a friend in the Tissue Bank. She knows Jo.'

'So I know Jo. So what?'

'Jo persuaded her to help out. The guy's virtually dead anyway. Drummer in a rock band. Came off a bike. Going too fast. Big machine. 1000 cc job. His brain is knocked about but that's not what's killing him. His body was almost cut in half by a lamppost. They can't save him. He'd signed a donor form. He won't last more than a day.'

'Christ, you said close. This is it. Where do I go? How am I supposed to collect it?'

'You'll have to get to a hospital in Banbury. North Oxford.'

'I know. Horton General.'

'That's correct.'

'Then what?'

'You'll have to be there when the time comes. You go in and get the tissue. I'll fax you the papers.'

'That's all?'

'No, there's a lot more we have to do. This is where we begin, Chris. This is where Charlie starts his journey, I think. Get some sleep. I'll call you in the morning.'

Chris broke one of his new rules and had two more beers before going to bed.

George slipped outside and stood alone outside the garage doors. He heard nothing. Charlie must be asleep. Then he went back inside the house, and opened the door to his operating theatre to have a quick look inside. He sighed. All was in order. 'Not long now Charlie, my boy,' he said aloud. 'Not long.'

George shut the door quietly, and went upstairs to sleep alone. Sleep would not come. He kept seeing Charlie's head being opened. He didn't know how much to cut out, how much to leave in. Bringing Charlie back alive would be the greatest challenge he had ever known.

TWENTY-FOUR

Chris got kitted up the next day with a Tissue Bank badge and paperwork relating to the poor man who'd been in collision with a lamppost. Badge and paperwork came from Jo's friend who worked in Imperial College. It was a big risk and a big gamble. If it was a gamble, they'd already had a big slice of luck. Jo refused to say who her contact was, only that Chris could collect all he needed from the Grand Café on The High.

Chris turned up at seven in the evening. He was tempted to order one of the half-price cocktails, a double even, but sanity came to his rescue just in time. He had a half pint of lager instead, and walked very self-consciously back to a table next to a large plant. It looked like an indoor palm tree. He was to sit with his back to the palm, facing the door, and leave an orange on the table. The bar was full of students enjoying their drinks so, although the idea of an orange on the table was a strange one, probably no one would notice.

Chris had the peculiar feeling of being a lemon sitting next to an orange. No one sat at his table, but soon two girls did. One had short dark hair, the other was blonde. The girl with dark hair leant over to scrutinise the orange. Chris saw she had something pink like a birthmark on her neck. She was astonishingly pretty in a classical way. She was so slim-hipped she could have been a boy.

The girl picked up the orange and juggled it with her friend. Chris asked her to stop but they took no notice.

'Would you leave that orange alone?'

The girl put it back without a murmur.

'Thanks,' Chris said, and looking at the girl with dark hair, added, 'What are you studying?'

'Forensic science,' the girl replied with a smile. 'Do you mind telling me what you plan to do with that orange?'

Chris was getting worried. At least it was still on the table. 'I'm saving it for a friend,' he said, which was almost true. 'He's mad about oranges. In fact, he's coming in soon to collect it.'

The girls looked at Chris as if he had half his brain missing. Just then, a tall man came in, holding a briefcase under his arm. He looked foreign. He walked right up to their table, his eyes intent on the orange. 'Is that beauty for me?' he asked happily.

'Take it,' Chris said. 'You have something for me?'

'Sure thing, boss.' The man opened up the briefcase, and pulled out some papers and a small envelope. 'This is what you need, I think. You don't have much time, let's say less than ninety minutes. Good luck.'

The stranger took the orange as if it was something really critical. The two girls looked bewildered. Chris said he was sorry, he had to go. 'I'll see you,' he called out.

In The High, he opened the small envelope, and took out the Tissue Bank identification badge, reading the instructions without wasting a second. He was to go to Horton General, wearing the badge, and then to the pathology lab with the paperwork. He should ring a bell if no one was there, and wait till someone arrived. He would hand over the paperwork, and say he'd come to collect something for the Tissue Bank.

George would be waiting for him in the hospital car park.

Chris took a taxi back to Headington Hill, calling in at the John Radcliffe to sign off work and get a change of clothes. He kept the taxi waiting, and then told to driver to go to Banbury fast, hoping he would make the thirty-mile drive in less than forty minutes. Chris got there at ten to nine.

George was waiting in his Rover in the car park. 'How much?' he asked the driver.

'Fifty pounds guv, to you.'

George paid the driver, and immediately turned on Chris. 'What took you so long? You could have ridden a cock horse to get here for the time it took you.'

'I came as fast as I could.'

'You've got the badge and the paper stuff?'

'Yes.'

'Get in there then. We have no time.'

'There's just one thing. I have to go back to the Radcliffe to get some things out of my locker.'

'Shit, you could have told me before. We have to start the operation within four hours and, before you ask me, Charlie's ready too. He's been on nil by mouth for at least twelve hours.'

Chris swallowed hard. 'I'm about as ready as I'll ever be. How do I look?'

'You look just like a Tissue Bank operative, for Christ's sake.' George adjusted the identification badge slightly, and then held Chris's shoulders with his hands. 'Go to it, young man. Let's get that brain. It's the right hemisphere only – the other half is going to the Tissue Bank – so it looks like they're getting something.'

With his heart seeming to beat more than usual in his chest, Chris went straight into the hospital. At the reception desk, he waved his form, and said, 'Tissue Bank collection'.

'Have you been here before?' the receptionist asked, holding her arm out for the form. She took a quick look, without stopping for a reply. 'Pathology's down at the end of the corridor opposite, up the stairs – or you can take the lift – to the first floor. Just follow the signs for pathology. You can't miss it.'

Chris thanked her. He took the lift, and finally got to the path lab window. A note by a bell read, 'Push ONCE for attention.'

Chris pressed the button. His heart was fluttering. He tried to pull himself together with a couple of deep breaths.

After a minute or two passed, a man appeared. He slid open the window. Chris proffered the form. 'Tissue Bank collection,' he said, trying to sound as if it was nothing much. 'Here's the paperwork.' He could see the man scanning him, looking at his ID badge but Chris didn't flinch. The window shut. There was nothing to do but wait.

In the car park George was fidgeting. He called Jo to thank her. 'Hi Jo. It looks like we're collecting any moment now. You know how much I owe you. Can you be at the house by eleven tonight? Open up the theatre. Switch everything on. You can give Charlie a pre-op sedative if you like, at eleven or just past eleven. If you want to wait for me, that's okay. We'll be there about ten to twelve.' George snapped his phone shut.

He had to wait only a few minutes more. Chris came out with a big grin on his face, holding a metal box by a pair of leather straps. 'I got it George! I got it!' Chris shouted.

'Okay. Okay. Did you have to sign anything?'

'I just scribbled a name on the form. They didn't bother to look. It's packed in ice. We have about four hours. Where do you want it?'

'Strap it to the back seatbelt. Don't cover it.' As soon as Chris had made the box safe, George exited from the hospital car park. 'Chris, I'm going to push this old car so don't expect an easy ride back.'

After just under forty minutes, they reached the John Radcliffe Hospital. Chris took off his ID badge and went inside to empty his locker. No one noticed him, except the CCTV cameras.

George had imagined in his mind getting out of Oxford to the sound of the one hundred and one chimes of Old Tom but by the time they got there Old Tom was silent. Great Tom had already sounded. George checked his watch. It was 9.50 p.m. 'The line of festal light in Christ-Church hall' that the Scholar Gipsy saw was to them invisible on the light-polluted A34. Soon they were on the road to Newbury, heading south to Winchester, then on to Bournemouth and Poole.

The severed brain, now no more than a collection of neurons swathed in moist tissue, sat in its icy container on the back seat. It was going on a very peculiar journey. It was going to make history.

TWENTY-FIVE

Jo got to the house at 10.10 p.m. She'd been unable to wait any longer. George told her to run through what they had ready in the operating theatre, and to make a list of tasks for the night ahead. As she turned into the drive, her headlights picked out a raucous crow that cawed three times from the top of the garage and flew off.

She wondered how Charlie was. It was a chill evening, typical November weather, gusting and blowing. In the harbour the swell was rising inexorably, with sea spray billowing over the harbour walls. Jo went into the house, opened up the laboratory, and got to work. It was not easy to be confident. There were so many risks to neurosurgery, even with the best equipment.

*

Any operation involving the brain can cause systemic paralysis, irreversible brain damage, and even death.

A wall-mounted, multiparameter monitor would measure Charlie's vital signs, such as recording ECG for cardiac output, electroencephalogram (EEG) to measure brain electrical activity, blood pressure, and dissolved gases in the blood. Although the human brain weighs only 2 per cent of the entire body, it uses 20 per cent of the oxygen in the body, and probably the same amount of glucose, so maintaining satisfactory oxygen levels would be especially important. The measurements wouldn't be too far out for Charlie, although the chimpanzee's brain volume is much less than a human's. The latest genome-mapping has shown that we share 99 per cent sequence identity in genes and proteins.

On standby would be an infusion pump to infuse fluids, medication or nutrients into Charlie's bloodstream; medication could include short-acting intravenous sedative agents, such as propofol, used for general anaesthesia and sedation. Other drugs that George might use were ketamine, rompum, or etomidate; analgesics for pain relief; diazepam for initial sedation, morphine intraoperatively. Then there would be anticoagulants, antibiotics, immunosuppressive drugs...

They would measure Charlie's heart rate, as well as oxygen saturation, via pulse oximetry (to measure oxygen levels in the blood), urine output, temperature, and neuromuscular function, via peripheral nerve stimulation monitoring.

There was also a vast array of surgical instruments, including forceps, a rongeur to open a window in the skull (also used for gouging out bone to expose areas for operation), clamps, callipers, cannula, nerve hooks, surgical hooks, tongue depressor, mouth gag, occluders for blood vessels, mechanical cutters, retractors, scalpels, drill bits, high-speed drill, bone chisels, dilators, specula, suction tubes and tips for bodily fluids, injection needles, 'tyndallers' to wedge open damaged brain tissue, titanium microclips, scalpels, powered devices for cutting bone, scopes and probes, scissors, an endotracheal tube to assist breathing, atraumatic or minimally invasive needles (with absorbable sutures attached to the eyeless needles for closing incisions on the skull). It was a very long list...

*

Jo was confident George had most of the necessary equipment. The problem was that brains are delicate creatures. Intraoperative complications during surgery, *at the very least*, include haemorrhage and traumatic perforation of the organ, which may have lethal sequelae.

However, all seemed in place. She could only trust in George's professional expertise, though his surgical skills had barely been exercised for years.

Jo thought it time to get Charlie in, bring him inside the house, at least give him a pre-op. She decided to call George. 'Hi George, it's Jo. You okay?'

George seemed a long way off, and concerned about something. 'Yes. We're okay, and that's including what we have on the back seat. What we need right now is an ice age, to cool that boy down. Poor guy. We don't know anything about him except he rode fast bikes, and was a drummer in a rock band.'

'George, theatre's ready. That's most of the stuff I know about. The rest I'll leave to you. Should I sedate Charlie, like you said?'

'Yes. No reason why not. Procedure would be initial sedation 1 mg/kg diazepam administered rectally to the chimpanzee. How much does he weigh now? We need to know that.'

'About 150 lb. Can you tell me how I'm supposed to administer rectally, for God's sake? Charlie won't take no for an answer. Well, you know what I mean. He won't take anything for an answer unless he likes it.'

'You can wait if you like. I don't think you'll get very far in Charlie's cage with a rectal syringe.'

Jo agreed.

'In fact, Charlie's so strong he might try it out on you!'

'Cut it out, George, will you?' She heard George chuckling to himself while Chris sniggered in the background. 'You men are disgusting.'

'We have to laugh, don't we Chris?' said George. 'You know that as a doctor. Without humour we'd want to get on that plane to Switzerland, use a sharp unwisely, or raid the drugs box. Anyway Jo, I've got to thank that friend of yours for doing such a fine job. We haven't checked inside the container though. Should be perfect for the job.'

'Hurry up George, will you?' said Jo, an anxious tone in her voice. 'I'm worried about Charlie. Shall I go and see him?'

'Yes. Good idea. Remember nil by mouth, not even water. Try to cheer him up. We're only about forty minutes away.' George clicked off his phone.

Jo pulled down the garage keys. She went outside, and towards the garage apprehensively. Perhaps, she thought, if Charlie had died, that would be an end to it. It might be better for him. She hadn't seen him since he'd thrown himself prostrate on the floor of his cage in the garage, his arms flailing the air.

Gingerly, she pulled back one of the doors. Almost instantly, she heard a pant-grunt from Charlie. He might have recognised her in the doorway or smelled her scent. Chimpanzees can make over thirty different calls, but all can be broken down into four main call types: grunts, barks, screams, and hoots. They have a fairly good sense of smell, and will identify other troupe members via pheromones, urine, faeces, or gland secretions. Each individual has a distinctive smell.

'Charlie, are you there? Are you okay?' Jo called out softly.

Charlie shook his cage in response, and made a '*Hoo, hoo*' sound that indicated he was pleased to see her.

Jo switched on the light and there was Charlie, his face pressed up against the bars of his cage, brown eyes looking pleadingly at her, lower lip hanging down, showing he felt relaxed. If he could get any closer to her, surely he would, and when Jo saw this, she threw away caution, picking up the padlock to his cage. She hesitated. Charlie looked at the padlock in her hands, then at her. He wanted to be free.

'You won't harm me Charlie, will you?' said Jo quietly. She found the key to the padlock, where George hid it, and as she turned the key in the lock, it was as if she knew she was opening up more than just a lock. It was a link in the causal chain that led to Charlie being strapped down, his head shaved, pinioned by a metal clamp. Charlie would lose something of himself, how much or how little nobody could have known, and gain in return something that once belonged to someone else – a young human being. Whether Charlie could make use of this gift was unknown. The gift might equally be a curse.

Jo opened the cage. Charlie stepped out, and held her hand. They came out of the garage together, and took their solitary way, Charlie knuckle-walking with his one free hand with slow, wandering steps, back to the house.

TWENTY-SIX

George Waldren was pushing the old Rover hard. It was 11.05 p.m., and there was less than twenty-five miles to go. George turned to look at Chris. He was wide awake, which was surprising. 'Looks like you've been having nil by mouth too,' George remarked coolly.

'Do you have a penchant for particular fruits?' Chris asked in return. 'Why go for oranges?'

'Easy to find someone if there's one on the table,' George laughed. 'And easier than carrying around a water melon or pineapple.'

'I hope you are still going to pay me,' Chris said a trifle mournfully, 'as it was Jo's friend who came up with the brain, not me.'

'Don't worry. Of course I'll pay you the money. You played your part, and you've still more to do,' George said.

'Whatever got you into this?' Chris asked suddenly. 'If I have more to do, you might as well tell me.'

'Look,' George began, obviously eager for the chance to explain, 'chimpanzees have been studied for more than sixty years now. Why? Well, one reason is because they're phylogenetically closest to humans. The circuitry and structure of the chimpanzee brain is closer to the human brain *than any other living primate*. There's a lot of behavioural data now from the wild but the neural basis for what I call cognitive processing isn't fully understood. Scientists are trying to understand the evolutionary and neural basis for human cognition. Cognitive scientists want to examine the brain in action. Chimpanzees can help in that study, but invasive techniques have fallen out of favour. There are practical difficulties trying to conduct non-invasive measurements on awake individuals.'

'I'm none the wiser really, George. It wouldn't be so bad if Charlie had something wrong with him – like a brain tumour he was going to die from. But he's healthy. He could live for fifty or sixty years. He could also be dead by tomorrow. Chimps may be close to humans but when it comes to skulls and what's inside them, I mean, don't you have to know about cranial indices, things like that? They're not the same, are they?'

'No,' George replied sullenly.

'All the more likely the parts won't fit and Charlie will die.'

'I know,' George responded, with a heaviness in his voice that was not typical. 'I know. I'll hurt him, past all surgery. I might kill him. In fact, I'm very likely to. It's odds on he will die. This is not elective brain surgery with informed consent, for Christ's sake. I don't have Charlie's permission.'

'That you don't,' Chris sighed.

'You know, in some of these animal experiments, guess what they have to consider now?' George didn't wait for an answer. 'Is it acceptable to do "reversible harm", create a mild, treatable infection, sedate a chimpanzee just like you would a child, to allow therapeutic procedures? The harm is reversible anyway, and yet they're asking if they can do it! Charlie, poor Charlie, there won't be anything reversible about his treatment. The therapeutic procedure he's getting is probably going to fuck his brain up, beyond any question.'

'Then, why George? Why worry about screwing up the poor creature's brain when you're probably going to kill him?'

'Because it's such a slim chance, I'm going for it. Do you remember that oil guy called Gulbenkian? They named him, "Mr Five Percent". Five per cent revenues from a few oil deals made him one of the world's richest men. He always liked to retain five per cent, the crafty old bastard.'

Chris chuckled, evidently enjoying the history lesson.

'When he died in the 1950s he left at least $500 million, probably more,' George continued. 'And then there was the son of Mr Five Percent. He was a lazy bastard. They said of him he was so tough that every day he tired out three stockbrokers, three horses, and three women.'

'What's the connection, George?'

'How much you can do on five per cent. Well, I'm different. I'm going for far, far less. I'm Mr 00000.1 per cent. That's what makes it such a challenge.'

'You're crazy George.'

George violently swerved the car. 'Thank you Chris,' he said sarcastically. 'Why haven't you got any faith? Look, will you promise me you'll concentrate, for Charlie's benefit? You're going to assist a surgeon who's got to somehow make this work. We have to pull out all the stops. And as well as taking the risks we have to proceed with utmost caution.

'Just you wait. Once we get inside the skull, the cranium, there's the dura, a tough leathery sheath – well, the outer barrier – to get through. The three meninges, the three coverings. When we get past the outer barrier, it's onto, or rather into, the inner barrier, the blood–brain barrier. The blood–brain barrier, for what it's worth, allows free passage of certain molecules, and restricts others. The process is known as homeostasis. Under the dura, there's the arachnoid membrane; this houses the fluid that surrounds the brain, the cerebrospinal fluid or CSF. Eighty per cent of the brain is made up of water, as you know.'

Chris coughed.

'In adults the total volume of CSF is about 125 ml, some of this being around the spinal cord. Adults produce about 20 ml of CSF per hour. The CSF circulates in the brain, the cerebrum, in spaces called ventricles. The cortex, which means bark as in tree bark, is the grey matter, the brain surface, a few millimetres thick. The cortex has folds to accommodate all the nerve cells, they're called gyri. Valleys in the gyri are called sulci. In the sulci...'

'...Please! George. I've got one hell of a headache,' Chris interrupted. 'I'm just a tissue bank operative, and a suspended, failed GP, remember? For the love of God stop! Before the nerves in *my* brain give out. They feel like they're breaking down!'

'Breaking down!' George interjected angrily. 'About to have a neurological episode, are we? You big baby. Okay, I won't tell you about, let's say refresh your memory, on the forebrain, hindbrain, the hemispheres, the corpus callosum that joins them, the cerebellum, the cranial nerves, basal ganglia, the brain stem, the lobes of the forebrain – frontal, parietal, occipital, temporal – the brain at any one time receiving 20 per cent of the heart's blood output, the carotid arteries, the vertebral arteries, the circle of Willis, internal jugular veins, the glia, the synapses, the dendrites, the white matter, and the rest – and that's just touching on the beginning, the basic nuts and bolts.'

In the car it fell suddenly silent. Chris yawned. George continued driving fast, his body language indicating a man obsessed, obsessed with getting to Charlie in time, in time to give his operation a chance of success.

It was Chris who spoke first. 'George, I do actually remember most of that because I had to learn it at med school. I have to say, "So what"?' If you really care about Charlie and the great apes, why don't you try to save the rainforests, set up a trust to work against the bushmeat trade, take on board Prince Charles' idea about convening power? You could do so much more. You're not helping chimpanzees and the other great apes. You're sacrificing an innocent animal for your own personal mania with warped experiments, experiments that no right-thinking scientist would endorse with the word "scientific".'

'I know. I know,' George answered with more than a hint of petulant frustration. 'I want to do this, to see if it can be done. To bring Charlie into the world with a new kind of cognition. A first for science. Do you know, even a first in the goddamn universe but that's not important. It will not be perfect. It will be an imperfection of sorts, an approximation of what one day might be possible if...'

George's train of thought was suddenly interrupted. 'By the way, Chris, I've only been able to get hold of human stem cells. I bought some online. Bloody expensive.'

'How much?' Chris asked.

'About seven hundred quid for pluripotent embryonic stem cells, including neural cells. It's probably better than mixing them up with chimp stem cells. The immune system might still reject them but it's worth a try.'

'I know how to get rich,' Chris chortled, 'without doing any work. You just pay me the ten grand. The odds of you succeeding must be about one hundred to one. If I could find someone to place the bet with, and you're successful, I'll be a millionaire.'

The distance had been eaten up. George almost rammed the car into his driveway, just missing a corner post. He parked the car right outside the back door, and with Chris following, walked in to the house, holding the container firmly under his left arm.

'Jo!' George called out in the kitchen. 'We're back!' He pushed open the door to the dining room, and his mouth fell open. Jo had placed a tray on the dining-room table. In George's usual chair, Charlie was sitting back comfortably, holding a mug of tea. When he saw George, Charlie hooted. He flung the mug up in the air and incredibly when it fell to the floor in a corner of the room, it found Helga, right on her nose. Helga sounded her anguish, and then fury. She stood up, growling with lips drawn back over her little teeth, snarling straight at Charlie. In turn, Charlie made his fur bristle, as if standing on end.

'I told you it was nil by mouth. What are you playing at, woman?'

Jo didn't seem at all worried, other than slightly perturbed by all the noise. 'There was nothing in the mug, George. I just gave it to Charlie to keep him quiet.'

George blew out a big sigh of relief. 'Thank Christ for that. You haven't sedated him, I take it.'

Jo shook her head. 'Rather you than me.'

Charlie was trying to reach under and behind George's chair where Helga had defiantly sought refuge. 'Chris!' George yelled. 'Get me the oral sedative from the operating theatre. We've no time to lose.'

TWENTY-SEVEN

Charlie was given the cup to drink, with its concealed oral sedative. He drank it boldly, as if with purpose, as Socrates had, but only in the sense that lesser amounts of the poison hemlock were used for their sedative property, not as a means of execution. Like Socrates once did, he walked around a little on his legs, holding on to George with one arm, before the potion began to take effect, whereupon he sat down.

'Let not all the drowsy syrups of the world prevent thy return,' whispered George into the chimp's protruding ears.

Charlie passed a limp hand across his face, grimaced at Helga, who had emerged from under George's chair, and then slumped over, his body crumpling quite suddenly. George caught him swiftly. He cradled Charlie's torso while looking expectantly at Chris and Jo.

'This is one big chimp. God, he's heavy. Okay, this is it. Time check. Midnight plus five. We have between four and six hours to go. I suggest if you want something to eat, or a quick coffee, you take it now. Chris, give me a hand to carry Charlie through, will you?'

Chris lifted Charlie by his feet, and with George holding the chimp under his armpits, Charlie was carried through to George's theatre. He was eased onto the operating table, freshly laid with cotton and lint, and a new light plastic covering.

George surveyed the scene. The body of 'the patient' was correctly positioned. All the necessary instruments appeared to be in place, with the exception of a pinion, a metal clamp with three points that would stick into the skin of the scalp to hold Charlie's head in place. George began to scrub up, and called out for Chris and Jo to join him.

'Oh my God,' Jo said when she walked in holding the container containing the body part destined for the inside of Charlie's skull.

'Put that down and scrub up,' George commanded. 'If I needed to remind you, one hundred thousand bacteria lurk on one square inch of healthy skin. And make sure you wash your hands for at least twenty seconds.'

'Christ, just look at him!' said Chris, who was also told to scrub up.

'Okay, when you're ready. I will run through the procedure. Jo will place some intravenous lines. He will then breathe oxygen and anaesthetic gases, whereupon IV sedation will take place. He will safely and comfortably be put to sleep and intubated. The endotracheal tube as you know is for what, Jo?'

'The placement of the tube is through the mouth, into the trachea, for controlled ventilation during the procedure, as Charlie – the patient – will be under deep anaesthesia.'

'Correct. We may then have to consider placing an intra-arterial line in the wrist artery, to allow for continuous blood pressure monitoring. Actually, we're going to do this now. The longer we delay the less Charlie's chances are of recovery.'

In two and a half minutes Charlie had his IV lines in place and was intubated successfully, breathing the mixture of oxygen and anaesthetic.

'We're not going to bother with a central line,' George continued, 'to monitor his cardiovascular system. We'll have to chance that.'

Chris sniggered at the thought. 'Chance! Chance would be a fine thing in this case, with the odds stacked against us, cephalically speaking, to start with. There's not much chance of a chance, is there?'

'Shut up, Chris,' George thundered. He looked round the room, as if something were missing. 'Where the bloody hell is the pinion? We can't start sawing into Charlie if his head's moving about all over the place. Can't do a craniotomy without it.' George began to rummage through cardboard boxes on the floor at the back of the room. When a box didn't contain the thing he was looking for, he just kicked it out of the way. Finally, there was one box left. George put his hand in. 'Got you, you bastard,' he cried triumphantly.

'We are now going to position the head, pad the body, and secure him to the table. The three pins prick through the skin of the scalp, and are then pressure-adjusted to make contact with the outer skull bone.'

'Great,' Chris said.

'Too right. Now watch this. Hand me the shaver. I'm going to shave the scalp hair, to prepare the field, as it were.' George deftly handled the shaver.

'As good as Mr Teasy-Weasy,' Chris put in, in his usual sardonic fashion.

'I shall now apply antiseptic solution, drape in a sterile manner, and begin the incision.' George picked up a scalpel from a side table and made a scalp flap, which he then turned to give good exposure of the craniotomy site.

Jo crossed herself. 'Good luck, Charlie,' she said.

'The sixth extinction event plus one,' said Chris mordantly.

George continued with the operation, as a conductor might move through a musical piece, full of concentration, not taking his mind off a thing, yet supremely relaxed in his professional skills. 'You can see the bone flap is now exposed. We shall remove this using a high speed drill.' George quickly made small holes in the skull, known as burr holes.

'Quick point, George,' Chris interrupted, 'should an antibiotic prophylaxis have been given before the incision?'

'Thanks for reminding me. Yes, better late than never. Jo, inject Charlie with this, will you?' George handed her a small bottle of clear liquid attached to a syringe.

'And another thing,' Chris said, 'make sure it's the right side.'

'Quite,' George replied. 'That would be a real disaster, ending up with two identical hemispheres, a real cock-up. Imagine trying to put a right arm on a person's left. It's actually advisable to use a marker pen beforehand.' He stopped to look down at Charlie on the operating table, so helpless, moments away from the most invasive surgery possible. George sighed because there was still a long way to go. He wondered if Charlie would ever walk again. If he would ever wake up.

'What now?' Chris asked expectantly.

'We remove the bone flap, expose the dura, and open this sharply like so, using scalpel and dural scissors. We reflect this out of the way, and then, look, the brain surface is exposed. The brain cannot feel pain itself, having no pain receptors.'

'God, it's very pinky red, isn't it?' Jo said, feeling a little sick. 'How on earth are you going to cut through all that? Blood vessels, fat, veins, arteries?' Jo saw the shiny surface of Charlie's brain, glittering with cerebrospinal fluid; red arteries and blue veins crisscrossed its surface like river systems seen from space.

'Well, this operation is my interpretation, you understand. It's neither an anatomic nor functional hemispherectomy, something in between. The first is complete removal, the second partial, but there are variations of both. I intend to leave some portions of the lower brain intact, and slot in, as it were, the upper part of the hemisphere from the donor. The corpus callosum is supposed to connect the two hemispheres. We're going to remove the central cortical region, temporal lobe, other bits and pieces I won't go into, like the parasagittal cortex, the cingulate gyrus. Far too complicated.

'I was going for some sort of cranial enlargement but the risk of infection would be too great. It's better to use less of the donor's tissue. This whole experiment is just one big great approximation, after all. When I've cut out the tissue, removed it, stopped the bleeding, what we have to transplant from that poor unfortunate donor will be put in place, not all of it because we won't need the entire hemisphere. That still has to be carved up to make it fit!

'After I have negotiated the numerous blood vessels, which is half the job really, among the one hundred billion nerve cells in the brain, the new underlying and adjacent tissues will be sutured together, the dura sutured, the bone flap replaced. We have a titanium miniplate and screws to affix the bone flap. The scalp is closed, staples or sutures used for the skin closure. Before the bone flap is restored, I will decide whether to flush in neural stem cells. This should improve plasticity of both existing and new material in the brain.'

'George, my old mate,' Chris said with some emotion, 'you're a fucking genius.'

'Open the box!' George cried. 'Let's get that brain out now.' Chris opened the box gingerly, and removed the piece of donor brain. It was not a beautiful sight. Yet, the alien-looking organ was still 'alive', presumably still held memories, might yet be capable of giving a sense of being and consciousness.

George deftly removed a few slivers of tissue. What part they played in the brain's circuitry would never be known. It was easy enough to slot the hemisphere into the ape's skull – the hardest part was always going to be the intricate connections needed, the surgeon's steady hands trying to do this via *his* brain, with as little damage as possible to the tissue and the maze of blood vessels. Hours passed. Then it was done.

*

No sound was heard, other than the monitors, the machines overseeing Charlie, recording his vital signs of life. George was still and very silent but he was also very tired. He ignored Chris and Jo and, placing one hand, encased in a surgeon's blue nitrile glove on Charlie's chest, he said solemnly, 'The sands are numbered that make up your life, Charlie my boy. Go well. Long live Charlie. Into this world you go alone.'

*

In the new world that Charlie now inhabited postoperatively, he did at least have the benefit of quietness but it was a quietness that he was as yet unable to appreciate. Most intensive care units or ICUs are busy environments but Charlie's was a one-patient only room. There were the usual lighted displays and sounds from a single monitor, showing the vital signs of heart and breathing rate, blood pressure, and level of blood oxygen. An IV line stand held IV fluid and medication for pain. A catheter drained his urine.

A thin plastic drainage tube exited from the back of Charlie's head, which was surrounded by a head wrap, a bandage that would apply pressure around the incision to the head.

It was evident that Jo and Chris were frankly amazed to see Charlie actually alive, although there was still a real likelihood that being alive would ultimately amount to nothing more than lying comatose on George's operating table. The breathing tube was still there. If Charlie had been strong enough, and had met all the requirements for extubation, it would have been removed. Charlie would remain on a mechanical ventilator for at least the next 24 hours.

He was uncannily still for a chimpanzee who often liked to romp about and play, who, when in better mood, was into every corner looking for the next trick. He lay on his back with his sizeable balls seemingly shrunken a little, his head thrown back, the prognathous snout jutting out, legs akimbo, arms splayed helplessly at either side, and weaving in and out of his body all the snaking tubes necessary for his earthly existence.

George Waldren had excelled himself, carrying out over three hours of microsurgery, without benefit of the latest neuroimaging procedures by which surgeons can see into the brain, like magnetic resonance imaging, computerised tomography, or positron emission tomography imaging.

His face, however, seemed drained, as if he had made an unwelcome pact from which there was scant prospect of return. He looked in pain, Jo noticed, as did Chris. But it was not fatigue. It was the pain of not knowing if Charlie would ever return and if he did what would he be?

TWENTY-EIGHT

Dr Waldren made some notes at the end of the first day. He reported 'no significant neurological change'. At the back of his mind he had questioned the truth of what he had written down. In truth, there was no minor or insignificant change – there was none at all. On the other hand, there had been major neurological change at the time of the operation – major if not colossal trauma.

Chris and Jo were deputed to look after routine care of the patient, monitoring pain medication, fluid administration, positioning, and hygiene. Together they shared ventilator and urinary catheter management. Recovery was expected to be slow. George disappeared for a rest. He had noticed a dull pain down one side of his head, not a good sign. He hoped it was nothing more than fatigue from excessive concentration over many hours, and lack of sleep.

Several times Chris pinched Charlie's toes quite hard but there was no response. The ape was breathing satisfactorily via the ventilator. His vital signs were good. Cognitively, however, and here Chris smiled painfully to himself when he came up with the words, Charlie could be a no-brainer. Chris was angry with George because George had refused to activate any EEG readings. He wanted to switch everything on later, hoping it would all be fine. How could they tell, Chris thought, if Charlie were actually alive? He might be brain dead, with a flat or straight-line EEG. If no tests were done to ascertain brain function, the electrical signals within the brain, he might as well, in his present state, *be* dead.

While George rested, Chris took sixteen electrodes and attached these to Charlie's scalp with sticky paste, linking them via wires to a laptop. Chris knew, as long as some waves were detectable, to be normal both sides of Charlie's brain ought to show broadly similar patterns of electrical activity. Chris fixed the last electrode anxiously.

There was a few seconds' wait for the electrical activity coming from Charlie's cortex to be recorded. Delta waves (and some theta waves) of less than three cycles per second were there. *'Christ, he might still have a chance!'* Chris thought excitedly.

He got Jo to look at the graphical results on the laptop. However, the two sides of Charlie's brain had very different electrical activity, which was abnormal if hardly surprising. The right hemisphere, which had been operated on, showed sudden bursts, or spikes, of activity, though these were faint. They would have to wait for signs of real recovery, particularly movement, on Charlie's left side.

'I can hardly believe he's still alive, can you?' Jo said.

'No, I can't. Lab chimps have a worse time, you know. All those knock-downs when shot with dart guns, repeatedly anaesthetised, often over many years, sometimes decades. They get complex PTSD symptoms. Some scientists suggest that chimps undergoing severe laboratory-induced trauma need similar psychiatric care as provided for humans. It always starts like that. Someone makes a "suggestion" because humans don't like their dominance being undermined. Like those suggesting "human rights" for apes. They only suggest it at first.

'Of course, humans can't even sort out their own human rights problems – look anywhere in the world today. Chechnya, Russia, Palestine, Iran, Syria, the Congo. In the Congo it's kill or be killed, and if you're a woman, they rape you first. They'll kill your husband and children too. Nearly six million dead. They'll gang rape you. They even rape three-year old babies. Bonobos are much more civilised. That makes us all irretrievably damned. Killing, raping, murder, it's all there, every day.'

'Do they go crazy?' Jo asked. 'I mean the animals.'

'Wouldn't you? The knock-downs are not comfortable to watch. They know what's coming, especially the chimp elders, who've often been locked up in animal prisons for years. They'll urinate and defecate involuntarily, eat their own faeces, scream, make desperate attempts to escape but they can't.

Some start compulsively pulling out their own hair, or slap themselves.'

Jo felt sick again. 'I'm glad I know only a little about some of the experiments on chimps and other non-human primates. Many are truly gross. Like blinding the poor chimp in one eye, and then finding out how the other eye manages on its own. Being put into the ultimate sensory deprivation cage – that makes the animals go insane.

'Brain experiments when the animals are fully awake must cause terror, like when they put them in restraint chairs or plastic tubes. You know, Chris, an early chimp experiment I read about was nasty but I think most of them lived. Its title was, "The effect on the chimpanzee of rapid decompression to a near vacuum", conducted way back in the sixties for space research. The report was marked "Approved for Public Release". What about the ones that aren't approved?

'Eight chimps were used, six males and two females. They were all measured, weighed, and trained beforehand at an air force base in New Mexico. The chimps' ages were determined by dental eruption. They had names like Jim, Duane, Shirley, Lulu and Jake. All had implanted electrodes. They survived rapid decompression from a pressure altitude of 10,000 metres, and rapid recompression but got back to normal within a few hours with only slight facial oedema, and no CNS damage. Guess they were lucky. Only one chimp died. He was excused because he already had a damaged heart – probably a result of other experiments on him earlier.'

'That's enough,' Chris said quietly. 'If it makes you feel any better Jo, Charlie so far has not felt any pain, as far as we know. He has not been mistreated, before his operation. If he ever wakes up, that's when we'll have a better idea of what's happened to him.'

'Do you have to go back to Oxford soon?' Jo asked.

'I do,' Chris replied, suddenly thinking that the chance of George handing over £10,000 was looking remote, 'but not for a few days.'

'We need rest,' Jo said drily.

'The door to the operating theatre opened. George walked in, rubbing his eyes. 'Any change yet?'

'I took an EEG, because you wouldn't and I had to see.'

'The results!' George shouted. 'What about the results? The rhythmic activity, the transients – you know, spikes and sharp waves. The meninges and CSF can play around with the signals – obscure the intracranial source.'

'Charlie's still with us.'

A big smile broke across George's face. 'Thank Christ! Thank Christ for the mercy. He's still with us then. But by how much? Any movement in the lower limbs yet? What does the EEG show?'

'Activity in both hemispheres, if unequal. The right is getting its fair share of spikes. Looks busy.'

'Good,' George said. 'Must be the stem cells. And cortical remapping. Give it time. We must give it time.'

'That's right,' Chris agreed. 'You can't hurry this. It's hanging in the balance.'

George came over to Charlie's supine form, and touched his bandaged head. 'So you're hanging in the balance, are you, Charlie boy? I know you'll do it. I know. I know you will, Charlie. You'll make it. Whiles yet I look after you. Whiles yet the cooling, temperate wind of grace…They say all beasts are happy, when they die, because their souls are soon dissolved in elements. *What have I begot in thee?* But you Charlie, soon you'll be up. Walking around, using that new brain of yours. We'll say, "Arise Charlie and walk! Arise Charles, my simian cousin." We will, won't we?' George's eyes implored his two fellow doctors to agree with him.

'Aye, we will George,' Chris said with sincerity. 'Aye we will.'

But Charlie just lay there, in the exact position he had been in for hours, intubated, breathing on the ventilator machine, his snout still thrust skywards. He couldn't see the stars through the roof, the sky-points of light he had seen in the Cameroonian forest; he couldn't even see the roof or the ceiling beneath it. He couldn't see anything. He was totally oblivious to the world.

TWENTY-NINE

'Do you have faith?' George asked Chris. 'Faith moves more than mountains, doesn't it?'

'Try moving the mountain first. If that moves, I'll listen.'

'I suppose you're right,' George sighed. 'You see, sometimes you can believe in yourself or in what you do but, if you're a surgeon, it just depends where you make the incision – the cut. If you cut in the wrong place, belief in your own skills is worthless. If you cut through the sinoatrial node, for example, you're going to interfere with the heart's rhythms, possibly seriously. In the brain, it's serious too. Cut out the wrong tissue and you could paralyse your patient, condemn him or her to a shuffling gait for life, take away the power of speech, or cause paralysis down one side of the body – and worse – as you know. You can make a mess of it in no time.'

Chris and Jo were not looking at George as he spoke. They were staring at Charlie. 'I don't know yet if I've ruined Charlie for ever, or given him a totally new life, mentation he has never had before, something no non-human primate has ever possessed.'

'Don't take it out on yourself,' Jo said quietly. 'Don't let it destroy your life. Let's get organised, start thinking. As far as I can see, unless Charlie recovers soon, he's going to need a feeding tube. Can he safely support his own airway yet? Who's going to check his urine samples for signs of infection? I notice he's been defecating directly onto the bed sheets. What about oral hygiene? If he stays in this position for much longer we need to think about avoiding deep vein thrombosis, DVT. We don't want a pulmonary embolism to stop Charlie from being whoever he is, whoever he's going to be.'

A tear splashed down George's face. 'Bless you, Jo. God, what a woman you are! God bless you. You have faith in Charlie, haven't you, Jo?' George inhaled deeply, as if to gain strength for a new and determined course of action.

'Okay, let's take this further. There's no need to consider chest percussion therapy yet. We're not ready for a feeding tube either. We may or may not need the endotracheal tube. Body position is acceptable. No pressure-related injuries to the skin. The catheter tube may or may not be dispensed with later. We must maintain the dignity of our patient. He will have regular bed baths, sponge or cloth baths, whatever, including attention paid to hair, skin and oral hygiene.

'DVT, there's no evidence of swelling. Give him some IV blood thinners. Massage his calf muscles to circulate blood in the region. Is there any CSF leakage? Apparently not. Withdrawal of support, WOS? No! When Charlie leaves here, he must be able to walk safely and independently, eat and excrete, have no pain or at least only controlled pain, and a clean and intact incision site. Sutures will be removed within ten to twelve days. Wound healing is an important aspect of surgery and must not be ignored. Pain and numbness…'

'…George, don't! Stop it.' Jo cried. 'We all know you mean well, but what is Charlie going to do about it, you know, contribute? Look at him! He's as good as gone, isn't he?'

'What will be, will be.' George was resting his case, as a lawyer might, but he was a surgeon and different rules applied. '*Res ipsa loquitur*' was what he might have said in law. 'The thing speaks for itself.' But whereas the surgeon would only be interested in the outcome, and perhaps the procedures involved in reaching that outcome, the lawyer would be arguing for a presumption that the defendant had acted negligently, simply because a harmful accident had occurred. No more details would be required. The proof of the case is self-evident. Charlie would not be brain-dead without the negligence of George Waldren, BM, MRCGP, MRCS.

What caused the harm, cutting into Charlie's brain, was an operation exclusively under the control of the surgeon at the time of injury. There could be no other reasonable explanation as to how Charlie's brain had been irretrievably damaged.

Chris and Jo were both exhausted, having had little rest since George carried out his operation. Only George was full of energy, possessed of urgency. 'Is this to be fortune's fickle will?' he said softly at first. 'Where's your mettle, Charlie? Where is it? I say there is none of you so mean and base, that hath not noble lustre in your eyes.'

Jo gasped, thinking George had gone mad but George leaned over Charlie, and pulled open an eyelid. There was no movement from Charlie. Just as George turned away, a slow flicker made its way across Charlie's mouth, like an involuntary tic, spreading in unhurried waves down over his chest. Charlie's limbs twitched, his fingers curled, and then began a shaking, a dreadful shaking of all his body.

'Hold him down,' George shouted. 'Hold him! Quick before he falls.'

Chris and Jo struggled to restrain Charlie, to contain his quivering.

'See if you can get a reading, an EEG.'

The single monitor above Charlie's bed became a fairground of lights and sounds, of protesting bleeps and buzzers, as if whatever it was that was hooked up to its terminals had gone very awry.

'We've got something,' Chris said moments later, 'widespread electrical discharge from both sides of the brain. It must be a seizure.'

'God, when this fellow comes back,' George said, 'he comes back with a bang. His heart rate has shot up, but his breathing is normal. Extubate him now, please Jo. Get these wires off him. Wait, leave one line for sedation.'

Jo started removing the IV lines. She disconnected the ventilator. 'His heart rate's better now, some atrial fibrillation though. Pulse rapid but strong mostly. I'm sedating him now.' Charlie visibly calmed as the diazepam went straight into a vein.

'I think we've stabilised him,' George said. 'Yes, look, his heart rate's dropped. Blood pressure and sats? How are they doing, Jo?'

The monitor over Charlie's head had stopped making so much noise. 'Blood pressure's normal. Charlie's oxygen saturation level is 98 per cent.'

'Remove the cannula, Jo.' George turned to face the prone figure of Charlie. 'Welcome home, my boy, Charlie. Welcome back my little jackanapes. Can we give him water? He'll take it. I'm giving him some water now.'

George gently lifted Charlie's head, and tipped some water into his mouth. It seemed as if Charlie savoured every drop. George poured a little more, and Charlie swallowed. Then he let Charlie sink back, as gently as he had raised him. 'He must rest. He's mending now. I'm sure of it.'

This time Charlie was sleeping unaided. He had glimpsed for a few moments the world outside the prison of mind and body. He had felt George's arm behind his head, and drunk cool water. It seemed good to rest.

George felt something rush through him. He was tense and flushed. 'I have to lie down,' he said. 'I can stay in here, to be near Charlie.'

George pulled over a couch from the wall and placed it near the supine chimpanzee. 'Get me a blanket, Jo, will you?'

Jo took a blanket from an airing cupboard, and draped it over him.

'Thank you. God bless you.' George looked up at Jo's tired but to him still beautiful face. He smiled warmly but she scarcely noticed. George was at Charlie's side. Charlie was going to survive, so the good doctor was happy. The operation, it was too early to say, but it was looking good. He must wait and see. George touched Charlie's right hand, which fell into his.

When Jo and Chris left the room shortly after, George was already snoring, seemingly without a care in the world, while Charlie snuffled contentedly in his sleep.

THIRTY

'I'm concerned about his diet, Chris. What's he going to eat?'

'He'll get by, my Jo. He has done so far. For what it's worth, it's something like 65 per cent fruit, 30 per cent leaves from trees, and shoots, and around 5 per cent animal matter.'

'So George was gorging him on lambs' legs?'

'Useful protein but they don't eat too much meat. They like termites, you will have heard about that famous research, using twigs to tease them out, Jane Goodall at Gombe Stream. They also eat termite mound clay for the minerals. Actually they're very good at self-medication too, eating varieties of plants and leaves, chewing bark as medicinal cures for illnesses, worms, intestinal parasites, diarrhoea, and so on. Chimps with roundworm infections eat plants – bitter-tasting ones with no nutritional value – because they have anti-parasitic properties. Most of my knowledge comes from listening to George.

'They'll go for small animals, birds even but they're also good at killing other mammals. They form organised hunting parties. They go off in a large troupe, track down colobus monkeys or bush pigs. Sometimes they'll ambush another chimp troupe just outside their range; they'll close in on a young chimp or a weak female. When they catch the animal, it's torn to pieces. The kill is shared but among high-ranking members of their own family first, very nepotistic. They also share preferentially with females and females with sexual or perineal swellings. The chimps squat high up in the tree canopy, and tear the flesh apart. It's a bloody sight.'

'Funny, I just can't see Charlie doing that.' Jo flung herself down in a chair. 'I need some sleep.'

'I'll join you,' Chris said. 'We'll use the spare beds upstairs.'

*

Charlie opened his eyes. George was still asleep. The ape removed his hand from George's, and stared up at the ceiling. He did this for several more minutes, and then looked down at his hands. He moved his fingers, turned his hands over, and opened the fingers. Then he turned his hands over again, straightening the fingers once more, still looking intently at them. He pushed out his right arm. His reach was long. He touched George's face, ran a brown mottled finger back and forth, stroking George's cheek.

Soon George's eyes opened. He was at first calm, then a little frightened as Charlie's brown eyes stared into his. The ape continued to rub George's face with his outstretched finger. 'Charlie, how are you? You may be feeling a little pain in your head but don't let that worry you.' He was worried because Charlie was unrestrained and weakly sedated. However, he'd had no food for almost three days, so he was unlikely to be strong enough to become dangerous.

George got up circumspectly. He decided to remove the last IV line, give Charlie some food, and get him walking. Being ambulatory was essential to help circulation and prevent blood clots in the lungs and legs. 'Come on, my boy,' George said, 'let's get you downstairs, and give you some food.'

It took a while to get Charlie on his feet. His left leg was dragging a little. George took Charlie by the hand and led him downstairs. Charlie obliged remarkably, clinging to George for support. In the dining room, the doctor sat Charlie in his comfortable chair. His left side seemed less agile than the right but in general, Charlie was already exhibiting strong signs of recovery.

Helga appeared from the kitchen and, very warily, approached Charlie's feet. She was quiet, unusually so, thought George. She jumped up, putting her front paws on an arm of the chair. Charlie turned his head slowly, and glanced at her. He began one of those odd chimpanzee yawns that start off with a slight opening of the mouth and end as a cavernous jaw-opening, teeth-baring exercise. Helga dropped back to the floor and went to the kitchen. She didn't seem to take any interest in Charlie.

Jo stumbled into the kitchen. She said she didn't get much sleep.

'Can you help, Jo?'

'With what?'

'Mash some banana. Then I'll spoon feed him. He's going to need pain medication every few hours or he might be difficult. Limbs on the left side are not so good, but thankfully it doesn't look completely serious. He limps a little, and he can't lift up his left arm more than a few inches. He needs plenty of rest, good food, and exercise.'

'Where have I heard that before? He looks good, considering,' Jo said. 'In fact, I'd say it's totally amazing, if not a miracle. He seems to have his faculties. His muscle tone is good. I mean, it's incredible he's functioning at all. That's got to be a success so far, hasn't it, George? I mean none of his body movements could take place without the instructions getting to and from his brain.'

'That's true Jo, very true, but we're very much fingers crossed at the minute. He's going to need help a while yet. He'll feel weak, he may have difficulty swallowing. Notice the way he keeps screwing his eyes up, and rubbing them. He could have problems with his vision. Balance and coordination are very fair in view of what's happened to him. With neurological issues you can never really tell. It's usually a question of time.'

Jo mashed three bananas, mixed in a little sugar.

George began spoonfeeding Charlie. In between mouthfuls, Charlie curled his upper lip with enjoyment. He seemed quite relaxed, taking in his surroundings, albeit watchfully. 'I think we could give him some weak tea as well,' George suggested. 'Jo, can you make some? Only a few leaves.'

Jo made black tea in a mug, added half a spoonful of sugar, and some cold water to cool it down.

Charlie took the mug readily when Jo gave it to him. He sipped the tea with a slurping noise.

'He's enjoying that,' George said happily. He turned to smile at Jo but Jo's face displayed alarm. George looked at Charlie. 'Oh, Christ,' he said.

Charlie was trying to hold on to the mug of tea with both hands.

He was shaking like a leaf. The tea was spilling over his large testicles, which made Charlie wince, and shake even more. His whole body stretched out in the chair. He was convulsing from shaved head to opposable toes. Helga found it of some interest. She growled and whined at the same time, unsure what to make of Charlie's discomfort.

'He's having a seizure,' George yelled with alarm. 'We've got abnormal electrical activity in the brain. We'll have to put him on anticonvulsants if he recovers. It could be a generalised tonic-clonic seizure, and if that's the case, it might not happen again. Don't try to do anything. There's nothing we can do, except try to stop him hurting himself.'

Chris came into the room. He looked worried. 'If he turns blue or stops breathing, you'll have to position the head to stop the tongue from blocking the airway. Hey, George, are you going to perform CPR if he needs it? Rather you than me.'

'No, you can if you like. Jo, do you want to volunteer for cardiopulmonary resuscitation?' Jo looked sick.

Charlie's seizure suddenly stopped. His breathing slowed to normal.

'He might just be okay now,' George said, obviously relieved. 'He's going to feel confused, drowsy, and have a headache.'

Chris laughed, almost contemptuously. 'He's already got one George, a fucking big one, and you gave it to him!'

'Shut up, Chris!' Jo spat out the words with venom. 'That's not fair comment, especially as you provided the means in that box you brought here. Who are you to criticise? Why don't you have another drink?'

'Cocky little bitch this morning, aren't we?'

Jo found one of George's whisky bottles and held it up in the air. 'I should brain you for saying that,' she said, waving the bottle just outside Chris's reach, 'but what's in your brain is hardly worth the effort.'

'Calm down Jo,' George shouted. 'Chris, apologise for that now. Or you'll be on the next train to Oxford – without your expenses.'

'Sorry, no harm done,' Chris replied cheerily.

'Jo, put that bottle of whisky somewhere where Chris can't find it. Charlie needs observing after this. We should do another EEG. It could be he's had a sudden burst, excess electrical activity in the brain. I'm not keen to find out why. I think it's too early to imagine that what we did – what I did – to his brain has had any chance to pull together yet. It takes time for new neurological networks to be laid down. There's cortical remapping to be done, that sort of stuff. It's a slow process.'

'Let's get him into the recovery position, shall we?' said Chris, wanting to take part, to stop George changing his mind about the money.

'What are we going to do with him?' Jo pleaded. 'He can't go back to his cage yet.'

'Good point Jo,' George responded. 'Look, we'll bring a bed in. He can sleep in here with Helga. We'll sedate him, just enough to make him rest some more. Four hours from now he should be given water and food. We'll work something out.'

They agreed it was the best course of action. Chris pushed in a bed that just squeezed through the doorway. Charlie was awake. He allowed himself to be lifted onto the bed. Jo went to the garage to get his woollen blanket. It was draped over him. Charlie was very observant, and didn't seem tired. It was as if he had completely recovered.

'Do you think it's safe to leave Helga with him?' Jo asked. 'I mean, chimps are meat eaters, aren't they? Suppose Charlie wakes up hungry, and decides to hunt Helga. That could be nasty.'

'I don't think we need worry about that,' said George confidently. 'I think we can safely leave that to providence – God's foreseeing protection and care of his creatures. You don't mind, do you Helga?'

Both Chris and Jo thought it was ridiculous of George to ask Helga if she minded, as it was to invoke providence's care, but animals and their owners have a habit of being closely attuned to each other's minds. Helga got up and trotted to the bed. She climbed up on her hind legs to sniff Charlie's face, and then licked his mouth. Charlie pursed his lips so Helga could lick them the more, closing his eyes as if glad of the company. He was quickly asleep. Helga stood by the bed, wagging her tail, not furiously, for she was not overjoyed. Her little tail wagged slowly, a little faster when George was looking.

Chris was plainly quite stirred by the idea of providence coming to Helga's rescue because he stood up, as if about to address an audience. He raised his voice in a grand manner, as when he and George had passed near Wren's sundial at All Souls. 'We are taking this current when it serves, are we not, George? If we take this tide with Charlie, to paraphrase that mighty writer, taken at this flood, we'll find our way to fortune. That has to be better than a life bound in shallows and miseries, hasn't it? Fuck providence, George, that's what I say, even on this full sea. Ah, but to catch the tide and be equal to it, that's providence too.'

George was staring at Chris, his mouth open in astonishment. 'Good on you, Chris. Good on you. I didn't think you had it in you. I'll write out a cheque now. You've earned it.'

'Screw the money for the time being, George. You can help in other ways. It's Charlie we must care for now. He's on that tide too.'

George went up to Chris to shake hands, and then held his shoulders. 'I love you, Chris,' he said. And then George embraced him, and they stayed locked together for a few moments, each man holding the other close, each man's heart beating with a rare goodness, and a common cause.

THIRTY-ONE

'Do you know the great apes laugh?' Chris was sitting in George's comfortable chair. George was asleep upstairs, exhausted. Charlie was also sleeping, on his new bed in the same room. Next to Chris, sitting on a wing-end of George's chair, was Jo. 'Aristotle thought that only the human animal laughs,' Chris said, looking directly at Jo, 'but Samuel Butler, well he wrote that all animals, except man, know that the principal business of life is to enjoy it. If you can't laugh, how can you enjoy life? Apes can laugh. They also like being tickled, like this.' Chris picked up Jo's legs in both hands, knocked off her shoes, and began to tickle the soles of her feet.

Jo screamed, almost falling off the chair. 'I hate being tickled. No! Stop it!' Charlie snorted in his sleep. Chris tried the same tactic again. He scratched his fingernails, gently but with purpose, right under her toes. Jo screamed. Charlie woke up and pant-hooted too. Helga howled mournfully from under the dining-room table.

The door crashed open. George stood there, defiant, the picture of an alpha male. He banged his fist down on the dining-room table and, if you could have seen it, Helga winced, as she buried her wet nose in outstretched paws. Charlie sat up, alarmed by George's posturing.

George looked furious. His face was livid pink. 'What the hell's going on? Are you playing games, charades? Do you fancy my ex-wife? Is that it, Chris? As soon as I'm sleeping, you're playing around with Jo. It's worse than a common menagerie in here. Poor Charlie, he's just had his brain fixed. You might upset him.'

Jo stood up. 'You're right, George. Anyway, Chris was attempting to tell me that apes laugh. Is that true?'

'Bloody hell, of course it's true,' George shouted. 'They're laughing at the great bloody mess we've made of everything. They just sound different, because they don't have the same voice box. They have no speech, like us. They make noises, pants, in and out, so when you wrestle one, play chase them, or tickle them, you can hear them laughing, in their own unique way. They can also drink and breathe at the same time, unlike humans.'

All looked at Charlie. He had opened his mouth wide as if grinning from ear to ear.

'You see!' George said. 'That bastard, that lovely chimp, he's grinning his head off. He must think this is fantastic. Grown humans arguing like hot-headed apes!'

'Hear, hear,' Chris put in. 'Chimps haven't got the same degree of breath control Jo, and of course their anatomy is different. We laugh while breathing out. Try saying, "ha-ha-ha". We chop an outward breath to laugh. Chimps laugh when breathing in and out – one sound for each inward and outward breath.'

George had calmed down but only a little. 'Have you two been taking any notes on Charlie? This is supposed to be a scientific experiment. We need data, observational data. Chris, I appreciate your knowledge of the great apes but, if I may say so, when are you due back in Oxford?'

'Two or three days at the most.'

'At least one of us will have to be with Charlie for the next few weeks, all the time. We can't take any chances, or leave him for long periods on his own.'

Charlie meanwhile had reclined back on the bed, drawing his blanket up to his nose, peering over the top to see around the room.

'I suggest,' Jo said, 'that we let Charlie sleep. He has to recover. We must feed him. You told me, George, about the variety of food chimps eat in the wild. Leaving aside the lamb and bananas, you only gave him fruit and nut bars from Waitrose. I like your choice of supermarket, however. I suppose Charlie could eat seeds, nuts, fruit, flowers, leaves, insects, honey, eggs, resin, galls, and the pith of some plants... What have we got for him? Water and banana mush! Whom the gods wish to destroy, they first make mad. Charlie will go mad soon – with his monotonous diet!'

'Jo, I hope you're not right,' Chris said. 'The mockman eating one of God's lambs, his legs. Sorry. Where did you get those lambs' legs from for Christ's sake?'

'From our local butcher. He'll be gone soon, he can't compete. I'm hoping that by feeding Charlie the occasional raw leg of lamb that I haven't mistakenly turned him into a carnivore. We'll soon find out. If we find Helga's leg bones all chewed up one morning, we'll know it was the wrong experiment. Come to think of it, it's time for him to have a meal. Jo, will you get some fresh water from the kitchen? I don't think we'll give him any solids just yet. More banana mash enriched with protein and vitamin powder should do it.'

Charlie was lifted by George to a sitting position, two pillows propped behind his back. He ate the banana mash in a rush, as if the food might suddenly run out or be taken away.

'Have you any more experiments planned, George, I mean immediate ones, with Charlie?' Chris was keen to know what lay round the next corner.

'I have some we should carry out. It's still too early, so we can deduce nothing really. I'd like to carry out some experiments with music, what precisely happens to Charlie's cognition, if anything, when he gets a blast of, say, Mendelssohn or Mozart. I'd also like to try the mirror self-recognition test again, but not yet. Charlie needs several weeks of rest, some gentle massage, and a little exercise.'

'I think I'll pack now, George,' Chris said, 'and Charlie needs to rest up a while, like you say.'

'I'll drive you to the station, if you like,' Jo said. 'George and I will have to cover for Charlie in turns. We both have to fit some work in. You should take some time off, George. You don't look well.'

'I don't feel well. I'm thinking about Charlie. Normally, in the wild, he'd be in a band of chimps, anything from 15 animals to 150 strong. I'm worried about him in a new way, so to speak. First, he's in a band of one – himself – then he's got us.'

'We're not much help, are we?' Chris said. 'We've cut his brain open, and we still don't know if he'll ever come out of it, or if there'll be any significant change in cognition. As we know, cognition is made up of many differing elements. For all we know, we might as well have lobotomised him. It's incredible he can even walk.'

'What I mean to say,' George continued, 'is that I'm not at all sure if Charlie's going on that journey I planned for him. If he lives, he might be better off in one of those ape rescue centres, you know, like the one near here. They take chimps that have been mistreated, had their balls cut off to make them more manageable. They take chimps that have been used as photographers' props in Spain. They come to the centre and they get given a home. They get free welfare, free veterinary treatment, free food, the comfort of other chimps. They've even got space to roam around in.'

'I don't understand what you're getting at, George?' Jo was concerned. 'You wanted to do the operation, didn't you?'

'Of course I did. But Charlie, what sort of life is he going to have? He's going to be a freak. Not fully a non-human primate, if you get what I mean. Not a kosher chimpanzee. How's he going to mix with the other chimps?'

'Stop worrying, George. Time's the great healer, isn't it? It's probably better sometimes to let time get a look in. Being treated by someone who's sworn the Hippocratic Oath or just by the passage of time, both could conceivably work, equally well depending on the circumstance. You need a rest too. You're making yourself ill.'

'Thanks for the concern, Chris. I think now Charlie's had some food and water, and before he rests, I'm going to try the mirror test again. Could be a little early but never mind. Jo, where's that mirror?'

'It's in the garage.' Jo looked unusually worried.

'Go and get it will you, please?'

In a few minutes she was back, carrying under her arm the round wall mirror shaped like a ship's porthole. 'Here you are, George,' she panted.

George made a point of dusting the mirror with a yellow duster from the kitchen. 'Let's make this easy for him, so he can see himself without any mistake.' George blew on the mirror, and then wiped it clean with the cloth duster. He walked across to Charlie on his bed. He took a deep breath, and then held the mirror in front of Charlie's face. 'Last time he spooked himself. He screamed his head off at the moment of recognition.'

Charlie took the mirror with both hands, and looked at the reflection. There was not a glimmer of visible emotion on Charlie's face as the face gazed back at him. He sat up a little on one elbow, so he could face George. Then he turned the mirror round, holding it right in front of George's face.

George's gaunt eyes looked haunted and very tired. 'Christ, is that me?' he said. Then *he* turned the mirror round in Charlie's hands so that Charlie could see *himself* again. Charlie took the mirror, placing it face down on his bed, but only for what seemed like a very protracted moment. Then, with an effort of great deliberation, he slowly picked it up, turned the mirror round once more, and pushed it right into George's haggard-looking face.

'He's trying the mirror test on you!' Chris exclaimed. 'Son of a bitch!'

THIRTY-TWO

Health for Charlie was like a slow boat to China. He took a very long time to heal. Invasive surgery as was visited upon Charlie is not an everyday event. As for George, he was not the man he was. His face was often flushed, like Chris's, but he wasn't an alcoholic. Chris and Jo knew the problem was arterial blood pressure that was way too high.

In that respect, Chris was lucky. He had stopped drinking the volumes of alcohol that could have killed him. He was becoming more sensible. George couldn't remember the last time he saw Chris with bleary eyes, sozzled to the hilt, pissed out of his mind.

He was sorry to see Chris leave, but Chris had to get back to Oxford. The John Radcliffe Hospital needed him, if only to move acquiescent bodies on trolleys in lifts, from one floor to another, or to place a body past caring with quasi-reverence in the mortuary. Christmas had little cheer. Jo worked right up until the day before Christmas Eve in her surgery.

George had tried to get to his surgery but made excuses, claiming he was ill, so a locum was found, which meant George could spend more time at the end of Charlie's bed, looking at him, analysing him, working every day like an NHS Trojan on his recovery.

Charlie was beginning to walk, very slowly. He could just about hobble along, his left side weak, unsteady. He tended to hang on George's left arm for support. Charlie spent a lot of time looking at the Christmas lights, so carefully put up by Jo on a six-foot artificial tree. He had also inspected the tree, but soon spat out its revolting plastic needles.

George thought about wrapping up some bananas and placing them under the tree as a Christmas treat for Charlie but on second thoughts, it was a silly idea. If only they could get through the winter and spring would come, and he could go out with Charlie into the garden. Charlie would knuckle-walk under the solitary apple tree, and round the large oaks at the back. His strength would return, and then in the warm spring sunshine he'd set some tasks for his 'ape–man protégé', and try to find out more about the chimp's state of mind. If there was any great change, or if he could show improvement in mental ability, however small, then Charlie would lead them both to fame and fortune. Life would be exceptionally busy, and money found for many more experiments.

What a tide that was likely to be! Never mind the publicity waves that would sweep through the scientific establishment. The wash would knock them off their feet! 'Oh Charlie boy,' George said aloud in the kitchen, 'when are you going to get well?'

Charlie must have heard because he hooted from the dining-room. George rushed in to see how Charlie was doing. He was fine. Ten days had already passed. It was time to remove the sutures. The hair on the back of Charlie's head was growing back. 'Charlie, I need to remove some clips from the back of your head.' To George's astonishment, Charlie turned round in his bed, pointing to the back of his head, as if expecting George to do something.

'I'm not sure I can do this Charlie, without sedating you. You might get angry. You could hurt me, so, so easily. Sit still, Charlie, will you?'

Charlie shifted in his seat, as if making ready.

'I am now going to remove these sutures. You might feel a slight pinch but nothing more.'

Charlie again pointed to his head, where the incision wound had nearly healed. Perhaps it was painful for him but if it was he showed nothing. Not a murmur. Not a trace of reaction to pain. He bore the removal of the sutures stoically.

'That's it, my boy,' George said. 'Well done. Your head is as good as new. In fact it might be better. Think of those people who say, "How ridiculous and how strange to be surprised at anything that happens in life!" Is that the point? They will be surprised when they see you, Charlie. When people see you, they will be shocked out of their cosy little lives. Life will grab them by the throat. And you, Charlie, you'll be squeezing them hard by the jugular, by the neck!'

*

George's two children were coming back for a Christmas break, but not until the New Year. Alice played the violin passably well, well enough to earn money busking. She had already bought herself a nice car. John was studying biology, Alice music and English. George didn't know if he should tell them about Charlie. Charlie might need to go back into the garage soon, especially if he recovered his full strength. He decided it was easier and safer to say nothing about Charlie's brain.

Wavy lines in George's vision were the first sign that all was not well. He had been clearing out Charlie's cage in the garage when he noticed almost half the field of vision in his right eye had gone. He had a raging headache. It was difficult to walk the short distance back to the house. His balance was wrong, coordination poor. As he got to the house, fear began to stalk him. He broke into a cold sweat. Charlie looked alarmed. He bobbed up and down on his forearms, as if doing press-ups, and made soft panting noises.

George got into the dining room and collapsed into his comfortable chair. 'I had hoped,' he began, 'I had hoped. I had hoped to play you some music. Would you care to listen to some now? How about some Beethoven? Für Elise? A bagatelle, easy to listen to. I read it was really for Therese. Or the Moonlight Sonata?' He slipped a disc into a CD player. 'We'll start with the Moonlight Sonata. I think you may find it comforting.'

Charlie was listening hard, rocking on his haunches from side to side. He knuckle-walked gingerly towards a speaker, and sat by it. His head made odd sideways movements, as if appreciating the sound and rhythm of the music.

'Beethoven went deaf, Charlie. Milton, well never mind about Milton. I don't suppose you want to know. Hell, Charlie, I feel peculiar. Down my right side, it feels numb. Christ, Charlie, I know what's happening to me! Classic warning signs. I don't want to die, I don't want to die.'

Charlie bounded across the room to George. He patted George on his knees. Then he found a gap at the top of George's socks, below the end of his trousers, where he could see hair growing. Charlie used his fingers and lips to search through George's leg hair. He was looking for ticks, dirt, and flakes of dead skin stuck to hair. Charlie smacked his lips, and made clacking noises with his teeth. Beethoven was still playing.

There was a sudden pain behind George's left eye. He looked down at his body, saw Charlie intently grooming him. He looked at his hands; they had become like claws. His headache got worse, everything slowed down, became silent, mute. George's right arm grew numb, almost impossible to move. George was certain he was having a stroke. He didn't need to take the FAST test, the face-arms-speech test. Weakness in the face, abnormality in speech, and weakness in the arm – these three typical symptoms were stroke symptoms, no mistake. He decided somewhere at the back of his mind it was probably an ischaemic stroke affecting the right hemisphere, and causing left hemiplegia – paralysis in the left side of the body. He wanted, strangely, to tell Charlie he was having a CVA, a cerebrovascular accident but the words in his head suddenly lost all meaning. Perhaps the part of his brain known as 'Broca's area', responsible for speech, had been compromised.

The blood supply to his brain was being interrupted by a blood clot. Without clot-busting drugs, George could be faced with a serious neurological deficit, and possibly much worse. By moving his left arm in what seemed like a seriously complicated and neurologically long-drawn-out activity, George was finally able to ring 999.

THIRTY-THREE

George was just about conscious. It was ironic that he was now in intensive care fighting for his life, as Charlie had been only weeks before. His mind went back to the garage; to the cage he had constructed to house Charlie.

He wanted to touch Charlie. Just for a second he thought he saw the ape at the end of his bed, his face grinning with mischievous glee. George sat up and tried to call Charlie, but no sound came from his lips, except a garbled growl. He couldn't speak.

George sank back into the soft hospital pillows.

*

Jo picked up her mobile. 'Hey Chris, George has had a stroke.'

'Is it serious?'

'It's not looking good. You could say as cerebrovascular accidents go, it's a bad one, a frontal lobe stroke. He's also got severe aphasia. He can't speak to anyone. If he pulls through, it could take him months to recover. I don't know what I'm going to do because someone will have to look after him.'

'The poor bastard!'

'What are we going to do?'

'About what?'

'About Charlie, of course. We can't keep him with George out of the equation. He'll have to go.'

'George won't like that.'

'He's not in a position to mind any longer, one way or the other. Personally, I don't fancy someone finding out about Charlie or the kind of operation he's had. If the wrong person gets to know, we're likely to be suspended, and then what? Forget about any medical career. If someone finds out what part you played, Chris, you'll be thrown out as well. How are you going to earn a living?'

'I refuse to panic. Jo, if that happens, I'll revert to being an alcoholic. You know the definition of an alcoholic, don't you?'

'Yes,' she answered, sounding bored because she'd heard it so many times before. 'Someone who drinks more than your GP.'

'Correct.'

'But what are we going to *do*?'

'It seems to me,' Chris began, 'that we have a number of choices. We could sedate him mercifully, so the future wouldn't concern him any more. Knock him out, like they do in that Swiss clinic. However, we know that's not on. George would sooner die.'

'Be practical, Chris. It's not just about how we deal with Charlie later, it's about now. Someone's got to feed him, keep him occupied.'

'Can you manage him for the time being? By the way, did the paramedics see him?'

'No, fortunately George had crawled to the front door.'

'That was lucky. Look, keep on with his diet of fruit and nut bars, I mean nut and date bars, and fruit. Short walks, once or twice a day, if you can manage it. Be very careful, Jo. If he turns on you, you'll be following George to hospital. Make sure he has plenty of fresh water. Fit that collar to him as well.'

'When can you come down?'

'Maybe the end of the month, beginning of February. When is George coming out?'

'About the same time, if he's lucky, according to the rehab team.'

'Okay. Call me if you have any problems. You'll have to tell the children. Hope no one sees Charlie in the meantime. Have you thought, by the way, that both Charlie and George are both going through the same process?'

'Meaning?'

'They're both trying to relearn disrupted cognitive functions. I wonder who'll come out of it first.'

'It's not looking good for George, that's for sure.'

'Take care.'

Jo didn't like the idea of having to care for her ex-husband, and for Charlie, all at the same time. She didn't know what she'd say to Alice and John. Charlie would have to be moved back to his cage in the garage.

*

George called out from his bed. He wanted to ask for a glass of water. He tried to speak but managed only an appalling groan. A nurse saw him. George pointed with his left arm to the water jug by his bedside. The nurse poured him a glass, and held it while he drank.

He tried to say thank you to the nurse. She was small and neat and pretty. She'd bathed him a couple of times behind the curtains in the first few days after the stroke, when he'd had a catheter tube stuck into his penis. She had bathed him very gently. He wanted to say thank you but the words were impossible to form. Instead, tears streamed down his face in an excessive bout of silent crying. He didn't know why he was crying.

*

'Come on, my beauty. Come out of there.' Jo was calling Charlie, who was hiding under the dining-room table. 'Be a good boy, Charlie, will you?'

Charlie wasn't interested so Jo broke off a banana and dangled it over the end of the table. 'Want some of this, Charlie? It's yours, if you come out and get it.'

Faster than she could move it away, Charlie reached out and grabbed the banana from her hand, hooting with the excitement. To Jo's incredulity, the banana, which had disappeared under the table, came back into view, sticking up like a yellow periscope. It moved up and down and along the rim of the table, an invitation by the non-human primate to play.

'So Mr Chimpanzee man, that's your game is it?' Jo waited a few seconds, and when the banana was within striking distance, she lunged and caught it. But Charlie came with it. He hung on to the other end and emerged from under the table. Then, in one swift movement, he pulled Jo towards him, and with his other arm reached out behind her, effectively trapping her in his arms. He stood up on his two hairy legs, and pushed his mouth towards her, kissing her on the lips.

Jo suppressed an urge to scream. Instead she bravely pouted her lips in return, being careful not to show her teeth. She patted Charlie on his arm, trying to reassure him. For one moment she imagined there would be this flicking, tapered pink object in front of her or that she should turn round and engage in social presenting; adopt a quadrupedal stance and display her rump, with gluteal creases, except it wasn't nearly pink enough. Neither was there any anogenital swelling to take Charlie's mind off the whole thing.

Much to her surprise, Charlie gazed at her with what she took to be a 'play face'. There was no threat. He kissed her again very gently, and said, '*Hoo, hoo*'. Then he dropped down and knuckle-walked over to George's comfortable chair. He sat down in it, threw back his head, stretching his legs forward. Helga came out of hiding and sniffed the ape's feet, then licked his toes. Charlie seemed to be quite happy. He ignored Helga. He picked up a mug that George used for his tea, holding it up, as if expecting Jo to take it.

To her amazement, she did. She made some tea in the kitchen and brought it back for Charlie, thinking she'd allow one treat before taking him back to the garage.

Charlie slurped his tea like an old hand. He loved it.

Jo switched on the TV. She thought Charlie could watch while he drank the tea. Then she slipped outside to get his leash. Charlie was not pleased but seemed to accept being taken outside with good grace. He went into the cage without a sound. Once inside he squatted down on his haunches. He scratched his head idly. Jo gave him a blanket. The chimp threw one end over his shoulders.

Jo knelt down too, outside the cage. 'Now look Charlie, you've got to stay here a while because George isn't well, and he can't take care of you. I don't know how long you'll have to stay here. It just depends.'

Charlie didn't seem to mind. He lay down on one side, resting his head on both hands. He seemed withdrawn but he followed every move Jo made from the corner of his eyes.

THIRTY-FOUR

George got a little better but not much. He lay in bed for hours staring at the ward ceiling. Every now and then he scratched his head as if rubbing out pain or the memory of it or in wonder as to exactly what had happened to him. When Jo came to visit, he took little notice of her.

He could walk, after a fashion. His right side was weak, and made him limp like an old man. He could speak a few words, if he got them out, although a succession of speech therapists came daily to coax sounds from him whose meaning he did not fully understand.

No one, not even the most illustrious doctors in the hospital, the consultant surgeons, no one knew if he would ever speak again, so that he could be understood. It became apparent after two months that not much more could be done for George, but he could go home. So after ten weeks, George was driven home by Jo. She nursed the old Rover into the drive just like George, nearly knocking off a corner post.

She got George out of the car in stages. Feet first swung onto the driveway, legs swivelled round, an arm into the car to pull him forward. George emerged from the car interior as a man might emerge from a cave, not having seen sunlight for many months. His head turned from left to right, then back again. Jo led him to the front door. George staggered into his own house.

He made his way painfully through to the dining room. Jo helped him into his chair, thinking that it had almost become Charlie's favourite chair too. George opened his mouth, trying to say something but only a horrid garbled snorting and snuffling emerged from the doctor's dry lips and nose. His eyes pleaded with Jo's, and then he held his head in his hands and began to cry.

Jo made him some tea. George took the mug gratefully. He made awful slurping noises too, just like Charlie, but this was because he could not control all the muscles on the right side of his face.

Alice and John arrived later. They had both visited George in hospital earlier. Alice threw her arms around George. John held back.

'He's had a hard time,' Jo said.

'He doesn't really look that well. Is he getting any better?' Alice asked.

'Yes, but it's very slow.'

'What's he got in his hand? It looks like a photo.'

'Just something he keeps with him. It's nothing.'

'Can I look?' Without waiting for an answer, Alice leaned over and quietly removed the photo George was clutching close to his chest. 'What on earth is that? *An ape?*'

'Yes,' Jo said.

'Can I see?' John took the photo. 'Hell, he's got some friends then, friends he hasn't told us about.'

'Do you want to meet him?'

'If you like,' Alice said.

'Bring it on!' John said.

Jo left the room. She took Charlie out of his cage. When he got to the kitchen, he screamed once. Inside the dining room, Alice and John froze as if they had heard a ghost but George's eyes shone brightly, and he tried to get up from his chair.

On a leash came Charlie into the dining room where George rested in his chair, as Alice and John looked on in plain astonishment. 'Here he is,' said Jo, 'not man's best friend, for that is reserved for the dog, but the animal most close to our own genome, and as you know, the difference is about 1.4 per cent. *Hail Charlie.*'

'Aren't you being a little theatrical?' John asked.

'Not a bit of it. God made him, and he can almost pass for a man. Charlie's birthplace is the rainforest of West Africa, from the Cross River area of western Cameroon. He is an exceptional ape, intelligent, and fun. George has been caring for him, but I can't tell you more. George is claiming patient confidentiality, except that George can no longer speak, so unfortunately he can't confirm any of this. He's asked me not to go into details.

'The truth is that George's stroke has really got to me, even though we haven't been together for years. The whole situation has made me feel a little crazy, as if I'm losing my mind. Charlie's just incredible. He adores George by the way, though if you knew the whole story you'd definitely have to question Charlie's sanity.

'If he could speak, God knows what he'd say. I think he'd make inappropriate comments, like Phineas Gage, who ended up on the receiving end of his tamping iron, with a hole in his head.'

'Are we supposed to know who Phineas Gage was, Mum?' Alice asked.

'Never heard of him,' was John's riposte.

'He was a 25-year-old railroad foreman who had a metal rod almost four feet long and over an inch thick blasted through his skull. It was a freak accident. It went through his upper jaw and out of the top of his skull. The metal bar landed about 80 feet away, apparently smeared with brain. Naturally, he wasn't the same afterwards.'

'You can say that again,' John said sarcastically. 'Who would be?'

'The point is that it changed the way we thought about the brain, mind, and behaviour, even though after 150 years or so we can't say much more than that massive injury to the brain produced a massive change in behaviour.'

'I don't understand,' said Alice. 'What's all this got to do with Charlie?'

'I'm not saying any more. You can ask Chris Grailing when he comes down, one of Dad's medic friends. All I'll tell you is that Charlie has some titanium screws in his head. George operated on him, but made me swear not to tell anyone. I've already told you too much.'

Alice and John looked suitably shocked.

Charlie had quietly been holding George's left arm. He stroked and patted it. Then he looked at Alice, then at John, visually appraising them. They were new members of the group that Charlie knew, and he needed to know their status. Charlie's body hair bristled, a signal of excitement known as piloerection.

*

Piloerection is an autonomic response not under conscious control of the animal. Blushing is a similar mechanism in humans.

An alpha male will often show hair bristling when in a group, although neither excited nor afraid. It makes the chimpanzee seem larger. When a chimpanzee has fear induced by the presence or behaviour of a dominant male, piloerection never takes place. Instead, the hair appears incredibly sleek, which also makes the animal look smaller, and less of a threat, less likely to evoke an aggressive response.

*

Charlie was very quiet, almost silent. He turned his attention to George, straddled his two outstretched legs, and embraced him.

'Isn't that dangerous?' asked Alice.

'It could easily be,' Jo answered. 'I think it's coming to that time when close contact is inadvisable. He's getting too big.'

'You can't get much closer than that.' John was laughing nervously. 'Look at him now.'

Charlie had leaned forward with his lips puckered so he could kiss George, who was enthralled. Charlie then stretched out his long brown fingers so he could stroke the sides of George's head. There was evident tenderness in Charlie's feelings.

Tears quickly massed in George's eyes, dropping down his cheeks, having nowhere else to go. His mouth opened in a vain attempt at speech but all he could manage was another kind of gargle, while slivers of saliva dripped in shiny silver columns from the corners of his mouth.

'What an incredible animal,' John said sincerely this time. 'Look at him!'

Charlie was cradling George's head in his arms.

THIRTY-FIVE

From the moment Charlie embraced and then kissed him, George was riding on a wave. It was true he had lost a great many of his faculties but the intellect that gave him the chance to qualify as a doctor, become a surgeon and a GP, that intellect was fragmented but still intact in places. It was only his body that was weak. Certain movements were beyond him. Speech had left him. His brain was attempting to repair the damage caused by the stroke, but healing always seems to come at its own pace.

George could still understand the enormous mercy Charlie had visited upon him, by accepting him after what had happened, and by his displays of affection.

Charlie was probably recovering the faster. Cortical remapping was accelerating. Indeed, when Charlie climbed off George, much to George's chagrin, and had stood alone in the centre of the room, he felt a degree of confidence, a way of looking at the world that had been absent before. Of course, he didn't know what that world was, but in the immediate vicinity of his surroundings, in his reaction to them, in the interplay between the other primates in the room and himself, there had been a subtle change. He was more aware, noticed more. His idea of 'self' had changed. He commanded more, though of course he commanded nothing. It seemed as if he were more in control. Yet he was also more hesitant, wanting to understand the behaviour of those around him before rushing to demonstrate his uncertainty.

The wave that George had been riding soon changed too. It beached itself ignominiously. Charlie had other things on his mind. First he turned his attention to Jo, pulling her arm so he could inspect it closely, but that soon tired him, because he found nothing. He turned towards Alice. This time he reached out with his right arm and felt her breasts. He didn't know what they were.

'Ugh,' Alice cried. 'He's a dirty old man besides!'

'No he's not you silly girl. He's just appreciative of nature.'

'Thanks for the lesson, John. It's not funny being fondled by a hairy ape. Mum, where do you keep Charlie?'

'At the moment he stays in the garage. George built him a cage.'

George turned round in his chair and mouthed, 'Yes, I did.'

'I think we'd be safer if he went back there now,' Alice said, a hint of anxiety making her voice crack. 'Chimps are a lot stronger than humans, aren't they Mum?'

'Between three to six times stronger.'

'You'd certainly never fight him off if he took a fancy to you,' John smirked.

'Or you. He might be gay!' Alice laughed, showing her lovely white teeth.

Charlie saw her teeth and it seemed to set something off in him. It could have been that Alice's bared teeth implied a threat, even if small. He grabbed her by the arm, and held on tight. He stood up, and with his other hand snapped a plastic branch off the Christmas tree, pulling it from its socket. The ape creature shook the branch wildly over its head, staring at Alice, with legs flexed and slightly splayed.

Jo had an idea that Charlie was displaying affection to Alice. It appeared to be an attempt to initiate consortship with her. The absence of an erect penis, making flicking or tapping movements in the air, might be a sign that Charlie did not intend to try to initiate copulation.

George was twisting in his chair as if supremely uncomfortable. Alice looked embarrassed. John was taking pictures of Charlie with his phone.

Charlie then saw the speaker on the floor – the same one he had listened to when George introduced him to Beethoven. He picked it up with his right hand and held it to one ear.

'He likes music,' Jo said. 'Play him some music to distract him. Then I'll take him outside to his cage if I can.'

Alice was intrigued to discover Charlie liked music. 'Hang on.

I'll get my violin,' she said. 'It's in my car. I'll play him something.'

Charlie suddenly became noisy and excitable. He made several pant-hoots. He kicked the speaker.

Jo called out, 'Hurry up!' to Alice, when she came back into the house.

Alice unzipped the case as she walked in. 'Get a load of this,' she said to Charlie, pointing the bow at his head. Charlie tried to grab the bow but wasn't fast enough. Then Alice positioned herself, brought the violin to her neck, and began playing.

Immediately Charlie became still but alert, watching the bow move over the violin, curling his lips, pricking his ears at the sounds it made, and squealing with repressed delight.

Alice played Massenet's *Méditation* from *Thaïs*. Her face was full of concentration. Light brown hair fell lightly onto bare silky shoulders. Her eyebrows were dark, eyelashes long, and above them her eyes were made up. She looked beautiful, full lips glistening with lip gloss, eyes pale blue, diamond earrings, hair tucked behind her ears. Sometimes she frowned as she played, then her face lightened, but not for long as the effort of concentration brought back a gentle furrow to her brow. She closed her eyes for what seemed like minutes, and then opened them, to gaze directly at Charlie.

Charlie was mesmerised. He sat on his haunches, folded his arms, then put both hands together and placed them at the side of his head, as if resting his head on his hands. It was five and a half minutes of bliss.

As the bow played its last downstroke, Alice remained quite still. George seemed to be in another world, his eyes glazed over. John and Jo wanted to applaud Alice but the extraordinary picture that presented itself in that room seemed to deter everyone from doing anything to change it.

Charlie lifted his head, and very gently uttered, '*Hoo, hoo, hoo.*'

'Look, he's thanking you,' Jo exclaimed.

Moments later Charlie grabbed the bow Alice had let fall at her side. He wrenched it away, loping back to the corner where Helga had hidden herself under a chair. Charlie poked the bow under the chair. Helga growled, then yelped when the bow prodded her stomach. A response from Helga enlivened Charlie. He thrust more strongly than before. Every now and then he was rewarded with a squeal or yelp.

'Okay, circus over please, Charlie!' said Jo crossly. 'George was supposed to have conducted this great experiment on Charlie, and all we've got is a naughty little schoolboy who can't behave. Come here, Charlie. Give me that bow!'

George squirmed in his chair. He was probably angry with Jo for talking to Charlie *as if* he could understand. Charlie retreated to the far corner, still holding the bow, waving it in the air towards them, as if fencing with a foil.

'You've got yourself a handful there,' remarked John gloomily.

George was trying to say something but nobody could understand what it was. George picked up a pillow and threw it at Charlie who simply fended it away with Alice's bow. Then the house phone rang. It was Chris.

'Thank goodness you phoned,' Jo said. 'It's a nightmare here. Charlie is behaving as if he's going to collect an ape ASBO any minute. When can you come down? And more to the point, what do you suggest I do to keep Charlie under control? He's absolutely full of himself.'

THIRTY-SIX

'He's come out of it remarkably well,' Chris said. 'His hair's grown back to almost cover the titanium miniplate and screws. In all other respects he appears normal. I don't think George ran any cognitive tests, did he?'

'None as far as I know. He has an inordinate interest in music. Alice played him a piece on her violin and he was off his head, sent, raptured.'

'I'm wondering if this is right for him here, Jo. I mean, if George has had some miraculous luck, and the tissue has taken, it will take some time to express itself. I just think he'd be better off in a group – like that ape rescue centre near here. I don't think George is going to recover in a hurry. And we're running too big a risk keeping him. I say we've got to get him out of his cage.'

'You're right. We can't keep Charlie indefinitely. Anyway, he's getting too strong to handle safely.'

'We can't just hand him over either. They'd be questions to answer. It's a miracle we've come this far without Charlie being reported by anyone.'

'I agree, Chris, but where do we start, in this imbroglio? I know for sure we have to let Charlie go. Give him some space.'

'We have to get him into that ape rescue centre so that nobody knows where he came from. That won't be easy. We can't just turn Charlie loose in the New Forest either.'

'I think we could do that,' Jo said calmly. 'I mean give him to the ape rescue centre. We'll donate him. We can go there now if you like, check it out.'

'We can't just hand him over.'

'I know, Chris. We have to give him away without anyone knowing. I think it's a question of disguise and deception. A bit like you at the John Radcliffe.'

'We could turn Charlie loose near the enclosures, and have someone find him, but I think it would be cool to try to get him inside, and then up and over, if you get my drift. As for disguise, how about kitting up Charlie like Mrs Doubtfire? A change of clothes and a wig should do it.'

'You are a clever bastard, Chris. Come upstairs now if you like. We'll start looking for clothes. But nothing else. Am I clear about that?'

'Of course not!' Chris retorted.

They started upstairs in Alice's bedroom. 'Sorry honey. Chris and I are looking for some party clothes for Charlie. We're going to dress him up. Have you still got those wigs from the school play?'

'I think so, Mum.' Alice rummaged in a bottom drawer. Triumphantly, she pulled out a black wig, quite long, curly. 'Hey look at this! It would suit someone like Beyoncé or Alexandra Burke, wouldn't it? I don't know about Charlie.'

Jo grabbed hold of the wig. 'That'll do just fine, thank you. Now for the clothes.' They left Alice looking both surprised and bemused, and headed for Jo's bedroom. 'I think we need something that will come off easily, a dress rather than a trouser suit. We can cut the dress and stick it together with Velcro so we won't actually have to undress Charlie.'

'A college scarf and a sunhat, and a very long cardigan to hide his hairy arms – not forgetting a pair of gloves – we don't need to go over the top with Michael Jackson sunglasses. I haven't had so much fun for ages,' Chris sighed. 'Being suspended is really horrible. I feel as if I have no useful work to do.'

'Don't worry. You'll be all right. Now throw me that scarf.' Within ten minutes they had all the clothes that Charlie needed for his entry into the ape rescue centre. 'I think we're ready for the dress rehearsal.'

Chris followed Jo downstairs with the clothes, which were put in the dining-room ready for Charlie to try on. Charlie was brought on his leash from the garage, and to make him more amenable was first given a mug of tea and a spoonful of honey.

Jo sat next to Charlie, who'd placed himself in George's chair, and held his hand. 'Charlie, we need you to dress up. It's for your own good, you see. You need to try some clothes on.'

Charlie yawned, displaying some significantly large canines. He looked at Jo as if she were slightly potty.

'Do you think it's safe?' Chris asked suddenly. 'Suppose he's not amenable to cross-dressing?'

'Let's see, shall we?' Jo began with a flowery skirt showered with Van Gogh irises, Velcro'd at the sides. It was very long. Then a wrap instead of a cardigan, pretty and pink. Chris put on the wig. For a moment there was a look of consternation on Charlie's face. Black curls fell to his neck. Then a blanket to cover his knees and feet, while the college scarf was draped round his neck and shoulders. On his head Jo placed a faded straw sunhat. 'Where are his gloves? We have no gloves.'

'Never mind just now, let's just put his hands under the blanket or under the wrap. It'll take too long to get them off.' Chris stood back to admire Charlie's get-up. All of a sudden a strange mood came over him, as when he had made his speech near the sundial at All Souls, and later, in the same house. Charlie was a little perplexed by his behaviour.

When he could see he had gained the attention of Jo, and perhaps that of Charlie, Chris began speaking, his voice swelling deep and growing in power: 'Oh, what a piece of work is a man – and this woman – how noble in reason, how infinite in faculty! In her dress how exquisite! In form and moving how express and admirable! In action how like an angel! In apprehension how like a god, or a goddess! The beauty of the world! The paragon of animals!'

'Most noble ape. Most learned noble ape!' Jo continued the peculiar soliloquy in her own fashion.

'What the hell...' John and Alice had the door ajar and were looking in, open-mouthed in astonishment. 'Look! A motley crew! If there were ever such a thing,' cried John, 'this is it.'

Both Chris and Jo blushed and Charlie's hair bristled.

'Mum, have you lost it? What's going on?' Alice pleaded.

'Chris and I must ask you to say nothing about Charlie here. The noble ape, this noble savage ape, who has suffered for surgery and for science, is he not nature's gentleman? Look how kindly he takes to his new outfit. Unfortunately we cannot keep him here any more. He has to be smuggled in unnoticed, hence the peculiar garb he's wearing.'

'You what?' said John. 'Smuggled in, where?'

'The ape rescue centre,' Jo answered.

'What, dressed like that? The other chimps would, well they'd probably scream in terror. They'd kick him out in no time.'

'It's not quite so simple,' Chris said. 'We need him in disguise to get him into the place. Look, the plan is we're going to get him inside, in a wheelchair. They have lots of wheelchairs and scooters for elderly people at the centre. Some have dual controls. They're powered scooters. Charlie's going in on the back of one of 'em. Then, when we've chosen an enclosure for him, it's off with his clothes, his shreds and patches, her rags and feathers, amid the garbage and the flowers – and up and over the fence! There's bound to be somewhere, some corner, where we can slip him through unnoticed.'

'Good luck,' said Alice. She and John were doing their best to suppress hysterical laughter. 'When are you taking him in? I want to say goodbye to him.'

'Tomorrow,' Chris answered.

Charlie was quickly disrobed. He made no complaint. He was given a nut and date bar as a reward for his cooperation. There was an eerie feeling for everyone in the house that night. Charlie was taken back to his cage, but he was very quiet, as if he anticipated all was not going to be the usual routine.

In the morning Charlie was led in to see George. Jo told George it was for the best, and she whispered to him that his operation had been a success because Charlie was fit and well. She told him that he had dreamed by day, and that he was a brave man. Charlie touched George's face with his lips and hands. George smiled weakly.

Alice came to say goodbye to Charlie but was shocked to see him already back in his disguise. Jo explained that they couldn't very well sit in the car dressing him. People might think something funny was going on and call the police. They'd had to sedate him, just a little, for the car journey.

'He can borrow my iPod if that helps,' Alice called out. 'He can listen to my music.'

John and Alice waved goodbye when George's car drew out of the driveway. Charlie was ensconced in the back, earphones on his head, listening happily to Alice's music. Anyone passing the house as the car drove away would have seen a man and woman in the front of the car, the man driving, and another woman in the back, but they would have seen little detail as Charlie's college scarf and straw sunhat hid most of his face, apart from two large brown eyes curiously taking in the world.

THIRTY-SEVEN

As George's old Rover sped towards the ape rescue centre via an ancient walled town, Charlie lounged cheerfully on the back seat, content to see the world go by his window. He hadn't seen such variety since leaving West Cameroon. Of particular interest were the open spaces of green fields, many dotted with cows and sheep, and the number and types of trees in copses and woods. The type of tree did not of course matter to him, only whether the canopy would provide cover, if any of the trees were fruiting, what else might be lurking there. The trees also reminded him of their importance in a life he no longer knew. Sometimes he watched birds flying overhead, ducks in a skein or a pair of swans with purposeful wingbeats heading overland. There were many people, some on foot, and there were cars, like the one he was in, driving and arguing noisily in the traffic.

Jo turned round to look at Charlie. 'There's one happy creature. I think we should've had a dummy run by the way. Don't we need to reconnoitre as well, and then get Charlie in? It's taking a big risk to get it right first time.'

'It's a risk but nothing like the operation on Charlie,' Chris said.

'Have you ever been to this walled town?' asked Jo.

'Yes, strangely enough, I have – many years ago, when I was a student. I was in a café one Sunday morning with some friends. One ran a farm not too far away. A huge terror struck me. I still don't know what it was. I think someone in the café put acid in my tea. I just walked out and into a tiny Saxon church.'

'Maybe you were in love with someone.'

'I had been. I thought my life had ended but, when I was inside the church, I broke down because of the pain of losing her. Tears covered the floor. I thought I'd lost everything.'

'Had you?'

'In a way I had. A girl with Titian hair. Of course it was a waste of romantic energy, looking back, something I don't like doing. A priest comforted me. It was horrible. I remember an effigy of Lawrence of Arabia, all in white marble. He's clutching a curved dagger, in an elaborate sheath, to his chest. There's this big slab of marble on the church floor. It was all bleak. There was nothing to hold on to. Even what he had was gone. There was nothing left.'

'Take me to it,' Jo demanded. 'I want to see it.'

'We can go if you like.'

Chris parked the car below a solid-looking town wall on a forecourt. 'It's up there,' he said, and Jo looked up to see a great wall, and this tiny church. They found the entrance, approached from the south side. It was quiet, apart from the noise of cars on the road. 'By the way, did Charlie seem okay to you?'

'He looked fine. I gave him a couple of bananas. He'll be okay. He's still mildly tranquillised.'

The door to the church was shut but Chris pushed it open. He had expected to feel pain inside him, but there was none, even after so many years. There was the smell of time encapsulated in the stonework. When confronted by marble and stone, effigies and death, was it right, Chris thought, to remember the colours in her cheeks, the shape of her mouth, the pallor of her translucent skin, the radiance of her red hair? He had not kissed her lips for decades nor would he want to now. 'What is flesh against dust, even quintessential dust? It was all bound to end in doom, in Hardy country.'

They found Lawrence's effigy, noting the three books placed by his head, the full Arab dress, his head resting on a camel saddle. 'Look at that poor man,' Jo said. 'All that effort, drawing tides of men into his hands. He said he wrote his will across the sky in stars, isn't that just another human deception? You know, chimps are good at that. Deception. They can pretend things are not as they are, to gain advantage.'

'I don't think deception is the right word, Jo. Delusion is better. It's impossible to write your will across the sky in stars. And anyway there'd be no point. It's because we are dreamers. Stars are where they put you when you're dead. You write your will on land, by dreaming in the day, by action, and when you become famous, they put you among the stars. As Virgil wrote of Aeneas – exalted to the stars – that is, treating him as a god, after his death. That's the only explanation I can think of.'

Jo shivered. 'I don't want any dreams,' she said. 'Stuff the dreams. I don't care if Charlie finds it. Even if he has the tiniest part of the head that Lawrence had, he's still going to end up as dust, isn't he?' She burst into tears.

'It's not all gloom, Jo,' Chris said quietly. 'It's the quality of that dust. Sometimes it's all we get. All that's left. Even if you're a reductionist to the core, suppose it's about the richer dust. Think of Charlie far from home, his home, and if he dies in this forgotten corner of England, there will be *here* some richer dust concealed – that is forever Cameroonian! Might there not be bugles over the rich dead, when Charlie is laid to rest?'

'Stop freaking me out, Chris, with all this weird stuff. I know you and George acted together a long time ago, I like the poets and Shakespeare too, like you do, but no more extravagant melodrama please, the quotes...' Jo's voice dried up; she'd made a few herself.

'I can't seem to stop them, at least when I care about something to make me rise above my cups. It's like numbers, Jo. Certain numbers stay with you all your life. Have you ever felt that?'

Jo looked perplexed.

'The number of the house you lived in on a certain street becomes your lucky number. Phone numbers of friends. The phone number of the house you grew up in. The number of your lovers. Numbers on a roulette wheel. Numbers on cards. The number they gave me at school, it still resonates. I think it was 449. The phone number of a girl I loved once was 33, this little village in France, you asked for the village and then the number 33. My phone number at home, it was 1032. One thousand and thirty-two.

'Numbers on cars are meaningless. All these numbers together mean nothing until your number's up. When your number comes up, whether its horses, cards, investment or death, what do you do? You either laugh or cry depending on what those numbers mean to you. If you're dead, you can forget it. It's the same for me with literature. Certain writers and authors have stuck with me, and always will. For the most part, I don't care that much, except when the words come together and mean something. Then I remember. Then I take part. Then it makes sense.'

'If you like numbers so much, what are the odds? What is going to become of Charlie? Is it his time?'

'Too soon to know, Jo. Who knows if we're abandoning the poor guy or liberating him? All we can do is give him the time to flourish, and then *his* number might come up – well, not in that way, I mean he gets lucky. Hey, we'd better get back to him.'

They left the church, Lawrence with his head in the clouds, at least it seemed like that because his marble eyes looked closed, and he could have been dreaming, or asleep, or dead, or all three. They ran down the small hill to the car, only to find it surrounded by children, boys and girls from the town, about five or six of them, peering in at Charlie.

'He's gross,' said one girl. 'Ape man,' shouted another. A third made snickering monkey noises. They were smacking the rear windows near Charlie.

Charlie was glowering, hugely angry. He pulled off his wig and banged the windows back. He jumped up and down on the seat, hitting his head on the car roof. He didn't care. Charlie stuck his nose against the glass, baring his big canines, and one of the girls screamed.

'Charlie,' Jo shouted as they reached the car, 'what have you done?' The taunting girls and mitching boys melted away, leaving just one girl with short black hair who stood by the car with her tongue stuck out at Charlie.

Charlie didn't seem to know where to look. He contrived to stand up, in the foot well behind the passenger seat, and lifted up his skirt. He tried to press hard against the window, so he could show off a pink spiky blob of flesh flanked by two enormous testicles. The girl pulled a prank face, as if she were sick. 'Ughh,' she screamed as she ran away, 'ughh!'

They got back in the car. Charlie calmed down a little. 'Give him a sweet or something,' Chris said. Jo broke off part of a nut and date bar. Charlie took it greedily. She rearranged his wig, strapped him in, and they set off. In the town centre they turned right at traffic lights. Several boys on a corner outside a pub pointed at the Rover as it passed by, gesticulating and hooting with laughter. 'If this gets out, there'll be a description, you know. They could find us easily.' Chris was worrying again, fearful that his suspension by the GMC would be extended if the facts of Charlie's operation and abduction ever became public.

As he pondered possible outcomes, Chris glanced in the rear-view mirror, and there caught sight of Charlie looking straight back at him. It was the strangest sight – Charlie in a black wig, pink wrap, a college scarf, and a pair of eyes peeping out. It was weird, thought Chris, horribly weird. 'Not long now, Charlie,' he said, as if to comfort himself too. 'Soon you'll be free. Plenty of space to roam around in with your new friends.'

Charlie grunted.

'You'll be a free man Charlie, won't you?'

Charlie pant-grunted again, still peering at Chris in the mirror.

'How much further is it, Jo? I can't take much more of this. It's Charlie. I need a drink. Hell, I haven't had a drink in three days! Of course chimps can't read minds, can they?'

'Of course not, Chris! You really do need a drink. There's no time to stop now. We have to get Charlie in soon, while it's still light.'

'If you say so, but the way he keeps looking at me, it's freaking me out, Jo. Have you ever thought how chimps would look if they had to shave like us? Actually they don't have a huge amount of facial hair.'

'Like you, Chris. Women don't shave except in some very private places.'

'Okay. Okay. Let's do it.'

Chris accelerated hard so that Charlie momentarily lost his balance. They drove on and on, down long straight roads with low trees on either side, until they reached a roundabout. Chris slowed the old Rover, let it purr along. At the roundabout they went right.

Charlie sat comfortably, even graciously, on the cream leather upholstery, considering what had been done to him, no hint of malice in his eyes, no hint of dissatisfaction with his keepers. He had his sunhat on his lap, relaxing in the back of the Rover like a royal visitor to a colonial settlement in the countryside.

They drove into a large car park, looking for the entrance to the ape rescue centre. A sign read: 'APE CENTRE this way'. 'Here we go,' said Chris. He drove a little closer to the main entrance. 'Looks like we have to drive as near as we dare to the gate. Go and buy two tickets, Jo, two adults, no three adults, and get one of the powered scooters, they should have dual control ones. Don't use a card. Pay cash. You'll need something with an address on it, so I've made one up. Here, have a look. MISS ETHEL GOODLIFE, 3A GRANTCHESTER TERRACE, LINGFIELD L53 3XS. I don't think they'll input any data into a computer. Say it's for your aunt. Tell them you need to take the scooter to the car.'

'Have you no nerves, Chris?'

'Not just now. Don't tell me I need a drink though. I'll check Charlie over. We could have given him some more diazepam, enough to take the edge off him. If he reacts as we go in, I don't know what we'll do.'

Chris sat in the car, his heart drumming in his ears as Jo walked towards the entrance turnstile. He saw her talk to a cashier, hand over some money, show the letter with the address, and get change and tickets. The person inside pointed to a row of three powered scooters in smart maroon livery.

Then he saw Jo walk back to the cashier, presumably to ask a question. Jo nodded. She returned to the scooters and sat on the nearest one, looking at the controls. It must have been easy to operate because the next time Chris looked up, Jo was heading out through the turnstile straight towards him at a steady four miles an hour. 'Oh my God,' he said. 'Charlie, I'm taking you in, do you hear? I'm taking you in.'

THIRTY-EIGHT

As Jo swung alongside the Rover, Chris detected a glint of triumph in her eyes. Perhaps she was proud to have mastered the scooter so easily.

Chris opened his door. 'I've told Charlie we're taking him in. He hasn't said a word.'

'Did you ask him if he can drive one of these as well, you boffin? What time is it?'

'It's nearly twelve, well five to. High noon. Reckoning time. Charlie has no shoes but we don't need any. We'll cover his feet with a blanket.'

'We should leave the music on. That's the only thing that will keep him quiet.'

Jo opened a rear door. 'Come over to the window, my little darling. Let's get you ready.'

Charlie was coaxed from the back seat after his attire was checked. A blanket covered most of his lower body. The flowery Van Gogh skirt was visible, then came the pink wrap. Around his neck and mouth the college scarf hid his simian features. Black curls fell down to his shoulders. 'You're the battle king, not the baffled one. You must compose your own life from now on. Hell, I need a drink.'

With help from Chris and Jo, Charlie managed to get out of the car and onto the scooter. His straw sunhat was placed on his head, and Chris took the dual controls at the back. He remote-locked the Rover, and turned to Charlie whose eyes had suddenly gone very large. 'Steady as you go, Charlie, just stay still and don't start pant-hooting. This will be your new home for now.'

'Love you Charlie, though you don't understand,' Jo whispered.

Charlie extended a hairy arm and grasped Jo. He held on to her hand, and then let it go. He looked ahead. He was ready. Jo tucked his hand back under the blanket.

Chris steered the scooter towards the ape centre. Next to the turnstile entrance a barrier slowly lifted to let them through. With mini speakers in both ears, Charlie could not hear the raucous calls of apes and monkeys. The centre housed many different species of primate – chimps, shaggy-haired orang-utans, black gibbons with long arms, perfect for brachiating through the tree canopy, and along play poles, woolly monkeys and odd-looking, stump-tailed macaques who looked like old Chinamen with whiskery faces.

There were moments of hushed silence from the animals as Chris manoeuvred the scooter along a central path, the enclosures on either side, but the calm was shattered every few seconds with strange, otherworldly cries, haunting screams, and the pant-hooting displays of male chimpanzees.

They were an odd trio, as they made their way forward, Jo to the left of the scooter, anxiously keeping an eye on Charlie, touching him every few moments in reassurance gestures. To the casual eye Charlie must have looked like a feeble old grandmother, dressed in eccentric clothes. Chris was scouting the enclosures, noting the ape houses that looked like small bungalows from the outside. It was virtually impossible for an ape to escape from them but far easier to get *into* an enclosure, since this was an eventuality that had never been explored. Wire fences surrounded the enclosures. Galvanised sheet metal extended down inside from the top of the wire fences, so an animal attempting an escape would just slide back down again.

Each chimpanzee enclosure was grass covered with climbing and swinging posts spread over a wide area. There were even small hills, which would have allowed various foraging behaviours to be expressed reasonably naturally.

Because of the time of year, early February, there were few sightseers at the centre. They moved around in small groups. Sometimes a child would run ahead and the mother call the child back. A black gibbon watched alone from its cage in the trees, the animal's eyes following the human primates as they walked past. Monkeys gibbered in small, secretive groups. Chris wondered who in this modern menagerie was watching whom.

There were several feeding centres for the human visitors, providing water, hot drinks, and food as well as resting places. Chris decided on a risky strategy. They would push Charlie into a covered area where visitors could look in on the chimpanzees in their houses – the bungalow-like structures, also equipped with climbing frames, rubber tyres, bedding straw, and the welcome of warmth in winter.

A woman ahead of them was engrossed in the behaviour of a large male chimp resting his body against the heavy glass floor-to-ceiling viewing window. She opened her handbag, showing its contents to the chimp. He wanted her to take out more. Finally she found a hand mirror, and held it against the glass. The big chimp glanced nonchalantly at his own image. Chris had the feeling the chimp had done this before. He had probably watched very odd human behaviour over the years: children pulling funny faces at him; fat old ladies giggling, pointing shiny, braceleted arms at his thin penis with its bulging testicles (capable of producing 200 times more sperm than gorillas, and 14 times more sperm than orang-utans); old men scratching bald heads in disbelief.

Then the great ape turned his head. His eyes fell on the frail old lady riding on the scooter. Perhaps he saw Charlie's brown-gold eyes peeping out from behind his college scarf. Whatever it was, it had an unsettling affect on him because the great ape thumped the floor with his hands and feet, screaming like a demented mental patient. Then he banged hard on the glass window, still screaming, baring his long canines, staring at Charlie.

Charlie had frozen in his seat. Jo felt him stiffen. She had the fearful thought that Charlie would leap off his seat and crash into the glass window in a display of strength. The game would be up. But Charlie stayed motionless on his seat. The big chimp took off round his ape house, swinging on ropes like a circus acrobat, crashing from side to side against the wooden walls. He even jumped up so high in the roof he hit his head but it didn't seem to harm him.

'Whoa!' Chris yelled. 'He's gone mental. Come on dear,' he

said to Charlie as if he were speaking to an old grandmother, 'let's get you away from here before that chimp goes ape.'

Chris took the controls, and steered Charlie away as fast as he could. The enclosure next to the chimp house they had just visited would do fine, even if it meant Charlie having to share with the angry alpha male they had just encountered. But how to get Charlie in?

Jo suggested they stop for a drink at one of the human feeding and drinking stations. Charlie was parked in a corner with his back to the counter. Chris ordered two coffees, and a tea with a spoonful of honey added, which was somehow conjured up by the staff. Charlie drank the tea greedily. He had been remarkably good. Jo decided it was time to remove the earphones. She fed Charlie with a banana she'd brought from the car, and she and Chris worked out their next moves.

At the side of the ape house that housed the bolshie alpha male, a post at the side of the building could give an agile intruder access to the top of the wire. When there seemed to be no one near, Chris parked the scooter. 'This is your moment, Charlie. *Go for it!*' He touched Charlie on the arm, only later thinking it was silly to talk to him like that, but nevertheless Charlie felt reassured. Jo stroked his chin, and behind his ears, which he liked, to prepare him for the suddenness of the move.

'*Now!*' cried Chris.

Jo yanked the blanket, pulled off the skirt, enveloped the wrap in both arms, then unwound Charlie's college scarf. She left the sunhat on until the last moment. Chris lifted it off saying, 'Go now, Charlie. Beat it.' He threw a banana as bait over the wire fencing, and almost pulled Charlie over to the post he was supposed to climb.

Charlie looked unhappy. He was glancing to left and right, lacking confidence. 'Go well, Charlie,' Chris said, trying to thrust Charlie up the post. Charlie appeared glum but, not having had a play opportunity for a very long time, he began to climb the post. He surveyed the scene, feeling confidence return. Then he jumped!

Straight over the top of the wire fence, sliding down a galvanised panel, rolling onto the grass below like a commando.

Chris and Jo felt out of breath, as Charlie might have done in his new surroundings. He looked back towards them, and then swung his arms from side to side, ignoring the thrown banana. After a moment he knuckle-walked away, aiming for the top of a small hill in the enclosure.

Chris was overcome with emotion. He saw Charlie reach the knoll of the hill, sit down, and calmly look back again towards them. Chris drew himself up, as if addressing an audience, which he was of sorts, although they were a strange audience, a few scattered groups of chimpanzees inside the enclosure, with Charlie on his vantage point alone. With a deep voice, he spoke aloud to Charlie. 'Go and find your piece of grass to lie on. Untroubled, Charlie, above you only the vaulted sky. Here it is, this world, fretted with golden fire. Don't travel blind, Charlie. Let not the searching eye of heaven find you out. This is a new place for you to dwell. Be warned, from this bourn there is no returning.'

Jo gasped. 'Chris, what are you saying?'

Chris looked ahead to Charlie on his hill, taking no notice of Jo, speaking more fervently than before, his voice swelling commandingly. 'This is the end of lonely street, it's crowded but you'll find some room.' He was crying. In a sudden change of tone, he spoke softly, as if to himself. 'Sweep up these jokers. Don't be just another Joseph looking for a manger. You won't find it, or any peace, or the blaze of light in every word. Oh Charlie, I wish you could speak! Go and find your piece of grass. May your life be filled with great adventures! This is where you must be now. Live well, Charlie. Bide your time. Have patience. Fare thee well! Try in your own way to be free.'

'What on earth was all that about? You soppy old doctor – suspended doctor,' Jo said. 'It's time we left. Like a chimp on the wire! *You're* the drunk in an old midnight choir.'

Chris was still in a daze.

'We'll park the scooter over there. Dump it. Forget the deposit. Do you want the deposit back?'

'No,' said Chris. 'By the way, I haven't had a drink yet.'

No one in the centre seemed to have noticed anything. Charlie had been successfully repatriated, if that was the correct word. They looked back, when they were not far from the entrance, and there was Charlie, on the small hill, four square to the world, calling out, pant-hooting with immense fervour, announcing his arrival. He was his own master now.

THIRTY-NINE

'I have to tell you, Chris, I don't like all that Leonard Cohen shit, although I've been as guilty myself. Did you spend hours listening to that guy when you were young, trying to make out what he was saying?'

'That's just it, Jo. Isn't it who you listen to at the time? I mean, no one read any Blake poems in my ear, in the pub, but those soulful songs, you could visit friends and crash out, and they'd play them. Roll a joint, try to make sense of the lyrics. Impossible.'

'I think we'll move on from that, Chris. No more, okay?'

'We all have memories, Jo. We are all rooted in the past as much as we yearn for the future. There's nothing we can do about it. Dreams come in all sizes. The cream always rises.'

'To where, Chris?' Jo was baffled.

'To the top.'

'And what does that mean?'

'It means what you want it to mean. It's just a song and I like the words. We should get the hell out of here, before they discover Charlie. And what's happened to his brain.'

'Could they find out?'

'Sure. There won't be any other creature within a thousand miles of here like Charlie. Even more than that. It hasn't happened yet. It's called plasticity. The brain's ability to learn and grow, modifying neurons, creating new ones, and the connections – the synapses – the brain constantly changes and adapts, even after injury. It takes time. What wound did ever heal but by degrees? There's a big story coming out of this, Jo. We'll see what happens to Charlie!'

The Rover was still there. Dependable, after a fashion. They got in the car. Chris didn't start the engine but draped his hands over the steering wheel, looking back to the ape centre. They could hear, but not differentiate between, the calls of monkeys, apes and prosimian vocalisations but suddenly, from one of the chimpanzee enclosures, came the sounds of frenzy – pant-hoots, high-pitched screams and guttural pant-grunts.

'Sounds like someone's having fun,' Jo said.

'Yes, that's about right,' Chris replied. 'It's all about the alpha male rising to the top, the *new* alpha male, that is, the new leader. Dominant chimpanzees have more serotonin in their brains than their less successful, low-status friends in a group. It's like a reward for being top of the pile. I've always wondered which comes first.

'Do they need the extra serotonin to get to the top, or is it produced by them because they *are* on top? In fact, you can artificially boost the social status of a chimpanzee within a group by giving it doses of serotonin. Anyway it's going to be a test for Charlie but I expect he'll come through it all right.'

*

They drove away, unable to see Charlie, defiant on his small hill, encircled by a troupe of chimps some fourteen strong.

Those in front were pulling at branches on the ground, stamping, drumming on tree trunks, rocking from side to side, and at the head of the troupe bristled the big alpha male from the ape house, a roar erupting from his throat, teeth exposed in a menacing snarl.

*

Back at home they couldn't find George, which was alarming. Helga was barking by the garage, which gave them a clue to his whereabouts. Chris opened one of the doors. The sight that greeted them was upsetting. George must have climbed into Charlie's cage. He had stray wisps of loose straw on his head, and he was clutching the wire bars, shaking the cage aggressively with his good right arm.

Helga ran in, barking. She jumped up against the cage but after sniffing the bars and seeing her master, began to whine piteously. When George shifted his feet, Helga let out a grim growl at the bizarre apparition of George, a scarecrow inside a cage of his own making.

'George, you poor thing,' Jo cried. 'What on earth are you doing? Come out of there!'

'Be careful he doesn't bite,' Chris said. 'I think he's lost his marbles this time.' As Jo took George's hand and led him from the cage, George lunged at Chris savagely, just missing his chin with a right hook of surprising strength.

'Sorry old man. Really sorry. Anyway, there's some good news for you. We've repatriated Charlie. We've reintroduced him, not to the wild, but to a wilder state than he was in here. He's gone to the ape rescue centre. We got him in. No one saw anything.'

George's eyes lit up, and a smile cracked his face. It was only a half smile because the muscles on his left side would still not work properly but there was no doubting George's happiness. He nodded his head over and over, as if retelling himself that Charlie had gone home, that the news was good.

'Let's all go inside, shall we?' Jo suggested. 'We'll have tea. I'm sorry Charlie isn't here to share it with us but he's better off where he is, at least I think he is.'

'Yes, yes,' said Chris, 'much better. He's got everything going for him now, wouldn't you agree, George?'

George could understand everything but speech was not easy. George pointed to his head with a long, limp finger and tapped it three times. Then he lifted his right fist and stuck his thumb up. His eyes were twinkling. It was obvious he was talking about Charlie, and the successful operation he had undergone. Of course the irony was not lost on Jo or Chris. The surgeon whose own brain had been catastrophically damaged by natural causes had gone into an ape's brain and forever changed it. What magic or mystery had been uncovered or revealed was as yet unknown. The change sought operated at the cellular level, which would take time to manifest. It was Charlie's behaviour that would decide whether the operation had been successful or break new ground.

Both Jo and Chris were already missing the chance to study

Charlie, in his now more natural habitat. They wondered how he would sleep in the ape sanctuary on his first night, how he would fit in with his group, what part memory would play in his development, either of his memory of life in the rainforest in western Cameroon, near the Cross River where his mother had been brutally killed, and he had been captured, or his rescue from a zoo, his memory of life with George, his incarceration in a cage, and the day he was taken into George's private surgery for the world's first human–ape partial brain transplant. Charlie was alive, and they wanted to be with him, to understand him the more.

*

On his small hill, confronted by the mob of angry chimpanzees, Charlie in his own way took stock. He was surprisingly cool and unconcerned. The big male from the ape house led them.

While lower-ranking males and females held back, behind the alpha male were several younger males eagerly taunting the intruder, their heads bent and drawn into their shoulders, backs rounded, all adopting a quadrupedal stance. The big male swayed from side to side, standing on his two legs, shoulders hunched, hair bristling because of piloerection, holding out his arms – a bipedal swagger – in a direct threat display to Charlie.

While the approaching chimps screamed, grunted, and barked, Charlie was silent. Before long the other chimps fell silent too. The silence became menacing because the atmosphere had changed; it was now hushed, soundless, the calm before the storm. Charlie's eyes searched the grass covered mound, whether for an escape route or a weapon, he didn't know. Luck was with him because there on the ground lay a thick, knobbly branch. He reached out, grasped the heavy branch, and held it to his chest. The next step was easy. He just hurled it around his head.

The big male jumped back, and then tried to reassert his authority. But it was to no avail. He walked right into the whirling bough. Charlie caught him square on the side of his head. With a great scream of pain, his opponent dropped to the grass, felled by a single blow. A monstrous tumult sounded from the remaining assailants. Several took hesitant steps towards Charlie but quickly lost their nerve and turned back. The big male was still prostrate on the grass, attended by several females who fussed over him making plaintive, whimpering cries, and licking the wound on his head.

Charlie stood up, charging the females tending the big chimp so they scattered in several directions. Then he turned towards his victim, the thick branch still in his hands.

He stood over the fallen body. For the other chimps, all was uproar and confusion. Charlie was strong enough to drag the chimp by his heels round the enclosure, if he wished, as a triumphant Achilles dragged Hector through the dust. He lifted the heavy branch as if it were a monstrous club, then knocked it against a nearby wooden post like some grotesque swashbuckler revelling in the din and glory of battle. Charlie roared. The big chimp roused himself from the grass but Charlie clubbed him back, and this time his body fell like a sack to the ground.

Charlie prodded the big chimp's face. There was no response. Blood trickled from his nose. Several females hesitantly made their way towards Charlie, and when they came close, adopted social presenting, showing their rumps to Charlie while in quadrupedal stance. Other females in the group demonstrated open-mouth grinning, looking over their shoulders at Charlie at the same time, a submissive stance assumed after an attack. The mouth is open, the corners drawn back, the large canine teeth showing.

A few females bowed to Charlie, facing him quadrupedally, with their elbows bent lower than their knees – the head is lowered but the rump is in the air. One female pressed her lips to Charlie's groin in a submissive kiss of affection, bowing at the same time. Although male chimpanzees often sniff and smell at the anogenital swellings of females, Charlie showed no interest.

Several young males embraced him, and then began social grooming, looking for parasites or dead skin to remove. Charlie seemed quite disinterested. He stood up on his two stocky legs and roared again, which made the chimpanzees back away.

He swung the branch he had used as a club around his head and then let go. It went high in the air before falling onto the ape house roof of the same enclosure. Several chimpanzees inside the ape house pant-hooted frantically at the noise. Charlie grunted. He seemed very satisfied.

Then he made his way to the ape house at the bottom of the hill, a confident, assured creature. He was the alpha male now, and no chimp dared stand in his way.

*

'I wonder how Charlie's getting on,' Jo said to Chris before he was to leave for Oxford. She invited him to stay for drinks, so Chris scuppered his latest plan for not drinking.

Within half an hour he had fallen into George's chair, clutching a bottle of George's malt whisky. George had retired to bed early. 'He used to like sitting here,' Chris sighed. 'I mean Charlie, of course.'

'Fancy a Chinese takeaway before you go? Mongolian lamb, sweet and sour chicken, crispy duck?'

'Great idea, Jo. We can sing and dance a galliard, in remembrance of the mallard, as the mallard does in Poole, let's dabble, dive, and duck...'

'...the booze got to your brain already?' Jo asked.

'Not yet. It's an old song from All Souls. I seem to have picked up loads of trivia since I've been working in Oxford. Here's another. "Know ye her secret none can utter? Hers of the Book, the tripled Crown? Still on the spire the pigeons flutter, still by the gateway flits the gown, still on the street from corbel and gutter..."'

'...we were talking about Charlie!' Jo put in.

'"Faces of stone look down". All right, Jo. Look, I'm not crazy about poetry but something got me. Ever since George and I stood in the gateway of Brasenose, and we just looked at the light in the quad.'

Jo sipped her drink slowly.

'You know when the Romans really wanted to get the crowd going, they'd tie a chimpanzee on the back of a horse, and set dogs on both horse and chimp. It was tried in London. The sight of a screaming ape on a desperate horse, both animals being ripped apart by dogs, was supposed to make the crowd laugh themselves silly.' Chris paused for a moment. 'I am really hoping for Charlie. And for George's sake, too. I'm hoping he'll make something of himself. If his new brain knits and holds together...'

'Is it *so* new?' Jo asked. 'What's new about the human male brain, or should I say, the human primate brain? Of course it may be a new combination, of ape and human, and for that it's worth celebrating as a scientific triumph.

'I don't think Charlie's going to start by being a saint. Religions invent saints, for the most part. Many in the past died for their beliefs, of course, and still do. Once you establish the need for some kind of principle by which you live your life, it's not really worth the candle if you're not prepared to die for it. Bully for them who were prepared to die but there were so many reasons why. In Oxford, Cranmer died, burnt to death, along with Latimer and Ridley, the Oxford Martyrs. They were tried in that beautiful church, St Mary the Virgin. Cranmer refused the pope as Christ's enemy. Anyway, I don't believe in saints and miracles. How can Charlie come together other than by the human part of his brain assuming control, and manifesting itself in a way that is *not* part of the lives of non-human primates?'

'It's asking a lot, I know,' Chris replied, clutching his whisky glass as if it might save his life. 'If Charlie does something, anything, that's *not* part of, as you say, non-human primate behaviour, shouldn't we be ready to applaud him, take him on board, welcome him into this world of ours?'

'Maybe. I'm not so sure. Males, humans – on the one side you have empathy, sympathy, altruistic behaviour, and what's on the other? Murder, mayhem, mass rape. Some of the women raped in the Congo so badly mutilated after being gang-raped by half-a-dozen humans at a time – I won't call them men – and that's after shooting dead the husbands, and the children as well, so they were raped over the dead bodies of their families – the women had to have their wombs surgically removed later because their wombs, cradles of life, were so badly bruised and beaten, ruined by men beyond hope of repair, by animals, beasts really that call themselves men...'

Jo sat down, in tears, shaken.

'I understand you Jo,' Chris said. 'It will be a miracle if Charlie can be anything other than a brute. What will he care? He's probably got more chance of being a saint if he were just a chimpanzee, asking no questions, not being fatally flawed like the average human animal. Isn't it strange how we despise humans by calling them animals and yet there is no more vicious, dangerous animal on the planet.'

'I suppose we'll have to see,' Jo replied. 'I'm still wondering if he's sleeping in one of the ape houses yet, curled up and comfortable, if he's been accepted by the group we left him with, if he ever thinks of us or George. We'll have to go back soon to check on him, if there's been no trouble in the meantime.'

Chris drained the last drop of his whisky. 'Come on then,' he said. 'Better get me to the station.'

FORTY

It was not until the following morning just before the eleven o'clock feed that the ape's body was discovered. A wildlife assistant had driven into the enclosure with feed – tiny protein nuggets to scatter in the grass. When the animals looked for them, it was as if they were foraging naturally, picking up the nuggets as they would small insects, grubs or edible leaves.

The man threw the feed pellets over part of the enclosure area, near where the public passed by, so as to give the visitors more chance to see the animals close up. The chimpanzees were kept away from him by a series of interlocking gates.

He saw the crows first. Five carrion crows perched on the ape's body, pecking at the creature's eyes. With a shout he accelerated towards the top of the hill where Charlie had battled the big ape. 'Good God almighty,' the man said out loud. 'What's got you, what's got you?' The black crows melted away into the trees surrounding the park. He pulled the ape's head round but could see it was no use. The ape's body was already stiff with rigor mortis.

He rang the ape centre's head, a rather reclusive director with a PhD in zoology and conservation studies. 'One of the apes, sir, has gone.'

Dr Dylan Stevenson, a burly barrel-chested man with a shock of shiny black hair on the crown of his head, not unlike the sheen on the pelage of the chimps in his care, rounded on him. 'Gone, what do you mean, gone? And who was it?'

'It was Michael, sir,' the name given to the big ape who had once posed on Playamar Beach, Torremolinos as a photographer's prop. 'Michael's kicked the bucket, sir. He's dead.'

'Bring the body down – no, leave it where it is. I want to see for myself.'

Dr Stevenson hurried down to the central enclosure. The great apes had been kept indoors so it was safe to enter. Once inside the enclosure, he saw the silhouette of Michael's body on the skyline at the top of the small hill, with the ape centre worker standing over it. When he reached them, Dr Stevenson pulled on a pair of sterile plastic gloves whilst kneeling down to examine the ape. 'There's a wound here, on the side of the head. The cranium looks damaged, as if it's taken a hit of some sort. Shame, he was the top animal here, you know. We'll load him up on the trailer. Let me take a few pictures first with my phone. Can you get a body bag?'

'Of course, sir. Right away.'

The man left to find one. He came back a few minutes later and when Dr Stevenson had finished taking photographs together they pulled and pushed the heavy chimp into a body bag, then lifted it onto the trailer. 'Take him back to the vet's, will you? He'll do a post mortem. I'm going to check the chimps in the ape house. It's possible some of them could be hurt as well.'

Dr Stevenson walked towards the ape house. There was a strange silence from the usually noisy chimps. He decided to look through the viewing windows at the front of the ape house. He was immediately struck by what he saw. He counted thirteen chimps sitting, squatting, almost in a circle, and in the middle was a chimpanzee he couldn't remember ever having seen before. The chimps kept their distance but were visibly intrigued by the male animal in their midst. He was sitting with his legs tucked up, in what could be described as the lotus posture, casual and calm, like a king about to hold court.

The chimps surrounding Charlie moved towards him one at a time, none with any confidence. There were no bipedal swaggers. Each chimp came close to Charlie, bowed, or briefly held out an arm, before snatching it away, and returning to the circle.

Charlie saw a curious face at the viewing window. It was Dr Stevenson's, his face a study in consternation. Charlie's head hunched down in his shoulders. Immediately, he knuckle-walked towards the viewing window, contemptuously brushing aside a couple of chimps, although they were hardly in his way. Both chimps let out piercing shrieks as he passed, the others remaining silent.

Charlie drew himself to full height, grasping a steadying wooden strut with his right hand, to stare at the face in the window. Dr Stevenson was now very close to the chimp and as he gazed back at the animal he saw the hair growth on the chimp's skull was unequal. It must have been shaved recently, he thought. Although he couldn't see the titanium screws and miniplate, when Charlie's crown was held at a certain angle it did look as if there was something bright behind the silky brown-black hair.

'And who are you, then?' Dr Stevenson asked out loud. 'Where do you come from?'

*

If Charlie could have spoken then he might have told him he came from western Cameroon, north of a town called Mamfe. Mamfe was where the bush still began. Villages in the area had unusual names like Basho, Obonye, Mblishe, Matene, and Esengi. They were part of a larger whole, the forest reserve of Takamanda, comprising an area of 67,599 hectares. The reserve and the neighbouring Okwangwo region in Nigeria were designated as important areas for many large mammals, including the Cross River gorilla, and the Nigeria-Cameroon chimpanzee, to which subspecies Charlie belonged.

The region encompassed lowland forest to montane savannah and was criss-crossed by many streams and rivers. When Charlie's mother was killed, a road was in the process of construction from Mamfe to the north, and this development probably led to the death of Charlie's mother. Habitat fragmentation and hunting with guns, to supply the ever-growing demand for bushmeat, were the largest threats to the unique biodiversity of this African rainforest.

The eyes of Dr Stevenson and Charlie met. Who can say what were the parameters of recognition, of identification? What flowed between human brain and the ape with human tissue sewn into its brain, replacing part of the original? Was it species recognition?

Communication between humans and animals is a fact: a dog lover can behold the animal it loves, and understand what he or she sees in the animal's eyes. Love, not just beauty, is in the eye of the beholder. Love sees if only blindly.

A young man riding too fast on a motorbike, a chimpanzee from the Cross River in Cameroon, a surgeon who now practised as a GP, the big ape whose skull had been crushed, Chris, the disgraced GP, and Jo, still practising as a GP, Alice and her music, Dr Stevenson, they were all involved. What *was* Charlie now? Could anyone say? 'Who was he? Who *is* Charlie?'

*

Charlie gave an answer, his answer. He lifted up his right arm, curled his hand into a fist, and with the flat underneath part, hit the viewing window with a shuddering crash. He moved his face towards the glass, staring proudly at the face in the window. He did not flinch: there was arrogant defiance in his eyes, confidence in his manner.

Dr Stevenson was clearly taken aback. His mouth had opened into a pouting shape, not unlike a chimpanzee about to pant-hoot. Dr Stevenson's right hand fell palm uppermost towards the glass window. He let it fall. Charlie copied the action, placing a brown, mottled hand in the same spot, but using his left hand. Both hands came together at the window, as if in a peculiar attitude of ape–human prayer, divided only by a pane of glass, an odd apparition.

Charlie then bent his head down, still leaving his hand where it was but showing the crown of his head. He tapped it lightly against the glass; there was an unusual sound, as if someone were striking the glass with a metal object. Charlie was banging his head gently against the glass window, and in the process the titanium plate and screws made contact with the glass.

'And *what* are you made of then?' Dr Dylan Stevenson asked. Again Charlie stared defiantly but then seemed to grow tired of the game, if it was a game. He dropped down, and knuckled-walked back to the group. This time he reclined on a rubber tyre for comfort, stretching himself out as if on a chaise longue, while several chimps attended, grooming his arms and legs, stroking his skin, and uttering soft *'hoo hoo'* cries. He was king of his new castle, at least for the time being.

Dr Stevenson called a fellow director at the ape rescue centre. 'Can you get down here fast, Matt? There's a chimp here I'd like you to have a look at. I don't recall seeing him before.'

Matt Brookes, a brilliant young zoologist from Cambridge, said, 'What's that?'

'I said I've never seen the animal before. He's a creepy sort too. We've also got one dead chimp, Michael, the alpha male. Looks like he's been killed. Something heavy. Skull crushed.'

'Oh God,' Matt replied. 'Stay there. I'm coming.'

Matt reached the ape house after only a few minutes. Despite his academic talent and ambition, he still looked like a boy, a fresher, not someone who'd already gained his master's in natural sciences, and was now a doctoral student in zoology.

'The body's been taken to the vet's office. I'll wager he was struck by something. That chimp over there, look at him, that's the one I was telling you about. He's taking it easy on that rubber tyre. Funny thing, he came and looked at me through the glass. He banged his head on it. It made this kind of metallic sound. His head's been shaved too. He's a cool customer all right. He looks right through you. Very strange.'

Matt was trying to take it all in.

'We need someone to observe him for the next few days. If we don't find out who he is, we'll have to box him up and take him to the vet's or maybe into town for a scan.'

'A scan?' Matt asked, perturbed by the unknown. 'Why would he need one?'

'The shaved crown and the metallic sound it made on the glass are highly unusual, to say the least. It's possible the chimp has been the victim of something nasty, animal experimentation, vivisection, something along those lines. Of course he may just have been in an accident. Perhaps he's been patched up.'

'This enclosure has fourteen animals, doesn't it?' Matt asked.

'You're one short with Michael dead, so there should be thirteen.'

'We'd better count them now,' Dr Stevenson rasped.

After a trip round the enclosure and the ape house, Matt said, 'I make it fourteen.'

'Impossible.'

'I've checked off all the names. It may be impossible but I think we have a new alpha male. Look at him. He keeps looking over here casually from time to time but you sort of get the feeling he's the boss round here, and he's taking everything in.'

Charlie was indeed taking everything in. He might have missed George but the ape enclosure had so much more room than a cage in a garage. He was also the subject of intense interest, both from the apes inside and the humans outside.

In the enclosure he remembered the grassy montane savannah, the high valleys with pockets of dense forest and open grassland of western Cameroon. He had gazed at the open vista of grass and forest that led to the far horizon and a remembrance of his past flooded into him. Yet now his senses seemed much more acute. He had not so much come to life but moved on to a new life. Every blade of grass in the new encounter threatened to overwhelm him because the sensory input he was experiencing presented all things anew.

Charlie's brain was more than ticking over. Completely new neural connections were involved in cognitive processing. With every second that passed, cortical remapping was reshaping him into something rich and strange.

The aphorism that might apply to Charlie had been inscribed in gold letters over the portico of a temple of Apollo at Delphi more than two thousand years before. It was hard for Charlie to follow it: *'Know thyself'*, a saying that has been attributed to many ancient sages, including Heraclitus, Pythagoras, and Socrates.

Charlie was trying in his own way.

FORTY-ONE

Dr Dylan Stevenson deputised Matt Brookes and another young assistant to keep watch on Charlie. He was to be subject to the closest scrutiny. A post-mortem examination of the dead male chimp revealed he had likely been hit with a heavy object to the side of the head. The skull was fractured, and bleeding inside the brain killed the ape.

Charlie became a suspect. However, no one knew anything about him. None of the ape rescue centre staff had ever seen him before. He was an outsider, an intruder, a mystery. CCTV covered only the outside perimeter and a few other areas within the centre.

The new great ape seemed to have settled in well. The beta males regarded him with respect. The higher-ranking females continued to groom him, occasionally presenting their rumps in submissive sexual gestures that appeared to leave Charlie strangely cold.

*

Normally, just the sight and faint odour of a perineal swelling would be enough to arouse a male chimpanzee such that his filiform penis with its tapering pink tip would awaken to the task with vigour. It is true that Charlie was not a bonobo, his cousin the 'pygmy', dwarf or gracile chimpanzee (*Pan paniscus*), for then the lack of interest would have been more disturbing. Sexual intercourse in bonobo society plays a major role. It is used as a greeting, as well as in conflict and post-conflict resolution. Bonobos have been observed engaging in the widest possible range of sexual activity: face-to-face genital sex, or the missionary position, was common. (A chance sighting of a pair of Congolese gorillas was the only other instance of non-human apes seen in such activity.)

Bonobos have also been recorded as tongue kissing, and

practising oral sex. For some groups of humans, the missionary position had been eponymously recommended as allowing face-to-face coition, permitting the man to take the 'superior' or dominant position, and leaving dorsoventral mounting to the 'unclean' animals.

*

Charlie was having none of it. When allowed out of the ape house, he liked to hoist himself up onto tall wooden climbing poles where he performed acrobatically enough, even though it was apparent he was not equally supple in all four limbs, his left side tending to drag, but only marginally.

Several times, when Charlie reached the top of the climbing structure, he peered out to the far distance, as if searching the horizon. He also began to develop a keen interest in the humans who came to the ape rescue centre to see the chimpanzees and other animals.

It was noted by Matt Brookes and his assistant that Charlie himself scrutinised all thirteen chimps in his enclosure. Each chimpanzee was singled out, when alone, especially when Charlie could dominate by controlling any possible exit route, and he would then subject the chimp to the closest examination. Charlie ran his fingers over the head and face of each chimp. He peered in each animal's eyes, holding their gaze. He would then appear to snort and turn away, as if he had lost interest. Matt recorded that there seemed to be nothing similar in the research literature.

One morning Matt's assistant came to relieve him from observational duties. She was a young girl, working part-time at the ape centre and studying at college. She'd brought a packed lunch. Charlie watched her eating a cheese and ham sandwich. On her way to the enclosure she'd picked up a littered newspaper. A couple of pages blew away while she was eating. They lifted with a gust of wind, and paper-planed into the enclosure, only a few feet away.

None of the chimps outside, quietly feeding on food nuggets thrown onto the grass, noticed anything, but Charlie was quickly there. He plucked the paper from the grass, and squatted down to pore over the newsprint. He turned the pages over repeatedly, flicking from one page to the next. One page displayed a semi-naked girl with large breasts. Charlie seemed intrigued by it because he tossed aside one of the two sheets of newspaper, keeping the other pinned down with his right foot.

The girl gasped when she saw Charlie's penis appear as if from nowhere. The ape was masturbating over the newspaper, or more correctly, over the picture of the half-naked human female.

Charlie's lips curled and the girl uttered a cry. 'Oh my God,' she said, 'you filthy pervert!' Charlie scrunched up the paper and stuffed it around his penis. She called Matt and tried to describe what had happened.

Matt came to look and made more notes. 'Are you sure that's what you saw? It sounds like deviant behaviour but maybe it's not. It can be stress related.'

'Can you explain it?' the girl asked.

'I'm scratching my head trying,' Matt replied, the irony of the situation becoming aware to him, as he remembered the great apes' habit of scratching as a displacement activity if they were uncertain about something or what to do next. What was worse, his own penis stirred as he noticed the girl's nipples stiffen through her top. He tried to concentrate. 'Chimps in zoos, more often in labs when they're used for experiments, exhibit aberrant behaviour, such as swaying from side to side or head-bobbing. Most have to deal with total boredom daily. They are supposed to get environmental enhancement, or environmental enrichment, to promote psychological well-being. In practice it's rare. It costs too much. Animal research is a business really. It's all about funding, getting the next research grant.

'So they harvest a few more monkeys or monkey parts for biomedical research. Who cares? Along come more painful and invasive procedures. The traumatised ones end up in a bad way – self-biting, pacing, or hair-pulling is common – just as it is with humans who've been tortured or suffer from PTSD.'

'Oh,' said the girl.

'But that chimp, I'm not so sure. He appears normal enough. He's holding his own in this group – in fact he's the alpha male, now that Michael's gone. Highly unusual though. He's not supposed to get off on the human female form. It's totally bizarre.'

'I agree, but you know, I think he's sound,' the girl responded. 'I mean, not being a zoology student, just a keeper, he doesn't seem to have suffered too much. I know that's weird, what he's just done, but couldn't there be reasons to explain it? He might have been adopted by a human family. I mean, he doesn't have that deep sadness that some chimps have in their eyes.'

'What's your name?' Matt asked.

'Nat. Short for Natalie.' The girl was pretty, a little unwashed, even plain, but she had spirit, which Matt liked. She also had insight. 'Shall I tell you more about what I think?'

Matt urged her on. 'Please, I'd like to hear everything you've got to say about this chimp.'

'I think he's not one of those chimps who've suffered repeated knockdowns, that kind of stuff. Some chimps have been through the procedure over three hundred times. Someone fires a dart gun loaded with anaesthetic. There's all the noise and din of the lab, doors slamming, bars clanging, you know about all this, don't you? Sometimes they need to shoot several times to down a chimp. The chimps never forget. They always live in fear. That chimp's different to me. He's had some kind of pain to be sure but not enough to knock him back. He's full of himself. He's, well, he feels like, I'm sure he feels as if he's getting somewhere. I know it's a funny thing to say but I think he's proud of who he is!'

'You like him, I can tell that.'

'I respect him, because he respects himself. We all make mistakes. I don't suppose we can blame him for that.'

'He's also our chief suspect in a murder case, Nat. Something hit Michael with very great force. We've yet to establish what happened here.'

Matt and Natalie seemed to bond a little in those moments, but it was not unnoticed. Charlie, who looked as if he had been sulking at the base of a climbing pole, came over to the observation window.

'He's looking at both of us now,' Natalie said.

'You seem to know a lot,' said Matt, intrigued.

'Monkeys, chimpanzees, gorillas – I've cared for all of them. The new chimp, have you seen him make a nest? I haven't yet. I know that gorillas, like chimps, make a nest each night. The mountain gorilla is the rarest. There are only about three hundred and fifty or so individuals in each location where they're found – in the Impenetrable National Park in Uganda, and the Virunga National Park in the Congo. They call them critically endangered. What a joke! Less than seven hundred individuals in those two areas! Nearer critically extinct is more like it.'

'What's this got to do with him?' Matt asked, nodding in Charlie's direction.

'Most of the chimps use straw bedding or blankets to make a nest at night but I haven't seen him do anything like that. A lot of the time he just lounges in that rubber tyre, being groomed, or else he's stalking round the enclosure.'

'He seems to take a keen interest in you,' Matt said. Charlie had come close to the glass window again.

'Hello,' Natalie said. 'What's your name?'

Charlie's big, liquid brown eyes stared back at Natalie. Just for a moment he eyed Matt but it was only a momentary glance, as if he found nothing of interest. But Natalie's face, while she was watching Charlie, was in itself very expressive. Charlie was fascinated by the dark curls that framed Natalie's face. Now and again she shook her head back, and the curls followed. Charlie stretched out a hand and placed it palm-flat on the glass, in front of Natalie. Natalie felt compelled to do the same, and their hands met.

'I'd say that's a demonstration of a certain kind of empathy, wouldn't you?'

'From whom?' Natalie asked. 'Me or him?'

'Both of you.'

Natalie couldn't resist the idea that came into her mind. She took her hand away. Charlie did likewise. Then she leant forward, bending down a little to be at Charlie's height. She pursed her lips into a kiss and pressed them against the glass. Charlie followed suit. It was not a very attractive sight; thin lips and a hairy chin with a garishly pink inner lining. Nevertheless, Natalie held her lips to the glass, and Charlie did the same.

As she was about to turn away giggling, she saw the result of Charlie's operation – the metallic glint of the titanium miniplate and screws. 'Hey, you poor thing,' Natalie exclaimed. 'You must have been in an accident!'

Matt called Dr Stevenson. 'I think we should box him up, Dylan. Give him a scan or maybe an X-ray. Natalie says she's seen something on his skull – like a metal plate. Whatever else he is, he's certainly bright.'

It was then that Charlie reached out his right arm in a circular motion and brought his hand in the air. His index finger was extended, a mottled, brown, very long finger. He held it to his head and pointed.

It was now Matt's turn to be astonished. 'Good God,' he said. 'I don't think I've ever seen that before.' He was thoughtful. 'I saw Ronaldo tap his head like that once, after he scored a goal. There's something else about this chimp. Doesn't it remind you a bit of ET, I mean the finger?'

'It really does, doesn't it?' said Natalie.

'There's at least one major difference, as well as ET being virtually hairless. The chimp doesn't have a little light at the end of his finger,' Matt said. 'And there's another thing.'

'What's that?'

'He's not asking to go *home*.'

FORTY-TWO

George Waldren had navigated to his garden in an electric wheelchair, very much like the one Charlie rode on for his entry to the ape rescue centre. The doctor drove slowly over the lawn towards the single apple tree, thinking of Charlie, and what had become of him. He glanced up to the tall oaks beyond, suddenly remembering Charlie brachiating fearlessly in the canopy's upper branches. As his head lifted towards the crowns of the oaks, two silvery columns of saliva dribbled leisurely from each side of his mouth.

There was a sad emptiness in the air, it was late June. Roses, mostly blown, hung their splendid heads limply, as if caught, impaled, on the point of exhaustion. George felt tired too. Strange to say, he missed Charlie, not because Charlie was a chimpanzee, and therefore something of a 'pet', an attraction for a lonely man, but because their relationship was that between doctor and patient, where confidentiality amounted to deep, abiding trust, and even beyond that. At least it was like that for Dr Waldren. He had Charlie's best interests at heart. But no one could say the same for Charlie because there was not a single person alive who could guess the outcome of the operation – whether an ape with a partial human brain implant would be able to teach anyone what it was like to be human, or at least partly human.

George was dreaming in the mellow June afternoon light. He was dreaming of Charlie reaching out into the world, finding his place and, if he allowed his thoughts to reach a little further into the unknown, it was of Charlie realising his cognition too – if only the two parts would marry together! A poem by Robert Herrick, or rather an epigram on dreams came clearly to mind, such that, even after the terrors of a stroke, he could see the words etched, as in bright ink, in front of his mind's eye:

Here we are all, by day; by night we're hurl'd
By dreams, each one into a several world.

The sun was going down slowly, turning the western sky pink, and darkening into a blood-red sunset. Thoughts of the primeval world came to him, of chimpanzees and gorillas, great apes of the forest each day following haphazard trails, foraging for food, the chaos of different troupes competing for shelter and sustenance, the never-ending quest for power, dominance and position.

Alas, no more did Charlie play with him under the oaks or climb the apple tree. 'If only I could see him again,' George thought. 'If only I could see him!'

*

Dr Dylan Stevenson was worried. He called Matt to his office. 'Hi, Matt' he said warily. 'I want to ask you a straightforward question.'

'Go ahead,' said Matt cheerily.

'I want to know what you think about our new friend in the ape house. Ape house number three.'

The look on Matt's young face visibly changed from happy to concerned. 'He's a strange one. I was chatting with Natalie about him. She thinks he's okay, that he's well in himself but...'

'...but what?' Dr Stevenson interrupted.

'The fact is we're no nearer knowing who or what he is, his identity, or even where he came from.'

Dr Stevenson pursed his lips.

'What's more, he has some odd behaviour,' said Matt.

'Can you explain that?' Dr Stevenson frowned. 'I know about the way the new chimp carried out a kind of identity parade on all the other chimps in ape house three, if that's what you mean.'

Matt's face softened a little as he rolled his eyes from side to side with embarrassment. 'How can I put it?' he began. 'He was jacking...I mean he was getting all excited about a woman's picture in a newspaper.'

'You mean he tried to eat it?'

'No! I mean he had an erection, he was sexually excited but he was doing it over the girl's breasts, in the picture. He had one foot on the newspaper, to hold it down, and one hand rubbed this...' Matt's face registered the extent of his consternation. 'If he's doing that to a newspaper, what will he do if he ever gets hold of Nat?'

'Come on, Matt, I feel that's a little far-fetched. I think it's reasonably unlikely the animal was sexually attracted to whatever it was he was looking at. I mean, suppose he was holding the paper down with his foot as some kind of displacement activity?' Dr Stevenson asked doubtfully.

'The fact is Nat says the chimp, the new alpha male, was staring at the picture on the grass – beneath his foot! All he could see from there, she said, was this girl with long blonde hair and big breasts. He certainly wasn't reading the newsprint,' said Matt, with a note of exasperated conviction.

'Okay,' Dr Stevenson said. 'Let's take it further. That chimp needs to be boxed up. We'll get him to a vet, there's a radiographer with the right equipment not far away. We need to have an X-ray to find out what's going on with his head. Why does it make that *sound* against the glass?' Dr Stevenson asked.

As if to echo his question a commotion began in one of the ape houses, the din quickly spreading to other enclosures. Normally the two men would have scarcely noticed the racket as over time they became conditioned to noisy primate groups in their charge. This time, however, Dr Dylan Stevenson and Matt Brookes cringed. Just as suddenly the noise abated until there was left only an eerie silence.

The two men hadn't moved. Matt was about to say something but there came from ape house number three a hideous, tumultuous roar. It had to be a belligerent, anthropoid ape. Twice more came the mighty roar.

'My God,' said Matt, 'is that the new alpha male?' Then a new sound hit their ears. A series of massive thumps shook the inner frame of ape house number three, as if a biblical Samson were testing the strength of the ape house.

'Come on!' Dr Stevenson said. The two men rushed to the ape

bungalow to find Charlie in bipedal stance threatening the huddled members of his group with a heavy wooden rafter, torn away from the roof of the building. With the rafter held aloft his shaggy arms, Charlie started smashing everything in sight, his posture the very picture of a dominant alpha male.

*

George burst into tears often but not for long. His mood swings irritated Jo but she could do nothing. He would sit in his wheelchair and remember in his mind a visit to the theatre twenty or thirty years before yet, if asked to say what he'd had for breakfast that morning, he'd have no recollection.

His speech was returning slowly. His main gripe was the continuing pain on his left side. Jo had to hide the Rover keys, as he'd forget his impairment meant he couldn't drive as before. He had to be watched: the sage, shrewd doctor had become an impulsive liability, almost as reckless as Charlie had been in the garage, before he'd left, before the operation.

One day Jo brought him a mug of warm tea. George asked for a mirror. He managed to get the word out, and with his right arm made combing gestures over his head.

Jo frowned but gave him one anyway, from her handbag. George put down his mug of tea, settling back in his chair as if about to watch the TV. His right hand picked up the mirror from his lap, and he looked at himself. He wondered who was that strange man with white hair and bushy eyebrows with the gaunt, haggard face, like a man haunted by unknown ghosts.

*

Chris Grailing had decided to ask George for some of his 'reward'. In fact, he'd emailed Jo asking for £1,000. She knew about their arrangement, so she decided to send Chris the money. It was only a tenth of the original sum anyway, and if George got better soon, he could decide on the rest.

In Oxford Chris tried to work happily but one day merged into another, and he felt like the tiniest cog ever in the giant Ferris wheel that was the NHS. He still worked as a hospital porter. He helped himself pass the time by mentally making a separate diagnosis or prognosis for each live patient he moved on a trolley. One day, he hoped, not too long in the future, his suspension would be lifted. He would be free to practise again as a doctor.

Drinking was still enjoyable but eating well had assumed greater importance in his life. He now had no single favourite pub but there were so many in Oxford, you were always spoilt for choice. He had one new passion for a hotel restaurant in a stately pile on the corner of Beaumont Street. The maître d'hôtel was a tall, courteous man who held court in a great, sumptuous room bedecked with fine paintings. The food was excellent. Chris liked to visit when he could afford it, drink fine wine and eat good food, and opposite him from time to time stood the courteous maître d'hôtel, slightly arcane, like a mysterious apparition of Don Quixote.

Chris wanted the panel interviewing him to lift his suspension to be somehow like the maître d'hôtel – courteous, considerate, and even chivalrous.

*

Dylan and Matt stared through the viewing window. Charlie had pinned down two beta or less senior-ranking males. He raised his right arm above his head, holding aloft the jagged roof timber.

'Christ,' said Matt. 'He looks angry enough to kill them both.'

'He needs to be boxed right away,' said Dylan, the black hair on his head standing on end – a weird copy of chimp piloerection.

Charlie was in full bipedal swagger. He beat one of the two cowering chimps on its legs, and then smashed the rafter against the wall behind it. As soon as the other tried to escape, Charlie blocked its exit. He snarled a couple of times, baring his long canines at other male chimps in the group behind him, who had been edging closer. They screamed at Charlie but quickly backed off.

'Get the vet down here, and that girl Natalie!' Dylan shouted.

Matt phoned. 'The vet's coming now. He's not far away.'

After what seemed like only a few moments, Natalie came

running towards the ape enclosure. She ran straight to the viewing window. 'Hey, just look at him,' she gasped.

Charlie tossed aside the roof rafter contemptuously, as if it was of no further use. Chimps scattered in a dozen different directions, leaping against the enclosure walls, swinging on poles, stamping on anything, including other chimps. Still with his bipedal swagger, Charlie rushed the viewing window with enormous force. Natalie stepped back, totally in awe of the new alpha male.

FORTY-THREE

Dan Holder, BVetMed, was enjoying coffee by the river, in the same town where Lawrence of Arabia's effigy reposed like a sleepless Arab eremite, the lids of his marble eyes eternally apart.

Snapping shut his mobile, he got up and swore. 'One crazy bloody chimpanzee! Sedation recommended.' He walked swiftly to an old Series III Land Rover. 'That'll be tiletamine-zolazepam, 3 mg per kg,' he said, speaking to himself. He climbed in, having first made sure all his equipment was in the back of the Land Rover. He called Dr Stevenson, only to be exasperated to discover the ape centre had no record of the animal's weight.

'You try finding the right dose,' he exclaimed to Dr Stevenson.

'I guess he's around 175 lbs. He's not fully mature either, he's just big. We have a cage here. I'd like you to X-ray him too.'

'Where?' Dan asked.

'His head, top of skull.'

'Any injuries?'

'Not yet!'

'Why the X-ray? Precautionary I guess.'

'You could say that,' Dr Stevenson replied. In truth, he was baffled by Charlie, to the extent that any kind of rational analysis amounted to an empirical leap into the unknown, a place where the usual formulae of zoological evidence and knowledge simply had no application.

*

Charlie's head was directly opposite Natalie. Spellbound, she gazed into Charlie's liquid gold-brown eyes. Charlie dropped on all fours, grabbed a rubber tyre, and rolled it right against the window. Then he pulled over a lower-ranking male chimp, making him crouch on the floor. After making sure the chimp dare not move, Charlie dragged another screaming chimp to the front of the tyre. This chimp was pushed into a similar posture, the animal's back bent forwards, face to the ground, head hunched but its eyes still able to look ahead to the faces of Natalie, Matt, and Dr Stevenson.

*

The Land Rover drove into the centre. Dan jumped down, grabbed a medical bag, and ran towards ape house three.

Charlie scrutinised the human faces at the window for a few seconds, and then casually squatted down on the tyre. He placed both feet on top of the prone chimpanzee in front of him, and then carefully let his back rest against the other. Charlie looked utterly relaxed, his body supported by the tyre and the two chimps, as if he were in George's favourite chair. One arm fell limply at his side, the other slowly scratched his prepotent testicles.

Dan joined the others, holding his vet's bag under one arm. Charlie had attracted quite a crowd of onlookers. Dr Stevenson decided to cordon off the ape house.

'Hi Dan,' he said. 'This is the one. He's calmed down a bit since we called you.'

'He looks kind of strange,' Dan said. 'I thought you said the ape had gone crazy.'

'You should have been here five minutes ago. He smashed up two of the chimps with that rafter.'

Dan took in the scene. Several females tended and groomed the two chimps struck by Charlie. There was little blood to be seen. Apart from probable bruising, Dan's prognosis was that serious harm to the two chimps had not occurred. It was common enough for chimpanzees to fight in the wild. Most times serious injury was avoided.

'I think you've been very lucky,' Dan said eventually, his experienced eyes reading the animals' mien and behaviour patterns for interpretable signs. 'But the question of this chimp, the one in front of us, quote unquote, "in repose", I cannot fathom.'

'Which means?' asked Dr Stevenson agog.

'Normally when an animal like this has undergone such a recent psychotic episode, recovery to this behaviour, this level of tranquillity is improbable. By psychotic, I mean on the margins, disturbed, vicious, out of character.' Dan paused. 'How well do you know this chimp?'

'That's the strange thing, we don't.'

'This repose, the way he lies there trusting, even laid feet to back, is *that* the wild chimp or are we talking about another one?'

'That's him,' said Dr Stevenson assuredly. For a moment he thought he saw a strange glint of triumph in Charlie's eyes. It couldn't be, could it? The two other chimps hadn't moved from their uncomfortable positions, appropriated, commandeered by the dominant alpha male for his own comfort and satisfaction.

'Bring the box down, will you, Matt?'

'But do we *need* to do that?' asked Natalie, her manner as earnest as a mother enquiring about a wayward but much loved child.

'I'm taking no chances,' said Dr Stevenson resolutely. Matt manhandled a metal cage towards a side entrance.

Dan had to make a choice between a hand-injection for Charlie to sedate him or darting, which is more stressful. Darting would mean setting off pandemonium in the ape house.

Charlie 'arose' from his slumbering position, the two chimps sent away with a solitary flick of his long fingers. He made his way towards a side corridor leading to the outside enclosure, an area where chimps could be partitioned and controlled as necessary. Matt was waiting with the portable transport cage.

'Hello there,' said Matt, wide-eyed.

Charlie saw the enclosure outside and suddenly wanted to be free. At least in his thinking it was an emotion rather than fact. His eyes took in the grassy banks, the wooden play structures, the trees behind like a distant forest. Matt was but a short way off with the cage. The ape remembered. More than anything he wanted freedom, freedom to range, forage, explore; not to be imprisoned, confined. Like the distant forest, the memory of freedom was distant too. Yet the eternal forest into which he could happily plunge himself called strongly in quick bursts of memory but there was no way there. Only half understood came the dim realisation he had to get through this present state, to survive and live, and that anger alone would not lead to the freedom he desired.

As if in a semi-trance, the ape moved forward towards Matt and the waiting cage, accepting there was no real choice. He must bear it out. The ways of humans he must live with, for the time being. Charlie leapt onto a low wall, screamed once at nothing in particular, raising his shaggy head towards the sky to vocalise, and then loped down, knuckle-walking towards the cage.

Matt retreated beyond the enclosure, safety being preferable to foolish bravery. To his astonishment, Charlie approached the cage, found the hinged door, opened it, and went inside. He even pulled the door shut behind him.

The most surprised member of the human group watching Charlie was the vet. Surprise turned to amazement when Charlie stuck out the fingers of one hand through the cage bars. Dan Holder walked over to the cage, locked it with a bolt, and very cautiously touched Charlie's fingers. It might even be possible to hand-inject the ape to sedate him but he decided against it.

Dan, Matt and Dylan were able to load the cage onto the Land Rover where it was secured. To the clamorous hooting and roaring of the chimps in ape house number three, chimps in adjacent ape houses, and various other non-human primates including a hirsute, reddish-brown orang-utan who hung with great unconcern from a high vantage pole, Charlie was driven away, on another extraordinary journey, this time to have his skull examined, tested and X-rayed. He surveyed his exit calmly, and felt a strange sense of relief as the Land Rover passed out through the gates.

FORTY-FOUR

Dan Holder drove straight to town. Matt and Dylan sat next to him. In a cul-de-sac, not far away from Charlie's temporary home in Dr Waldren's garage, Dan steered the Land Rover towards a colleague's animal surgery, commandeered for the tests.

Once inside, Charlie was sedated by a simple hand injection, tolerated by the ape remarkably well, although it was clear he scrutinised the new surroundings carefully.

'We'll start with a brief examination of the skull, followed by X-ray,' Dan said. 'Are we all in agreement?'

'Yes,' was immediately chorused. Charlie drowsily nodded his head, as an ironic after-event. Velcro pads and binders were affixed to the ape's arms and neck to assist immobilisation, necessary for high quality diagnostic imaging. Cursory examination of the head revealed recent hair growth and a ridged structure bounded by rectangular scar tissue, evidence of healing.

It was the X-rays that were most telling. A dorsal view of the frontal and parietal areas showed the curved, convex shape of the titanium miniplate, *in situ*. It extended from above the supraorbital ridge over the eye sockets to just before the occipital bone. Bone regrowth surrounding it was evident, as it was along the cranial sutures. The cranial surface was relatively smooth with no evidence of a sagittal crest, which runs lengthwise along the midline of the skull.

'If I'm not mistaken,' said Dan with a hushed voice, 'that's the head of a screw. Look, four of them!'

'By Christ,' whispered Dr Stevenson, 'he has history then. But how far, how far back, and why?'

Matt scratched his head. Charlie stirred. Outside it was raining unseasonably hard, sluicing and sleeting on the road, as well as through the deciduous and evergreen canopies in the gardens of the cul-de-sac. You could hear the wind soughing in the trees, the incessant pattering rain drops.

*

Charlie would have remembered. Deep in the forest, from Takamanda in western Cameroon right up to the wooded slopes of the Obudu Plateau in Nigeria, his home range would have been at least 20 square kilometres, over a mosaic of highland and lowland forest. The seasons, wet and dry, would dictate variation in ranging. Availability of surface water for drinking and ripe fruit for eating would be taken into account.

Whether he ranged in woodland savannah, riverine forest, montane forest or the rainforest, he would know the location of thousands of individual trees, memorised from an early age, when with his mother. He would return to certain core ranges, especially in lean times, to locations taught by his mother. Cognitive representations of the landscape in his mind enabled him to harvest fruit, travelling directly from resource to resource.

*

'We'll let him recover,' Dan said. 'I wonder if we can keep him here over the weekend, run some more tests.' Matt found a secure room next to the waiting area, and Dan hurriedly cleared Charlie's stay with his colleague.

*

In Oxford, Chris Grailing was becoming increasingly impatient. Although his friend George was the principal mover in the whole affair, Chris felt more and more responsible for Charlie. George was not going to recover fast enough to help the anthropoid ape.

Chris began researching the taxonomy of Charlie's species to pass the time until his suspension from practising as a doctor was lifted. He felt alarm when he discovered the subspecies was listed in the IUCN's *Red List of Threatened Species*. If the International Union for Conservation of Nature were on their tail, or was it trail, he, George, and Jo would be on another kind of red list, starting with the word, *WANTED*.

Chris snapped his fingers lightly in the grand restaurant with its sumptuous wainscoted walls, high ceiling and elegant paintings.

'Yes sir, how I can assist you?' queried the comically chivalric figure of the maître d' looming over him.

'Wine, more wine. I am trying to understand...'

The maître d' seemed puzzled. 'Understand, sir?' he asked.

'The relatives of the taxon. Who or what are they hypothesised to be? In this particular case, I am not sure all the ranks can be completed.' He poured himself another glass of red.

The maître d' just smiled warmly.

'Bring me some condiment sets, will you? About seven or eight.'

A trolley was swiftly wheeled over and eight salt and pepper condiment sets appeared on the table. Chris arranged them in neat lines. Furthest away from him, he placed the first pair saying, 'Kingdom', lifting up the salt and replacing it, then, '*Animalia*' for the pepper. He followed in the same order with Phylum *Chordata* (muttering 'with backbones'); Class *Mammalia*; Order *Primates*; Family *Pongidae*; Genus *Pan*; Species *troglodytes vellerosus*.' There was one set left over.

'I could add suborder,' he said, 'like *Anthropoidea*. Or a superfamily, *Hominoidea*, which includes apes and humans. Even a subfamily, *Ponginae*. But I'm not sure what to do with this last set.'

The maître d' clearly didn't understand a word of it but he said suddenly, 'Do you have anyone in mind?'

'As a matter of fact, yes, I do,' Chris said, warming to the idea. 'I do have someone or something in mind. His name is Charlie, by way of Takamanda, a forest deep in another land.'

But the maître d' had his own suggestion. He picked up the last condiment set, placing it down squarely on Chris's dessert plate. 'I think this one's for you, sir. Curious *Man!*'

Later that evening, when over the shock of the restaurant bill, Chris began further research into the furry ape from Takamanda Forest, at least that's where George told him the species came from. He was thrilled to learn about one of the most intriguing ape stories ever told. The chimp had been named *vellerosus* or furry in 1862 but in 2009 a doughty primatologist by the name of Oates (sharing the same surname as that 'very gallant gentleman' who walked to his death in a blizzard with the words, 'I am just going out and may be some time') unravelled its true origin. In 2009, the species was renamed *Pan troglodytes ellioti*.

Chris wanted to tell George the tale. It ran from Fernando Pó to Gabon, and thence to a small village in western Cameroon called Basho. The story even included mighty Mount Cameroon, *Mongo ma Ndemi*, its native name (Mountain of Greatness). He was so excited he nearly rang but the thought of George not being able to properly understand prevented him.

*

In his new confinement Charlie sulked. He was left little to eat, just a hand of bananas, and a bowl of water, like one generously left out on the pavement for passing dogs. Fully recovered from the sedative he had been given, and sensing the uniqueness of the moment, before the next set of experiments and tests due in the morning, Charlie grabbed the metal bowl and hurled it against the wall in front of him. He was in a small room, not a cage, and he swayed from side to side with increasing vigour.

'Escape' was an abstract concept he could not yet fully understand. It was more to do with a lack of confinement, not to be caged but in the wild heartland of natural life, the song of the forest where the trees and leaves 'spoke' their truths and mysteries to him (if not trailed with daisies and barley, then strewn with epiphytes, ferns, and fruit). Even with the threat of danger, it was better to be free.

Charlie reached up to the single window frame. The supposedly secure, double-glazed unit came away in his brawny hands, wrenched and twisted aside, as though nothing more than aluminium foil. Then he reached down for the metal water bowl, and with renewed determination jammed it through the remaining glass pane. Instincts deep inside him literally forced his arms and hands, as he pushed still harder until the outer frame gave way, and fell to the tarmac outside. With one leap Charlie was free. It was 5.00 p.m.

FORTY-FIVE

'*Yaay!*' Chris cried on opening the letter. Oxford University Hospitals NHS Trust had decided to lift his suspension with immediate effect. He began to sing out loud. '*For he's a jolly good fellow, for he's a jolly good fellow. And so say all of them! Hurrah!*'

In ebullient mood, Chris snapped open a bottle of cold beer. 'Are we ready?' he shouted, echoing the Mayor of London at the time of the 2012 Olympics. 'By Christ, I'm ready,' he told himself. But then he paused, remembering Charlie. He called Jo.

'Chris! I like it,' Jo exclaimed. '*Dr* Grailing is back in business. George will be pleased.'

'How is he?'

'I think he's depressed. He can't do very much.'

'How's Charlie? Have you been to see him?'

Jo sighed. 'That poor ape, God knows what's happened to him.'

'You know Jo, that ape, he's not furry after all.'

'What do you mean?'

'The species was called *vellerosus* or furry, say hairy chested, after the explorer Captain Richard Burton, who was consul at Fernando Pó, sent skin specimens to the British Museum. They were thought to have come from the Cameroon Mountains. He said, the old male, Nchígo Mpolo, excuse my pronunciation, was as hairy as hell, and it's still recorded in the Natural History Museum. It's got a number: 1862.6.28.1. Don't ask me what that means. A man called Gray named it in 1862.'

'You're giving me a lecture on the nomenclature of West African chimpanzees?'

'Yes! I just think it's a fabulous story. Burton was supposed to have collected them from the slopes of Mount Cameroon. He went to Gabon a month later, and then shipped his specimens to London, but somehow got them mixed up. In 2008, a scientist discovered it really came from Gabon, once called "Gaboon Country", not from Mount Cameroon, after studying mitochondrial DNA from the skins.'

'And?' asked Jo, a little wearily.

'A German captain called Jasper von Oertzen collected another chimp near Basho in 1905, that's a small village east of Takamanda Forest Reserve. Someone else called Matschie later named the chimp *ellioti* in 1914 after a primate researcher, Elliot; the specimen is still in the Humboldt Museum in Berlin.'

'What's the point of all this?' Jo demanded.

'The point is that, according to someone called Oates and other researchers (2009), Charlie is not *Pan troglodytes vellerosus*, he's *Pan troglodytes ellioti*.'

'Wow! Does it make that much difference?'

'It's really of question of taxonomic names. Charlie still has his hairy chest but his name has changed. If in time we, or others, venerate him, it's *ellioti*, not *vellerosus*. I know it doesn't amount to much. There aren't many chimpanzees now in or near Basho, that's for sure.'

'Where is Basho?'

'I think you have to go to a town called Mamfe first. It's a settlement north of there.'

'I'm hoping you'll come down soon so we can go and see Charlie.' Something was worrying Jo. Perhaps it was empathy for Charlie's plight, locked up with a troupe of rescued chimpanzees. Or was he happy with new friends? 'You will come, won't you?'

'Of course, Jo.' Chris said he'd be down that weekend. He had things to celebrate and organise, now he was able to practise as a doctor again.

*

Charlie's eyes darted from side to side. He was imaging in his mind the mental map made for him by the billions of neurons in his cerebral cortex. The same 'fight or flight' response as in man quickly kicked in, the sympathetic nervous system organising the release of hormones as well as maintaining constant homeostasis.

Charlie's heartbeat accelerated, his pupils dilated, lung action increased, fat and glucose were released for muscular action, and there was piloerection of his black-brown hair.

Initial hesitation gave way to flight – across a car park, under a bridge, down a road. Sometimes he took cover for a few minutes in hedges but always he was urged on by instincts deep within him. In just a few minutes he had covered almost 500 yards. A giant Monterey pine loomed ahead, its gnarled trunk causing alarm until the opening he found, a cut between holly and privet. Down this escape route Charlie scampered, less nervous now, and with no humans in sight, although he knew nothing of the white bindweed trumpets, the purple foxgloves and holly lining the path.

Moments later he emerged from the cut onto a road and he could hear water. It was late July, early evening, shadows already lengthening, though the sun was still high. He avoided two cars, crossed the road, and found a wooden walkway leading beneath a canopy of leaves – the red and green leaves of a Persian ironwood tree – until there he was, in the sunlight, in a meadow fringed with weeping willow, still on the walkway, hemmed in by tall, fluffy meadowsweet, white flowering valerian, buttercups grown high, and purple loosestrife with magenta flower spikes rising above the long grasses.

A lone green woodpecker bounded up into the air, sinking and rising again by starts, uttering its yaffling cry of alarm.

Charlie looked behind him. His shadow frightened him. He heard the noise of cars, the voices of children, wood pigeons. He kept on the walkway. Pink Himalayan balsam lined a stream in the middle of the green valley. There were unusual trees he had no memory of. The ape turned right onto grass, seagulls mewed above him, and then he found the stream, about five feet across. He saw a bridge ahead with sunlight glittering on the water beneath it. A wren scolded him, a magpie skulked.

A girl with a dog walked near. Charlie froze. When they had gone, he drank from surface water, found a litter bin with a half-eaten sandwich, and turned right by a copper beech, back down the valley. On his left a red fuchsia in flower, on his right the quietly flowing stream. Tall cow parsley vied with the pink balsam to see who could be highest. Along the bank he saw purple flowers, like tiny five-pointed stars, the earth still muddy in places after rain, then climbed a weeping willow as a young couple approached.

Beside a stand of yellow ragwort next to the stream the couple kissed. Charlie kept still. Apart from the swishing of leaves he heard little more than the tumbling rivulet and the noise of squirrels eating pine cones, the cores and stripped scales dropping steadily down. When the couple had gone from sight, Charlie bounded back on the grass, continuing to follow the stream. He saw a fallen tree several metres long, and with one leap landed on its smooth, worn bole. He walked up and down on it bipedally, his arms raised. Several cars drove down and up the one-way crossing in front of him but he remained out of sight, stamping his feet on the tree in a display of dominance – or perhaps something akin to delight at his new freedom. Charlie wisely kept from vocalising, which was as well, since chimpanzees' hoots and hollers can carry more than one mile. He liked the sound made by the hollow tree. He drummed with the flat of his hands instead of his feet for a while, and was entranced.

His goal seemed to be to follow the greenway. The great ape ducked under the contorted branches of another Persian ironwood, and finding no humans on the road, he quickly crossed. There was yet another refuge beyond. The stream ran beneath the road into a pool, a vista of parkland trees, and the beckoning valley.

Following the stream it was like foraging in lush grassland except Charlie noticed no fruit. To his left rose up a dark shape, a red brick, gothic Victorian water tower, surrounded by lush cultivated blooms, a forest of purple agapanthus or African lilies, flaming bottlebrush flowers, hydrangeas, and yellow iris. To his right was a red-painted bridge, reminiscent of a Japanese garden.

The sun was setting slowly. Charlie explored around the water tower, crossed the bridge to where the multiple trunks of a Zebrina

Western red cedar, with its distinctive pyramidal shape, creamy-yellow variegation and fibrous bark provided cover and shade, so that he could see past the stream to the path beyond. Occasionally cyclists or walkers passed by and were gone. Charlie rested.

A song thrush singing from a nearby tree in full-throated melody roused Charlie once more. There were new sounds in the air. Sirens, more cars, planes in the sky. A huge portentous moon billowed through the trees in the west. The grass was already wet with dew and by 9.00 p.m. another footpath behind him was lit every 30 yards or so with old street lamps.

The damp earth smelled clean, fresh. Blue dragonflies and damselflies, common by day, had all but disappeared, replaced by tiny Natterer's bats that seemed to fly without any purpose of direction.

Charlie's heart was at peace. The sound and sight of water trickling was like a blushful bourn, with the sun sliding down the sky adding russet-red hues. He wandered beyond to a group of giant gunnera plants, surrounded by tall yellow polyanthus flowers, near a patch of white, pink and blue hydrangeas. There were some flies but not enough to bother him. He hadn't had much to eat but he didn't feel hungry. His metabolism had already adjusted to the lack of abundant food by slowing down.

Then Charlie did something he had not done for a very long time. He scraped together leaves, ferns and small branches. He made a nest, not in a tree but there on the rich earth. And he slept by starlight.

FORTY-SIX

At 9.35 a.m. the next morning Dan Holder's mobile rang. With the phone by his ear, his face soon went white. He called Dr Stevenson moments later. 'All hell's let loose,' he said, his voice shaky. 'Guess what? Charlie's gone. He's gone AWOL.'

Dr Dylan Stevenson was so shocked he was speechless. 'Christ,' he said after a numbing silence. 'Christ almighty! So much for that place being secure.'

Dan said, 'They've already searched the surgery buildings. There's no sign of him. They say he must have forced his way out. This is serious. People are at risk. The way that ape went crazy in the ape house…'

'Where's Matt? Get Natalie over too. We need help.' Dr Stevenson ran both hands through his black hair, then sighed heavily. His phone rang again about an hour later. This time it was a reporter from the local newspaper. 'Hi,' he said, wondering how she knew his name already. 'Yes, that's right. No, we haven't called the emergency services yet. Look, please don't print any wild stories just now, okay? A lot of people could be frightened by this.'

It seemed that no matter how hard he tried to explain to the reporter not to splash the news all over the front page, she was already explaining that in the public interest, they would have to run a major story. And it would be headlined something like, 'CHIMP ON THE RUN' or 'CHIMP ON THE LOOSE', whatever the subs decided. Was the animal dangerous?

'This creature – this ape – he's very special, you know. Well, I hardly know him but, no, he's not dangerous. Not exactly.'

The reporter sensed she was onto something. 'Maybe we should say he's dangerous just to protect people?'

Dr Stevenson hung up.

George was in bed in his dressing gown, propped up with pillows, having breakfast, watching TV. He was just about to slice at a piece of bacon when he caught sight of a chimpanzee at the end of his bed. He screwed up his eyes, opened them, and realised it was on the TV.

'By Jove,' he cried, 'Ch-Ch-Charlie!' His tray of food slipped off the bed. 'Oh God,' he said, 'I can't even look after...my own breakfast.' His stomach had warmed to the slice of bacon, now on the floor, but the gurgling sound it made was not to do with food. It was his Charlie, his very own Charlie.

'I'm sure it's you,' he said to himself. 'I know that face, I'd know it anywhere!' Poor George was beside himself. It wasn't ecstasy, which is to stand outside one's self, just beside himself. As his breakfast had tipped over, he did the same, ending up face-down on his plate of egg and bacon slices. His mouth opened slightly.

One of George's canines rested against a nub of bacon, the tomato buried on his nose. The egg was a hopeless afterthought. George cursed whoever cooked it.

Then Jo walked in.

'Did you cook that goddamn egg?'

'Quiet, George. Let's watch that. Is that Charlie?'

The story about the chimp was very short. There were terse 'No comment' statements from the surgery staff and Dan Holder. It was put down to speculation, like the stories of big cats glimpsed on Dartmoor. It was in fact a clever ruse to keep a lid on the story and find Charlie before he got into trouble. The only evidence was hearsay and so far that didn't amount to much. The picture of the chimp was a stock photo, and not Charlie, Jo was sure.

George sank back on his bed, still depressed. A voice from Eden, or one that breathed over it, that's what he wanted to hear before he died. Of course, it wasn't a voice, more of a stir or a sigh or a sough in the great trees of the forest, and then a gentle '*hoo hoo*' in his ear.

He began to dream, a daydream, not quite 'dreaming by day' as a prelude to action but remembering what he knew. Although his stroke had compromised some of his physical abilities, his intellectual faculties were still quite sharp. Perhaps some of the words that sprang to mind were not immediately recognisable or wholly understood but reason and good sense had not left him entirely.

He was thinking how all the pieces of man's ancient past were beginning to fit together, how new fossil human species were being discovered (the first fossil chimpanzees had also been found in Kenya), helping to unlock the secrets of our human past. How genetics was opening its vast libraries of treasure, all those billions of base pairs – 6 billion letters of DNA, 46 strands of DNA, the chromosomes, and the letters ACGT making up the digital encoding information in an ordered sequence of just four different symbols…

*

There was the little hobbit man, *Homo floriensis*, who managed to survive until about 12,000 years ago. This diminutive creature was a dwarf human, nicknamed 'The hobbit', whose remains were found on the Indonesian island of Flores in 2003.

The heavy, thick-set, large nosed, flame-haired Neanderthal, *Homo neanderthalensis*, discovered in the Neander Valley in Germany in 1856 made its last stand about 28,000 years ago. Climate change and/or competition from modern humans (and perhaps having too much of their brains devoted to eyesight at the expense of cognitive areas) drove the nemesis of our closest extinct human relative.

Neanderthals knew how to control fire, made hunting tools, sometimes buried their dead, with pierced shells and red ochre, put flowers on their graves, quite possibly were cannibals when it suited them, are thought to have had unique songs, and a few interbred with modern humans some 50,000 years ago. Their lineage stretched back to a common ancestor with modern humans around 500,000 to 200,000 years ago. Between 1 to 4 per cent of the Eurasian human genome comes from Neanderthals, so in this way they live on, are not totally extinct.

Perhaps there was a time when there was just a handful alive, confined to a cave near the shoreline of Gibraltar. Then just one. If he or she could sing, what a sad, poignant last song, pitifully sung, drowned by the unstoppable wave of evolution.

*

Jo shook George gently. 'Where are you?' she asked, thoughtfully.

'In a reverie of sorts, my dear. I feel as if I am on the vast plains of Africa. Charlie's out there somewhere, you know.'

Jo patted his good arm, saddened by the blight of stroke, not knowing that underneath that ageing skin was a man making more progress to recovery than she realised. 'Chris is coming soon. And Alice and John, they're coming down to see you.

'Splendid,' George replied, returning to his disrupted reverie with more vigour.

Jo quietly let herself out of the room.

*

His thoughts turned to the many different species of man's ancestors. In the west were Neanderthals, but in the east, a strange creature known as *Homo denisovensis*, or Denisovans, an ancient hominin named from a cave where their remains were found, in eastern Siberia. They are thought to have coexisted with Neanderthals and humans around 50,000 years ago.

The Melanesian (the region to the north and east of Australia) genome contains around 4 to 6 per cent Denisovan DNA as well. This group is thought to have shared a last common ancestor (LCA) with modern humans and Neanderthals one million years ago, the so-called 'divergence date'. (A living entity with a genome was 'living' around 3.5 billion years ago, known as LUCA, the last universal common ancestor – of all life.)

This amounted, George knew, to at least four distinct types of human, that is, genetically distinct, still living 50,000 years ago. Anatomically modern humans emerged around 200,000 years ago, but for the past 25,000 years at least (with the exception of Red Deer Cave people from China, dated to 10,500 years ago), humans

(*Homo sapiens sapiens*, the subspecies of archaic *Homo sapiens*) are alone on the planet, with no close relatives alive any more. George suddenly thought of Charlie, and a smile crossed his face.

Apart from all that, there had been *Homo habilis*, *Homo erectus*, *Homo rudolfensis*, all co-existing around 2 mya. In our evolution as a species, there had been great early diversity. A new hominid had been discovered, on the same path that led to our own species. *Australopithecus sediba*, found in 2008, is a transitional fossil, in our own lineage, a species of *Australopithecus* from the early Pleistocene, dated to 2 mya. Or consider *Ardipithecus ramidus*, who lived over 4 mya, and there are some far older still. Incredible it is to think that we have all evolved from a common ancestor we shared with Charlie's kind, the chimpanzee.

George chuckled, thinking back to the fossil human species found on a Richard Leakey expedition to Kenya in 1972. This species of the genus *Homo* (with a remarkably flat face, from eye socket to jaw line) was later named *Homo rudolfensis*. The specimen was a skull with an estimated age of 1.9 million years, dug up on the east side of Lake Rudolf, now known as Lake Turkana. It was given a name and number, Skull 1470 (KNM ER 1470). In his student years George thought the 'ER' might have had some reference to the Queen but ER stood for East (Lake) Rudolph. Was that east of Eden?

So many apes in the earth's story, the first ones dating back 23 million years. The Australopithecines or southern apes, like *Australopithecus afarensis* (one representative of this extinct genus of hominids being the gracile AL 288-1, known as 'Lucy', discovered in 1974 in Ethiopia; her 140 or so bones rested in the earth for 3.2 million years) or *Australopithecus africanus*, to name just two from the family, Hominidae, or Great Apes, from many more.

Millions of years of evolution had been slowly passing before the first humans migrated out of Africa 130,000 to 50,000 years ago. (Certainly there had to be more things in heaven and earth than could ever *possibly* be dreamt of in the paleoanthropologist's philosophy; the incredible diversity of life, from the grotesque ferocity of a dinosaur to the indulgence of a dormouse; and the great tides of climatic and cultural change, continually sweeping over the earth.)

There were still so many questions to answer. When did early hominids stop climbing in trees? (The term 'hominid' is the traditional classification for modern humans and their ancestors but because of new molecular testing the preferred term is now 'hominin'. The new system of classification recognises the close relationship between chimps and humans, placing orang-utans, gorillas, chimps and humans in the family Hominidae (thus hominid), with chimps and humans in the subfamily Homininae (so hominines). Humans are placed in the tribe Hominini (hominins). Hominoid refers to members of the superfamily Hominoidea, past and present.) Recent analysis of fossilised shoulder blades from a three-year-old girl who died 3.3 mya, from the same species as Lucy, also found in Ethiopia, has shown that the shoulders of the species were still well adapted for climbing, although they already walked on the ground, suggesting these apes probably abandoned life in trees later than thought (or possibly went back into them).

Was it really possible that *Homo erectus* had controlled use of fire one million years ago? George knew that sites in Asia and Europe confirmed this. How much we have learned already from the study of mitochondrial DNA, which is passed down the maternal line only.

As for 'mitochondrial Eve', what would she have made of Charlie? George sighed like the old man he was. There were some things in life that would always remain unanswered.

*

Chris packed the last of his few belongings, having decided to leave Oxford for good. George was expecting him, and there was the question of Charlie, which nagged at his conscience. If George was incapable, it fell upon him to act as Charlie's keeper. The ape was too precious to be abandoned when no one knew his potential.

As the taxi drove him once more from Headington, over Magdalen's beautiful bridge, and along The High where he had waited, with an orange on his table in the Grand Café for news from the Tissue Bank, past the glorious façades and on towards the west, and Oxford train station, he found himself declaiming a few lines by James Elroy Flecker:

Proud and godly kings had built her, long ago,
With her towers and tombs and statues all arow,
With her fair and floral air and the love that lingers there,
And the streets where the great men go.

The taxi driver said, 'What's that, Guv?'

Chris was trying to stand up in the back, to see as much as possible but then he sat down, and simply said, 'Oh, nothing.'

As soon as the train reached Dorset, Chris was in for a shock. As he climbed into another taxi, he saw a newsstand poster. It read: WILD CHIMP ESCAPES, ON THE RUN.

He spluttered a question to the driver. 'What's that all about, escaped chimp?'

'Don't ask me, Guvnor,' said the man, 'just started my shift.'

Chris kept as quiet as a mouse in the back. When the taxi stopped outside George's house, Chris nearly forgot to take his suitcase. Struggling with the heavy case, he stumbled towards George's front door.

Jo let him in. 'What's up?' she asked to a breathless Chris.

'The chimp, on the run. D'you suppose it's Charlie? Who else could it be? I mean what other chimp?'

George staggered into the hallway. 'I know. It *is* Charlie!' he said, his eyes wild, his white hair floating over his head, as if under its own gravity.

'There's no proof yet, George,' Jo shouted.

'Where's the whisky?' Chris yelled over the top of everyone. 'That's what we all need, a drink, to think this through.'

'Whisky?' whispered George. 'You think the malted grain tells more? Fate is fate. Believe you me.'

'Then fate it is then. We'll drink to that!'

FORTY-SEVEN

Fate it seemed was converging on Charlie. He had woken early, refreshed, drank a little water from the stream. Being diurnal, like humans, each day begins anew. The receding night left wet morning dew. Fingers of white mist lingered in the shrubs and trees. Charlie braced himself, stiffening his posture in involuntary movements of reassurance. He stood up to see more, grunted, and then set off down the valley, in the direction of the sea.

In a summer of rain, the good weather that day was a respite for holidaymakers and tourists in the town. It was still early in the morning. Charlie followed the stream. Further down he skirted more golden weeping willows, giant stands of gunnera, and a Chusan palm with hairy matted trunk, not entirely unlike the palm trees of West Africa. When Persian ironwood trees caught the sun's rays, the leaves glowed like dark rubies.

Just about all the trees were strange to him. The swamp cypress, giant sequoia, and Caucasian wingnut, with its hanging catkins, belonged to other continents as did the coast redwood, sweet gum, fragrant mimosa. The same went for the handsome tulip tree, whose trunks were used by Native Americans to make canoes, the Mexican weeping pine from the cloud forests of east Mexico, and the hardwood hornbeam. Foraging under the trees brought him little; wild crab apples, grubs, few leaves worth eating, and sore feet from brushing against spiny thorns on the bole of a honey locust.

Hunger drove him on. It was not serious yet, the lack of food, because in the gardens he found more discarded crusts of bread and nuts left out for squirrels. He avoided several walkers and runners with his usual cunning, melting in an instant into cover. He felt no fear, as he had in the rainforest of Cameroon, when his mother vainly fought for her life, slain by a hunter's gun.

He pressed on down the valley still following the stream. He quickly crossed another road, joining the stream again on the other side. A flyover loomed ahead by Corsican pines. He edged closer, unable to see the cars passing overhead. Charlie must have presented a strange apparition of life under the reinforced concrete pillars that supported the dual carriageway; a black-haired wraith with muscular arms and legs, staggering in short bipedal bursts. The town quietly beckoned, drawing the ape forward to his future.

*

Dan Holder was distraught. He'd got everyone he could find to start searching for Charlie. Surely he wouldn't be too far away. It was true there were extensive pine woods stretching all the way to sandy chines by the sea. There were large houses with gardens. Some had ponds with ornamental fish; the water was drinkable, the fish easily caught. Giant rhododendrons flourished. There were parks, civic gardens, and a six kilometre stretch of greenway. If Charlie adopted the tactics of urban foxes, he could find plenty of shelter, and food enough to survive.

Matt was worried too. They were hiding information from the local authority, the directors of the ape centre, from the press…Natalie broke the stalemate by urging a coordinated search. It was all very well to talk about finding Charlie but how would they catch him?

*

Jo and Chris were similarly agitated. George appeared the same morning in a bizarre outfit, dressed for grouse shooting on the open moors; his best tweed jacket and trousers, hunting boots, a doeskin waistcoat, and tweed cap at the ready.

'Where do you think you're going?' Jo asked.

'I'm going to find Charlie. I saw him on TV,' George urged.

'We're not going to shoot him, you know, if we find him,' Chris said. 'Looks like all you need is a gun. In fact, George, why are you kitted up like that?'

'I admit it's a bit strange,' George responded slowly. 'At the same time there is logic.' He paused, as if catching his breath. 'It's like being on a drive, isn't it? You are the beaters, and I'm going to catch him.'

'Any one of us might,' said Chris, thoughtfully. 'I say it has to be a team effort. We'll spread out, and then home in on him, once there's news of a confirmed sighting. We might lure him with food. I'm worried stiff he might be discovered by someone else first. Imagine if he's in a bad mood...You could lose an arm just thinking about it!'

'Blasted business this,' George rasped. 'Goddamn blasted business.' He buried his head in his hands and sunk further into his favourite chair.

Suddenly he struggled to his feet. His eyes lit up like twin sparklers on bonfire night, alive with incandescent, preternatural energy. 'Now!' he shouted. 'Get the car out. Why on earth have we wasted all this time? We're going to see Charlie at home. If he's not there, he must have escaped!'

'The car is already out,' Jo said tetchily. 'If you remember we can't park the car in the garage because of Charlie's cage.'

'Oh, all right! All right!' He turned to Chris. 'You drive.'

Once again the old Rover made haste towards the town where Lawrence's noble effigy reposed, his head pillowed by a camel saddle.

George urged them on. *'Faster, faster, goddamn it!'* He sat in the back in a peculiar re-enactment of an earlier journey when Charlie was conveyed like a nabob to a colonial outpost.

When they got to the ape centre a subtle change came over George. He heard in the near distance the hoots and screams of monkeys and chimpanzees, the eerie, other-worldly cries of gibbons. It was if all his remaining senses sharpened. There was a keenness in his step, the limp from the stroke all but disappeared.

They went to each ape house in turn, in case Charlie had been moved, and to number three last. Three pairs of human eyes scanned the enclosure. A desultory group of chimps wandered aimlessly inside. It was if they could find no rest, pacing up and down, forwards, sometimes even backwards.

'There's no dominant male,' Jo whispered.

'I can't see him. I can't see him!' George wailed.

A figure of a well-built man came up beside him. It was Dr Stevenson. He turned to George and said, 'Can't see who?'

'Charlie! I can't see Charlie.' Involuntarily, George tapped his own head, and looked into Dr Stevenson's perturbed face. 'You know him, don't you? He's...'

'...what?' He's what?' Dr Stevenson's eyes implored George's for an answer.

Chris and Jo quickly guided George away, trying to show they were caring for an invalid. George's face went knotted purple, contorted with rage. 'I know it's him!' he shouted. 'He's my boy, Charlie boy. The screws, the titanium...all my own work!'

Dr Stevenson followed them. When they reached the Rover, George was swiftly pushed onto the back seat. Dr Stevenson hit the rear windows. 'Tell me! You can tell me,' he shouted through the glass, his face a picture of bafflement and fear. Chris accelerated hard.

There was not just consternation at the exit gates. From within the ape centre came a mighty climax of pant-hoots, shrieks, and primitive howls – a cacophony, an animal bedlam – as from a time 'when fishes flew and forests walked'. Chris was thinking as he drove away from the ape centre, 'Why were they making such a furious noise? Were they talking about Charlie? Surely that wouldn't, couldn't be possible?'

FORTY-EIGHT

With a determination that could only be described as resolute, Charlie headed to town. He had no idea of course where he was going other than that something drew him southwards, towards the coast, down the valley, to the sea – the place where the stream at its mouth found the bay. He had no knowledge or recollection of the sea except distant vistas glimpsed from the oaks at the end of George's garden.

He recognised water but what was the sea, what it was made of, having never known the bays, the sandy coves below Mount Cameroon, like Ambas Bay where huge breakers roll in over landlocked, rocky islands, and where monitor lizards search for prey (if not caught by traders, sold online) because he was not born near the coast but in the forests of Takamanda.

By the cunning he had learnt from the forest, Charlie moved ever southwards. He missed nothing. Just as he followed the valley to the sea, he saw skeins of ducks racing inland, following the valley northwards. There were trees and more trees, none that he knew.

He could still hide from people in undergrowth, from cyclists, walkers, lovers. Soon he passed the spongy, bulbous trunks of dawn redwoods, a tree that was thought extinct, and known only as a fossil, until discovered growing in China in 1941. Later there was a memorial to death, to human death, of no account to him. He reached changes in the path, a pergola, the noise of people and cars growing in his ears.

He decided to break cover. A café had set out tables and chairs, a stretch of greenery offered safety, a group of Africans singing, dancing, and drumming had attracted a crowd. He slipped by as one dancer moved to the front, swaying her grass-skirted hips like a girl beneath a coconut palm, working hard for a Yankee dollar.

Then he burst through into the lower gardens past pillars of palms, the stream flowing nearby, and a large balloon-like object tethered to the ground by steel stays.

Charlie kept going until he reached the next tree line on his left. After pounding through the pines, he found himself in a maze of cages where bright birds squawked, taunting him with their gaudy colours, trapped, contained, with nothing better to pass the time than gossip, as birds do. A horrendous screeching and screaming greeted the great ape, suddenly confronted with creatures, some of them at least, whose existence he was familiar with, like the African grey parrot.

Charlie bounded towards the nearest cage. It was full of silly budgerigars, showy cockatoos, and drab female pheasants pecking the stale leaf litter. One African grey saw him, inclined its head, and kept repeating the same two words. 'STUFF IT, STUFF IT', followed by, 'STUFF THE BLOODY LOT!'

Even Charlie was aghast, and not understanding a word. He stretched out his arms as if embracing the cage in a vision of primate horror, a mock-predation through the wire mesh. The birds screamed themselves silly. They hated it. Then Charlie screamed too, a deep anthropoidal roar, a wild primordial scream of the dark forest, the gnawing vastness, as if he feared nothing. All the birds fell silent. Charlie grunted, satisfied, and moved on.

Despite his fearlessness, he had already been marked. There had been copious sightings of a black, furry wraith, who moved with incredible daring, among the garbage and the flowers, the pine trees and shrubs.

Still he roamed freely, either not noticed, or dismissed as a phantom by unseeing eyes, a spectre amid the pines, behind Purbeck stone blocks, a wraith in the rockeries, elusive. The urge to vocalise was strong but the need to escape was stronger; not to be confined but free, as he had been in the African bush.

That day Charlie took another risk. He crossed a road silently like a padded apparition, although you could hear the noise from the seafront – the pier, the promenade, the side shows and fun fair rides – a mixture of music from the rides and cries of joy from the beach. Then he plunged over a wire fence to the sanctuary of the cliff top, densely covered in shrubbery, wild sweet pea vines, gorse and stunted trees. The sweet pea blooms were a soft rosy pink backdrop to the blue of sky and sea.

After climbing up and along the cliff face, hidden from view, eating sweet blackberries on the way, he found somewhere to rest and sleep.

*

In her corner of the lounge, Helga stirred in her sleep. Night was falling and even though the wind had dropped a little, the leaves of a white poplar by the garage shimmered, as if tousled by invisible hands. She woke with a start. She moved to the kitchen door and barked. Dr Waldren came in. 'Quiet girl now. What is it?' he asked.

Helga turned her face to him and whined plaintively, her way of saying she wanted to go outside. The doctor opened the kitchen door, and let Helga out. She raced ahead and did something of a handbrake turn, managing to shoot forwards from the kitchen door and veer to the right. She went straight for the garage doors. Once there, her head went up, that is her head arched in the manner of wolves. There followed from her a howl such as no one wants to hear – long-drawn out, mournful. The doctor questioned if it was a song of loss or happiness. Wolves howl not just when they are sad but also when happy.

It was then Dr Waldren realised Helga was not barking at strangers, or a cat, or some nameless wraith. Helga's howl was about Charlie, and the garage where he had lived was the connection. To test his theory, Dr Waldren unlocked the garage doors. Helga bounded in, ran to the empty cage, sniffed the bars, and then howled again. She sat down by the bars, and whined sadly, her head resting over her front paws, eyes staring worriedly ahead.

*

Chris had taken Jo into town the day after. They decided to visit an art gallery near the cliff top. They entered a great room with a long dining table, with places set for diners, as it might have been in Victorian times. In another room they were dazzled by nymphs on the ceiling in a blue sky, a painting of a wood nymph by a stream in another, and upstairs a naked 'Shiva slave'. There were many more rooms filled with treasures. In another was a bed. Chris lay on it.

'They'll throw you out.' Jo looked worried. 'An old lady probably died in it.'

'I was thinking of Charlie, if he came here. He could bang his cutlery in the dining room, on that table, and sleep in this bed for free. Wake to that view behind the blinds, the curving bay, the headland. Not much of a life really,' he sighed. He got up from the bed to tweak the bedroom blinds, to look through them. There was a garden below with a red-painted Japanese bridge, rose arches, and statues of Roman gods.

Just then a black form flitted across the end of the garden. Chris rubbed his eyes, and looked again. He tore back the blinds and forced open a window. He called out, 'Charlie! Charlie!'

Jo ran to the window, her heart fluttering at the expectation and pure joy of seeing Charlie again.

'It was nothing, I guess,' Chris said. 'It moved so fast, whatever it was, I had no time to see.' He lay back on the bed, the window still wide open. Jo slumped into a chair.

Into the silence of the room drifted the sounds of people on the beach, and in a reverie of sorts Chris listened to the background hum of noise, the human vocalisations in their hundreds, if not thousands, all calling to each other, communicating, expressing a myriad of gestures and feelings. Then he heard it, above the chatter and din from the beach and the fun fair by the pier, a unique long drawn out greeting call from about one hundred or so yards away, in the pine trees of the pleasure gardens. *Hoo, hoo, hoo!*

*

Dan Holder drove into town. Matt was tied up at the ape centre, along with Natalie. He parked the Land Rover. It was a short walk to the centre. He was more interested in the long, green valley that snaked up the ornamental gardens a couple of miles inland. If the chimp was to hide successfully, he would need space, trees, and not too many people. The trail he followed, however, was already cold. It was only later in the day that he thought of turning round, going towards the sea instead, in a peculiar kind of reverse logic. Where there were more people, though the risks would be greater, there would be more food to scavenge.

*

Chris and Jo rushed from the building, ran down a hill, and turned right into a car park. They crossed a road, and were soon in amongst stands of pine trees. There was another open stretch by a fountain, and then more pines and rockery gardens. They passed near the caged squawking birds until they saw below them the stream on its way to the sea, and in a Victorian bandstand, a small group of musicians. The music was fairly typical: loud, sprightly, almost jingoistic.

Chris noticed the red and blue balloon moored further up the gardens. It was a helium-filled tourist attraction, 6,000 cubic feet of helium, used to take flyers in a suspended gondola five hundred feet above the town.

'I'm going up in that,' Chris said, excitedly.

'Why? You silly boy.'

'Because of what I'll see from up there! The whole town laid out before me. If luck is with me, I might find Charlie!'

Jo smiled. 'Trying to see Charlie from up there is hardly practical. You might as well hunt a gadfly or the snark. You couldn't catch him anyway.'

'Oh sod it! I'm going.' He set off towards a kiosk to buy a ticket while Jo's eyes searched the pine banks. She felt more and more helpless. She worried about George back at home, too. It seemed as if they were doing everything wrong. Their plan, well, she said to herself, there is no plan. If it all goes wrong and Charlie plays up, he'll probably be killed, shot on sight. How could they ever save him?

A red admiral butterfly landed briefly on her hand. She saw its perfectly symmetrical wings, the orange and white markings on the forewings, the two slender antennae erect, and she thought of the fragility of life, and yet the strength within it.

Her mobile rang. It was Alice. She said her father was in the garden on his electric wheelchair. He wouldn't stop driving it, round and round the oak trees at the end of their garden.

'I'll come as soon as I can,' Jo said.

FORTY-NINE

Chris Grailing climbed aboard the gondola, refreshing himself with the pure sea air, breathing in deeply, keen to get aloft. There were eight other people, clutching the metal handrail. Then a man who was the 'pilot' locked the twin gates, ready for takeoff. A recorded voice droned on with facts and features of the forthcoming flight. He could still hear the colourful singing, and the deep drums of the African band, as well as people cheering and clapping from time to time.

After a few minutes he realised how absurd his idea was about looking for an ape from a balloon. But it was too late to get off. There were hundreds of people strolling through the gardens, trees, bushes, buildings, hiding places – how was he going to spot a single chimpanzee? The gondola bumped a little, it was going up.

'Christ almighty!' Chris covered his mouth with his hands in astonishment. 'Stone the flipping crows!' Some of the female fliers uttered short gasps.

Bounding from the tree line came a dark creature, possessed it seemed of terrifying speed. It was coming straight at the balloon.

Chris strained against the guardrails. The gondola was lifting. Still the black-brown apparition came hurtling towards them.

'Oh my dear God,' Chris whispered. Then he shouted, 'Charlie!'

The creature that was Charlie crossed the divide between them with one giant leap, easily gripping the padded rail above the gondola's cage. Chris looked up to see Charlie's dark, brown-yellow eyes staring at him through the mesh of the cage. He stared back. How strange. Humans inside, the chimp outside; humans caged and safe, the ape free but perilously placed with just his strong grip between life and death. The balloon had already risen 50 feet or so above the ground.

'How on earth did you find *me*?' Chris uttered the words in astonishment. Whether it was his clothes, a familiar scent or smell, or pure chance, he would never know. Charlie pant-hooted but he held on, glancing down but his eyes always coming back to Chris. The pilot had already stopped the ascent but it was taking a few seconds for the braking system to work. The recorded voice kept talking, pointing out views and historic landmarks. Chris glanced north, seeing the green valley, and then south to the sea.

He began to feel dizzy. He looked up at Charlie. He seemed a strong as ever, even as if he were enjoying the ride. Occasionally one of the women fliers would scream briefly until silenced by one from Charlie.

'The mother church of the town,' the voice continued, 'is to your right, in the east, the spire reaches 202 feet. Mary Shelley is buried there…along with the heart of the poet Shelley.'

'*Cor Cordium!*' Chris exclaimed. 'I must tell George.'

'We're going down!' shouted the pilot. The descent was too rapid, the onboard computer overridden by an emergency system. However, back-up braking was soon triggered. Once more balloon and gondola felt safer, if not quite becalmed.

Chris was still dizzy, his mind making up images that seemed to flash past him with no sense or reality. Charlie was like some strange albatross of the skies, clinging to the balloon's shrouds. The balloon had caught not a great bird of the sea but an ape of the jungle. Would it drag him through bitter gulfs, bringing him to the deck, which was the Earth?

Yes, Charlie would be teased and taunted, if he were caught. They would mimic and mock him too, this once king of his jungle, and laugh at him. Like the giant bird, though he scorns the bows and arrows of captivity, he would be powerless in the nets of his shouting capturers.

'Oh Charlie,' Chris said softly to him. 'Just hang on tight!'

*

Dan Holder had all but given up the search. Perhaps it was time to call 'the authorities', who would probably call the ape centre for advice anyway. Whether to use guns or tranquilliser darts – if there was any immediate threat of harm to the public, which was highly likely, the ape would be shot dead. Matt phoned with news of press interest, and more sightings of the chimp in the town centre. He returned to the parked Land Rover.

On the way to town, he saw the great billowing balloon plummeting, and swerved to avoid a woman in the road. It was Jo. She looked anguished. 'Sorry, I wasn't looking,' she explained. 'If you must know I'm looking for an animal.'

'Don't tell me – it's a chimpanzee.'

'Yes! He's a brute and a gentle hero.' She decided she liked him, enough to trust him. 'I'm here with a friend. We're trying to find the chimp. That one on the news! We call him Charlie. There are things I can tell you about him when there's time, just not now.'

Dan nodded his agreement. He saw the balloon about to land. They couldn't help watching, though the Land Rover was partly blocking the road. It was only for buses and taxis. He hadn't noticed. The African band was still playing. Three drummers brought the sounds of Africa to the seaside town, but conveyed no messages to the listeners, as they do in some African villages and in the bush.

*

The balloon landed safely. The pilot told everyone to stay where they were but Chris had other plans. He lunged at one of the two metal gates, swiftly unbolting it. He stepped out, turning back to look up at Charlie. Women screamed lustily. A cheer went up from the gathering crowd. Whether because the balloon hadn't crashed or the chimpanzee was unharmed, Chris neither knew nor cared. He stretched out his right arm. 'Come, Charlie. Come with me!'

Charlie grabbed his arm, swung round, and held on to Chris's left arm instead. Chris had no idea which way to go but the crowds on the main path made way for them, so they headed north. They were a curious pair, Chris urging Charlie on and Charlie gesturing repeatedly with his left arm, touching his head and chest again and again.

There was a lump in Jo's throat when she saw them coming.

What did they remind her of? They weren't exactly running, more like hobbling upright, supporting each other – glimpses, she thought, of *Midnight Cowboy* or *Rain Man*. A line drawn somewhere between 'Ratso' Rizzo and Raymond Babbitt.

They came up a slight incline on the path, past ten pillars of palm, five on each side. The more Charlie grunted and pant-hooted, the more space was made for them. Jo heard police sirens getting closer.

'That's him!' she said, panting with excitement.

Three or four taxi drivers were becoming impatient. Dan said, 'We'll have to move soon.'

'You *have* to wait! That's the most remarkable ape ever.' Despite protesting drivers caught up by the Land Rover, Jo jumped down in the middle of the road. 'Here Charlie, Chris!' she shouted.

Chris didn't hesitate. He clambered into the back, grateful for the slight feeling of protection from the canvas hood. Charlie manhandled his way aboard with gusto. 'Okay,' Chris yelled. '*Go go go!*'

The Land Rover bucked into life like an aged bronco. Dan's right foot pressed on the accelerator as if pressing on a deadly insect he wanted to obliterate. Luckily people scattered in time. The Land Rover lurched several times, and Charlie was thrown sprawling onto Chris, who didn't seem to mind. Charlie said, '*Hoo, hoo,*' which was a good sign, as if to tell Chris not to worry.

Dan pushed the old beast up a steep hill. Chris pulled back a canvas flap. He told Jo and Dan to head straight for George's, not to stop for anything or anyone.

Meanwhile, Charlie had slid towards the tailgate. He stood up in the back, a little bent. He waved one arm wildly in the air like a bronco rider. Some people saw the chimp, a swagger-figure in the back, an easy rider. To some he must have looked a demonic adventurer, with his defiant gold-brown eyes and shaggy limbs.

Whether Charlie had sensed or glimpsed a vision of freedom, no one could have known. But Charlie once again strode his cramped stage with more than a hint of triumph, perhaps even a sense of victory. He pant-hooted to a screaming climax, his feet drumming on the floor of the Land Rover for added effect. His was the roar and the song, the holler of the alpha male, the prodigal coming home, and no one could stop him.

FIFTY

Alice and John had cornered George by the oak trees, whereupon he abruptly ended the game. He managed to stand up. He kicked his wheelchair hard. 'I don't need the damn thing anyway,' he said.

'Let me help you, Dad,' Alice said. He lent on her for support. Helga began to bark, suppressing growls only with difficulty.

'You hear her?' asked George querulously. 'That dog has a sixth sense. It won't be long now.'

'Long, Dad?' Alice's brow furrowed as she led George back to the house.

'That's right, my girl. Not long now.'

Alice said, 'I don't understand.'

'I can tell you in riddles,' said George with a chortle. 'You see, this old brain of mine, it's still working, isn't it?'

'Yes it is but go on, Dad. Please.'

'A Japanese poet who flourished more than three hundred years ago. His name was Matsuo Basho. He said a few things worth remembering. D'you know the one about the bell?'

Alice said, 'No, Dad. I don't.'

George said, '"The temple bell stops but I still hear the sound coming out of the flowers." Reverberating, like drums resonating. I don't really know what he meant but sometimes you hear echoes from the past. I know that's what will happen to Charlie.'

'Charlie's not here any more, Dad, is he?' Alice helped George to his favourite chair.

'He is near, that's all I'll say. He's already made ripples in the world, not too many yet, but Charlie will strike a drum in people's hearts, you know. Perhaps I should say a chord, but the sound, Alice, will go on and on, reverberating, long after I am gone.

'Take the instance of…Helga, do be quiet!'

The dog had taken off round the room like a crazed rabbit, a canine torpedo loosed. Suddenly, Helga herself stopped in mid-flight. Alice held her breath. George's head went up, as if straining to hear something.

First, there was the sound of screeching tyres, a pounding, dull noise from the road. Then a high-pitched scream that got worse the closer it came, followed by squealing brakes and crashing gears.

'What is that roistering?' George demanded.

Dan's Land Rover careered into the driveway, grinding over a corner post.

George led the charge, although he was quickly overtaken, and almost felled, by Helga. Alice and John were more wary, and hung back. George stood in the driveway, walking stick held aloft. The Land Rover had stopped just in front of him. Chris and Charlie leapt out together, Jo tumbled to the tarmac.

Dan leaned his head out of the side window. 'I need to hide this fast. Can you help me? Any room in there,' he shouted, pointing to the garage.

'No, it's full.' As soon as he saw Charlie, George's posture stiffened, as if he gained an inch in height. '*My boy Charlie!* Oh, filial tender! Little body with a mighty heart. My lambkin, imp – no, chimp – of fame!'

Dan seemed not to hear the remark about the garage. 'Open the doors,' he yelled. 'Open the bloody doors!'

John ran to pull them open. Dan accelerated hard, thrusting the Land Rover forward. He saw the metal bars of Charlie's cage and decided they would be no match for four-wheel drive.

Normally sensible, the pressure was telling on him. He rammed the Land Rover into the garage, neatly crushing Charlie's cage. It folded up into a tangle at the back of the garage.

'That was Charlie's home, for God's sake,' George cried. 'Did you have to?'

Dan looked sheepish for the first time. 'I just panicked,' he said.

George said, 'Close the garage doors anyway. I don't want Charlie to see.' He coughed, feeling a dull pain in one arm. 'Shall we all go inside for tea?'

A strange mammalian group went into the house – six human primates, one non-human primate, and a dog. To everyone's surprise, Charlie led the way into the kitchen. He paused, as if scouting around for food, and then loped towards George's chair in the dining room. He sat down with his legs stretched out, perhaps copying George's usual posture. He placed an arm on each corner as if about to chair a meeting. The small group was eyeing the great ape closely, none more so than Helga.

George was forced to sit elsewhere. 'I think he probably knows the word "tea" by now,' he said with quiet satisfaction.

Jo agreed. She motioned to Dan to grab somewhere to sit. 'I'll make some now.' Alice helped her.

'Shush!' George said to silence any conversation. 'Let's keep calm, no staring at Charlie, let's wait for the tea to come.'

'You know, George, Shelley's heart, the ashes, they're in the town.' Chris kept his voice low.

'What else did you discover?' George asked. 'Seems to me you came back with the goods.'

'Charlie found me, the clever ape. I think he just wanted to go home. You can see how much he loves it here. Anyone would think that's *his* chair.'

Jo and Alice came in with two trays, mugs, and a large teapot. John got up to help his mother and sister. Jo also brought some bananas. She cut them in half. 'We're all going to have tea, including Charlie. I think it's best we eat the bananas together, as if we're sharing in a group, so to speak.' She brushed her hair back as if seeking grooming reassurance.

While they drank their tea, and Charlie munched on a banana, slurping his tea like an old hand, Chris began to explain to Dan why he must keep a secret, as if his life depended on it. Dan was shocked, of course, to learn that the relaxed creature in the room, the great ape known as Charlie, might not be altogether ape, but consisting of parts, most belonging to the apes but a significant part human. He would be sworn to secrecy before the afternoon was out.

Throughout the intense conversation that followed, Charlie made no sound. He groomed himself from time to time, as if trying to remain detached, yet still a member of the group.

George put down his mug with an air of finality. 'This is it,' he said. 'Charlie has to go home, you know, he cannot be appreciated here for what he really is. He needs the freedom, of his own dear country, the land of his birth. Remember,

Breathes there the man, with soul so dead, who ne'er to himself hath said, 'This is my own, my native land!'

I say breathes there the ape who has not longed for canopied galleries, the open road, for life among his own countrymen?' George was evidently overcome with emotion.

Charlie snuffled in his chair, as if bizarrely in agreement.

Chris threw down a challenge. 'Countrymen? Isn't that a bit rich? For an ape? Even with his pedigree?'

'Of course, of course!' George responded quickly. 'I know, I'm off the mark. But who are his countrymen now? I say, we send Charlie back, to the great forests of Takamanda. Let him roam free. We must pick him up, lift him from the worm-holes of forgotten days!'

George rose to his feet. 'Let him have not oaks as in this garden but his own giants, mighty lords of high plateaus and coastal forests, my liege Charlie, Mountjoy of an oak, in the form of an ape!'

Jo was laughing. She explained to Dan that sometimes George could be 'theatrical'.

Chris said, 'You're right, George. If he stays here, he'll just be a curiosity. In order for Charlie to find himself, he needs the challenge of making his own life. Somehow we have to find a way of sending him home, to be repatriated, if you like.'

In reply, George said he thought there was a way. In the meantime, a 'family' celebration was called for, at least when Chris began searching for a whisky bottle, that was the general assumption.

The six humans drank several tots of whisky each while Helga and Charlie looked on. They raised their glasses, toasted the safe return of Charlie, and they drank to his future.

FIFTY-ONE

The next morning George was busy phoning and emailing. He was looking at ways to send Charlie home. It might mean bribing a few officials along the way but had to be worth doing. His quarry was finding an old cargo ship still running between Liverpool and Cameroon. Sometimes old coasters went up the Bonny River to Port Harcourt, Nigeria and thence on to Limbe port in Cameroon, once known as Victoria. There was one old sea dog of a captain who might help, if he hadn't already retired.

George was thrilled to receive a reply the same day. It read:

> *Hello George,*
> *Good to hear from you, my old son. I'm still with the company for my sins, sailing out of Liverpool to Apapa and sometimes on to Limbe in Cameroon. Business is not what it was, plenty of room. We still take up to 12 passengers. The cargo you mention is an odd one. You'll have to clear it with the port agents, with appropriate dash, of course, to help things along.*
> *Let me know*
> *Tom McDonald*

Chris came in to the office cum operating room. 'What's the plan?' he asked expectantly.

George pushed back his chair. 'I think I can get Charlie on a boat – a cargo ship, MV *Tarkwon* out of Dundee, gross tonnage 7,416, and 498 feet long, 59.3 wide. She's a cast-off from Elder Dempster Lines, one of the old banana boats. Used to ply up and down the coast. She'll do.'

'You know someone?'

'He's been in the Merchant Navy since I can remember.'

'There's a law governing the transport of chimps from their native countries – the CITES convention, on international trade in endangered species. It might not apply the other way.'

'I don't care if it does or doesn't but you're right. Perhaps they didn't imagine a great ape, sent back.'

Chris stared hard at George. 'I'll go,' he said. 'Send me. With the rest of that money you promised. I'll take care of him.'

George thought hard, placing both hands on his desk. 'He is special cargo, you know. Tell me why you think it's best for him, to go back. Suppose he's so valuable we shouldn't lose sight of him. Doesn't he need our protection?'

Chris considered their options, trying to remain objective. 'He stays here, we can learn more. However, he's something of a freak not of nature but of our doing. Remember what happened to the Elephant Man? Not a particularly apt analogy to be sure but to be considered nonetheless. What is in *his* best interests? As doctors we're always asking that question.'

George coughed. He felt the same pain as the day before, a dull ache in one arm. 'I grant you, he's more ape than human. We can't speculate about the future, development in his mentation, at least for now. My view is that we send him back to a more natural life, and to put it bluntly, see if he can make a go of it. Without risk, there is no progress.'

Jo came in. George turned to her, and said, 'Jo, meet Dr Livingstone. Do you want to go to Africa?'

Jo's lower lip trembled. 'Did you mean that, George?'

'Of course. Chris needs someone to help him take Charlie back. You can go on a cargo ship, Liverpool to Limbe. Then fly back if you want to.'

For several seconds Jo held a picture in her mind, of days at sea passing one by one. When they'd got past the Bay of Biscay, it would be calmer, such a change from the demands of the surgery. There would be mangrove lagoons and swamps and palm-fringed, surf-washed, white beaches...

'How long does it take to get there?'

'Imagine 30 days' full board, meals on the captain's table.'

'What about Charlie? How's he going to travel?' Jo worried in case this was another of George's pipe dreams. She knew the ape would never be allowed in a cabin.

'All taken care of,' said George proudly. 'Well, it will be if my captain friend Tom successfully smuggles him aboard. I've been reading up on how chimps used to be sent back here. I found this piece in a book by Sir Richard Burton. Shall I read it to you?'

Chris and Jo nodded vigorously.

George pulled up a page onscreen and began to read.

> *Perhaps the best way to send home so delicate an animal would be to keep it for a time in its native forest; to accustom it to boiled plantains, rice, and messes of grain; and to ship it during the fine season, having previously fitted up a cabin near the engine-room, where the mercury should never fall below 70° (Fahr.). In order to escape nostalgia and melancholy, which are sure to be fatal, the emigrant should be valeted by a faithful and attached native.*

'You will be the faithful, attached natives,' quipped George, smiling broadly. 'For "cabin" read "cage". I don't see why Charlie can't be accommodated on deck somewhere, in a cage that can be covered up from prying eyes.'

'I wonder how his mental state might change on the voyage. He's not being taken away from his home, he's going back. For nostalgia, read happiness?' When nothing more was said, Chris continued, 'We're going, George, and we won't look back.'

'Hadn't we better check on the passenger?' Jo queried.

They left George's office and went straight to the dining-room, where Charlie had another makeshift bed. He made a greeting call but it seemed his attention was directed outside to the garden. They let Charlie out and hoped the neighbours wouldn't notice. He went straight towards the single apple tree, swung up to the first canopy of branches in one easy movement. He grabbed an apple and ate it, sweet juice trickling down his chin.

There was an air of seasonal change; it was warm but the sun no longer had the same power of heat. It was like the end of summer, going back to school, a new term. Alice and John would leave the same night. Dan Holder had to return to work. He said he'd leave the Land Rover where it was for the time being, until the fuss died down.

George prevailed on him to speak to those he knew at the ape centre, especially Dr Stevenson and Matt. He didn't expect the vet to stay quiet for ever, just enough time to get Charlie safely out of the country. There was a sailing, he said, in late September, getting nearer to the dry season, which began in November.

Once again Charlie climbed to the top of the oak trees at the back of the garden. George guessed the ape sensed something, a change coming. He soon descended to one low branch just above George's head where he rested.

George spoke up to him. 'Charlie boy, you have a job to do. Steel your heart and be brave.'

Charlie began to make soft '*Hoo, hoo*' sounds as if in a state of delight and appreciation.

'Time to test the noble sinews of your new powers, my liege Charlie! My puissant ape whose veins run with new strength, are you not ripe for exploits, and mighty adventures?

'You're going into that bosky heaven – that bosky wild. Of what do I speak I hear you say; I speak of Africa and golden joys. So go on this tide, ebb back to the sea and be carried home.'

Tears were streaming down George's cheeks. Chris and Jo, Alice, John and Dan were all watching, in silence.

George picked up a stick and held it above Charlie's shoulder. For one silly moment Chris thought George was about to dub the ape knight, but George withdrew the stick, and with it made a sweeping bow. Not looking directly at Charlie, but looking down at the grass he said, 'Not for you the idleness of apes! Mere jesting monkeys! No canopy of costly slate, but green canopies of trees in great forests, their branches, leaves, over your horizon spreading. You will touch the wings of greatness, Charlie. Go well, my boy.'

The emotional strain must have got to George because moments later he staggered back to the step outside the French windows. Down from the tree, Charlie followed. The polytunnel had long since gone, leaving more room on the patio.

Jo brought out more tea. 'You two look like good old friends,' she said. They were sitting side by side on the step, shoulder to shoulder.

*

In the days that followed into and through September, Charlie and George often spent time together in this way. Sometimes Charlie rested an arm on George, and sometimes it was the other way round. Charlie nattered to himself or pursed his lips, and pouted. He groomed George from time to time, stroked his face, and was fascinated by his balding head. An observer would be sure that shared communication between them was a palpable fact.

It was all falling into place. Jo and Chris packed in earnest, got some vaccinations, applied for visas. George assured them he would bribe half the coast of West Africa no matter the cost if it meant Charlie would get home.

Over a last mug of tea, George gave out his instructions, where to take Charlie, who to hand him to, names to contact such as port agents, and a safe house in Limbe at a place called Bota. Then there were contact details for a forest guard to be met at Kumba, and a forestry officer in Mamfe. They would also meet the chief medical officer in Mamfe who had agreed to hand over essential medical supplies. Finally, they were to pick up two 'small boys' from the Limbe Wildlife Centre, John Embai and Smoky Joe. They would accompany them to the bush beyond Mamfe, to the fabled land of Takamanda. Where Charlie was to be taken would only be known when they left Mamfe. George left the location details of Charlie's release into the wild in a sealed brown envelope.

So it was that one morning in late September (first flagged by Helga's excitability several days beforehand) a small convoy left

Dr Waldren's at 4.00 a.m., bound for Liverpool docks. Chris had hired two short wheelbase vans, one for their luggage, driven by Jo, and one for Charlie. George waved them off in the driveway, Helga in his arms whining.

Charlie couldn't see him from the back of the van but just before leaving George had hugged the great ape. Charlie in turn embraced George, pressing his open mouth against the top of his balding head.

As the vans turned into the road, George walked to the end of the driveway. He stood like a lonely sentinel, an old man getting to the end of life, sending out his new experiment into the world. He was illumined in the road by the moon, star points in the night sky, and two streetlamps. He felt a lump in his throat. As he turned back, when the vans sped from sight, he clung tightly to Helga. He felt himself shiver, not because of the cold but some other delight, an anticipatory keenness, a premonition of good things to come, and he said quietly into the cool night air, 'Now it begins!'

PART II
GOODBYE CHARLIE, AND GOOD LUCK

FIFTY-TWO

Tom McDonald welcomed Chris and Jo on board. A big man with a white beard, flinty eyes and a weathered smile, he shook hands as if he meant it. A crane lifted a square-shaped wooden box into one of the cargo holds. Later it would be transferred onto an upper deck, within sight of the captain's bridge. This was to be the ape's new home for a month of sailing.

Later that night MV *Tarkwon* weighed anchor, and slipped out of Liverpool docks, the long blast of its horn reverberating, making the old ship's timbers shiver and creak.

Life at sea acquired a routine all its own. Wake early, shower, breakfast, followed by a stroll on deck. Check Charlie, feed and water. Lunch at the captain's table, a rest after lunch, then afternoon tea brought by a white-suited African steward. Another check on Charlie towards the evening, then drinks from the tiny bar, followed by a three-course dinner with the ship's officers at the captain's table, or another table next to it.

There was little to do during the day except make plans for the expedition from Limbe to Mamfe and from there into the bush. All day long the ship churned through the steely seas and followed the stars by night. One day Chris was asked by the captain to read a lesson in front of crew and passengers at a Sunday service, and for the closing hymn they all sang, '*For those in Peril on the Sea*'.

The ship's purser kept an eye on Chris's slate at the bar. It had burgeoned since he had struck up a friendship with the ship's surgeon or doctor, a single man in his fifties who smoked untipped 'Senior Service', and who was usually drunk by midday.

Chris nearly slipped into his old habits, sharing rounds with the ship's doctor who liked a cigarette burning in his left hand, a bottle of Scotch in his right. His speech slurred by late afternoon as they stumbled to stay upright when the sea was heavy.

Just as Jo had surmised, their passage smoothed after the Bay of Biscay. Leisurely they made their way around the coast of West Africa, the ship's top speed of 13.5 knots rarely being achieved. Occasionally flying fish or dolphins ranged alongside. Once a submarine surfaced, remaining on the surface for an hour before diving. Names of ports were posted outside the purser's office: Dakar, Conakry, Freetown, Monrovia, Abidjan, Takoradi, Tema, Lagos, Port Harcourt, and Limbe.

Under arc lights, cargoes were offloaded and winched aboard through the night at Freetown and Takoradi. Gangs of stevedores running with sweat swarmed over bales of oil seeds, nuts and kernels, cocoa and coffee, crates of bananas, and aluminium. The noise of trade and commerce, the cranes, gantries, the crew and the gangs of dock workers rang out in the stifling, humid night.

They sailed up the Bonny River to Port Harcourt. Chris and Jo watched natives riding on precarious boats and canoes, willing to trade fruit and fish with anyone. The banks of the Bonny were crammed with the tangled, twisted roots of mangrove trees. After the brief exchange of more cargo, the next stop was Limbe.

Chris was allowed to bring Charlie out on a lead for exercise if the weather was good. Most days they sat together, as Charlie had with George, and just watched the sea passing. The closer they moved towards the tropical coastline, the more Charlie's lips would curl up, and his nose wrinkle. His pelage now had the warmth of the tropics and Chris noticed it shone with health. He wondered what Charlie sensed in the ozone clarity of the humid air. By night he would have seen the starry points of light as though someone had scraped away cataracts from his eyes.

He watched Charlie grasp the deck rail, and saw how the great ape nearly always faced the same way, towards the distant shoreline on the port side.

Jo came to see Charlie when they were on their way to Limbe. The ape shuffled up against her, embracing her with open arms. She followed Charlie's gaze to the far horizon. The massive bulk of Mount Cameroon loomed, rising over 4,000 metres from the south Atlantic sea on the Cameroon coast. It rose from surf-washed plinths of volcanic rock on the seaward side, clad in moist, tropical rainforest, its summit bare, windswept, and occasionally swept by snow.

'It was first seen by Hanno, a Carthaginian navigator in the fifth century BC,' said Chris. 'It's active too, sometimes you get lava flows cutting off roads or ending up in the sea.'

'Isn't it one of the wettest places on Earth?' Jo asked.

'Over 400 inches a year at Debundscha, a village on the coast.'

Jo couldn't care less about the rain. The tropics had enveloped her in sensuous warmth, even at night she felt caressed by the heat.

Chris was anxious to put Charlie back in his cage, and join the doctor by the hatch that also served as a bar. He was near the ship's prow. Suddenly, he jumped onto a capstan and, finding himself able to stand, addressed the gusting wind. 'O wild tropic wind! Convey this cargo home, to palm-fringed shores, this darling ape that carries our hopes and dreams.'

Jo hugged Charlie who seemed for once slightly frightened by Chris's theatrical posturing.

'They say paley flames issue from the mountain's heart. Think, the same pale flames live in Charlie's heart and creative fire in his brain. Speed him on, equatorial winds, and tell the proud people of Cameroon, "Accept this great ape, dash extraordinaire, the gift of gods and surgeon George, to your dear homeland."'

Chris strained his eyes, as did Jo and Charlie, to see beyond the waves to the land of Cameroon but it was too distant, though the Mountain of Greatness, *Mongo ma Ndemi*, towered into the sky.

*

At home George fumbled at his keyboard. He wanted to send an email. Although Jo and Chris had agreed to keep in touch, he was anxious to know how Charlie would stand up to the voyage. Winter was coming. He wanted so much to learn that Charlie had made the journey and survived. 'The white man's grave,' he said to himself, 'those days have gone.' He paused. 'Except for white farmers in Zimbabwe. Today it's the black man's grave too, because of AIDS.'

George knew that, although chimps have their own version of HIV, known as SIV (simian immunodeficiency virus), the origin of the HIV virus that plagues humans has been genetically traced to nonhuman primates – wild chimpanzees from Southern Cameroon, near the Sanaga River.

'At least it was the central chimpanzee, the subspecies *Pan troglodytes troglodytes*,' he muttered, 'and not *vellerosus*. I mean *ellioti*.'

He tried to remember the email instructions Jo had given him. Emails from friends and relatives sent to the vessel's email address were transmitted free of charge to the passenger/recipient. No attachments allowed. The use of email, fax and phone was at the Master's or Captain's discretion.

George sent the message. It was a simple one, typed in capitals.

M.V. TARKWON – TO DR CHRIS GRAILING SAILING LIVERPOOL – LIMBE
PLEASE ADVISE CURRENT STATE OF PLAY WITH CARGO AND TIME OF ARRIVAL LIMBE.
ALL THE BEST
GEORGE

*

Captain Tom McDonald came on deck with George's email. 'The old boy's still alive, I see,' he said, handing the message to Chris.

For a moment, Chris thought he must have meant Charlie but then the captain said, 'When I first met George I thought, there's a man. They'll either hang him or he'll die famous.'

A grin lit up Chris's face. 'It was either him or me,' he said. 'When do we arrive at Limbe?'

'About seven hours' sailing time. You should be ashore by 6.00 p.m. or thereabouts. I want you to get that creature inside his cage. Have you got any way of keeping him quiet? We're going to have a visit later from the port agent. There shouldn't be too much of a problem if George got things right.' The captain smiled wryly.

'You'll be taken ashore by lighter. Bota? Is that right?'

'Yes,' Jo said suddenly. 'Bota.'

There was an odd calmness on board. The ship made her way, a good wind and her engines carried her, with no need of a guiding albatross. The crew were mostly unseen, below deck, each with a job to do.

'Come Charlie,' Jo said. 'You'll have to go back in your cage.' The ape moved, pulling so slightly against his lead that it seemed no one would notice. Before she knew what was happening, Jo was being hauled along by Charlie.

He pant-grunted softly but as he moved closer to the ship's port rail the pant-grunts became pant-hoots, growing in intensity. Soon enough Charlie gripped the rail, standing bipedally, screaming in full-throated voice. His body turned towards the coast ahead.

'Christ, he wants to get there badly, doesn't he?' Alarmed, Chris pulled on the lead with Jo. Charlie turned towards them, one hand on the rail, the other clutching his lead. He roared defiantly, and with one great pull, yanked the lead from their hands.

Chris walked slowly towards the great ape, calling softly to him. 'Patience, Charlie, patience. Soon you *will* be there, in the rainforests, your home.' He extended an arm to Charlie, repeating the gesture several times. All that stopped Charlie from jumping overboard was an inherent dislike of water, and when the ship was buffeted by a wave, it sent unpleasant salty sea spray into his face. He was brave but not so reckless as to lose all self-control, and the decision he made was correct. Just as Chris had gestured to him, Charlie gestured to the waves, the sea, and beyond to the end of what he could see and sense. A faint bar of land to their left appeared, perhaps ten miles off, but Charlie had seen it. He stood upright again, pointing, chattering to himself with excitement.

Jo said, 'He can see land, Chris. It's incredible.'

Captain McDonald muttered gruffly, 'Sort him out, will you.' There was a look of suppressed anger on his sea-roughened face. He said he had a ship to run not a circus.

Charlie turned and knuckle-walked over to Chris, as calm as

could be, relaxed, the tension gone from his muscles. Once again, the two walked together arm in arm. Charlie and Chris were busy vocalising to each other like two bickering adults. Outside his cage, Charlie hesitated, looking up at Chris. Then, with a grunt and a bark, he went inside. The ape was resigned now. He must let things take their course.

'Send George a message, please Chris,' said Jo. 'And give him my love. What shall we say?'

'We'll say, "The cargo is well, landfall imminent."'

FIFTY-THREE

Barely six hours later, MV *Tarkwon* dropped anchor in Ambas Bay, among small islets, forested and rocky. Surf pounded along the black-brown volcanic beaches. A few fishing boats and canoes out of Limbe dared the waves.

Chris and Jo watched a lighter come alongside. Before they had time to take in what was happening, the ship's bosun had thrown over a sturdy pilot's ladder, and the port agent clambered aboard. All the paperwork necessary for a clean bill of health appeared in order. When the landing permits, bills of lading, passports, customs forms, and the various documents, instructions and formalities had been arranged or concluded, suddenly there came the realisation of leaving, going ashore. Mount Cameroon was obscured by cloud but smaller hills were visible.

The captain shouted, 'Get that box off smartly there!' Charlie inside his box was winched down to the lighter, along with items of luggage. Chris and Jo followed, separately, in a bosun's chair. The port agent wasted no time, ordering the lighter crew to make for a landing stage opposite the residential quarter at Bota. The lighter chugged away, some of the ship's crew waved goodbye, the captain too, prominent on his bridge.

Suddenly, the shock of reaching land, seeing the forest creeping right down to the water's edge, the odorous perfume of the tropics, the flight of strange, coloured birds and, as dusk was falling, the scintillating green glints of fireflies, the deafening noises of unseen insect life, all came together in a flowering burst of consciousness. This was the magical reality of life in the tropics, the steaming red earth, the lush abundant vegetation, the mingling nostalgia of wood smoke, a huge resplendent sun crashing into the southern Atlantic.

'My God,' Jo said, almost in awe as the lighter hove to and

someone threw a mooring line to an African boy wearing just a pair of shorts. 'Talk about the torrid zone,' she said, wiping her forehead, discovering her body pouring with sweat.

In a rush, they landed. 'George, old boy,' Chris shouted, excited even beyond his usual enthusiasm. 'George, can you believe it!' He looked down at Charlie's cage, which had just been hauled onto the jetty. 'Cargo landed,' he said triumphantly. He fell onto the decking, on his back laughing. 'What a journey!'

'How long do we have to wait?' said Jo, worried by the sudden nightfall. The lighter had already pulled away. The waves near the shoreline softened their patter. There were several bungalows with red corrugated iron roofs dotted on green lawns, nestling under palm trees, evidently a prosperous part of the town. It was quiet, the hour around dusk, yet still the insect life kept up its deafening chatter, as though the fecundity of life would not be denied.

'Is that for us?' Chris asked when a green Land Rover nosed cautiously towards the jetty.

A swarthy middle-aged African in shorts and red shirt opened his door, got out and walked across the narrow tarmac path. A smile spread across his face. '*Na yu o! Yu don kam?* Greetings. You have the animal?' He took one look inside the cage, and said, '*Eh-eh! Husay yu comot? Husay contri?*'

Jo looked perplexed but Chris said, 'He's asking where Charlie comes from.'

The man laughed. '*Mek wi go fo hos, chop, res smol. Yu no sabi tok Pidgin? Kamtok. Limbe Kamtok?* That's Pidgin language, Cameroon talk. Plenty people still use it in Cameroon. Well, my friends, it means, "Let's go home, eat, and rest a little." Hurry, it's not far. You can stay overnight in the rest house.'

They had only a short drive to a bungalow fronting the sea. Jacob, their driver, parked in a compound at the back. Charlie was hustled inside. Chris let him out. Immediately, the ape made for the nearest wicker armchair where he reposed in comfort. He looked around earnestly, as if enquiring about his new accommodation, then threw his head back, opened his mouth, to show his teeth.

'Is he laughing or threatening me?' Jacob asked.

'The former,' Chris answered. 'I think he's tickled pink.'

'Tickled pink?' Jacob scratched his head.

'That ape there, you know he comes from Cameroon originally. He can't believe his luck that he's come back.'

'Mista Chris, we have to tell the Forestry and Wildlife Ministry and the conservators that this animal was missing. He came to the wrong place. I've been told to say he was sent to Limbe Wildlife Centre when he should have gone to Mefou National Park, near Yaoundé.'

'You mean an admin mix-up?'

'Yes. It's in the paperwork. Enough people have been paid, dashed, to swing the story along.'

'To make it stick,' Jo said.

'Correct.' Jacob scratched his head again. 'In Pidgin we say, "*Di ting wey ma eye see, mi mouth no fit tok am.*" That means, "Words fail me."'

'Why?' Chris asked bluntly.

'That ape must be a very special animal. If he was in the bush, he would *chop bullet* by now – get shot. Just *bushbif*. I mean, why is he so special? All the money that's passed hands for him!'

Charlie looked over at Jacob from his wicker chair as if to say, 'Mind your own business.'

'The thing is he's not going to Mefou either. He's to be sent on to Mamfe. We stop at Kumba first to pick up a forest guard.'

'Thank you, Jacob,' Chris said. 'When do we leave?'

'We leave for the bush tomorrow, in the afternoon. I know it's short notice but better to get going. You can shop in the morning for food from the market. For your chop here, there's plenty in the fridge, and bottled water. There's a separate generator if the electricity cuts out – we say if *cease light* – power failure.' Jacob smiled warmly. 'There's a houseboy in the backyard. Ask him if you want for anything. Keep him in the house, always,' he said, staring hard at Charlie.

After shaking hands, Jacob left. They waved from the veranda.

Jo and Chris immediately went inside the bungalow and locked the door. 'It seems,' Chris said thoughtfully, 'it seems they don't know *why* Charlie is so special. Just as well, I'd say.' He looked around the sparsely furnished room, the wicker arms chairs, a coffee table, mosquito gauze in the windows, a solitary ceiling light, a view towards Ambas Bay and the small rocky islands not far offshore.

'Let's check the kitchen.' Jo went into another room, opened an old Electrolux fridge, and found six cold beers, some bacon, butter, eggs, plantains, and tomatoes. In a box by the sink were two hands of ripe bananas and a bowlful of groundnuts. 'Shall we have a drink? A toast to Charlie, and to the man who sent him here, my dear husband Dr George Waldren.'

'God! A drink! In all the excitement I'd forgotten about it. Get those beers out. Let's make some tea for Charlie too.'

'I can't find a bottle opener,' Jo said.

'Here, give it to me.' Chris grabbed a bottle and ripped the cap off with his teeth.

'Be careful,' said Jo.

'It's okay really. In Africa most people have got fantastic teeth, they find it easy.'

Jo screamed. 'What's that?' She pulled her hand away fast from the banana box. Suddenly, a greeny-brown house gecko jumped out. It clambered up the nearest wall, stopped and peered back at her, using its specialised toe pads to cling easily to the vertical wall. As Jo watched, its long tongue came out and licked its eyes to clean off any dust.

'You can get another top off for me, please Chris. This is the tropics, right? Do we need to check the beds for snakes as well?'

'It's pretty safe, I reckon, just need to keep your wits about you. Have you seen the bedroom?'

'No,' Jo said.

'There's one large bed and a pull-down mosquito net.'

'Oh great!' Jo said glumly. 'I hope you can sleep on your side without bothering me.'

Chris came over and clinked her beer bottle. 'There are so much more important things in life, Jo. Let's drink to George, our absent friend, and to Charlie, our "man" in Limbe who's about to be posted to the bush. We'd better check on Charlie too.'

Next door they found Charlie had moved to the window overlooking the bay. Night clothed the foreland, it was inky black. Just as they had seen the huge disc of the tropical sun sinking into the ocean, now the moon arose, lavishly scattering silver bars over the water.

'Look at Charlie, Chris,' Jo said quietly.

Chris saw Charlie looking upwards. He was muttering a little, sometimes the ape said, *'Hoo hoo hoo'* softly and clicked his lips. They followed Charlie's gaze.

'He can't be looking at stars, surely?'

'He is,' Chris nodded. 'I know I can't believe it but it's a long time since he saw that sky.' As they gazed upwards there were indeed star-bursts of light dashed over the Cameroon sky, a huge reckless scattering, the stars and planets that Charlie once lived under, in the forests of Takamanda.

There was a knock from the kitchen door. Jo went through and saw the houseboy. *'Na welkom,'* he said. *'Welkom.'*

'Hi, I'm Jo. How are you?'

'Ah de fayn. Ha fo yu?'

Guessing, Jo answered, 'I'm fine, thank you.'

He was very young, perhaps fourteen or fifteen. He wore flip-flops, a t-shirt, and a pair of tattered shorts. His voice was almost a whisper. The boy said he would come back *'monin taym'* to *'go fo maket'*.

'Sure, okay,' Jo said smiling.

The boy turned to leave. Then he said, *'All Europeans enta for dis Cameroon contri, dey na automatically blessed bi God.'*

Jo laughed but when she went to say goodnight to the boy, he had disappeared into the blackness. The sound of insect life was still deafening, and from the town and its hotels and bars she heard music with its own plangent rhythms. Was it *Highlife* or *Makossa*? She didn't know.

'What did he say?' Chris had come in for another beer.

'He said any European who enters this part of Cameroon is blessed by God – automatically. And he's coming in the morning so we can get some things in the market.'

'Charlie's been blessed by God then. He's *part* European, isn't he?'

Jo chuckled but suddenly her face was serious. 'It's scary. I hardly ever think about it now…can you imagine it? The young man on the motorbike…some parts of him, cells, neurons, have new life, now, right next door?'

'That's right,' Chris said, 'from Headington to Limbe. Are you ready for bed?'

'Have you looked at Charlie?'

'Yes, he's still in the wicker chair, and everything's locked. He should be all right until morning.'

'Bags the side near the window.'

Soon all that could be heard from the rest house by the sea was the sound of contented snoring, as the three travellers were gently lulled to sleep by plashing waves and waving palm-fronds, each deep in their separate dreams, waiting for morning time.

*

At 7.00 a.m. the houseboy, Solomon, knocked and brought in two cups of tea, and a tin of condensed milk. As he left he heard Charlie pant-grunting from the front room. His eyes rolled with fear. With obvious disquiet in his voice he said, '*Wai dat man beef di hala so?*'

'He's fine,' Chris said. 'Do you want to see him?'

'*Acting big man Jacob, e tell mi dis bif get plenti power.*'

'He is a chimpanzee from your country,' Chris explained.

'*Ah no wan look dat kain ting,*' Solomon said. '*Ah de fear. If yu toch am, e go chop yu.*' His eyes rolled wide again in sheer terror. '*If e get chance, e go bostaut fo room, go kill yu. No bi tru?*'

Solomon could not be induced to look at Charlie.

An hour later they were in the market, marvelling at the array of wares displayed, the variety of local produce from the farms and forests. Mammies with colourful headscarves, often with a piccin or two slung in a harness on their backs or suckling at the breast, chatted away *'time no dey'* – time was unimportant.

Jo was busy buying various stores. She'd made a list. One by one, items were ticked off. Sleeping bags, groundsheets, kerosene lamp, socks, boots, mosquito nets, fishing rod and reel, water filter, matches, torch. There was so much needed. Bars of soap, flannels, towels, tinned milk, plastic plates, washing bowl, a cooking pan, one kettle, two mugs, two glasses, one kitchen knife, toilet rolls, tins of coffee, packets of tea, sugar, salt, pepper, rice, cigarettes (to be given as dashes), one washbowl, toothpaste, toothbrushes, cooking oil, Maggi cubes, oats, biscuits, lime juice, marmalade, jam, a bottle of whisky, tinned meat – it seemed the list would never end.

'How long Chris? How long are we going for? You said about a week; supposing it's more? And anyway, where are we going?'

Chris was buying a pack of beer. 'Jo, I really don't know. George gave me the letter. I have to open it in Mamfe. God knows why.' He didn't seem to care. 'He said it would need a few days' trek to get there, so I reckon two to three weeks, there and back.'

Solomon was packing things into boxes. By one o'clock they had most of the equipment needed. Anything they couldn't find they could look for in Kumba or Mamfe. They had to hire a taxi to get everything back to the rest house.

Just before leaving, an old woman who was sitting in the dust reached out her arm, pleading to be seen. *'Massa, mi ah no bi well. Ah bi ol wuman. Mi ah need dokta. Abeg massa, find mi dokta!'*

Chris looked at her, noticed her imploring eyes, the pain in her expression. 'Mammy, what is it, *ha fo yu*? *Weti bin hapin?*'

'Ma bodi no fit waka, ah no get power pass smol piccin, long taym weak fo bodi. Na ma fut hurt bad bad ah tel yu.'

Chris checked her over quickly. She was well apart from a leg infection, caused by an ugly abscess. He told her to wait, and found a chemist's shop. He bought some penicillin and dressings. With so little time, he decided to send her to the local hospital straightaway. He pressed three 10,000 CFA franc notes into her hands. Another taxi driver who claimed to be the *broda* or brother of the first one took her.

The old woman was very happy as she left for hospital. She called out, *'Massa, tank yu. Papa God e go bless yu plenti. Waka fine.'*

'Your first patient in a long time?' Jo smiled at Chris warmly.

'It was satisfying. Just sorry I had no time to treat her myself.'

Back at the rest house, they were met with screams of delight from Charlie. At this, Solomon covered his head in his hands.

Jacob arrived with the Land Rover to start loading supplies. They got underway three hours later, the ape carefully hidden by draped blankets from the rest house, and drove straight to the Limbe Wildlife Centre. Chris was anxious to go inside; it had so many beautiful gardens, specimen iroko trees, even a stream in the Botanic Gardens. It was a pity there was so little time.

'We have to see some of this,' Chris told Jo. 'Perhaps when we come back. Maybe there's time to see the chimps and gorillas then. There's Charlie's kind here, *ellioti*, and Cross River gorillas too, *Gorilla gorilla diehli*, most orphans rescued from the bush.'

'It's dangerous to go inside,' Jacob said. 'Not when you have the chimpanzee in the back. We can't be seen. Let's get the two boys who are going to help you, that's all there's time for.'

'It's true, Jacob. Much as we'd love to visit, it's too risky.'

'I felt a shiver go through me, when you talked about orphans,' Jo whispered, dropping her voice in case anyone heard. 'What is even stranger is where the chimps in there come from. Some may be from Takamanda forest itself. They could be Charlie's cousins!'

A few minutes later Jacob jumped down from the Land Rover to greet two boys, not 'small boys' Jo thought, more like teenagers. With big smiles and evident joy the boys squeezed into the back. So it was that John Embai and Smoky Joe were hired to help convey Charlie home, though they would need extra help in Mamfe. With feelings of mutual and mounting excitement, they set off for Kumba town.

FIFTY-FOUR

The Land Rover pulled hard, climbing higher along a road that seemed to have more than its fair share of potholes but at least the road was paved. It had been raining and red, crumbling earth stacked up by the sides of the road. In the back of the Land Rover, hidden by the draped blankets, Charlie was brooding. So far he'd had enough food and water. He was not happy being inside his cramped box but from experience he knew that 'movement' meant change, especially movement in the back of a Land Rover, an experience with which he was already familiar.

As they passed through villages, horn blaring at sheep, or an odd goat, or a few Zebu cattle with their striking horns and fatty shoulder humps, Charlie's nose began to sense something rich though not strange. The ruts in the road meant he banged his head, and sometimes he was thrown from side to side. Something inside him decided against being a valorous chimp, trying to smash his way out with brute strength. Charlie now was much more cunning. He had seen more than most chimpanzees, and his mentation was responding, knitting together faster, what was within him was alive, expressing itself in new ways. There was so much to take in, to fathom, to understand.

The journey to Kumba took two hours. In the 'Providence Bar', Mr Benjamin Ayuk introduced himself, a thin, wiry old forest guard with a taste for 'African gin', a potent drink distilled from the juice of raffia palm trees. The so-called illicit gin was kept in a hip flask, which he frequently used to top up his beer. Jacob had already given him cash for his assistance, a tiny part of the train of finance that reached all the way back to Dr George Waldren. Mr Ayuk said he wanted to visit a cousin first but Jacob persuaded him to squeeze in the back.

'If you like we can visit Barombi Lake,' Jacob told them. There wouldn't be much time but it was worth a visit. They passed the garage where Charlie had been imprisoned after his capture in Takamanda. Jacob drove them towards the top of the volcanic lake, the road hemmed in on either side by rampant tropical growth. Ancient trees festooned with ferns and mosses, among enormous smooth black boulders, reached down to the edge of the lake.

Charlie was brought out, and made to sit on a woollen blanket. As a precaution, Chris tethered him to the Land Rover. He tried to explain to the two new boys not to fear him or make any quick movements. Mr Ayuk cradled his hip flask for comfort.

The most wide-eyed was John Embai, a bright boy with a happy nature and flashing smile. '*Ibabo! If ah go look am, afraid de catch mi.*'

Smoky Joe, his companion, had bursts of humour when he didn't feel too seriously about life. '*Dis na big big sumbu, chimpanzee. Dis beef e get power o!*' Smoky began to dance. He looked at Charlie, and said, '*Yu no sabi dans Makossa?*'

Charlie took a swipe at him.

In the distance Jacob saw some African villagers from the far side of the lake journeying across in canoes. He said, 'We must leave before they get here.' Rolls, sandwiches and bananas were eaten fast. After only ten minutes' rest, Jacob coaxed the Land Rover back to the main road, glad to leave the stygian quietness of the lake, known for its tiny cichlid fish, and 'mammy water' legend, a local water goddess or mermaid.

Soon they were back on the laterite road to Mamfe, thick forest on either side through which the road cut a deep gash, the earth a primal ochre red, a journey of four to six hours, depending on the severity of seasonal rain.

It was misty by the time they arrived. Jacob drove straight to a rest house, Charlie taken into a back room in his box. Mr Ayuk took Chris straight to see a Forestry Officer in an air-conditioned office nearby. He was a youthful, affable man in his thirties with short cropped hair, smartly dressed in a green forestry bush jacket. His manner was polite yet firm.

'Welcome,' he said. 'Julius Foucham, head of the department here, with responsibility for Mamfe Overside. Please sit down, Dr Grailing.'

Chris sat down in the nearest chair, and found himself lost for words.

'I understand that you are responsible for...' He hunted for the right words, and then continued...'a consignment. A very rare consignment, I believe, that was due to go to Mefou.'

'Yes,' Chris said noticing Mr Ayuk standing outside. Perhaps he was out of earshot. 'By some extraordinary chance, or mistake, the animal was sent to Limbe, or was to have been sent to Limbe. In fact, it ended up at Bota.'

The African's eyes narrowed to little more than slits. 'Have you got the letter?'

Chris played dumb at first. 'Letter?' He shrugged his shoulders.

'I think you have a letter, shall we say, from another doctor, from one doctor to another.' He laughed uproariously but then his face became set again. 'Open it!'

Worried and thinking he was about to be asked for a bribe, it was several moments before Chris realised the Forestry Officer was referring to the letter he kept carefully zipped up in an inside pocket – the one George gave him just before leaving.

'Yes, I do.' Chris was very surprised. 'You know Dr Waldren?'

The African leant back in his reclining office chair. 'George and I were at university together when I did my forestry degree. I am willing to do an old friend a favour. An expensive favour for George but he was always good with money. George is a very generous man. He's very good at *greasing palms*, when he wants to get his own way.'

'That's true,' Chris admitted, struck how the African made even the words sound greasy by the careful way he enunciated them.

'I know very well that you landed at Bota, and that you have no intention of sending the animal anywhere near Mefou National Park.'

Chris decided to be truthful there and then. 'Your information is correct. In that case, let me read you the letter.' He unzipped an inner pocket of his lightweight jacket and pulled out a brown envelope, opened it, and began to read:

Dear Chris
By the time you open this letter, if you have kept to your promise, you should be in Mamfe ready to discharge your duty to Charlie.

I have made various arrangements to make your path easier.

My wish is that Charlie goes back to his homeland, to the forests of Takamanda. You must see that he gets there, and you have a double duty, to care for Charlie and to look after Jo.

After deliberating on where to release Charlie, I want you to take him to a village, not too far inside the forest reserve. There, I want you to ask the local people where chimpanzees are still found in the forest, and with their help, you must take him wherever they say he (Charlie) should go to be with his own kind, in the safest possible place.

The village I have chosen goes by the name of Basho, a funny name to be sure. Take Charlie to Basho 1, which I am led to believe is deeper inside the reserve. Actually, the whole area is now a national park, so you will need passes etc. from the Forestry Officer in Mamfe, but that's not a problem.

Why Basho? Heaven only knows. There was a specimen collected from there in 1905 by a man called Jasper von Oertzen (we were talking about it), and another explorer, Paul Matschie, gave the sub-species the name ellioti *in 1914, resurrected by Oates and colleagues only recently.*

I think there is a kind of 'poetic justice' in sending him back to the very birthplace of the first specimen of his kind, but clearly you may need to trek further into the reserve to find an area not disturbed by logging, and so on.

I have arranged a bank transfer for you to collect from the Afriland First Bank, Mile 11, Limbe on your successful return.

God speed, with love

George

The Forestry Officer was quiet, almost brooding. 'This Charlie that George mentioned in his letter, is he here, now?'

Chris nodded. He got up from his chair knowing that the Mr Foucham would follow him. They trailed out of the office with Mr Ayuk, the old forest guard, bringing up the rear. Outside the rest house, Chris stopped, asking the two Africans to wait. After a minute he was back on the doorstep.

'Can we go in now?' Mr Foucham asked expectantly.

'Sure, follow me but please be quiet and don't make any sudden movements.'

They got as far as the doorway, Chris stepping aside so they would have a better look. Mr Foucham and Mr Ayuk seemed transfixed, as though they had seen a spirit.

'*Chai!*' wheezed Mr Ayuk.

Mr Foucham unexpectedly broke into Pidgin, and in a shrill voice exclaimed, '*E don kam!*'

Charlie looked round from the table where he was having his tea, sitting upright in a canvas chair.

'Good grief,' Mr Foucham continued sotto voce. 'Is that him? It looks like he can do just about everything except talk.'

Jo welcomed them. She said Charlie was fairly relaxed seeing that he had been cooped up for hours. Abruptly, Charlie banged his cup of tea on the table, not too hard but enough to be noticed. With a certain aplomb, he picked up a teaspoon and began to tap the side of the mug repeatedly. The expression on his face was one of long-suffering forbearance, as if his patience wouldn't last much longer.

'He just wants more tea,' Jo said.

'You seem to have him well trained. As far as I know the plan was to release him into the wild.' Mr Foucham looked concerned. 'Is he not too domesticated, if that is the right word, to go back? No one's going to give him tea – in the bush.'

At this last remark Charlie just as abruptly stopped rapping. He pushed the cup away. Then he turned his head towards the strangers. He fixed Mr Foucham with such a frightening stare that Mr Foucham might have been a rabbit caught in the sudden glare of the yellow-brown lights that were Charlie's piercing eyes.

Then the ape gave out a guttural growl that almost shook the room with its ferocity, his canine teeth bared, and his pelage bristling so much that he suddenly seemed much larger.

Old Mr Ayuk looked startled. '*Belle don fulup, hed no kohret.*'

'I'm sure he's just excited, not crazy.' Mr Foncham coughed nervously. 'It seems he *is* wild enough to return to the bush. Those teeth scare me. I'm going back to my office to get the permits. Collect them later, this evening.' Both men left in a hurry.

Chris showed George's letter to Jo. 'We're going to Basho,' he said. 'Note the bank transfer, could be useful. I have to hand it to him; he seems to have planned everything.'

'How far is it to Basho?'

'The Forestry Officer says it's about two to three day's trek. We cross the Manyu or Cross River on the old colonial bridge into Mamfe Overside. There's a new road being built but he said we should take the bush path.'

Jo glanced at Charlie, who was sitting very still. 'Look at him. All quiet now. You'd think he was listening intently, wouldn't you?'

'Anyway, we are supposed to leave the day after tomorrow. We need more supplies, medical things, and the main problem is going to be transport. It's got to be on foot, and I don't fancy carrying him.' Chris looked at Charlie, who stiffened in his chair as if reproached suddenly.

'I hope you have some good ideas,' Jo said glumly.

Chris went outside to find Mr Ayuk. He explained he wanted carpenters, and when he was met with a blank stare, took him to Charlie's box. He pretended to measure up a piece of wood and hit it with a hammer.

Benjamin Ayuk's face lit up. '*Ah sabi dat man! Ah de go kwik-kwik. Smol taym kam bak. Mek ah begin go.*' He stopped what seemed to be a friend on a motorbike and they left. About an hour later he was back, the small car bringing him announcing their arrival with a flourish of car horns.

'*Kari am fo bush?*' Mr Ayuk and the carpenter began to laugh so much they had to sit down by the side of the road. '*Ayyyyh! Dat bif get sens pass plenti pipol. E no fit waka dat Overside. Go kari am fo bush!*'

So it happened that the carpenter fashioned two long poles, strong but not too heavy. Each pole was simply nailed on under Charlie's box. Each end was sanded down to make smooth handholds. Four people could manage it. To some strong Africans who worked as porters, it would be an easy task to take Charlie into the bush, easier than carrying a heavy load on the head.

Jo came out to see it. 'Just a minute,' she said when it was ready. 'I'll get Charlie.'

The ape was led towards his litter. Small bars of ironwood were placed across the front, the wood at that end ripped off, so that he would be able to see as he was being carried along. He got in, turned round, without fuss. He was given a ceremonial ride round in a large circle in the rest house garden.

Chris and Jo were pleased with it. The carpenter was paid.

When they had brought Charlie back inside the rest house, Chris said, 'Kind of appropriate as a method of travel, wouldn't you say, Jo? A palanquin – for the peerless prince of Takamanda!'

'I wish George could see it,' Jo said sadly.

FIFTY-FIVE

It all started because of Mr Ayuk. At least, it became necessary to lay the blame somewhere. The old forest guard suggested there should be a party, a send-off, before they left for the bush.

The chief medical officer kindly donated all kinds of useful medicine and first-aid items. Extra supplies were bought in Mamfe market. Porters were hired. Permits were issued and collected. Mr Foucham helped. Advice was sought and received. Somewhere inside Takamanda, the ape would find his home, '*e on pipol*', as Mr Ayuk said.

It was the day before departure. With loads checked and porters due to turn up the next day, it was Mr Ayuk's plea in the evening that resonated: '*Mek wi go drink smol mimbo fo ton.*'

The best *mimbo* or palm wine was drunk when young, tapped by hand, being the fermented sap of palm trees, and usually stored in hollowed-out, dried calabash gourds. The younger the wine the sweeter it was, as it quickly becomes sour and acidic if not drunk soon after fermentation.

In the Mamfe Club, a relic of colonial days, the drinks flowed, not mimbo but cold lager and spirits. There were toasts to Chris and Jo, toasts to Mr Foucham, toasts to Mr Ayuk, toasts to others in the club but all listened to Mr Foucham, the Forestry Officer, when he got up to speak.

'My good country people, you see us here enjoying ourselves. We welcome Chris and his friend Jo, and we remember she is the wife of our patron, a long way from here, in UK. The doctor responsible for this incredible and momentous upcoming journey, to the bush, to Mamfe Overside, is the great Dr George…'

The applause and general back-slapping stopped him from speaking but Mr Ayuk said, '*Shh*', and it went quiet.

'We never know what is to happen in life. God hides things from us, from our own selves. We try to do our best. From the kindness of his heart, Dr George has decided to return to us a creature from our own forests.

'From here, excuse me Mr Chris, I use a Pidgin word, from here *sotey, so-teeeeey*, I mean very, very *far* from here, in the Takamanda Forest Reserve, now National Park, somewhere in all that forest, up to the border with Nigeria, the Cross River area, that is where this creature comes from. He is here now, in Mamfe, and I have just seen him!

'In the meantime, this creature, this *man beef*, we say in country talk, has been on his own journey. We all know what it is to be away from our own country, from our home, our homeland. People sometimes they cry, just to go home.'

'*Aye, dey de cri fo dem heart*,' nodded Mr Ayuk wisely, patting his own breast for emphasis.

'Our dear patron, Dr George is paying for our drinks! What is one man worth if he thinks not of his brother? Who *is* our brother? Is it just people in our immediate family, or does it extend all the way to the creatures we share the Earth with, who walk in the same bush, who breathe the same air, sleep under same sky?'

Silence fell on the small band of revellers. Most had drunk so much they no longer knew why they had become so maudlin, to the point of tears.

'*Wich kayn broda yu don tok nau?*' asked a man at the bar.

'My brother Charlie,' said Mr Foucham, with the gravest face imaginable, as if his smooth jowls were about to slide off his face. 'I don't mean *brother* in the literal sense, you understand.'

At that moment, Mr Foucham looked more like a headmaster than a forestry officer. To everyone's surprise his demeanour became even more academic, as he slipped a pair of reading glasses onto his nose, pushed them down a little, and then said stiffly, 'To be honest, more like *cousin*.'

'*Ah-hah!*' the onlookers exclaimed in unison together, as if that explained everything.

'Where is this cousin, you ask me?' whispered Mr Foucham.

All was hushed in the club apart from the cacophony of noisy insects and sporadic cockerel cries. Mr Foucham paused to look round, and then he said, 'Our cousin is right here in Mamfe town, at the government rest house. I can't take you to see him right now, as he is resting, and Mr Chris and his friend Jo have to rest too.'

The small group of people who had been listening were about to leave when Mr Ayuk jumped up, shouting, *'Wuna sidon! Evriwan na welcome. Wi go si am smol taym, de no bi wan. Taym we wi go leave fo bush, afta tumoro, yu go si am.'*

It was agreed. Those who wanted to meet the 'cousin' should gather in the early morning by the old colonial bridge on the day of departure. Chris and Jo walked back in the warm African night to the rest house.

When they had checked Charlie over, eaten some cold chop left out by John Embai, Chris poured two small whiskies, one each for the road, he said. 'If we have hangovers tomorrow, I'm going to blame poor Mr Ayuk. Jo, will you send George a fax tomorrow, if you can't text him. Tell him we're going into the bush.'

'I'm so wide awake, Chris. I should be exhausted but I just feel this is so incredible.'

'Me too.'

'You know I was reading about Richard Dawkins before we left. I meant to tell you. He thinks chimps and bonobos might be descended from the southern ape, *Australopithecus*. Not the robust kind but the slender, gracile-type – so that would point to *Australopithecus afarensis*, as the ancestors of chimpanzees.'

'I wouldn't risk telling Charlie that, at this time of night. He might be upset.'

'Seriously that's not all, Chris. Another professor, called Jared Mason Diamond, said humans are so very close taxonomically to chimps, more so than chimps are to gorillas, for example. If you take the genetic differences as your parameters, humans could be classified as a third species of chimpanzee, after the common chimpanzee and bonobos!'

'Oh my God,' Chris said. 'Doesn't that just explain so many things?'

'Like what?' Jo asked curiously.

'I'm too tired to think,' Chris said, suddenly overwhelmed by the need for sleep. 'It must be the emotion of months and months of getting Charlie to where he is now.' He stopped a moment, as he heard Charlie vocalising in the other room with a soft '*hoo hoo*'. He wondered if apes 'say' things when asleep. 'I do remember something about three million-year-old *afarensis* footprints found in Africa. The early hominid prints are virtually identical to modern humans, indistinguishable in fact. Yet the footprints are not like any other living primate. They also walked upright. So, there are conundrums to ponder...'

*

The next day more stores were bought in the market, some by John Embai and Smoky Joe. Groups of young children, aged between three to nine, dressed in an odd melange of school caps, colourful shirts, grass skirts and juju headgear, singing odd snatches of songs, some shaking old cans filled with rice, others imitating castanets with spoons, a hollow bamboo cane serving as a rudimentary drum, paraded past the government rest house. Chris handed out some money and a cry of joy went up. A new chant began: 'Money was made to spend!' Singing as one, the children ran across to the white sprawling sand of the Manyu River, undressed, and tumbled in somersaults, running, jumping, leaping, some of them backwards, into the river.

The following morning, Charlie was roused at 6.00 a.m. By 7.15 six porters filed up to the rest house entrance. Loads had to be organised; some of the carriers complained over heavy bags and boxes. The palanquin was brought out but its occupier was not. Delays were inevitable. At 10.00 the small convoy, this time with Charlie safely ensconced, left for the old suspension bridge, a German relic from the past, when Cameroon was written Kamerun.

Mr Foucham arrived to wish everyone good luck, as well as a

motley crew of 'unbelievers', who had come to see their cousin. Mr Ayuk was well to the fore, with a 30/06 rifle and ten rounds of ammunition, provided by the Wildlife department. A small crowd gathered, just as the palanquin began its journey to the bush.

An African held up his hand. '*Tanap!*' he cried. '*Abi na wetin?*' The palanquin and its guard were being told to stop, and explain just what they were. The four porters abruptly halted, placing the palanquin on the ground.

Those who had come to give their blessing looked down into Charlie's box. There were cries of unbelief, and howls of derision, with loud hooting and slapping of knees, as if struck by an enormously funny joke. '*Na dis, na ma cousin o! Wetin ya on nem, broda? Husay yu comot?*'

John Embai was cross. '*Comot fo road nau nau! Mek wi pass.*'

An onlooker, as perplexed as could be, took one look at Charlie and said, '*Weti yu kam du fo Cameroon?*' Another man spied the ape's strong arms and said, '*Dat piccin na big pass mi.*'

Chris was sorely tempted. If only, he thought, I could open the box, let Charlie out to greet them but when he saw the snarling scowl on the great ape's face, the brooding brown-yellow eyes, he reasoned it was unsafe. It was Charlie's own country, and yet they were asking him what he was doing in Cameroon!

Once the bridge and its perilous drop had been negotiated, the journey into Mamfe Overside began in earnest. Chris and Jo were soaked in sweat. The tropical heat was relentless. They trekked for two miles and already Mamfe town seemed remote and far away. They rested at a small village of about ten huts. An African appeared with a jug of sweet but strong mimbo, and it was emptied in seconds by the thirsty carriers.

The carriers began to sing, chant and amuse themselves with simple repartee. Charlie occasionally joined in. All were happy.

After trekking another five miles, the small column reached Eshobi village. The headmaster of the local school, who was on leave, invited all to drink mimbo again. Forest guard, Mr Ayuk, wasted ten minutes; he said his 'knickers' had torn and needed mending. At the same time he managed to down about six half-pint mugs of mimbo.

Six miles further was the village of Muboyong. The trekking was undemanding, and small streams could be forded easily. Then the River Mam was reached, about 20 yards wide. All except Charlie bathed in the river to cool down. Just over a small hill, John Embai and Smoky Joe led the team to the village of Muboyong.

The assistant chief of the village gave them a hut for the night. A tortoise was suspended mid-air by a length of twine. It clawed frantically, finding nothing to grip. It would be left overnight, then thrown into boiling water, and chopped.

Nobody wanted to do much except bathe again in the river to cool down. At 6.00 p.m. the local choirmaster took the new arrivals to a small church to hear the village choir. The church was an oblong mud hut about 20 yards long by 10 wide. Written on the far wall was the inscription, 'It is better to have a good name than riches.' The choirmaster raised his hands and the children burst into song, the rhythms uniquely African, vibrant, seductive.

In the chief's compound elders were dancing, drinking, and shouting. Chris dashed a packet of cigarettes. As a return gift another man brought a bottle of distilled palm wine – 'African gin'. 'One glass can make you see kaleidoscope stars,' warned Jo but she sank hers in one anyway.

Forest guard Mr Ayuk struggled through the door of their hut, struggling because he was drunk. More African gin was handed round. A Mr John, who said he was the landlord, came in with some friends, including a ribald, rotund man named Effiom. A party was inevitable. Mr Ayuk stood up to continue with one of his loquacious soliloquies, mainly about his prowess as a forest guard.

'Time for some fresh air,' said Chris, feeling his head reeling from the drink. He gave instructions to John Embai to cover Charlie's cage, which was outside under a palm frond awning, with a rug.

They made their excuses, and then walked through narrow, labyrinthine passages to the village centre. A kerosene lamp dimly lit the scene. A chief from another village, Nyang, had died in Limbe after an operation. The man had some connection with the village because people were celebrating his life with a 'cry die', a West African wake. Grief is openly expressed, often with floods of tears and wailing. After this, there may be a 'cry chop', when food is eaten together after the cry die. Mammies and young girls, some naked to the waist, danced conga-like, clapped and shouted to the sky, sometimes lit by an occasional flash of lightning.

Not wanting to make their visit seem like an intrusion, Chris and Jo headed back for their hut. The party was breaking up, but then it started all over again. A song was sung, roughly translated as, 'As you do us good by your visit, you shall see the things you want to see. The creature you have brought with you will find his home in the bush. God has willed that you stay in this house.'

The forest guard slumped over a table. A little while later he woke up with a start. '*Wi de go shap shap fo bush monin taym. Wi begin go fo sevin oklok. Goodnight sah!*'

In the same hut slept a small girl of about eight. Since birth she had been unable to speak. Jo gave her some sweets and a cup of coffee, and the girl embraced her.

*

John Embai woke Chris and Jo at 6.30 a.m. Breakfast was two fried eggs each and several cups of tea. Charlie had tea and two bananas. The porters caused some palaver, wanting more wages for carrying the ape. Finally, about 11 a.m. they got underway, all loads correct, John Embai having shouted, '*Dress, dress*' to get them all in line. A short distance from the village, they had to wade through a small river and once when a porter lost his footing, Charlie complained with a vicious pant-grunt.

Within a short time the column made its way through dense rain forest along a well-used path. Light dappled the leaves where the secondary growth was not too thick.

At Mile 8 from Muboyong, they halted in the dim, green and

mystic forest for a short rest. While Mr Ayuk argued vehemently about very little, Charlie was unusually quiet, almost meditative, his large brown-yellow eyes absorbed with the forest around him.

After only ten minutes, they continued along the bush path. Hornbills whistled and rasped overhead. Sometimes fallen forest giants like iroko or obeche trees blocked the way. Myriads of multicoloured butterflies flew alongside them. Unseen eyes peered from the forest canopy. Then a goat crossed the path, and Nyang village was near, after a trek of some fourteen miles.

A man ran out to greet them, and took them to a small but clean hut with a palm-frond roof and mud walls. It was several hundred yards from the village. Then all bathed in the river, except Charlie. Earlier, on the way to Nyang, they had passed two men, one standing, the other sitting cross-legged on the ground. Garbled, inarticulate sounds came from their mouths. Jo, frightened a little by the display, asked one of the carriers to explain. The story about a chief or dignitary from Nyang who had died in Limbe was repeated; they were mourning his death.

When they reached the village, the news had not yet come. Nothing was said. Then, walking back from the river, they saw the entire populace in utter confusion. Women and men rushed out from huts, wailing and moaning as though Mephistopheles had winged his way into their village.

'It's pure pandemonium,' Jo said to Chris. 'Their cheeks are glistening with tears. They don't seem to cry like we do.' That was true. Instead the Africans uttered continuous moans and wails, juxtaposed with choking sobs, while tears glided gently down their faces.

'We should keep away,' Chris said. 'We can't disturb them.' When they got back, children were already cleaning and brushing the packed earth floor. Others brought bananas and water from a stream. Jo bought a fish for a few francs; it was eaten with onions and two eggs from the village.

By 7.00 p.m. it was dark, dark as it can only be in Africa, in the bush, and no one wants to be in the forest where the spirits walk and live. After having been taken for a walk round the hut, Charlie met two mammies passing who cried out, '*Ibabo!*' He was led back inside but was supremely restless. It seemed as if he were fighting an inner spirit because he kept looking at the black night, and the trees in the bush.

Sometimes drifting smoke from fires inside huts made him cough. Once he recovered, his body tensed only to relax moments later. Still his gaze wandered through the opening above him in the mud-hut wall while bats, hammer-headed fruit bats, honked like crazed, love-sick frogs in the starry night, and insects loaded the air with their own strident sounds as the moon rose over the village.

Carried on the same air began another insistent rhythm of the forest, which was the sound of heavy beating drums, echoing from the forest places, secret messages from one village to another.

FIFTY-SIX

'Can you sleep?' Jo whispered in the dark. 'My sleeping bag is fine but it's so damn hard underneath.' The 'beds' in the hut were two raised blocks of hard red earth.

'No. I'm comfortable enough but those drums don't stop.'

The drumming from the village, four hundred yards away, was not in competition with the insect and animal symphonies of the night but added extra aural layers to the great heart of Africa, insistent, pounding and powerful rhythms in tune with the forest.

'John Embai told me that one old man threatened to kill any strangers in the morning.'

'Great,' Chris said. 'We can get Charlie to protect us.'

'Let's go and see, shall we?'

'Okay. I'll get the torch.' Chris rummaged in one of the boxes on the floor. They walked slowly towards the village. It was hard to find the way, even with a torch. The night was inscrutably black. White-orbed eyes peered at them in the dark. Of all primates, human eyes are conspicuous in their clarity, as if meant to be seen, probably for cooperative purposes. Apes do not have the same marked contrast between the white sclera, colourful iris and black pupil. Only humans have the defined whiteness of the sclera. In most other mammals the white of the eye or sclera matches the colour of the iris.

'I'm not exactly scared,' Jo said, 'more like petrified.'

They reached the village centre. About forty men and women danced round a wood fire, which flared up at intervals, giving the dancers ghost-like silhouettes. They edged closer, a hand touched Chris's shoulder. It was John Embai. He whispered something in Chris's ear.

Chris swallowed, turning to Jo to translate. 'He says the people are very wild here. They used to kill many Europeans, especially missionaries. No wonder one of the first questions the chief asked was whether we were missionaries.'

Heavy, thick-set men lunged nearer, hooting like Apaches, Jo thought. One native had hung a heavy brass bell from his belt that sounded with each movement of his buttocks. Some women wore leaves bound together around their middle, their skin oiled and shiny. Nearly all danced with bare feet on the dry red earth, as if shoes would be an impediment to the caress of naked feet on mother Africa. Cries, shouts, ululations rang out. The forest came quite close to some huts, like an invisible presence. A man fired an ancient Dane gun to the sky. There was more noise, pye-dogs barked.

'Let's get back,' Jo said. 'It's midnight already.' Charlie was wide awake at the hut. The noise from the dance echoed through the night, and twelve gunshots sounded at dawn.

In the morning they left the village at 8.30 a.m. One obese mammy threw her arms around Chris's neck. Villagers came to wave goodbye, though most scratched their heads in disbelief as Charlie was led into his box, and then carried away in the palanquin. It seemed so much of an event that many followed the small column until they reached another suspension bridge on the periphery of Nyang, smaller than the one at Mamfe but more precarious.

'*Eh-eh!*' several villagers cried as one, when Charlie looked sternly at them as he passed, as a king might deign to glance at his subjects. One said, '*Dem dey call yu o!*' This was to say the ape was beckoned by unseen forces, suggesting that juju was involved.

The carriers crossed the bridge with reluctance and threw down their loads on reaching the other side. Forest guard Mr Ayuk tried his hardest to get them moving but they would not budge an inch. One or two recalcitrant mutineers upset the balance. It was finally agreed the daily rate would be increased.

Once again they trekked through thick secondary forest, which was interlaced by a filigree of rivulets and streams. They did not rest on this trek until they reached Akwa, a tiny village of about 30 huts.

An old man directed Chris, Jo, John Embai and Smoky Joe, who had all arrived ahead of Mr Ayuk and the porters to a wide, fast-flowing river, where tired feet were bathed. John Embai discovered they could sleep in the school hut. Having moved in, sleeping bags were brought out, and tea brewed on a fire. Five small children brought water in calabashes. They rested in the indolent heat, the sun just over zenith.

They heard chanting in the far distance, which gradually grew louder. The porters had arrived, led by the forest guard, his rifle slung over his back. Their *esprit de corps* was high, after their wage increase.

Charlie's litter, or palanquin, was an object of much curiosity. At each village, the chief or headman in his absence had to be informed about the nature of the cargo. When it was explained that Charlie was going 'home', the old men nodded their agreement, talking among themselves, each person in turn making a ritual out of understanding with sage nodding, as if it were the most natural thing in the world for a strange chimpanzee to be carried through their village en route to his own '*contri*', to be with '*e on pipol*', as Mr Ayuk had said – his very own people.

When Chris asked how far it was to Basho, and how many days' march it was to reach Charlie's home in Takamanda, each man held up both arms to the sky, then dropped them, head sunk on chest in thought. Then one arm would be raised ever higher while the man looked over his shoulder, all the time saying, '*Yu go reach sotey* . . .' The duration of the word '*sotey*' indicated how far in miles and/or time it would take to reach Charlie's home. So, '*sotey*', pronounced '*so-tay*', became '*so-taaaaaaaaaaaaaaaaaaay*' and sometimes the sound lasted for several moments, accompanied by rolling eyes, and much shaking of heads.

'*Very far, massa,*' said Mr Ayuk gravely.

The boys busied themselves making chop. Smoky Joe wanted to buy a small bush dog. He bargained hard, buying a scrawny puppy for a few hundred francs. It was about four weeks old, very prepossessing, but weak from a poor diet. He took to Charlie quite quickly. After only a few days they sometimes slept or rested together. It was possible Charlie missed Helga.

That night swarms of ants invaded the hut. The pye-dog puppy yelped in pain. Chris extricated a huge black ant that had dug into the dog's flesh. All the stores were in jeopardy. Everyone cursed the black terrors, including Charlie – in the form of a high-pitched scream.

'Do you have any ideas how to deal with these things?' Jo asked, desperately trying to prevent ants getting through to Charlie by stamping on the ground.

'Get some wood ash from the boys' cooking fire, and spread the ash round in a circle. If they get to Charlie he might break out of his cage. Christ, if he charges through the village, and someone starts running, who's to say he won't take a bite out of a man's leg?'

'Smoky!' Jo shouted. When he came, she said, 'Ants, get fire, ash.' It seemed as if the boy understood because he left the hut and soon came back with a mound of smoking ash on a four-foot-long plantain leaf.

*

At daybreak Mr Ayuk threatened to sack the carriers for laziness. During the night the ants had found their way into nearby huts and the men were sulky with lack of sleep.

'Base camp is just a day's trek away now,' said Chris excitedly.

'So far there's been no sign of any chimpanzees,' Jo cut in, 'just occasional monkeys. That guy you were telling me about, what was his name, van Oertzen?'

'Von Oertzen. Captain Jasper von Oertzen.'

'Well how many years is it now, since he found that specimen in Basho?'

'A very long time, come to think about it.'

'Well, how long?'

'I think it was 1905. Over a century. And to think it's still in the Humboldt Museum in Berlin. Must be a sorry sight by now. His brother Alexander was the famous seafarer and geographer.'

'This is the day when we get to Basho, isn't it?' Jo's face was glistening with sweat from the tremendous heat.

'Yes, we finally reach there sometime this afternoon. It's about four or five hours' trek by my reckoning. We're aiming for latitude 6.1333, longitude 9.4333. I got that from George, you know. He's so bloody particular.'

'Bless him,' Jo said, a little wistfully.

At the sound of George's name, Charlie grabbed the bars in the front of his cage, and turned his head to one side, as if straining to hear. Jo had some saved nut and date bars from George. She gave one to Charlie.

Mr Ayuk arrived at 10.30 a.m. and asked if they were '*fit go waka fo dat bush*'. After Charlie was exercised on a leash around the hut, Mr Ayuk called out, '*Dress, dress*' at the carriers, and not long after the small column moved out.

They crossed five rivers in the first two hours before resting at a tiny village of six huts. They shook hands with a few elders and pressed on.

On the trek the noise of running water sooner or later broke through the forest's monopoly of silence. It drowns even the solitary, raucous hornbill and the steady insect drone that goes unnoticed after a time, when the rhythm of trekking engrosses all attention. At times they heard the sound a mile off; a constant, tuneless roar that filled the forest like a monstrous accordion endlessly driving air through colossal bellows. Sometimes the bush path ran parallel to the course of a river for several miles, the river itself hidden by a belt of trees. The path would suddenly dip round and down and there would be the river, revealed at the last step.

Rivers often gave the illusion of being the only living things: a river has volition because it moves; the forest is lost to everything except the time machine of its tardy metabolism. Iroko, mahogany and obeche trees take one hundred years to mature – billions of photosensitive cells reacting chemically to light, using the energy of the sun to form complex substances from carbon dioxide and water, carrying on a huge building process, programmed by genes from the seed.

At the sixth river a carrier slipped in the waist-deep water. He was unhurt but cigarettes intended as a dash perished by the time they made Basho. The seventh river, like the seventh wave, was even more daunting. Charlie was quite unconcerned, perhaps because the passage through the forest must have kindled all kinds of memories. Once the column froze for a few moments when they heard the trumpeting scream of a forest elephant.

Having crossed the river successfully, they were then smothered by a cloud of sand flies. In less than a second they can crawl under clothing, in eyes, hair, and ears. All the carriers beat a retreat into the bush with extraordinary haste, leaving poor Charlie alone in his litter, like a king suddenly deposed. Chris ran towards him, covering his box with a towel.

At 2.00 p.m. they were at Basho II, or Margow, a village of about thirty huts. On the skyline behind the mud huts, the distant cloth-green hills of Takamanda hinted at the changing terrain. They tracked round a plantain farm, splashed across a six-inch-deep stream, and there was Basho I, or Melayong, their home for a week or two until Charlie's future was decided.

A local teacher took them to a small hut, at the top end of the village, near a two-acre field where children played. The carriers were paid off, the little army demobbed. All were happy, though entering Basho a new song rang from the carriers' lips. It was *'Moni no dey o!'*

FIFTY-SEVEN

Their stay at Basho was to last eleven days, long enough to acclimatise to village life, take stock. Within two days familiar routines quickly establish themselves, imposing the idea of some sort of order to life. Shaving, washing, bathing, finding the hole-in-the-ground toilet in the dark, the morning brew of tea – all acquire the mystique of ritual in a strange country.

That first afternoon would never be forgotten. At least half the village came to inspect. The bravest among them looked right into Charlie's cage, saw him face to face. The village chief introduced himself, something of a tatterdemalion, inarticulate but canny, Chris suspected. The best thing about him was his pipe; a gold-braided leviathan, a monster briar about eighteen inches long. The shock of actually reaching Basho faded when someone brought a jug of fresh palm wine. They were all tired, and ready for sleep.

'I want to take Charlie out quickly,' Chris told Jo. It was late, two hours before midnight. 'I think he shouldn't see too many people, if we can prevent that. I don't see how he's going to get into the wild if people feed him bananas.'

'You're right,' Jo said from her sleeping bag on the floor. 'It must be restricted access from now on. If you take him out now, it should be quiet – but in the dark?'

Chris didn't answer but went to get Charlie from his cage and put on his leash and collar. They stepped outside into the dark. A few kerosene lamps lit the scene. Smoke drifted upwards through the palm thatch covering the roofs of many of the huts.

He took Charlie on a small path to the north of the village, round the edge of the large field. It ran towards a river on the far side of a small hill. The ape began to vocalise almost immediately but, for a chimpanzee, he was almost restrained: a few whimpers of suppressed excitement and, as they walked further from the village, the familiar '*hoo hoo*' sound but softly uttered.

Chris decided not to go very far. There wasn't any real danger. The gibbous moon provided enough light. There were neither lions nor leopards extant in the forest though leopards were found across the border in Nigeria, and isolated pockets of Cameroon, especially further north. A few lions survived in both countries, not in the hundreds but in the tens. There were forest elephants, and lowland gorillas (the latter called '*muki*') but they inhabited more remote areas of Takamanda. Snakes were common but most of the time they kept out of the way. African rock pythons up to twenty feet long lived in the forest, usually near water sources.

Charlie moved with him along the bush path, more aware than ever of the forest's presence. He reached the buttressed roots of a cottonwood tree, feeling them with his hands, as if caressing the exposed roots, like a blind man rubbing the surface of an object to discover its nature.

Before Chris could stop him, Charlie pulled on his leash, not to escape but to drum violently with his feet on one of the buttresses. The sound was muffled but the tree root was hollow, so the noise carried deep into the forest. He first uttered more '*hoo hoo*' sounds, then several pant-hoots before with one bound he leapt onto the root to drum with rapid beats lasting about fifteen seconds. Before jumping to the ground, the ape screamed to the black night, lifting his head to the darkness, the sky above him pricked with star-points.

Chris felt a shiver down his spine.

Without fuss or murmur other than contented coughs from Charlie, they made their way back to the village. At the hut, Charlie drank deeply from a water bottle, as if slaking a dry-season thirst, each mouthful more satisfying than the last.

Jo sat up in her sleeping bag. 'Is everything all right?' she said anxiously.

'You know Jo, I just had the most amazing experience of my life. It was dark out there. Charlie drummed on a tree with his feet. The sound would have carried almost a mile. Did you hear it? He screamed too, a climax scream, as if...as if to say, "I'm back." The night held no terrors for him.'

'I was sleeping,' Jo said. 'Wow, Charles announces his imminent arrival to the forest!'

'I think we could be lucky Jo. Heaven knows why he hasn't gone soft on lambs' legs and nut and date bars. It's as if he wants to return to the wild, to go back, to be his own *person* – if you'll forgive the little nod to George's surgery skills.'

Jo chuckled to herself and slipped back under her mosquito net. Chris hunted for more palm wine but there was none left. He soon fell asleep next to Jo, exhausted by the long day's trekking, and the huge excitement.

*

In the morning John Embai brought tea at 7.30. Breakfast was eggs, Ryvita, butter spread, jam and coffee.

'I like Basho,' Chris told Jo, 'it's like an Arcadian paradise.' It was true; a sylvan spot with small paths leading off into the bush in many directions, animal life reasonably plentiful. To the south west of the village a small river ran where most of the villagers bathed. To the north east a larger river flowed between worn black rocks, rushing down from higher valleys deeper into the reserve.

'You can practise as a doctor again right here,' Jo said, when several natives came looking for help with health problems, mostly boils, sores, headaches, arthritis, measles or abscesses.

The chief's son had an ugly leg abscess, which was treated with penicillin. The chief dashed a jar of mimbo. Another man, an innocent, demented court jester known as 'the lunatic' dashed three eggs, all of them addled.

'You *must* thank him for the eggs, Chris,' Jo said, 'as if they were freshly laid.' She'd found out every time the lunatic dashed something, it was nearly always off or bad.

The pye-dog Smoky Joe had bought was growing stronger. Charlie's coat shone with health. For much of the day he was taken outside. He sat in a camp chair delighting in the sun but found it difficult to keep still. Sometimes he rolled over and over on the dry red earth at the end of a length of rope, provided by the headmaster of the village school. Word was sent out via John Embai and forest guard Mr Ayuk that any hunters who knew where to find chimpanzees in Takamanda Forest should visit the hut.

Later several hunters came to talk about the animals in the bush, mainly about chimpanzees, gorillas and different kinds of monkey.

John Embai ably questioned the hunters. '*Dis chimpanzee, ha e go waka?*'

One hunter squatted down, placing his knuckles on the ground just as a chimpanzee or gorilla would.

'*Dis chimpanzee, na how e go tok?*'

The man gave an exact replica of a chimp vocalisation. The questions moved on to gorillas.

'*Dis gorille, e go fit pass chimpanzee?*'

'*E go pass chimpanzee.*'

'*E go beat am fo ches?*'

'*No, gorille no beat ches, na chimpanzee e get stik fo hit tree!*'

'*Dis gorille, wetin e go do when e fit see man dey fo bush?*'

'*E go chase yu and hold yu plenti.*'

John Embai questioned the hunter again. '*Yu bi hunter-man long taym?*'

The man was irritated. He looked straight at Chris, avoiding the questioner. '*Massa, tell yua piccin ah bi hunter-man since ah bi dis high!*' He pointed to Chris's knee.

It was agreed with the last hunter to search in the bush for chimpanzees. A price had to be fixed. John Embai said, '*If wi go fo bush and see no ting, wi go pay yu 5,000 francs.*'

The hunter nodded his assent but waited quietly to hear more.

'*Wi go pay yu 10,000 francs fo fit see chimpanzee. If wi fit see chimpanzee* and *gorille fo eye, wi go pay yu 15,000, and dash yu 5,000 more.*'

The hunter, a wiry, kindly-faced man about 50 smiled broadly. '*Tank yu. Na fayn fayn. A gri, massa.*'

Chris asked what direction they would take. The hunter, whose name was Gabriel, said they must wait '*fo monin taym*'. Then he would see the colour of his blood (which really meant how he was feeling), and know which bush path to follow.

There was much haranguing about the direction of travel. Chris found his compass but kept it hidden. Gabriel pointed to the northeast. Chris showed him the 32-point compass rose, and joked that it would be able to point to where the chimpanzees lived in the bush. Gabriel laughed out loud and said, '*White man get sens pass black man.*'

Smoky brought news that a woman in the village had died. In the evening another dance began. It would last until dawn.

All night long noise came from the village centre, disturbing Charlie the most. He became restless, whimpering in his box or, if allowed inside the hut, crouching like a withdrawn autistic child alone in a corner. The rhythmic beat of drums, ululating cries, and sporadic gunshots were broken only for a short hour when a storm shook the village.

Tall hunters arrived at intervals throughout the night, walking right up to the hut, covering their eyes with one hand, and wailing like devils – part of 'cry die' celebrations for the West African wake. Then, each would aim his musket skywards and pull the trigger. The effect was usually electrifying; the music came to an abrupt stop, cocks crowed, and vibrations shook the ground for several seconds. Like the visiting hunters, Charlie also covered his eyes but with both hands.

At dawn, long-barrelled muskets or Dane guns boomed seven times. When the light grew stronger in the morning, Chris and Jo watched as the dead woman's calabashes and eating plates were ceremonially broken over a stone. There were rumours that relatives of the dead woman conducted a primitive post mortem (to find not so much the cause of death but which juju or witchcraft killed the person) but nothing could have saved her. The old woman died of old age.

By mid morning the village was quieter but drumming still persisted. Charlie had recovered as soon as the guns had stopped shooting. Jo supplemented their meagre diet with food bought in the village.

*

The local fare was mainly fowls, eggs, plantains, bananas, mangoes, pineapple, limes, pawpaw, papaya, sugar cane, yams, edible mushrooms, cocoyams, ground cassava (*garri*), *fufu* (made from boiled cassava, cocoyams or plantains), fresh fish, smoked fish, mudfish, groundnuts, coconut, snails, crayfish, and of course mimbo.

Other side dishes were edible grubs (one favourite the big, maggot-like pupae of the rhinoceros beetle, eaten raw or lightly fried in palm oil), honeycombs prised from holes in trees, the bees smoked out, and fresh or dried bushmeat. This could be anything: monkey legs/arms, crocodile, crocodile eggs, tortoise, pangolin, porcupine, forest squirrels, smoked frogs, bush-cow (buffalo), cane rats, hyraxes, duiker, antelope, bush pigs, etc.

*

The chief came again with his son. He was given lukewarm tea, paracetamol, and a vitamin pill. The penicillin had cleared his leg abscess.

Natives began arriving from Basho II (1.5 miles distant) and Mblishe (6 miles) for Chris and Jo's 'surgery', mostly first-aid: bathing, washing, cleaning wounds, applying antiseptic cream, covering sores, sprains, boils or bites with a bandage.

Old women complained of headaches, probably from the huge loads of firewood they carry home from the bush on their heads. The chief sent Chris a leaf of tobacco, about twelve inches high and six inches wide. In return Chris dispatched John Embai with some Bisto cubes and more paracetamol for his son. A small boy arrived and dashed a bottle of mimbo.

In the afternoon John Embai and Smoky Joe trekked to Basho II in search of food. They returned two hours later with seven small fish, one pineapple, and some limes.

When Gabriel announced their visit to the bush to look for chimpanzees would have to be delayed by two days because his wife was sick, Chris and Jo used the spare time to walk to Basho II. They were up before dawn, left some water and bananas and the last nut and date bar for Charlie, and set off.

When they arrived the village was sleeping as they walked through, after a trek of just 1.5 miles. John Embai bought five leaves of tobacco and one small fresh fish. Jo picked ten limes from a nearby tree. Smoky Joe wasted a little time, flirting with a native girl. As they were about to leave, the chief of the village, an old man with eyes full of good humour, welcomed them with an invitation to drink wine.

'*Mi ah don get fayn fayn mimbo fo drink. Welkom!*'

'It's early in the morning to drink,' Chris answered weakly.

'*Pah! Pipol dey de drink mimbo all dey, twenty-four hour! Abi?*'

So they entered in to the chief's 'sitting room', a hut raised about four feet from the earth, about ten yards wide by eight yards long. Rush mats were abundantly strewn on the floor. At the far end of the hut a kind of juju frame, three feet square, hung on the mud wall behind him. Animal skulls, like bush pig, chimpanzee, dogs, and small drums, had been fixed to the wooden frame.

The chief pointed to it. '*When pipol go die, ma on pipol, mi ah go put am dey!*'

'*Ah ha!*' replied Chris, understanding the chief's pidgin. '*No bi spirits – juju?*' The old chief cackled with laughter at this and filled a pipe with tobacco and smoked. They sat still in the gloom for what seemed at least ten minutes before a young boy wearing worn shorts brought a quart jug of mimbo.

Unusually for Chris, one glass of the sweet mimbo was enough. Jo swigged at a water bottle. They thanked the chief, and then set off for camp, John Embai's small, bare feet noiseless on the forest floor. Later Smoky Joe borrowed a net to try his luck in a nearby river. He caught seven tiny fish; they were cooked for a late breakfast. The lunatic also turned up and dashed two addled eggs.

The chief was dashed one leaf of tobacco and he went away happy. Later the chief of Basho II arrived; he was treated to more mimbo and a leaf also.

In the evening before their departure for the bush to try to find chimpanzees, a boy arrived with a letter from the headmaster.

Dear Mr Chris,

I have arranged with two hunters for your excursion into the jungle tomorrow. They have accepted to do so. You may sleep there.

They have assured me that, God being with you, it will be easy to find the chimpanzees. Here are their names. John Ata and Michael Tata.

I have some headache and fever, hence I am unable to see you. This will be the best way of seeing the animals.

I have sent to you one cluster of plantains, to be prepared for you. My wife leaves on Monday for Mamfe. Sorry for the delay. No children to travel with.

Thanks
Headmaster, Basho

The scrawled signature was indecipherable. There was no doubting his generosity and kindness. One of the two hunters came to the hut. Chris questioned him. He said he had never seen, heard or shot a chimpanzee in his life. It didn't seem at all unusual for some of the hunters to mix up the character of monkeys, chimpanzees and gorillas.

Chris took the hunter to Charlie's cage. As soon as he saw Charlie, glowering back at him with yellow-brown coals for eyes, he shook his head, saying '*Na e! Dis bif get plenti power fo hed.*' The hunter left without a murmur, and neither he nor the other hunter provisionally booked by the village headmaster turned up the following morning.

In the evening a group of about thirty villagers, most of them very young, between five and twenty years old, came to dance outside their hut. Chris brought out two chairs. A kerosene lamp was placed on the ground and the villagers danced round this. Several bare-breasted mammies came with suckling piccins and joined in the fun. Nearly all suckled or nestled their babies at the left breast where the mother's rhythmic heartbeat is more clearly heard.

Young boys expertly played skin-covered drums cradled between brown thighs, beating them lightly and repeatedly. A girl in a thin white smock whacked her buttocks with a tambourine. There was much cheering, laughing, clapping, singing and dancing well into the night. One song, translated in part was, 'I am leaving home in the morning – be a good boy.' Another, 'If it wasn't for harlots, bachelors couldn't live.'

There was an interruption when Charlie vocalised from the hut, just loud enough for Chris and Jo to hear him. 'I'll take a look,' Chris said.

'What was it?' Jo asked when he got back.

'Charlie spotted a nine-inch centipede. Smoky Joe said it had come through a tiny hole in the wall.'

'Did you get rid of it?'

'Smoky said they sting so he killed it with my fishing rod.'

'Where's the pye-dog?'

'Curled up in front of Charlie's box.'

Soon after the party ended Chris and Jo climbed into their sleeping bags, looking forward to the journey into the bush to find signs of chimpanzee. Jo was to stay behind to look after Charlie. The entire village was soon fast asleep in the humid tropical night.

Only the ape was awake, brooding in silence, breathing softly without any effort, his brown yellow liquescent eyes glinting in the silver moonlight, ears randomly twitching, as if listening to the sounds of the forest, which tremor by tremor and vibration by vibration entered into his ears, and carried on into his mind the spirit of his jungle home.

FIFTY-EIGHT

'Thank goodness for tea,' Jo whispered to Chris when John Embai padded silently into the hut with two cups of tea. 'I just wish I could come with you.'

'So do I but someone has to keep an eye on him,' Chris said, glancing at Charlie who looked back open mouthed, baring his teeth in a kind of supercilious grin. 'I've decided there are definitely similarities between apes and us – whether or not they have had brain operations.'

'Oh yes,' Jo said drily. 'Do tell me.'

'Well, they vary between empathy and extreme violence like humans do. One moment they are grooming, the next tearing each other apart. There are also similarities with the tyranny of sex and hormones, jealousy, though some degree less for bonobos.'

'Very thoughtful this morning,' Jo observed.

'And they don't torture one another for the sake of religious beliefs, stone to the death for adultery, burn each other alive, break their bones on a rack, pull out teeth with pliers, or forcibly extract toe and fingernails.' Chris had indeed become very thoughtful. He sighed and there was silence. Then his eyes took on a glazed look as he said quietly, '*Ecce homo. Ἰδοὺ ὁ ἄνθρωπος.* Behold the man.' Then, he paused, saying '*Ecce troglodytes!*'

Jo laughed at his mock-serious face. She gently stabbed his chest seven times with her index finger. 'No! *Ec-ce ell-i-o-ti!*'

'It's about time that plasticity that George kept going on about started to work. God, what an operation! As it is, looks like we just have another chimp on our hands, very much like another. I mean...'

Chris stopped because Charlie had grabbed the front bars in his cage and was pushing against them hard. At the same time a blood-curdling scream erupted from his throat. He stared at Chris with the same malevolent glare he had once reserved for Mr Foucham in Mamfe. In just a few minutes the hardened wooden bars snapped as a growing child can snap a pencil.

Charlie climbed from his cage and shook his body, as if releasing all the pent-up energy in his muscles. With a bipedal swagger he quickly crossed the few feet to Chris, pinning him in a corner of the hut.

'Look, Charlie,' Chris implored, 'I didn't mean it, okay?' He cowered under Charlie's menacing stance, one of the ape's arms leant against a wall, the other free to catch him if he dared move. While Chris stood there with his eyes shut, fearful that Charlie might go for him, he called out, 'Jo, help for Christ's sake!'

The ape turned his head and snarled at Jo as if to say don't even try it. Then, with his free hand, he brushed Chris's face, slapping it from side to side but without real force, as if solely intended as a deterrent or warning.

Jo's stomach was suddenly queasy. She had to get to a toilet fast. She ran out of the hut, heading for the patch where a large hole in the ground served as a communal latrine.

When she came back, she saw Charlie suddenly back off, leaving Chris wobbly on his feet. 'Are you all right?'

'You'll have to stay behind now,' Chris gasped. 'Far too much of a risk leaving him on his own.'

Jo got the leash. She secured Charlie, taking his mind off any more outbursts with the expedient gift of several fat bananas and a plastic bottle filled with water.

'He really scared me, Jo. It was almost as if he was reading my thoughts.'

*

The plan was to leave in the morning for Obonye I, said to be the wildest part of Takamanda.

Chris called in to the chief's hut to say goodbye but he was away on a visit to a native court. His son had mouth ulcers. He was given an antiseptic mouthwash. Mr Ayuk the forest guard shouldered his 30/06, and together with John Embai and Smoky Joe and the intrepid hunter Gabriel, Chris left the village by 10.30 the next morning, with several pretty mammies acting as well-wishers on the road out.

The path to Obonye branched off from the Akwa road just half a mile from Basho. After an hour's trek through forest with rich vegetation, the path running beneath umbrella-like musanga trees, they came to an old wooden signboard, and written on this, hidden in parts by moss, the words TAKAMANDA FOREST.

By 2.30 a.m. after a ten-mile trek they reached Nfakwe, a village of about twenty huts, staying overnight in the chief's hut. Their goal was now Obonye II, said to be an even wilder part of the forest, close to the Nigerian border, after a hunter said he had seen chimpanzees there and reported that, '*Dis bush bi very bad bad, no man fit enta, plenti plenti bad bif.*'

'*Wich taym yu go see am?*' Chris asked.

The hunter replied, '*Bifor-bifor, long taym, soteeeeey...*'

'*Wetin kayn bushbif?*'

'*Cimpanzay, gerillerai – muki, tiga, antlope, elefan.*'

By 'bad bush' the hunter meant deep rivers, slippery streams, hills hard to climb, rocks strewn like giant boulders, dangerous animals, the remoteness, the forest thick and impenetrable in places, especially in the wet season rain and mist. Gabriel seemed convinced, however, they would succeed. His muscles were honed to corded perfection by years of trekking and hunting in the bush.

After a good night's sleep, Smoky brought eight eggs to share for breakfast and some coconuts, and a little porridge. On the way to Obonye was Assam, some 12 miles away. They crossed a small stream just outside the village and after an hour came to a large river where they stopped for twenty minutes for coffee.

Nearby were definite signs of the wily, small forest elephant. With their tusks the elephants had uprooted the ground in search of roots and wild yams. On the way to the nearest village, Takpe, the small bush path was blocked by a pile of elephant dung. Hornbills, when disturbed, noisily flew away on great wings. They found more elephant trails and 'rubbing trees' where the elephants had eased their giant carcases against one side of a tree, removing most of the bark. Broken and twisted saplings were more evidence.

The most startling confirmation, however, was to see 9 inch diameter, circular holes, sometimes a foot deep, where the soft mud had given way to several tons of animal weight. One 'monster' imprint measured 12 inches across.

This excitement spurred Chris on. Rounding a bend in the path, he saw what appeared to be chimpanzees brachiating through the lower canopy level. He wanted to shout out loud in a lung-bursting yell. *'Charlie, George, Jo – we've found them!'* But it was difficult to make out if they were chimpanzees or mona or patas monkeys, yet the way the dark shapes moved was so reminiscent of Charlie that he was convinced. It all took place in about four seconds, leaving just still-swaying branches. The apes, if they were apes, did not vocalise.

The small party eventually reached Takpe, a village of some ten houses. A woman brought out a reclining chair for Chris. Gabriel opened several cool coconuts with his machete, and they drank the juice mixed with a dash of lime. It was decided not to go back to look for the chimpanzees but to press on deeper into the forest.

Assam was now eight miles away. It was the most tiring part of the trek that day. Walking uphill from a small river near Assam, they emerged onto a level plain, an avenue of trees stretching towards the town, about 800 yards away from the school hut used for their overnight stay. Supplies of food were low but the chief exchanged a chicken for tea, coffee and sugar. A man offered to sell a chimpanzee skull. Chris bargained for it and packed it in a rucksack. It was the skull of a male chimpanzee, the skull darkened with age.

The next day they left early, negotiated a very wide river (the canoe man was absent) and arrived at Obonye 1 at 3.00 p.m., a distance of 15 miles. Before they reached the village, the sound of heavy drums drifted through the forest, the traditional African way in the bush of sending messages over long distances.

By custom, the chief's house is always open to strangers. They waited for at least an hour, the heavy drums resonating from the bush, but who were the drummers, it was impossible to see. Eventually the chief came. He asked for papers. Chris told him they had come to look for signs of chimpanzee in the forest, to photograph them. He nodded but his face remained reserved in character. Smoky Joe translated. 'I will call a meeting of my people. We will question you and see whether you can stay in our village.'

Chris sat quietly in the chief's house while the others gossiped outside. In another hut a group of ten men argued over their fate. Soon a demand came. Chris should come before the chief and his elders, assembled on their veranda. It was agreed they could stay – as long as they shot and killed all the animals they saw in the bush!

Meat was available after a hunter shot a duiker. Smoky bought sweet potatoes and ripe pawpaw. At dawn, everything was ready for the trip. Gabriel was quietly confident. The chief complained that his wife wasn't well and to help her get better, impaled a tortoise on a length of bamboo.

They trekked steadily and rested after the first five miles. A troupe of *sumbu* or drills, numbering five or six animals, scattered high in the canopy (the word *sumbu* was loosely used to mean 'monkey'). Gabriel stopped to make juju with large green leaves he'd picked. First he spat on the leaves, then pressed them into the earth, with a prayer they should find chimpanzees. They trekked another four miles, then stopped to have chop, resting on a fallen trunk, by the side of a river. Gabriel cut more strips of leaves, placed them flat on his machete and tossed them skywards. Depending on how the leaves fell to the ground would determine whether they found chimpanzees. The leaves must have fallen the right way because Gabriel smiled happily.

Then he took five pinnate leaves, made a screwball of them, found a larger leaf inside which he placed the former, put the whole collection on the sand near the river bank and pressed the caboodle into the earth. He began weird incantations. Chris heard the word '*cimpanzay*' three times. Gabriel then asked him to spit onto the remains and press them even further into the sandy earth.

He began cutting a path through the bush uphill. Chris, Mr Ayuk, Smoky Joe and John Embai followed, trying to make as little noise as possible. About four hundred yards up the hill, Gabriel whistled back, '*Na tiga*'. No tiger was seen but perhaps he meant a civet cat. He did say he had leopard skins at his house. Suddenly, to their right came a rustling in the branches above. A collared or red-capped mangabey monkey peered through the foliage, bobbed his head, and scampered out of sight. Then a bay duiker ran past very fast with Gabriel trying his aim in vain.

Chris saw two nests, about 40 feet off the ground, large enough for chimpanzees. Beneath the trees were clear signs of foraging, small plants stripped and a yellow fruit cracked open, the insides eaten out.

They moved on, as quietly as possible. Smoky heard more monkeys. A troupe of twelve mangabeys came close, dropping fifteen feet onto lower branches. Half the group branched off west, half to the east. Chris was praying Gabriel wouldn't shoot.

Instead the hunter mimicked duiker noises through his teeth. There was a huge roaring gunshot but he missed, the monkeys continuing to crash off into the bush.

Chris sat down, feeling exhausted. He was thinking of the incredible journeys he, George and Jo had all taken to get Charlie back to Africa. But it was no clearer yet in his mind *where* Charlie would find his spot of earth, his 'peace' in the forest, whether there was such an indefinably vague thing in the bush as sanctuary for chimpanzees, for gorillas even, for apes, when humans encroached from all sides, taking their habitat, destroying ecosystems, pushing species after species in an inexorable slide to extinction.

Gabriel started to reload, a tedious, time-wasting business taking five minutes but done with relative efficacy. His gun was over five feet long, with a four-foot barrel made from water pipe, no sights – a muzzle-loading shotgun, a cap shotgun, with one rusty hammer.

First, he opened his shooting bag – a tough pouch made from monkey skin, crammed with odd bric-à-brac. He took from this two miniature calabash powder-holders, held together with string. He emptied one measure of gunpowder from a small glass bottle, poured it down the barrel, used the ramrod, stuffed some wadding home, dropped eleven small lead balls down, then more wadding, cleaned the flash-hole, a little gunpowder there, put on the cap, and cocked the hammer.

Chris thought the best part of the Dane gun was its duiker-skin flash guard. While the indigenous people had such guns (nearly all made in Nigeria), animal life would survive – one shot only, five minutes to reload, inaccurate except at point-blank range. The natives were formidable hunters, able to get close to their quarry. But new guns were common in the forest now, and at cry dies.

After the reloading they pressed on. When he moved through the bush, every few yards Gabriel snapped the stem of a plant or fern so that he could always find his way back. They heard a frightening noise, like the sound of a forest elephant rampaging through the brush. Gabriel motioned to the others to catch up. They followed him into a small ravine where he shot a duiker that escaped into cover. Ten minutes later another shot, killing stone dead the forest's peace, birds' shrieking their alarm calls.

Gabriel came back to lay the antelope at their feet. Both male and female were in the covert, the female escaped. The dead animal, still warm to the touch, blood dripping from its nose, was bound with hide, fore and back legs tied together, a stick pushed through its nostrils to make a hole for twine, all tied up with hideous but professional efficiency.

They set off towards Gabriel's camp, not far from Obonye II, passed another troupe of about twelve mona monkeys, met further elephants trails, then climbed down a steep hill to reach Gabriel's hut, an idyllic site, 30 yards from a medium-sized river. Here were plantains, bananas and cassava, which he had planted. All bathed in the river, except Mr Ayuk who was hunting for his hip flask, while the '*bushbif*' was drawn and quartered by Gabriel. Chop that night was just potatoes, tea and meat going high – dried meat brought with them for the journey. 'Fresh' meat was rarely eaten. Dusk fell, and the small band huddled near a fire that burned in the centre of the hut (it had no walls; just a roof made of plantain leaves, and poles to support it). Perhaps there may have been a leopard prowling and forest elephants only yards away but all felt safe by the fire.

During the night it rained heavily. Lightning continually lit up the sky, in the few places where it was visible under the canopy. Swirling mist crept with tapering fingers through the forest. Chris lay wide awake. He felt the trees had a primeval aura about them, as though they had all descended into another world, a world where monsters took the form of twisting trees, where winds howled like dogs, and where the air was at times raucous with screeching cries and at others, pensively mute, listening to its own breathing.

The next day they left the camp early, crossed a large river and four miles later Gabriel pointed out buffalo, or bush-cow prints and duiker slots in the red earth. Gabriel moved with the agility and patience of a skilled tracker, his senses attuned to the forest around him. He showed Chris a troupe of around 15 mangabeys with several large drills among them. They crept as noiselessly as possible until they were right under the monkeys. Gabriel grabbed a small bush, swished it to and fro, making a hissing sound between his teeth.

Immediately, the monkeys vocalised, the big ones grunted harshly. Many were almost two hundred feet above in the canopy and quite safe from Gabriel's anachronism of a gun. So it went on for some 15 minutes, the bush shaking and vocalisations, until the monkeys eventually left staring after them.

More mangabeys were seen, about five, and then Gabriel stopped so they could listen to the unmistakable calls, the *pyows* and *hacks*, of putty-nosed monkeys. But there was no sign of chimpanzees.

After they began to climb a forested hill, a shot rang out. It was the deafening roar of Gabriel's muzzle loader, shattering once again the peace of the forest. A duiker fell, not quite dead. Gabriel throttled the antelope. He said they should go on a little further and they would be sure to find chimpanzees. He pointed out places where he had shot them.

A palaver was inevitable. They needed food but the shots would drive away any chimpanzees. Chris wanted to return to Obonye before dark but Gabriel said it was too far and that they would be hunted by elephants.

Gabriel stayed behind to return to his hunting camp, saying he would join them after a few days. Chris tried to remember the way back. Mr Ayuk could not be relied upon as he had secreted a full bottle of African gin in a pocket of his green forestry jacket, and was already half drunk. After four miles they met the pungent smell of elephant, and saw where the huge beasts had crossed their path moments before.

Weary from trekking and fearing for his safety, John Embai whispered, '*Na tru, massa. Dis bi bad bad bush. Ah tin se plenti juju fo dis rod.*'

Chris tried his best to show he was not frightened by the bush or the path or the 'road' through it. Suddenly there came the blood-curdling trumpet of an elephant in the thick bush, yards from their path. It ended with a whimsical scream. No one dared move. Daylight would soon be gone and forest elephants are very cunning.

They pressed on, waded through a small river and tired and exhausted reached Obonye I at 5.30 p.m. They were welcomed back by the chief and villagers. Chris sat down and poured himself a lime juice.

FIFTY-NINE

They were still two hundred yards from the village when the pye-dog yelped and ran outside the hut. His small, stocky legs carried him quickly to the outskirts of Basho. In the distance trekked a thin line of five souls, weary, hungry, but for Chris at least, happy at the thought he had had a sighting of wild chimpanzees at last. At least he had managed to convince himself that the black shapes briefly glimpsed through the upper canopy of the forest belonged to wild chimpanzees.

When they reached the village, Charlie turned his head, as if listening. He began the characteristic, species-specific pant-hoot, a long-distance vocalisation. It began with soft '*hoos*', increasing in volume, building to a call climax, with screams, occasional barks, then the screams died down to soft '*hoos*' once more.

John Embai came into the hut, looked at the ape. '*Mek yu no vex mi! Wetin dey do yu?*' he said, which was like saying, 'Don't upset me! What's wrong with you?'

Jo ran out too. When she saw Chris, she rushed to him. 'Did you see them, did you find any chimps?' she asked out of breath.

'We saw some, between Assam and Obonye. They were in the trees, far up, couldn't see much.'

Jo abruptly threw her arms round Chris and kissed him. 'I'm so happy you're back. We must tell George!'

'I'm still not sure,' Chris confided. 'There's so much ground, territory to cover. The best place for him could be twenty miles from here or fifty, and there's lots of hunting for bush meat.'

'What do you need to find?' asked Jo anxiously.

'We know what Charlie's made of, you and I. We know, don't we, that little imp, how he's George's peerless prince. I have to say he pushed his luck the last time he held me against that hut wall – in fact, how is he, Jo? Has everything been all right?'

'Charlie's been absolutely wonderful. I just wish I could read his thoughts. He's kind of very self-absorbed. He looks at the pye-dog as if he could kill him sometimes; it reminds me of Helga, but they usually sleep together, like friends.'

'What he needs is an established group in safe territory. Where are we likely to find that?'

'The way I see is that he's still got to go through the hierarchy business, hasn't he? Unless he starts his own group. Is that so far-fetched?'

'There's no saying. Did you see any unusual behaviour while I was away? Signs that George's oft-famed plasticity is working? It's been a few months now since the operation.'

'No, nothing to remark on. It's not so much *what* he does as the way he stares. His eyes bore into you, with an eerie knowing look, and you wonder what's going on in his mind.'

'I don't think Basho's right for him,' George said. 'He needs to go deeper, much further into the bush, maybe to the north and west.'

'Funny you should say that Chris,' Jo said. 'There's a hunter in the village who thinks the same way. I spoke to him while you were away.'

'What did he say?'

'He said that you need to take the ape to the edges of this reserve, way up, high – in fact you know he said – "*soteeeeey*", so I guess that's far. He needs to go almost as far as the Nigerian border, up beyond to places called, what was it, Matene, Esengi? Especially Esengi. There are few huts or quarters there. It must be all semi-montane forest, lush valleys, galleried forests, grass-covered hills, that kind of thing.'

Chris pondered. He was thinking if Jo was right, if the hunter really knew. Conditions near Takamanda and Obonye were lacking something. It was as if the forest was no longer virginal, not quite. Too many hunters had combed the bush for too many years. Charlie's Shangri-La would be in isolated valleys, in green places with plenty of water, surrounded by mountains, remote, almost out of reach. He pursed his lips in thought.

'Chris, what is it Chris?' Jo implored.

Chris strode to the field outside their hut, waving his arms to the distance. In a deep voice, watched by some curious, beguiled natives, he began to speak, as if addressing an empty theatre of earth and sky. 'So our chimp, our peerless prince, must from Basho town take his leave, and make his way to cloud-capp'd hills. Not foreign climes but the further bush beyond, *soteeey*, so far, to find his place. There will our Charlie meet his proper destiny, and his life be rightfully fulfilled. The hills summon him! The blue remembered hills. They call him back, this paragon of ape and man!'

A hunter appeared from nowhere, a man of about fifty-five, clad in very little, not even a shirt, just plastic shoes and tattered shorts, his Dane gun almost as tall as he was. He touched Chris gently, holding his arm. He spoke softly. '*Na dis place yu de tok nau? Esengi. Matene. Bush near dat place bi good bush fo yua piccin bif. Man cimpanzay? Chop, water, forest, no bi many pipol.*'

Chris looked at the man, nodding.

'*Ah-hah! Mi a don tell yu first. No bi so?*'

Chris smiled. '*Welkom. Yua on nem na weti?*'

'*Tank yu. Ma nem na Jonas*,' the hunter replied. '*Jonas. Mi tu kal Captain Tiko. Ah de ste no fawe fo Obonye.*'

'*Yu fit waka fo dat bush?*'

'*Yes, ah fit waka. Betta follow fo yu,*' said the hunter, wishing him good luck. '*Bring am fo Esengi bush, yua man bif.*'

Chris quickly made up his mind. They would take Charlie to the bush, near Esengi or Matene villages. There was no time left for exploring. The longer Charlie stayed in the hut, the harder it would be for him to adapt to life in the forest. Once there, he would be abandoned, left to fend for himself.

Suddenly the sound of drums started again in the village. 'Maybe someone's died,' Jo said. 'Or had twins, a girl married, we'll have to wait a day or two because there'll be no carriers for Charlie. Can you find out what's happening? What do you think?'

'How should I know?' Chris answered tetchily, feeling angry

because he couldn't leave immediately for the bush. 'They might mean anything – a visit from another chief, strangers, a marriage, a birth, a death in the village. I'll ask Mr Ayuk.'

Mr Ayuk was nowhere to be found. Instead, he sent John Embai.

'I think I'll take Charlie out for some exercise,' Jo said, thinking she'd discover why the drums were beating so much when she got back.

After ten minutes, John Embai returned. *'Massa, no bi cry die – cry chop, and big dans. Wuman go mari big man fo village. Na yong wuman – ngondele, titi.'*

Chris understood most of it. A young woman was to marry a powerful man in the village, and there would be dancing.

John Embai smiled coyly. *'Na danjumba,'* he said, which meant a serious love affair.

Jo changed her mind about taking Charlie for a walk, so Chris led him away from the village on the path north to a river. The ape stopped every now and then, and turned his head, as if listening to the beating drums. Charlie found the cottonwood tree with the buttressed roots, the one he had used for his own drumming, an important way for chimpanzees to communicate with one another in the forest. Chris let him go, it was only early afternoon, they had plenty of time.

Silently, Charlie climbed up the towering bole with the most intent concentration, all the muscles in his body seeming to propel him higher, with facile strength and agility. He reached the upper branches and when he had found a safe place to stop, looked out from his vantage point, much higher than when he had sailed skyward on the balloon.

Feeling the power in his limbs, Charlie must have felt a surge of his coming freedom, as if he anticipated he would soon be free. His gaze ranged over the forest north of the village, and because the sky was clear, he would have seen a vision of the great expanse of Takamanda Forest Reserve, wave upon unstoppable wave of trees climbing to the far distance, strange because the trees were going uphill, to the mountains, the highlands near Matene and Esengi.

There, in valleys and steep ravines, the forest fought to climb the hillsides, eventually giving way altogether to grass-covered hills, burnt off once a year, rolling ever on and on, as far as Nigeria and the Obudu Plateau.

Charlie looked down below to see Chris staring up at him. Then the ape's chest convulsed with his four stage, pant-hoot display, '*hoos*' leading up to staccato screams that exploded into the forest around them, a display of primeval power that made Chris suddenly think Charlie could scare off a gorilla, if he wanted to.

'Come down, Charlie, will you?' Chris called out. Instead of complying with the request, Charlie snapped off a thick branch near his head, and then thrashed the leaves around him into broken bits. From the depths of the forest Chris thought he heard a solitary cry, another vocalisation from beyond the river, but it might have been an echo, he couldn't tell.

Once again Charlie's head jutted out while he barked to the hills, shook his furry pelage, and with extreme adroitness plunged to lower branches, and then down to the ground by Chris's feet.

'What an ape you are!' Chris said out loud, amazed at the alert dexterity. Charlie put up one arm, and began to rub his head with one hand. Chris noticed he was rubbing the crown of his head, at the exact site of the operation.

'What is it, Charles?' Chris asked, suddenly immensely curious to know how the new cells the ape received from George were coping. It was as if the doctor in him had suddenly awoken to the prospect of all the synapses in the ape's brain firing, the plasticity George had talked about having come true.

Charlie held out his hand but just as Chris was about to take it, Charlie smartly pulled back and gripped Chris's wrist with a swinging counter move that took Chris completely by surprise. In the ape's grasp he could do nothing. Slowly Charlie began to twist.

Chris gasped. He felt powerless, and the pain from his twisted wrist was growing stronger. Without letting go of Chris's wrist, Charlie seized his leash, carelessly left on one of the buttress roots. He pushed one end through the hand loop, and then with one sharp flick threw it over Chris's head, and pulled. Now Chris was caught in two places, by his neck and wrist.

Charlie grunted. Slowly he released the grip on his keeper's wrist. Chris stood up but could see Charlie had no intention to let go. To Chris's astonishment, Charlie grabbed a small stick with his free hand and began to swipe at Chris's legs. Chris turned on the path. Charlie gave him slack, enough for him to start walking back to the village. 'Oh my God,' thought Chris, 'he's taking *me* in!'

Chris led the way back to the village. They passed two mammies carrying water calabashes on their heads. One said, '*Babo! Who born monkey?*' They took one look at Chris in harness and fled back into the bush.

Mr Ayuk was at the hut. He scratched his head in wonder. Jo ran out to see Charlie sitting in a camp chair with Chris squatting on the ground, held in check by the leash. He looked very sheepish. 'Don't ask me why, Jo. Charlie decided to restrain me. God, he's got a powerful grip.'

Jo pushed the leash over his head. Charlie didn't seem to mind. 'Mr Ayuk, bring me bananas!' The old forest guard scrabbled around in the hut and came back with two. He gingerly gave one to Charlie. At the same time, Charlie put out his hand to demand the other one. He sat in the camp chair quietly eating while Chris brushed himself down, ran his fingers through his hair, and said, 'Christ, Jo, I've just been through it.'

'I think it's curfew time for both of you, playing games like that,' said Jo, crossly.

'I had nothing to do with it!' Chris was getting upset now. 'That ape is responsible, entirely responsible. He went up a tree, came down, and I'm buggered if he didn't lasso me with his own leash! He also tried to twist my arm off, to make sure I'd be no trouble. George's idea of plasticity is getting out of hand.'

Jo tried to shrug it off. It made no sense. She looked at Charlie, and received in a return an almost reproving stare.

'Let's pack. After the celebration we have to get him to the bush.

When is the party, anyway?' she asked, the drums starting up again in the village.

Chris had no idea. Mr Ayuk said, '*Tumoro. Ah get fo res tude. Ah de taya.*' He was tired because of too much mimbo and African gin.

Charlie watched him leave for a nearby hut. The ape looked round as if bored and clapped his hands.

'What the hell? If he thinks he's summoning me, he can think again.' Chris picked up a cushion and threw it at Charlie. Charlie caught it and wedged it under his tiny buttocks, pushing himself into a relaxed position.

It was decided they all needed to rest. Smoky Joe asked for money to buy mimbo for the party, and then he left for the bush to tap a few palms.

After coaxing Charlie back into his cage, Jo and Chris lay down on their makeshift beds to rest but they couldn't because the drumming pervaded the village, even the walls of their hut.

Before dawn a few scraggy cockerels announced the day of the party. It seemed as if the whole village came to life slowly by degrees. Mammies began cooking in earnest. People came in from other villages. The pye-dogs sensed there was food in the air from the cooking smells, bushmeat wrapped in leaves and smoked over fires, the *fufu* made ready, the sauces, the rich red palm oil, and still the drumming persisted, not light drums but heavy wooden ones whose 'boom, boom, boom' carried into the bush, making even ponderous hornbills take flight.

The centre of the village was made ready for a tribal dance. Mr Ayuk had recovered from too much mimbo. He was already looking forward to the day's delights. Charlie was more relaxed than ever, sitting contentedly in a camp chair, his leash secured to a very large piece of wood.

Smoky began to sing a song. '*De ting wich ma mother tol mi, weti ma mami bin tell mi, e don kam tru. Wan ol man bin mari wan smol girl but de girl an ah bin bi frens bet de ol man don kam. As e don kam now, danjumba e da finish.*'

Another young boy joined in with his song, translated by one man whose English was good, a man originally from Buea. 'One boy is crying and saying, "Where shall I sleep? Where shall I sleep? People who are married have someone to sleep with, men get wives, but I have no woman – where can I sleep?" The boy keeps his eyes on the road all day long, looking for a girl to marry but finds no girl.'

Before the party started in the afternoon, Jo treated more people in her 'surgery'. A mother brought in an emaciated child of three who hadn't defecated for three days. A minute later, the child did so, onto the floor of the hut, and as soon as this happened a thin pye-dog rushed up and ate the faeces.

'You see that local dog,' the man from Buea explained. 'Nobody feeds them and so that is why they have to eat human faeces. Dogs here are little more than pariahs, outcasts.' The dog then licked the child's anus. Feeling sorry for the pye-dog, Chris gave it some cold boiled rice, which was wolfed ravenously. The natives laughed at this, saying in Bakweri language, '*Mokala! Mokala!* White man! White man! What strange things they do.'

The headmaster of the village sent a note asking for one jar of kerosene. Their supplies were almost nil. It was strange to be in such a paradise. Life was hard but the people were happy. Few complained. Hardly anyone wore shoes, as if trusting to the goodness of mother earth. From few resources, colourfully dressed mammies toiled over tureens, pounded cassava with outsize mortars and pestles, cracked palm nuts, prepared *garri*, mixed fresh leaves and herbs, made pepper soup. Fine cuisine was not sought after in the bush. Most villagers looked to being satisfied, so they could eat their fill, and say happily, '*Belle don fulup.*'

'What do you mean to do with Charlie?' Jo asked at lunchtime, which was several small fish caught in the nearby river, and vegetable sauce and *fufu* provided by a kind mammy, friendly with the headmaster.

'Our goal is to get to Esengi. Jonas says it's a small place, only four huts, high up on grass-covered hills but the bush is remote, two miles from the village, and that's where we'll take Charlie, as soon as Captain Tiko, Jonas, leads us to a chimpanzee troupe. I know if we were conducting a scientific experiment, we'd have to stay, keep an eye on him. I don't think either of us has the time, do you?'

Jo stared wistfully ahead, deep in her own thoughts. She wanted to hear from George, to speak to him but there was no reception so far into the bush. 'First there was one miracle,' she said slowly. 'That was George conducting his experiment and Charlie coming out fighting. Now we have to expect another miracle. Leaving Charlie to cope on his own, to somehow hope he will just merge into the bush, fade into the forest dim, find his feet, whatever. God, he doesn't seem to know the first thing about foraging for food. All he does is sit in our camp chair, and occasionally clap his hands!'

And while she thought, and Chris, also troubled, mused on what he would find at Esengi village, the fate of Charlie, village drums kicked into life, to more insistent rhythms, the signal that the celebration was about to begin.

SIXTY

The delay in moving out for Esengi gave Chris and Jo time to pack up and prepare for Charlie's transfer to a more amenable part of the reserve. By early afternoon excitement was building but it was not until 4.00 p.m. that a procession of dancers came through the village, dressed in multicoloured swirling robes and dresses. Carried through the village on her own elaborate 'bush chair' came the bride, dressed in a strapless, short white satin dress, her arms and neck dangling with gold bangles and necklaces.

Chris was stunned. 'She's like the Queen of Sheba,' he gasped. Small boys followed in the procession, weaving in and out of the crowd with their bare feet, clamouring to touch her. John Embai remarked that the bride price must have been very high for such a beautiful young girl.

Jo discovered that the bride had married earlier in Limbe but that she'd returned home to Basho for the village celebration.

Mr Ayuk was angry, having a big palaver with one of the carriers, after discovering a cache of mimbo he had bought the day before was all gone. Mr Ayuk had the man by the neck. He said, '*Yu bi tief-man, no bi kohret tek ol mimbo.*'

The carrier, who was only quite young, confessed, and said he was sorry. '*Ashya. Wi don drink all dat swit mimbo we yu bin bay am yestade.*'

The drumming continued through the afternoon. Everyone in the village joined in, carrying food on plates or plantain leaves to all who asked. The food was washed down with copious streams of mimbo. Chris saw one young man who had made a drinking goblet from a cow's horn. Hidden in huts, groups of old men shared round glasses of African gin. Gunshots sounded every now and then.

The newly-wed husband, an engineer from Buea, carried jugs of wine to the girl's father and mother – a few of which were possibly intercepted by the canny forest guard. To show her happiness the young bride began to dance at the head of a group of female dancers. She threw off her shoes, dancing with bare brown feet. Mammies clapped and cheered her on, the eyes of their piccins round and bright with glee.

The men of the village tried hard to take their eyes off her but most failed dismally. The girl was as lithe as the young trees in the forest, sinuous and nubile, fertile as a many-seeded pomegranate. It was a peculiar vision, a girl in a modern wedding dress prancing and leaping, stamping and beating the red earth with her naked feet.

Chris was inside his hut, packing things ready for the journey to Esengi. He found the chimp skull he'd bought at Assam. The bone was dark, not bleached like a laboratory specimen. He sat down, holding it up to examine it more closely. Some teeth were missing. The lower jawbone was detachable.

Turning the skull over, he saw the angled foramen magnum – the hole or opening in the skull where the spine joined it, the spine exiting it an angle. From there the spinal chord nerves connected directly into the brain. He reflected how the human foramen magnum is right under the brain case, as humans evolved to walk upright rather than the angled posture of knuckle-walking.

'Alas, poor *ellioti*...'

Suddenly John Embai rushed in. '*Massa, nyu dans begin, kam.*' John Embai grabbed his arm and pulled. Chris tumbled out. He saw fifty to sixty people setting up tables, preparing the ground outside their hut for dancing. Mammies brought still more food. Calabashes of palm wine adorned more rickety tables. Among the guests was the village headmaster, dressed like a master of ceremonies in a resplendent native gown, a fading bowler hat, white shirt and bow tie.

'This should be fun,' Jo said. 'Shall we bring Charlie outside too?'

'Why not,' Chris answered. 'I suppose one more exposure to

dozens of humans en masse isn't going to hurt. Make sure he's secured well. In fact, why not put him in a camp chair? He seems to like that.'

So Charlie was brought out in the late afternoon sun. He was settled in one of the chairs, to oversee the occasion. A circle of brightly-costumed dancers formed, and several times Charlie stood up, as if to get a better view. Graceful girls lightly stamped the earth, not dancing fast, but in the slow seductive shuffle most Africans seem to like best. A girl blew on a whistle stuck in her mouth.

Six young men with goatskin-covered, carved wooden drums called djembe drums assembled in the dance area. Two other men with much larger drums beat out an introduction. Mr Ayuk's face was creased with a certain kind of joy.

Chris was in charge of Charlie, making sure he was relaxed and safe. (In fact, Charlie's mood was fairly irascible, because he had helped himself to some pepper soup, and found it rather hot.) Then the young men, sitting astride their djembes, readied themselves. A hush fell on the crowd. The two lovers kissed.

The headmaster rushed forward with a cane held high in the air. 'God bless you both,' he cried. 'May you find all the happiness there is to find in this world!' One young boy drummer slapped his djembe for a solo turn and a great cry of jubilation went up.

A mammy carrying two jugs of mimbo passed close to Charlie. She stopped to look at the ape. Charlie pouted back at her until the woman bawled, '*Ah dey fear yu o!*'

Charlie seized an opportunity. He stood up and made a grab at the handle of a calabash. Before the woman realised, Charlie had it. He had often been given water from calabashes but had never tasted mimbo. He took one swig, swallowed, and sat back in his chair, tightly clutching his prize. Jo tried to take it from him, but Charlie menacingly bared his teeth. He took another swig, and his lips curled in appreciation. A cheer went up from the crowd when Charlie drained the calabash, and promptly threw it on the ground.

The children loved it. Charlie got up, tired of sitting, a spectator at his own spectacle. While the young men drummed, Charlie did an impromptu bipedal dance. There were more squeals of delight.

'Better get him inside,' Jo said but Chris wouldn't hear of it, so Charlie was allowed his time upon the stage of destiny.

*

The solo drummer caught Charlie's attention first. In fact he was mesmerised by all the drummers. The way their hands so delicately struck the middle of the drum head with palm and fingers, then new sounds made closer to the rim, where the drum head is tighter. The drummers at times held their fingers tightly for more tonal depth, or opened them for more relaxed sounds.

So much mimbo had been consumed and so happy were that throng in the African bush (a pageant in which it seemed all the souls of the village, the scrawny cockerels, the scraggy pye-dogs too, were entwined as one in the dance of life) – that none would have guessed the unfolding drama.

Charlie loped over to one of the drummers, constrained by his leash, but not enough to stop him. Seizing a drum with his hands, he scuttled back to his chair, stuck the drum between his legs, and began to pant-hoot. From gentle *'hoo hoo'* noises to the climax scream lasted what seemed an age as the crowd of revellers collectively held their breath. Then the ape shook his upper body as if freeing himself from invisible constraints.

'Charlie!' Chris shouted but the ape took no notice. Instead he fondled the drum, cradled between his thighs. Then he ran his fingers over the skin and a few moments later began tapping the drum head, slowly at first, then with increasing speed.

'*Eh-eh!*' the crowd screamed in unison.

The rhythm was compelling, so much so that Africans began to drum on anything they could find, on pieces of wood, on calabashes, each other. Then more drummers joined Charlie. He stared ahead, his shoulders set straight, drumming with incredible dexterity and speed.

Jo went up to Chris, her mouth wide open. '*Chris, he's in time! How does he do it?*'

Just then Charlie dropped his hands at his side. Then after a few moments he was at the drum head again, his mouth opening and closing, as if concentrating so hard, as if the drumming process involved other muscles.

The people screamed with delight. Charlie's pelage fairly bristled. He moved his arms higher, then lower. He stopped with one arm, and then started again. He drummed for five seconds, stopped a split second, then another five seconds, and on and on, all in time, varying beat and tone like a djembe master.

The sound was indeed wonderful. Maracas, like rumba shakers, beads or dried rice in calabashes, whistles, metal spoons, harps, larger drums, all joined in. Screams, ululations, cries of astonishment, none or nothing could deter or stop Charlie.

It was a tour de force for the ape. His upper body moved with the beat, his head on one side, and then the other. He was deftly able to alter his posture, sometimes leaning low over the djembe, then sitting up straight. His head shook from time to time but he always regained control. Charlie was in a trance, ecstatic. He made it look so easy. The ape glanced round now and again to see who was watching.

A few bold girls came to dance suggestively in front of him, which only engendered deeper and more complex rhythms from Charlie. What was amazing was the way he could hold the beat, then desist, one arm to the side and back again, then both hands going full speed, with occasional slaps in the centre of the drum head, always returning to the primal but fabulously satisfying tempo of the group, as well as initiating his own rhythms.

Chris noticed Mr Ayuk cheering to the heavens, and rolling his eyes, which were filling with tears and cascading down his cheeks. He went close to speak but Mr Ayuk put a finger to Chris's mouth, as if to say, don't spoil it, say nothing. Chris turned to see what Mr Ayuk was watching. It was Charlie in full solo flight, making magnificent music with his long, slender hands.

Mr Ayuk looked deeply at Chris for several seconds. Then he said, *'Ah noba foget tude. Di ting wey ma eye see, mi mouth no fit tok am!'*

Chris pressed him for more.

Mr Ayuk pulled out his hip flask and drained it of the last few drops. '*White man get sens pass black man but dis man bif, dis yua cimpanzay, e get sens pass white man* and *black man!*'

A few of the villagers looked worried. They must have thought Charlie had special powers, and that perhaps some strange juju was involved. It was no ordinary afternoon in Basho: an anthropoid ape giving a master class in djembe drumming

Old villagers believed in spirits in the bush, and devils, whether tall, short, tiny or gigantic. Some believed they were able to transform themselves into animals of any kind – elephants, hippos, gorillas, chimpanzees. Every man who believes this, for example that he can change into an elephant spirit, has his own private elephant in the bush, which sometimes feeds there or returns to the stomach of the man. While the man is alive, the elephant cannot be killed but as soon as the man dies, the elephant will lose its reasoning and can be killed easily.

The dance showed no signs of slowing. Charlie took a rest for a few minutes but no one dared approach him. Then he started again, beating the most exquisite djembe sounds, so that the crowd gathered closer round him, their eyes wide, staring in disbelief, slapping their sides or clapping their hands over their heads, exclaiming with glee like children at a funfair.

A rash young man offered Charlie a gift. It was a small calabash of palm wine. Charlie took it, and drank it in two gulps. Then he threw the calabash back into the crowd and more cheers.

'Did you see that, Chris?' Jo asked. 'It's time we stopped this, isn't it? It could get out of hand.'

'Yes, I agree, but I cannot believe my eyes. Can you? This is the proof, that good old George made it, with his last one great fantasy, I mean experiment. He actually did it!'

The village chief, dressed in a white robe, also paid homage. He carried a tray filled with fruit, and bowing first, he dropped on one knee before Charlie, holding out the tray. Charlie stopped his djembe drumming, took a banana, stripped the skin, and happily ate it. The chief stayed on bended knee. A few minutes later, Charlie picked up a pawpaw and hurled it into the crowd, then another, followed by several mangoes. The crowd screamed and some lucky person got the fruit, which now had magical status, as it had been dispensed by such a thoroughly remarkable ape.

Charlie resumed his beat on the djembe, and another roar went up. It was almost dark now, fires were lit in huts, and Mr Ayuk had very nearly passed out.

Chris was showing signs of bipolar disorder, then on an extreme high. He sank several glasses of African gin with the pure adrenalin rush of thinking that the success of George's experiment was fact, that would make its own history – and there he was right in the middle of it with Jo. 'Oh George, my good friend George,' he cried. '*You smashed it!*'

'Bring Charlie in Chris,' Jo urged. 'Remember where we have to go tomorrow. Now it's more important than ever to get Charlie into the forest, far away from villages and hunters.'

Chris was dancing with some of the Africans. He did one turn with the headmaster, another with a very large mammy, and the last with a sweet girl of eighteen. Mr Ayuk approved, as he called out, '*Na fayn fayn pretty baby.*'

Charlie ended with a flourish and a couple of screams. Chris saw his chance, and led Charlie back to their hut, with villagers following, not wishing the party to end. '*Res smol,*' he told them. '*Go slip.*'

More visitors came to wish them well. Charlie lay exhausted on the floor on a blanket. 'Let him stay there,' Chris told Jo. Chris felt so close to Charlie he couldn't stop fussing round him. Once he took Jo's only hairbrush, and lightly stroked Charlie's head with it. Jo herself was just about wasted after some serious palm wine drinking. The whole concept of George's 'experiment' had completely overwhelmed her.

The hunter called Jonas or Captain Tiko came to find out what time they were leaving in the morning. Chris pointed to his head, and explained they all needed a long sleep.

Jonas then introduced a man who claimed to be a native witchdoctor. He had some ideas about how to catch chimpanzees. It was originally a method of catching gorillas but the man said he was certain it would work for chimpanzees too. All you needed to do was place palm wine on the forest floor, with knives and cups. The hunters hide in the bush. Shortly after the gorillas arrive and drink the palm wine. Then they become excited, get drunk, beat their chests, pick up the knives and slowly stab themselves to death. Or perhaps injure themselves, enough to be caught.

In the village the carousing continued well into the early hours. Palm wine and African gin were in short supply by then, and anybody who had any left could have sold it at an inflated price.

'Let's not disturb him,' Chris said to Jo. 'He'll be all right till the morning. I daren't wake him up now.'

SIXTY-ONE

Well before dawn cocks crowed but the village itself was silent. Slight sounds came from the huts, snoring and soughing, some coughing amid the slumber. The villagers were in a kind of comatose stupor after the best party in a very long time.

Charlie was awake. His mind was clear, so clear that he felt unusually aware, sentient. He turned his head slowly to see Jo and Chris sprawled on their crude beds. At that moment he knew.

His eyes took in the room and its contents. There was nothing he needed or wanted. He thought of water, and immediately but very quietly drank from the calabash of water left out for him. The rest happened very fast. He gave himself little time to reflect, seeing only the doorway of the hut, the field at the back, the bush path leading towards the forest.

Like a black wraith he moved silently to the door, saw there was no one near, glared briefly at the pye-dog staring at him, then he was away, bounding towards the path, then leaping along it, to the river and the forest beyond. He knew the cottonwood tree when he passed it but there was no time to stop and drum.

At the river he found the narrowest part where dark, volcanic-looking rocks crowded together in the water made escape possible with just one jump. Then the black wraith headed along another bush path towards the north and east. His strength grew with every leap. His chest felt strong, his muscles invigorated by the freedom he was creating for himself.

For an hour and a half the black wraith travelled, sometimes in the trees, sometimes on the bush path, before he halted. He listened to the rainforest, his eyes glazing over because he could feel, because he could remember, because something inside him was giving him strength, and fearless courage beyond instinct. Then he plunged deeper into the forest, his ears hearing his own breathing and the magical resonances of animals, birds, insects – millions of living beings in the kaleidoscope of the African jungle.

The ape felt he must move higher, ever onwards, ever higher. He heard the call of *his* wild and for that whole day rested not once on his journey.

*

Bleary-eyed with an almighty headache, Chris literally crashed out of the hut. It was eleven o'clock in the morning and there was no sign of Jonas, no sign of anyone. A few moments before he had glanced down at Charlie's blanket, and seen nothing but an empty pile of wool. Frantically, he had pulled at the blanket but Charlie wasn't there.

Outside, he stumbled towards the field. Behind him, a sheepish Mr Ayuk and John Embai followed solicitously. 'CHARLIE!' Chris yelled at the top of his voice. 'COME BACK!' Then he buried his head in his hands, and sat down heavily on the ground.

Mr Ayuk said, '*Eh-eh-eh-eh! Massa, e don run.*' He shook his head disbelievingly, then muttered under his breath, '*Wi no fo drink ol dat bad bad mimbo.*' A taggle of villagers had come out to see what was happening, Jo among them.

'*Nau, wi ol drink garri,*' John Embai said, which was his way of saying that now everyone was in trouble.

Jo put her hands on the back of Chris's neck to comfort him. 'It's not anyone's fault,' she said quietly. 'Charlie just decided to go. He made his mind up, that's all.'

Chris struggled with what Jo had said for a few seconds but then raised his downcast head. He stood up, touched Jo on the shoulder as if to thank her, and then walked the few feet to the small wooden post that marked the beginning of the field. Jo knew he was going to do something, probably make one of his speeches. She was right.

Chris drew himself up to full height with an effort, and actually shook himself, just as Charlie had done the day before, as if releasing himself from a constraining force. Facing the bush path that led away to the forest, he began. 'Oh my hardy-daring, Charlie boy! Peerless prince of Takamanda. You have gone into the forest dim, like a light-wingèd dryad of the trees.'

He paused, as if thinking further. The Africans had come nearer to him, trying to catch what he was saying, although his voice was clamorous enough. 'Why then, the proper study of mankind is man but placed upon this isthmus, of a middling state, is yet another being, these creatures that share our family's genes, and this fair one who lately lived and flourished here in Basho, only now darkly wise, thanks to a surgeon's hand!

'And there he was before us, and rudely great. Played like a man those tender skins, stretched for the sounding, like only yesterday, reaching out to his most dear land of Takamanda!'

Solemnly, after pointing to the forest to the north, Chris turned back to the villagers. 'Charlie has gone, to his own people!'

The small group who were listening agreed, some saying, '*Na so, massa. Na so.*'

Chris lowered his voice and the crowd hushed. 'Our revels now are truly ended. Spirits among us have just melted into thin air! The pageant ended.'

Jo tried to comfort him again but Chris wasn't ready.

He looked at Mr Ayuk, John Embai and the small group of villagers, and then addressed them directly. '*It is not ended!* These revels are not, I swear thee! Charlie lives on in your great forests. Charlie lives on!'

Few, if any, understood his English words but in their hearts they knew what he meant.

*

A search party made up of Captain Tiko, Mr Ayuk, Smoky and John Embai returned empty-handed. Having already packed most of their equipment, Chris and Jo decided it was time to leave Basho and head back to Mamfe.

They stayed another two days, one complete day of which was spent saying goodbye to the villagers and one last final 'surgery', for anyone who needed it. Charlie's palanquin was donated for firewood. The young bride and groom were also returning to Mamfe, so they had some company.

On the morning of their departure, villagers walked with them to the village boundary. Hugs, handshakes and kisses followed and wishes for a safe journey. The headmaster took in the pye-dog, and promised to look after him well.

One mammy threw her arms around Chris and kissed him. She wouldn't let go. When she did, there were big tears on her face, and she said, '*Na so wi used to do am.*'

They trekked to Mamfe, following the same path they had taken to get to the Forest Reserve. No one was in a good mood. When they passed through villages, they were often asked about Charlie. Men and women would seek out the palanquin, and simply find it not there. If asked directly about his fate, Chris and Jo hardly said a word, as if they were reluctant to talk, and if they did, it was only sotto voce, '*Bak fo e on pipol.*'

They crossed the old colonial bridge into Mamfe. It was so busy and noisy after the forest quietness. The Forestry Officer was there to greet them.

'Welcome,' he said. 'Is it done?'

'All done,' Chris answered. 'Back, gone back.'

'Would you care for a drink?' Mr Foucham asked kindly. 'I imagine you have a thirst after your time in the bush.' Mr Ayuk's ears pricked up. 'Come then,' said Mr Foucham, 'we can have pepper soup too.'

They walked over to the Mamfe Club. Bottles of beer misting from an enormous fridge were brought to their table, opened before them as one might open the most precious perfume. As the tops came off, there was a hissing sound, and Mr Ayuk nodded his total happiness.

A few hours later, they sprawled out of the Mamfe Club. Mr Ayuk had been handsomely paid, and his heart was still happy. The sky was bright with star-points. On the road to the rest house, Chris paused to consider past events. He could not help himself. 'Where are you now, Charlie?' he asked. 'Which bush did you find?' The rest house was quiet without him.

The next day, Chris and Jo hired a car to take them south. First stop was Kumba, in the Providence Bar. Morning time came soon enough. A few hours later, they reached Limbe.

'We'll stay in that hotel by the beach,' Jo said, adding that she wanted nothing else. She remembered the cresting surf breaking on the black volcanic beach, and the islands in Ambas Bay.

'George will have to know. Phone him Jo! Now! Come on. Why did we wait so long?'

So they phoned George but the number they rang forwarded the call, and a voice answered, 'Canford Gardens Rest Home. Can I help?'

'I want to speak to George,' Chris shouted into the phone. 'I must speak to him.'

There was a distant silence at the other end of the phone. As if no one knew what to say.

'You can speak to him if you want, but he is very unwell. Just a few moments only.'

Chris held his breath. 'Are you there, George?' he said. 'Come on, you old bugger. I need to speak.'

Chris waited for what seemed an age. Then he heard a frail voice whispering. It said, 'Have you good news?'

'Yes! Charlie is home. In Takamanda, we got him in but...'

'No need to tell me. Just give my love to Charlie. Oh Charlie boy, I pray you are safe. That's all that matters.'

'Thank you, George, for everything,' Chris shouted into the phone. 'You know, I think the plasticity worked, I mean it started to show through. Charlie, oh my God, you should have seen him!'

'What...what was that?' George asked.

'History,' Chris said, short of breath with excitement. 'Charlie made it. I mean, if you could have seen him, what he did...'

The line went dead.

*

Two days later, they had the news: a text and a phone call from the rest home. George had passed away. He had rallied for a time after the call. The nurse meant to say he went with a smile.

In Limbe, Chris and Jo just wanted to relax. John Embai and Smoky Joe got paid, outside the Limbe Wildlife Centre, which was fitting, as that's where it all started.

They walked in the grounds first, saw some *ellioti* chimpanzees, and big dark gorillas without any palm wine to drink. Chris took Jo to a glass-domed restaurant near the sea. They drank together, and each shared their time, as if the other was the most important person in the world.

'Nothing is written then, after all,' Jo said. 'We are the ones who have to make it possible.' Then she kissed Chris.

Chris stared out to the tiny islands in Ambas Bay. 'So it's not the eternal mysteries, the sacraments, the symbols of the inner life that always point the path forward,' he said pensively. 'It's science that leads the way now, to new discoveries and new truths. It makes human progress possible and transforms our lives. Science drives technology and technology drives science. Science helps our everyday life, too. Think fire to candles to electric bulbs to lasers to solar lights powering learning in the bush.'

Jo found her gaze following. The vista of the bay seemed timeless even with an oil platform out at sea. Clouds covered part of remote Bioko island, formerly Fernando Pó.

'First the march of evolution; it's still relentless but to a degree it now moves hand in hand with science. The GPS systems on mobile phones only work because of Einstein's insight, his two great discoveries, general relativity and the special theory of relativity. Where will this all end? I mean where will it lead us? Out there in the bush a new primate variant goes in search of his territory… He carries with him the wonders, Africa and all her prodigies, and so much more.' Unusually for Chris, his voice softened to quiet intimacy, tears welling in his eyes. 'So, let's drink to our absent friend who had the courage to try, dear old George. A pioneer of science.'

They clinked glasses.

'And you know the best part, Jo?'

Chris placed his glass firmly on the table in front of him, a ready smile breaking over his face. 'Charlie lives. This is just the beginning of what might be possible. There's no way that ape could have mastered music, those incredible rhythms, to that extent without the plasticity having worked. The human part, the brain – Christ, Jo – it took!'

'Sweet,' said Jo.

'Even now,' Chris whispered excitedly, tears dropping into his wine glass even as he smiled. 'Charlie's almost certainly planning his next move!'

*

It didn't take long for Charlie to be found, by guards from the Wildlife ministry. 'Long' is of course a relative term. The group of rangers had to trek for days, stretching to weeks, way past Esengi – into ravines where waterfalls ran, where white mist curled over bromeliads and green ferns, where the bush was deep, and it was bad bush, if you were a hunter.

They say the ape ran fast when they met him, as if he didn't want any contact. From time to time, the black wraith is spotted but not near Basho. He is regarded as special, a spirit of the forest.

When the natives hunt in the bush near Esengi and Matene, they listen. They listen for a sound that carries through the forest, a rhythmical beat that could not be made by any animal. Other villages have followed suit, so that any hunter venturing into the bush always listens as he travels, for the djembe sounds, in case the spirit of the great ape returns.

They believe the '*man beef get plenti power*', and when they speak of him you can see something akin to empathy mixed in with apprehension in their dark, fearful eyes.

They listen for the spirit of the ape because they remember him, in Basho especially, indeed throughout Mamfe Overside, they still speak of him. The ape reminds them of their own lives, as if he were somehow like them, a creature caught midway between ape and man, and more than that too. Sometimes they shiver, the hair on the back of their heads rising at the wonder of it, even in the tropical heat, at their remembrance of him, the greatest of the great apes in Cameroon. If palm wine is there, it is drunk swiftly, as if to placate the gods of the forest.

And of Charlie's plans or his next moves, nothing is known but after a little more time has passed, to allow room for the ape to confront reality at his own pace, and some believe it will not be long in coming, who can tell?

They say he has found a mate, and sometimes he is to be seen at the head of his group; that he leads a troupe of some fifteen chimpanzees, and already has two sons. The researchers say he is shy, wary of human contact, and that he spends his time teaching his two sons, so they may learn the way of this world.

Further Research

Great Apes Survival Partnership (GRASP)
www.un-grasp.org

Chimpanzees in Nigeria and western Cameroon (*Pan troglodytes ellioti* website)
www.ellioti.org

Conservation Action Plan for the Nigeria-Cameroon chimpanzee
www.ellioti.org/ActionPlan/English/elliotiAP-mediumres.pdf

Africa's most endangered ape
www.crossrivergorilla.org

Working/volunteering in Cameroon
www.wcs.org/where-we-work/africa/cameroon.aspx

Creation of Takamanda National Park, western Cameroon
www.phys.org/news146929258.html

The Limbe Wildlife Centre, Limbe, western Cameroon
http://limbewildlifecentre.wildlifedirect.org

African Conservation Foundation (and volunteering opportunities)
www.africanconservation.org/great-apes/item/saving-cross-river-gorillas-and-chimpanzees

The Jane Goodall Institute UK. Learn about the pioneering research by primatologist Dr Jane Goodall in Gombe National Park, Tanzania, her Roots & Shoots groups for young people around the world, and community-centred development programmes in Africa, now with 23 offices worldwide
www.janegoodall.org.uk
JGI Canada
www.janegoodall.ca

Ayumu – the chimp with phenomenal 'eidetic' (photographic/total recall) memory
www.bbc.co.uk/nature/16832379
www2.pri.kyoto-u.ac.jp/ai/
Ayumu's researcher, Professor Tetsuro Matsuzawa
www.kyoto-u.ac.jp/en/research/forefront/message/rakuyu11_a.htm

Monkey World Ape Rescue Centre, Wareham, Dorset, led by Dr Alison Cronin
www.monkeyworld.org

A full list of organisations working to protect chimpanzees and other great apes, or involved in their care:
Chimpanzee groups
www.4apes.com/chimpanzee
Gorilla groups
www.4apes.com/gorilla
Bonobo groups
www.4apes.com/bonobo

Note to Readers

If you have enjoyed reading about Charlie and his extraordinary life, any reviews posted on Amazon.co.uk about this book (positive ones preferred!) will be gratefully acknowledged by the author.

You can also follow more news and conservation projects on the great apes by visiting: www.GiveMyLoveToCharlie.com – it surely can't be too long before someone posts a sighting of Charlie in the African rainforests!

Printed in Great Britain
by Amazon.co.uk, Ltd.,
Marston Gate.